BLO

# BLOOD BOUND

## BOOK SEVEN

### LINDSAY J. PRYOR

Bookouture

Published by Bookouture

An imprint of StoryFire Ltd.
23 Sussex Road, Ickenham, UB10 8PN
United Kingdom

www.bookouture.com

ISBN: 978-1-78681-061-8
eBook ISBN: 978-1-78681-060-1

*For Moth*

With special thanks to:

Those who have continued to support me since the beginning: Anita, Christine, Fiona, Incy, Kelly, Linds and Tima. Thank you for remaining by my side.

Tracey, *still* my Mary Poppins. No tears allowed! I'm happy to remain in denial if you are.

My awesome Darklings. Hilarious, passionate, relentless – I can't thank you enough for giving up so much of your time to get Blackthorn 'out there'. Your dedication and enthusiasm for my books, as always, means the world to me.

My incredible Facebook and blog followers as well as the 'Into the World of Blackthorn' discussion group, thank you for your interactions, your amazing sense of fun and, with it, for making Team Blackthorn what it is.

To every single reader who has enjoyed my books and been in touch or left me a review to say so, thank you for taking time out of your day for me. Your encouragement, support and kindness make such a difference.

And not forgetting:

Bookouture, my brilliant publisher, for bringing Blackthorn to my readers. Book seven – it's nearly over. What a long way we've come! Thank you for making this possible and for giving me the opportunity to share these stories.

# Chapter One

*Five hours earlier*

'We have to get moving as quickly as possible,' Kane said.

With Jessie close by his side, Eden followed the master vampire through the tunnels.

The morphed lycans' attack on the underground bunker was still vivid in Eden's mind. There was no doubt Sirius Throme had orchestrated the ambush. They'd saved as many as they could but had lost many too, the genetically mutated lycans having ripped through the tunnels like an unstoppable force.

With Jask still in recovery, Kane had resumed the helm immediately, taking Eden and Jessie with him.

'Now that Throme has located us, he won't stop,' Kane added. 'They could attack again at any point, and my bet is it'll be his specialist army that move in this time. I'll show you the route, and then I want you two to head it up.'

'Kane, with the technology the army has, they're going to map out the tunnel system easily,' Eden said. 'All they have to do is send a few drones in and they'll have an entire schematic within hours. Blackthorn's too small for us to hide for long enough.'

'That's why we're not staying in Blackthorn.'

Eden grabbed Kane's arm to step in front of him. 'You're taking us into *Lowtown*?'

'No.' His navy gaze was resolute and composed. *'You're* taking everyone into Lowtown. And then through Midtown and into Summerton.'

Eden's heart pounded as he stared at the master vampire. Hundreds of individuals to shift: humans, lycans, vampires. It was going to be like a military operation in its own right.

'Eden and I took that journey with Jask and Phia to go and collect Leila, remember?' Jessie said, her expression echoing Eden's unease as she stared at Kane. 'It was challenging enough with a small group of us. It's too much of a funnel. We're never going to be able to shift that many quickly enough, especially if Eden is proved right.'

'All the more reason to start as soon as possible,' Kane said.

And that's why he was so calm; that was why he was so composed.

Eden snagged his attention again. 'This was your back-up plan all along, wasn't it? When the war started, you were going to evacuate as many as possible to Summerton – right beneath Sirius's nose.'

Kane met his gaze with the resolve of someone who was never going to be defeated. Kane who they all knew had entered Blackthorn *after* the regulations had been put in place. Kane who could have escaped back that way any time he chose.

No one truly knew where he had come from, only that it wasn't *that* locale. For all they knew, Kane Malloy was the only non-Summerton resident who could go wherever the hell he wanted – and could take whomever he wanted with him.

'But if they find us *before* everyone gets through. . .' Jessie interjected.

'For now, we focus on getting everyone to Lowtown,' Kane said. 'Eden, you know every recess of it, as does Caitlin should you run into trouble once you're there and need to get above ground. She already knows exactly what to do. You'll also have Phia with you, which will be a huge advantage if you run into the same problem in Midtown. And she'll be invaluable once you reach Summerton. As for you, Jessie, you know we're going to need those angel senses and skills should there be fourth species to contend with too.'

'And you? Jask? Corbin?' Eden asked.

'We're staying here. Jask will be back on his feet in hours. We've got the strategy sorted this end – and the less bodies we have to worry about getting caught in the crossfire, the better.'

'I'm not leaving you guys behind to fight it out without me,' Eden insisted.

'I need to put those lives in the hands of people I trust,' Kane counter-argued. 'And you know as well as we all do that we have to prioritise getting you out of here, Eden. You *have* to get to Midtown. You have to find that doctor. And as walking proof of what angel tears can do to you, you are the *one* person who can prove what Sirius has been up to all this time – especially if he destroys evidence of his research at The Facility in the meantime.

'At this point the only way we're going to stop this snowball without bringing this prophecy into fruition is by getting the Global Council to call a ceasefire,' Kane added. 'I'm relying on you to get everything Caitlin needs in order to make that happen.'

Jessie squeezed Eden's hand reassuringly, her eyes capturing his in the process. 'We can do this.'

This was his chance to get Jessie out of Blackthorn, if he took the opportunity, and the rest of his family too – his brother Billy, Amanda, Honey. Eden looked back at Kane, his friend's gaze characteristically uncompromising.

'I know you're geared up for battle, Eden,' Kane said, 'and that's why I need you heading this up in case it comes to that. I need good leaders; people who are calm and strategic under pressure. Remember, I'm putting Caitlin in your hands too. Don't think this is easy for me either.'

Eden looked back at Jessie. Her hand was still clutching his, her eyes fixed on his in anticipation. If she didn't think it was a good idea, she'd already be insisting to the contrary.

He looked back at Kane and nodded. 'Show us where we're going.'

Kane slapped him appreciatively on the back as he stepped past him.

Unlacing his hand from Jessie's, Eden wrapped his arm around her shoulders and pulled her close so he could kiss her tenderly on the temple as they followed behind Kane.

'You know he's picked me because I'm the only one man enough to do this, right?' Eden whispered in her ear, knowing only too well he was far from being out of the vampire's earshot.

Kane's terse exhale echoed within the confines of the tunnel.

Jessie jabbed Eden in the side with a playful smirk, her light-hearted warning glance making it impossible for him not to grin back.

'Just saying,' he remarked, tilting her head so he could capture a fleeting kiss.

'I've picked the route with the highest number of adjoining tunnels until you get to the Lowtown border,' Kane said.

'Which also means more angles to be attacked from,' Eden remarked.

'Offset by giving you the best chance of multiple places to run should things get nasty. I'll have a full team of scouts lead the way and take the rear.'

Kane veered them left and then right again, the angel blood in Eden's system allowing him to navigate with night vision in what would have otherwise been pitch-black tunnels. The chill was still all-encompassing to his human – albeit *super*human – body though, the damp of the underground depths lingering in the air.

Beneath Blackthorn, the tunnels were a maze of underground maintenance systems, storage facilities, defunct tube and train stations, rivers and sewage systems. Their extent had always been an urban legend. The authorities had infiltrated more than once over the decades, especially amidst alarm from residents of Midtown and Summerton regarding the myth of the tunnels extending as far as their cordoned-off districts. But a maze was a maze, especially one reconstructed with hidden doorways and illogical routes. As such, the urban legend had remained exactly that – until Sirius Throme had found them earlier that night.

As they turned the next corner, Kane stopped abruptly, Eden and Jessie following suit.

The glow was subtle, but it was definitely there: flickering from a source somewhere deep in the tunnel to their left.

'Fourth species?' Eden whispered to Jessie, given her ability to detect the low-level thrum of their presence before anyone else.

She shook her head as she glanced from Eden to Kane, the latter also awaiting her confirmation.

But there was definitely an echo from something, the low-level buzzing intensifying in his sensitive ears as they all took a few wary steps closer.

Kane put his hand up to indicate that Eden and Jessie should stay back as he turned the corner.

Eden's heart skipped a beat when Kane froze as if hypnotised, multicoloured light dancing on the vampire's face.

Unable to wait a second longer, Eden stepped up to the end of the tunnel alongside his friend.

Spanning the tunnel ahead was what could have been mistaken for a summer night sky – the type of sky he'd only ever seen in books: the sunset igniting the clouds with lilac, deep purple and fuchsia.

But there was no sky. And there certainly wasn't a sun.

And this most definitely wasn't the Northern Lights either, even if the vibrant wall shimmied and pulsed like it was.

'Kane?' Jessie asked on his behalf.

'An electromagnetic field,' the master vampire muttered, almost to himself.

Eden stared from Kane back to the spectacular visual that would have been invisible to his regular human eyes.

Kane's frown deepened. His jaw clenched. He looked as if he was about to spit on something before he spun on his heels and brushed back past them.

Eden glanced at Jessie. As the multicoloured lightshow danced in her eyes, her concern matched his.

Grabbing her hand, Eden turned on his heels too. 'Wait up!'

But Kane ploughed forward, taking a left and then a right before marching along to the end of another tunnel.

The same sight lingered in the distance, bringing them all to a standstill again.

'Kane, what is this?' Jessie asked.

Kane shook his head. He slid his hands through his hair to clutch the nape of his neck. With a growl and a glower, he spun on his heels again, this time picking up even more pace.

Everywhere he led them, they came across the same thing.

Catching his breath at the pace and distance they had covered, Eden met Kane's gaze as they stopped once more, the master vampire's eyes worryingly lacerated with something between frustration, fury and despair.

'The cylinders,' Eden said, deducing for himself what Kane was already thinking.

'What cylinders?' Jessie asked.

'The cylinders I told you we saw erected on the Blackthorn border wall,' Eden clarified as he met her gaze.

He, Kane and Jask had seen them whilst they'd been lying on one of the rooftops a couple of days before, watching Sirius's army first take position.

Jessie looked back at the buzzing wall in front of them before her eyes locked on Eden's again, a flare of panic in hers now too. '*They've* done this?'

'More specifically, Sirius Throme has done this,' Kane said, anger resonating in his tone. He stared at the wall for a split second longer before spinning on his heels again. '*Fuck.*'

Eden cautiously approached the fluctuating waterfall of colour that rippled as if it were a sheet of loosely stretched silk in a breeze. Even from a foot away, sparks fired aggressively at his upheld palm, as if he'd set off sparklers. Sparks that warned him off amidst a multitude of pinpricks that became increasingly painful the closer he got.

'Eden, be careful!' Jessie demanded as she caught his arm to pull him back.

He didn't need her warning though. He understood enough to know that the tesla rating was through the roof. One attempt to step through and they'd be fried.

'A field of that intensity is impassable,' Eden said, pointing back towards the barrier as he turned to face Kane pacing the narrow space.

Kane's navy eyes met his. 'I'd deduced that for myself, Eden, hence the minor profanity.'

'Just how deep could this run?' Jessie asked.

Eden shrugged. 'Maybe miles.'

'And this has likely blocked off *all* the tunnel exits into Lowtown?'

'Every last one,' Kane said, his voice echoing in the narrow space. 'Those cylinders were around the entire circumference of Blackthorn.'

Jessie stared to Eden then back at Kane. 'We're *trapped*?'

'Trapped *and* fucked,' Kane replied.

Eden stared back at the lightshow that now felt like a noose around all their necks.

'There's a weak point in everything,' Eden said, his hand still stinging from getting too close to it. 'We'll find it.'

Kane's glare rested on the electromagnetic field. 'Sirius has been planning this for too long. If there had been a weak point, he would have discovered it and overcome it. We have to think of something else.' He looked back to Eden then Jessie. 'All suggestions are welcome because, as of now, I've no idea what the fuck we're going to do other than kick-start the very war Sirius wants.'

# Chapter Two

*Now*

As the steel door was unlocked from the other side, Xavier Carter instantly prepared himself for the worse. From his seated position on the floor, he braced himself for Kane Malloy to enter.

Kane had brought him there after he and Jask's pack of lycans had overthrown Sirius's army back at the compound. The master vampire hadn't disclosed his purpose for him yet. Instead he'd been left alone to recover from whatever sedative Caitlin Parish had pumped into him.

Forty years of trying to get his hands on the vampire and now *he* was the one trapped in some unknown location.

But it wasn't Kane who entered. Tentative relief was his instant response to Eden Reece's unexpected presence.

He'd heard Reece's name bandied around a few times since being there. Disappointment grated deep as the Curfew Enforcement Officer – who *he* had hired whilst in his role as chief of the Third Species Control Division – confirmed his suspicion: that the man he had recommended to Sirius Throme for one of their most important missions had gone rogue. Eden Reece had turned traitor to the organisation who had put food on his table and a roof over his head; who had given him the best opportunities he was ever going to get in life.

Eden strolled over to the wall directly opposite Xavier and sat on the floor. His subordinate mirrored him as he drew his knees to his chest and rested his wrists loosely on top, his head back against the wall.

He was subtly toying with a mint in his mouth. He regularly toyed with a mint in his mouth. He'd turned up to their recruitment day doing the exact same thing.

As Eden had sat alone in the small isolation chamber to take the aptitude tests, Xavier had ordered him through the one-way mirror to spit out whatever was in his mouth. He could remember it clearly, despite it being over ten years ago now. Eden had slam dunked it accurately into the bin from four feet away before leaning back, arms folded, to stare with indifference in Xavier's concealed direction – not unlike he was now.

He would never have got that far if he hadn't survived boot camp from the first round, let alone the combat round of the second.

A kid from the rough streets of Lowtown was a rare enough sight at open recruitment. Everyone expected the 26-year-old to fall at the first hurdle. But under the unassuming swagger, the self-assurance and the smart mouth, Eden could actually fight – and not just physically. He was smart, strategic, quick thinking, even manipulative. He read his opponents in a way Xavier had never witnessed in all his years at the TSCD. And when it came to the aptitude tests, his IQ was as impressive as the rest of his performance.

Regardless, the panel had wanted to fail him. Despite the 'open-house' policy once every three years, preference was always given to residents of Midtown or Summerton for the competitive jobs in the TSCD. There had been particular worry about how the others would feel about brushing shoulders with a Lowtowner – or Lowt as they nicknamed them – just as much as there had been concern over whether someone from that district could truly side with the TSCD. He'd had the final say though. Except now it seemed he'd been wrong all along.

'Eden Reece. I've overheard your name mentioned a few times and, sure enough, here you are.'

'There's an electromagnetic barrier that's gone up around Blackthorn. What do you know about it, Xavier?'

Eden's tone was as direct as his brown-eyed gaze. He'd never been overly compliant or one to stand on ceremony, hence having had more charges of misconduct than any other CEO in the history of the TSCD. But that had always been countered by his having the highest success rate too. Eden Reece, although the preferable alternative to Kane Malloy right then, was not one to be underestimated when it came to unpredictability.

'So Sirius has finally resorted to Plan B. And it's *Mr* Carter to you,' he added, the compulsion to pull rank too great. 'I don't believe I've had your official resignation as yet.'

Eden flipped the mint in his closed mouth again, his gaze unwavering.

Xavier glanced at the door before fixing his full attention back on Eden. 'Unless I'm getting ahead of myself. Maybe you're even smarter than I give you credit for,' he added quietly. 'Or you certainly can be. That barrier is impenetrable, Reece. This is all coming to a head right here and right now. You can make the right choice. You can get me out of here. I'm willing to place money on your ability to get Malloy out too. This could be the making of you.'

The CEO didn't flinch. 'Maybe.' He flipped the mint again. 'If I was wearing my *I'm-a-back-stabbing-traitor* T-shirt today. Let me know when you've finished borrowing it.'

His humour was as unappealing as the unwavering look of resolve in his eyes, especially as Eden had dared to go there thinking he could get answers.

'You do know Kane's going to kill me, don't you?' Xavier asked. 'Can you stand by and let that happen?'

'For orchestrating the murder of his sister? For slaughtering his friends in your continued attempt to capture him, as well as putting innocent people like my family on the line, all for Sirius's putrid ends? I can't imagine why you'd think that would make Kane want to kill you.'

Xavier swallowed back his temper. 'You could have had it all, Reece. You still can. I recommended you to this mission because I knew you were the best. You've always been the best. You and your family cannot survive this without my help. Get me out of here and Sirius's offer will still be open. I give you my word.'

'But as you've just confirmed, we're all trapped in Blackthorn now, X.'

The shortened use of his name, the dismissal of his offer, had Xavier forcing himself to curb his temper again.

'You either turn this around as of now, Reece, or you go back out there to your new vampire and lycan best friends. But this is the one and only opportunity I'm giving you.'

'What if this is the only opportunity I'm giving *you*?'

'You're Malloy's lapdog. You don't have any say over what the outcome will be – we both know that. Unless you take control now.'

'I'm asking nicely, X. If you know how to bring that barrier down, you need to tell me.'

'It can't be brought down, Reece. Not from inside. You know as well as I do how long Sirius has waited for this. His plan is infallible.'

'Maybe I should tell Kane that. After all, if you're telling the truth, that makes you defunct. One less piece of baggage.'

Eden eased himself up from the floor and turned his back on Xavier as he made his way across to the door.

'It was me who fought your corner to get you a place in the Curfew Enforcement Unit, Reece!' he called after him. 'They didn't want you. But I didn't judge you by where you came from, only by what you had to offer. Up to now you've made me proud – and that unit proud. I know your background. I know what you stand for.'

Eden turned to face him again, his brown eyes still unflinchingly resolute. 'Then you should know why asking me to choose the system that enforces it is a tad more than an insult.'

'So instead you become a part of the rebels – those who murder, who bully, who deceive; who want to bring everything down around us for their own ends?'

'And what was your intention when you sided with the rebels, X? You confessed to Kane for yourself about your involvement with Feinith. Does Sirius know about you using the Higher Order for *your* own ends?'

'I told Feinith what she wanted to hear. I told Feinith what I needed her to hear in order to gain disclosure from her. I know exactly where my loyalties lie, Reece. I don't bite the hand that feeds me.'

'Yet you confessed to it all whilst cowering on the floor in front of Kane Malloy. See, I know about *your* background too, X.'

'Come on, Reece. You know all about playing the game. You're a survivor after all. The kid orphaned at thirteen. Playing big brother to his older sibling, who was incapable of surviving those rough streets you'd been abandoned to. I know how your mother was beaten into a coma. I found it in the records. I know your drunk of a father ended it all soon after that machine was switched off because he couldn't cope with his own sense of inadequacy at not being there to help her.

'You were clever at manipulating the recruitment psychologists, I'll give you that, but your true underlying motivation for joining the TSCD didn't go unnoticed. You used the system you despised because you knew deep down that you had every chance of becoming one of the very people you loathed. The TSCD was your only way out; your only way to stop it happening. We were there for you, for your family, when you needed us. And yet this is how you repay us?'

'I've paid my dues. I didn't start this.'

'Sirius isn't a monster, Reece, despite you trying to convince yourself to the contrary.'

'Then how would *you* describe him?'

'We can't sustain this way forever. We all know that. Prophecy or not, sooner or later the third species were going to rise against us. Feinith knew we were putting the pressure on finding that cure. They were going to use the next election: put Amilek forward, knowing he would fail, so they could incite that uprising.'

'And Sirius planned to use this barrier to manage that?' Eden asked.

'But, more than ever, he wanted Kane out first. It's been Throme versus Feinith all the way, and you've been playing them both and keeping both your options open. Maybe I should check your arse for splinters from that fence.'

'He'll let you in on it too, Reece. You get me out of here and I'll see to it that it happens. You're fighting on the wrong side. Parish was warned, now you have been too. They're using you. They're using all of you. Kane can't be trusted. He's spun a line around you all.'

Eden stepped back over to join him. He crouched down in front of him, wrists on his knees again as he held his gaze.

'There's a weak spot in everything, Xavier, and that means there's a weak spot in that barrier – and in Sirius's plan too. If you don't want to help, then I can't help you. I just need to know if that's your final decision.'

'I don't know who I'm more disappointed in: you or Caitlin Parish.'

Eden offered him the subtlest hint of a smile. 'We'll both struggle to sleep tonight knowing that.'

He stood again and made his way back out of the room.

✳ ✳ ✳

Eden locked the door behind himself as Jessie backed up in the bunker tunnel.

'No luck?' she asked, her forest-green irises reflecting her concern.

'I take it you listened to all of that?'

'Of course I listened.'

And that meant she'd heard more than he'd wanted her to.

She reached for his hand, interlaced their fingers and squeezed as they headed back down the corridor.

Xavier's words clogged his mind and made it hard to swallow amidst his irritation at his former boss trying to manipulate and use his emotions about his family, his past, against him. The fact Jessie had heard the conversation grated even more.

It grated because of how true it was: how he could so easily have become what he despised. And he didn't need that pointed out to Jessie. He didn't need the girl who had spent decades trapped amongst the worst dregs of humankind, the girl he now loved, knowing how close he had been to becoming the very thing she despised.

'Whatever Xavier claims, I'm telling you an electromagnetic pulse will work,' he said. 'It'll bring the whole barrier down.'

'*If* we can get to the core circuitry, which we've already established is almost definitely on the other side. We're going in circles, Eden.'

She knew it. He knew it. They all knew it.

'Yeah, well it's better than standing still.'

'We don't even have time for that now,' Kane said, meeting them on the corner from the other direction. 'So I take it you had no luck with Carter?'

'Short of torture intervention, no. He's a stubborn bastard but he knows what we could do to him. He's insisting there's no way through. What's happening?'

'Sirius's army has moved from the border. They're infiltrating the streets and moving door to door as of now. They've started at the northern boundary and are sweeping downwards.'

'How many?'

'Over a hundred by the last count, and that's on top of standard military. They've got Curfew Enforcement Officers leading the way.'

'Using my boys as the expendable grunts as always.'

'And at the pace they're moving, they'll be infiltrating the hub within the next twenty-four hours,' Kane added.

This was finally Throme's decades-old strategy meeting Kane's – though Kane's had originally been intended for use against the vampire uprising, and certainly hadn't included a total blockage of any exit route outside of the confines of Blackthorn.

'Any news on Leila?' Jessie asked.

With Jask still unconscious, his pack beta Corbin had taken the lead on the hunt. Leila had vanished from the bunker five hours before – around the time they'd discovered the barrier.

Whether she'd escaped as herself or whether the serryn had already taken over – as it had attempted to with her sister Sophia – none of them knew. Ever since she'd conducted the spell to transfer Sophia's serrynity back to herself, they'd been preoccupied with the fallout of the attack on the bunker and then trying to pull all their resources together for a new plan since the barrier had curbed the last one.

Caitlin and Sophia – Phia to them – had remained on the case in-house, hunting for clues as to Leila's intentions. She'd been adamant she wasn't going to kill Caleb. Now none of them could be sure, especially as they had every reason to believe she'd left with Kane's Tryan-killing sword in hand.

If she *had* gone for him and she messed up, if Caleb killed her and claimed his Tryan status, the prophecy would be back on track. He would rise as the vampire leader and he *would* win. They'd be wedged between two almighty powers with no option but to succumb to the war they were trying to avoid. Caleb would end up destroying Blackthorn in his clash with Sirius Throme. And, if the prophecy continued on its path, destroy everything as they knew it.

'No,' Kane said. 'They've failed to find her anywhere. I've had to pull the teams back in. I can't risk it. Any third species they find on the streets, they're taking to camps they've set up in the north.'

'What has Phia said about that?' Eden asked.

'The air was blue for a while, and I fielded one or two punches, but she knows as well as we do that it's too high risk to keep searching. If Leila's gone to fight this battle with Caleb alone, there's nothing we can do about it now.'

'She'd better know what she's doing,' Eden said. 'Or we're all screwed.'

'She does,' Jessie said. 'Knowing she'll go the same way as Phia did, she'll be trying to talk Caleb round before it's too late.'

'Or she's handing the pending Tryan a ready-made serryn on a platter,' Eden counter-argued.

Jessie met his gaze with the glint of challenge that he loved about her. 'She had no choice. The longer she delays, the more the serryn will out. We all saw what it did to Phia. We should be applauding her, not doubting her.'

'I'm not the happiest camper that she fucked off without saying so, but I'm inclined to agree,' Kane said. 'Looking at the state of the streets, I'm betting Caleb isn't going to rein it in for much longer. At the pace the army is moving, we've got about twenty-four hours until they've cleared the north and reach the east and west. He's going to be a fucking time bomb waiting to go off once they hit his territory.'

'You still don't want to go for him?' Eden asked.

Kane shook his head. 'His building's on total lockdown. No one's getting near him without his say so. If we still had Leila, I would have had no choice but to try and bargain. If I go near him now, I may as well throw down the gauntlet.'

'If we could get near him, could you kill him *without* your sword?'

'*If* we could first find another way to permanently seal the fourth dimension to stop it blowing open? He's mortal like the rest of us, pending Tryan or otherwise.'

'So why do you need it at all?'

'Because killing him with that sword stops it jumping.'

Kane exchanged a swift glance with Jessie.

Jessie was the first to speak. 'Caleb's Tryan status works the same way as Leila's serrynity?'

'This prophecy is a determined bastard. His bloodline is the best conductor.'

'But Jake is dead,' Eden said. 'And their older brother died decades ago. You told us that.'

'And I'm not taking any chances. Killing him with that sword was the only guarantee that this ends.'

'Does Leila know this?'

'With her interpreter skills, she would have been able to interpret the writing on the handle. My bet is she knows exactly what it's for.'

Eden stepped away as a heavy sigh escaped his lips. 'Then we'd better hope more than ever that she knows what she's doing.'

'But we don't have time to wait for the outcome. Just as we predicted, Sirius's army aren't only infiltrating above ground, they're infiltrating below ground now too. They're already blowing holes through walls and sending sonar devices through every recess to map out what we've built.'

'They're going to herd us,' Eden said.

'Exactly. With the aim to localise us to whatever point they've chosen. My guess is they'll try to drive us south, to the most unfamiliar territory for us.'

'To the cons. We all know they've got a tunnel system of their own. If we blow through the wrong wall, Kane. . .'

'We've got at least forty-eight hours until it gets to that. If you're still convinced there's a weakness in this barrier somewhere, then I need you to work out what it is sooner rather than later. Until then, there's only one way to survive this and that's to keep moving.'

'Like one giant game of fucking Pac-Man,' Eden remarked. 'Except their ghosts can see through walls, in the dark and have the most deadly ammunition going.'

'What's Pac-Man?' Jessie asked.

'Geek reference. And another pleasure for me to introduce you to once this is over.' He knocked his hip playfully against Jessie's before he looked back to Kane. 'Tell me we're not just running but that we're going to do something to defend ourselves.'

'I'm preparing a defence team *and* an attack team – the former to hold them back and to distract where necessary and draw them away from the more vulnerable, the latter to lower the enemy numbers. But the attack team's the last resort for reasons we know. They might be in, they might be planning to fight dirty, but we stick to the plan: minimal death toll for as long as we have other options.'

'And when we're out of options?' Eden asked. 'And if Leila doesn't get through to Caleb in the interim? If he kills her?'

'We buckle down and we face this war head-on.'

'And everything we've worked for will be for nothing,' Jessie reminded him.

'If Leila fails, we'll have no choice,' Kane said. 'If Caleb becomes the Tryan, then at least the fourth dimension will be permanently closed again by default. That means it'll be open season on Caleb again – and I *will* kill him, sword or not.'

'And Sirius will still be coming for you. And you know he'll rip this place apart until he finds you,' Jessie said.

'Which is why we'll get as many away from here as possible. We buy Leila as much time as we can, we keep as many of our own as alive and safe as we can, and we find a way out of this.'

'Kane.'

The vampire looked across his shoulder as Caitlin stepped into view.

'I need to talk to you.'

Kane raked her swiftly. 'News on Leila?'

Eden caught Caitlin's subtle glance in his direction before looking back to Kane. 'Somewhere private.'

It didn't take any further effort on Caitlin's part for Kane to sense she needed him to do as she asked. And neither did it take any effort on Eden's part for him to realise that meant out of earshot of him and Jessie.

As Kane followed her out of sight, Eden looked to Jessie. Her pensive frown was as deep as his felt as she exchanged glances with him at their friends' elusiveness.

'Hey!' Eden called after them, quickly catching them up. 'Is there something we should know?'

'I need to talk to Kane, that's all.'

But it wasn't like Caitlin to avoid meeting his gaze.

His stomach churned. His heart pounded. As Jessie moved in alongside him, he instinctively reached for her hand to interlace his fingers with hers. 'About what?'

Caitlin's momentary hesitation did nothing to abate his unease.

'Caitlin?' Jessie interjected, the tension in her hand intensifying. 'What's wrong? Has something happened?'

Caitlin subtly wetted her lips as she glanced from Kane to Jessie and finally to Eden. Her brow furrowed, but she only hesitated for a second longer. 'Maybe you should come too.'

# Chapter Three

Sophia was sitting at the table. Her hands cupped her forehead in a dual salute as she stared down at the book in front of her.

Stepping closer, Jessie instantly recognised the book to be Claire McKay's diary: Sophia and Leila's mother's diary.

Sophia looked up as all four of them joined her. Her startled and questioning gaze locked on Caitlin's as if she wasn't expecting their arrival – Jessie and Eden's, at least.

Jessie glanced to Kane, who looked as perplexed as she felt. And the dense atmosphere in the room, the fact Caitlin had tried to take Kane aside, told her it wasn't good.

'What's going on?' Jessie asked.

'Let's all sit down,' Caitlin suggested as she pulled out a chair.

Jessie opted for the seat next to Eden, her hand almost crushing his as he held it out of sight in his lap.

'This was left on my bed earlier,' Sophia said, sliding the open book into the middle of the table for them all to see.

Caitlin was the only one who didn't lean forward.

'Leila must have put it there before she left,' Sophia added. 'It looks like she made some breakthroughs.'

'What kind of breakthroughs?' Kane asked.

'About Leah Par and the constant references to her throughout my mother's diary. As you know, we scoured whatever resources we had to find out who she is and how she might link to the research at The Facility.'

'And?' Eden asked.

'Is not a she, but a he.' She turned the page and removed the loose piece of paper inside – a piece of paper where the writing didn't match that in the book.

Amongst the pensive-looking scribbles were two words in bold, the letters overlaid over and over again: *Leah Par*. And then, underneath, one word: *Raphael.*

'It's an anagram. Leah Par spelt backwards is Raphael. And look what Leila's scribbled underneath.'

Leila had written it boldly: *the angel of healing.*

Jessie tightened her grip on Eden's hand at 'healing' underlined three times.

'Shit,' Eden hissed quietly.

'This is definitely it,' Sophia said. 'I don't understand half of my mother's medical references or coding information, but I bet this is the proof we need to bring Sirius down. My mother's been dead for twenty years. That means Sirius has known about the use of angel tears for all that time, if not longer. We have got to get this to the Global Council along with the rest of the proof we have about the angels' existence. If you're right about this doctor, Eden – this Cassandra – and she backs us up, we've got this.'

'*If* we can get out,' Eden reminded her.

'But this is great news,' Jessie said, looking from Sophia to Caitlin. 'You nearly gave me heart failure. I thought something was wrong.'

Her heart skipped a beat as Caitlin and Sophia exchanged glances.

The lack of exultation in both their expressions, even as they'd broken the good news, added to the tightness in Jessie's chest.

Caitlin's lowered gaze, the tension in her hands, turned Jessie's breathing ragged.

'Phia?' Kane asked as he glanced from Caitlin back to her.

'As you know, my mother was a haematologist at the lab. This diary talks about staged research. It talks about side effects. I don't understand enough of the terminology, but there were definitely repercussions.'

'Repercussions to what?' Eden asked, sliding the diary towards himself. 'The research into the tears?'

Jessie could see it in his eyes: he was rapidly catching up as he flicked through the pages. And it wasn't good.

'These symbols relate to calcium levels,' Eden said, looking at everyone but her. 'They used to be on Honey's medical reports whenever blood tests came back.'

'The diary is littered with references to them,' Caitlin explained. 'It appears that was Claire McKay's primary job: to monitor calcium levels in subjects.'

'Sirius's army?'

'The precursors to Sirius's army,' Sophia clarified. 'Human subjects before then. The notes reference one condition in particular: sarcoidosis. My mother had drawn a line through it several times, but I looked it up. It's a rare disease where the body's immune system is over-activated. The boost in the immune system causes an increase in calcium levels in the bloodstream. Too much calcium can lead to all sorts of complications. No one knows how sarcoidosis causes high calcium, but it does. It starts with a cough and shortness of breath. You can have sarcoidosis of the heart, the lungs. . .'

'What does this have to do with angel tears?' Jessie asked.

'Some of my mother's final notes refer to an unidentified liquid she describes as iridescent,' Sophia added. 'She mentions the subjects being given it. She talks about variables indicating this iridescent liquid as being responsible for the raised calcium levels – which she then had to combat to get the dose right.

'She put a line through sarcoidosis because she established it wasn't that, but she found something similar in all the subjects who were given angel tears. And, as with sarcoidosis, steroids seemed to counteract the side effects. It seems that her job was ultimately to find the right levels of steroids to bring the calcium levels in the subjects down. In some cases. . .'

Jessie's heart skipped a beat as Sophia glanced to her.

'In some cases,' she continued after a light clearing of her throat, 'the steroids weren't given. Purposefully. I think this is when my mother started having an issue with the research.'

'Because?' Eden asked.

Sophia glanced down at the diary before forcing herself to look Eden in the eyes. 'It can be fatal without them.'

Jessie's heart pounded.

Eden's complexion had already turned ashen, and she knew why: he wasn't thinking about himself, he was thinking about Honey.

'You're *sure*?' Eden asked.

'With lab animals, some are picked to die in the name of finding ways for others to survive. It appears that the same principle was applied to the human subjects. A few were definitely denied any treatment in order to assess the outcome.'

'I need to get out of here,' Eden said. He looked to Kane. 'I need to get to Cass. I need to get my hands on whatever that dose of steroids is.'

'Eden,' Sophia said, her sympathetic tone even more troubling.

Jessie stared at her. She wanted her to stop speaking. She wanted them all to stop speaking.

Sophia paused for a painful few moments. 'One of the findings was that the steroids have to be introduced from the outset or they prove ineffective.'

Eden's breath caught as he stared at their friend. '*Ineffective*?'

Sophia leaned forward to turn the pages. She spread two open and removed two folded pieces of paper before placing them in front of Eden and Jessie.

The word in bold letters meant nothing to her. Underneath it, the interpretation read *immortality*.

'Leila's an interpreter, as you know. She can read nearly every archaic language there is. Word origins were her speciality. We all know words change with time – and mistakes happen during conversion depending how expert the translator is. Our mother had come across this word in files that didn't belong to her. It seems Sirius *thought* he knew what the tears meant.'

Below the original translation, Leila had corrected the meaning from *immortality* to *lasts forever*.

In more scribbles, Leila had circled the word 'calcification'.

Eden stopped breathing.

Silence descended.

Jessie didn't need any further explanation. Bile was already rising at the back of her throat as her stomach clenched to the point of pain.

'Angel tears aren't a cure at all, are they?' she forced herself to say.

'No,' Caitlin confirmed, her eyes shrouded with sadness. 'All they do is heighten the immune system for a limited time, like a peak before the fall. A last burst of energy.' Caitlin's eyes glossed as she turned a few more pages. She pointed to a line. 'Claire stumbled on things Throme clearly didn't want her to. She found notes where they refer to it as White Witch Syndrome.'

Eden exhaled abruptly. 'Fucking *Narnia*? I used to read to Honey every time I went to see her. I've read that story to her. I always skipped the part where the witch turns people to stone in case it scared her. Are you telling me that my niece is going to die? After *all* this, she isn't going to make it whether we get out of here or not? Are you telling me I've already killed her?'

More silence.

Jessie tightened her grip on Eden's hand but he unravelled from her in order to place both palms flat on the table.

Eden's frown deepened. His jaw clenched. 'How long does it say it takes? How quickly does the body calcify without the steroids?'

'It varies,' Sophia replied.

'Roughly?'

'In some cases, weeks. In others, only days.'

Jessie's stomach plummeted. Her attention snapped to Eden.

Without looking at her, he kicked back his chair and ploughed out of the room.

# Chapter Four

It took him minutes to get back to Xavier's room.

It took him seconds to burst inside, shrugging Kane off in the process.

Xavier was already on his feet and backing up.

'There's a weak spot in the barrier,' Eden said. '*Where* is it?'

As unbridled fury swept through his veins, he knew he was displaying a weakness he shouldn't have allowed himself to reveal. Even when he was on a knife's edge, he was usually composed, methodical.

But Honey would always be that weakness.

Xavier's attention nervously flitted between Eden and Kane, who was holding him back again. 'I told you, Reece,' his ex-boss said. 'There *is* no weak spot.'

'Fucking bullshit!' Eden hissed, breaking free of Kane again.

Catching hold of Xavier's T-shirt, Eden slammed him up against the wall.

Xavier clearly knew better than to attempt a futile retaliation and held both hands up in an attempt to placate him. 'There is no way out, Reece.' But there was something in his eyes: a silent exchange. 'You know what I've told you,' he reminded him quietly.

His attempt to strike a deal; his nerve to *still* try to strike a deal had Eden tightening his fists on Xavier's shirt.

But Kane finally peeled him off before shoving him backwards, back towards the door. 'Outside,' he said firmly.

'I'm not done.'

'Eden,' Jessie said from the threshold, catching hold of his arm.

But his attention remained fixed on Kane as the master vampire closed and locked the door behind him.

'We've got Ziel,' Eden remarked through gritted teeth. 'He'll know a way around this.'

'Ziel doesn't know anything,' Kane replied. 'I've already asked.'

His heart skipped a beat. 'You've *already* asked? You *knew* about this?'

Kane's gaze didn't flinch – it was confirmation enough.

'You *knew* what the angel tears could do?' Eden persisted.

The master vampire's lack of denial only pumped more adrenaline into his veins.

Eden gave him a short, sharp shove to the chest. 'You did, didn't you?'

Kane's navy eyes narrowed on his, but the vampire held both his palms up, his concession nonetheless countered by his warning glare.

'Eden,' Jessie said, her palm flat to his chest as she stepped between them.

Eden's attention snapped to Jessie. Her eyes glossy with the tears she was struggling to hold back. Lethal tears that had saved his life – had saved Honey's life – only to mask their eventual poison.

'Did *you* know too?' he asked quietly.

Her eyes flared. 'Of course I didn't!'

He looked back to Kane. 'You should have told me.'

'To what end? *This*? I knew the effects, but this is the first I've heard of steroids being using to counteract it. I know it doesn't feel like it right now, but it's a ray of hope.'

Eden raked his hands back through his hair, berating himself that his own shock and protective instinct towards Honey had overwhelmed his thoughts about the impact on Jessie.

But as he turned to face her fully, he found she was already heading back down the corridor.

'Jess, wait!' he called out, pursuing her.

But Jessie ploughed ahead regardless, not even glancing in his direction.

'I know this is a shock, but I can't believe you asked me that, Eden.'

'I know you had no choice unless I was to die that night. And I know you were aware that Honey had no other options. . .'

She stopped abruptly then pivoted 180 degrees to face him. 'So I opted for *this*? To spend even more time with you and fall for you even more only to lose you anyway? To put that little girl through that?'

'That's not what I'm saying.'

'Then what *are* you saying, Eden?' she demanded, her irises claret with hurt.

'That I wouldn't blame you for acting in the moment and planning to find a way out of it later.'

'I didn't know,' she said firmly, her gaze steady on his. 'Okay? I had *no* idea. I'm hearing this for the first time, exactly like you are, and I'm having *just* as much of a problem getting my head around it.'

Her attention snapped back down the corridor at the same time as Eden's did.

Making his way up the corridor, Honey in his arms, Billy slowed, his eyes as quizzical as those of the six-year-old he was carrying.

His brother came to a standstill, as if tempted to turn around and go back the way he'd come. He cast a wary glance at Kane, the tension between them all thick enough for anyone to detect.

As his attention flitted between Eden and Jessie, he instead closed the gap.

'Someone wanted to give their Uncle Eden a hug before we leave,' Billy said, putting on a relaxed smile for Honey's sake whilst keeping his questioning gaze on Eden.

A pang resounded deep in his chest as he gazed into his niece's large eyes. The niece who always saw him as her hero, able to solve any problem that came their way.

But not this time.

Worse, this time he'd bestowed a death sentence on her.

He should have already been leading them across the border. He should have been leading them all across the border. Instead, being trapped had become an entirely new weight around his neck.

'Maybe we should come back in a little while,' Billy suggested to Honey. 'Just before we go. Uncle Eden looks *very* busy right now. And we know what important things Uncle Eden has to do.'

For Jessie, it was clearly already too much.

Billy's eyes narrowed quizzically as he looked over Eden's shoulder to see her hightailing out of sight. 'Eden? Has something happened?'

'I'll. . .' He looked over his shoulder just as Jessie vanished around the corner. He promptly closed the gap between him and his family and held the back of Honey's head as he kissed her forehead before attempting to pull away. 'I'll find you in just a little while.'

Her arms were instantly around his neck though as she displayed her best limpet routine.

'Love you, Uncle Eden,' she whispered in his ear before she finally let go. 'Tell Jessie I love her too.'

Eden couldn't look Billy in the eye again. He couldn't look into the eyes of either of them as he turned away.

Kane grabbed his arm before indicating for Billy to leave them be.

Billy took the hint, and Kane waited for him to disappear from earshot.

'I even asked Leila about it before she left,' Kane informed him.

'And?'

'At the time, she claimed to know nothing, which is why telling you wasn't going to help anything. Your focus wouldn't be on what you need to do.'

'No, my focus would be on my niece, who I've only just learned I fucking poisoned whilst trying to save her life. I can't even imagine what this is doing to Jessie.'

'Which is why we need to get you to this doctor more than ever now, as much for you and Honey as to bring Sirius down. Those notes are twenty years old,' Kane reminded him. 'There might have been advancements. Angel lore doesn't change, but medically you don't know what they've come up with. I will keep asking questions, starting with Carter, but you need to use that smart brain of yours to figure out the flaw in that barrier. Then I'll get your arse out of here and right into Midtown, I promise you.'

Eden watched Kane head back up the corridor before returning his attention in the direction Jessie had disappeared.

His heart ached at the recollection of his accusation, of the look in her eyes when he'd challenged her.

He stopped at the threshold to the open doorway. He berated himself for even letting the thought cross his mind that he'd find her curled up and crying.

Her eyes were red raw, yes, but curled up she certainly wasn't.

Standing in the middle of the room side-on to him, she tightened the shoulder straps of her backpack.

His heart and stomach simultaneously plummeted.

The prospect of her walking out of that room with rejection in her eyes had his heart pounding in a way he'd never known. He braced himself, knowing there was no way he was letting her leave; knowing it would be a hell of a battle if she tried.

The thought that he'd hurt her that much had him more than willing to swallow any ounce of pride he had to convince her he knew he'd been wrong; that he'd had no right asking her that now seemingly fatal question.

He could barely take a deep enough breath. 'Where are you going?'

She turned to face him, knuckles white as she held the straps of the rucksack. 'Back to the row.'

'The row? *Pummel's* row? Why?'

'For Toby's files. The ones I told you about: all of Toby's research into my kind.'

She'd told him about them a couple of days after they'd first met, at the same time she'd explained about her ex-guardian Toby, who had searched the globe for decades – back before the regulations were put in place – to find out more about her and her kind.

With her memory taken by the Angelic Parliament, that was how she'd discovered she was an envoi. It was how she'd learned of the healing powers of her tears – that angel tears were the permanent cure Sirius had been seeking.

Or what she'd *thought* was the permanent cure.

'He *kept* those files?'

As she held his gaze, he saw no indignation at what he'd accused her of despite her pain. Instead, her red-raw eyes were laced with the grit, determination and resolve that he'd come to love about her – the look that made it clear it was never over until it was over.

'I hope so. There's only one way to find out.' She closed the gap between them before attempting to slip past him. 'All I know is that in that research could be the answer we need to help you and Honey.'

Eden braced his arm across the doorway to block her exit. 'Even if he did keep them, the row's burned to the ground.'

'He didn't keep them in the house, Eden. He used to keep them in the shop opposite – the one I told you his family used to own. I don't know if they're still there, I don't know if they're any use, I haven't seen them in fifty years, since the cons murdered him, but I've got to try. He never took them from me, Eden. Toby never took my tears. My blood, yes, so he could protect me for as long as possible, but not my tears. I thought it was some moral standpoint, but maybe he knew something. Maybe our answers are somewhere in those notes.'

His gaze lingered on hers as the prospect sank in – that there was a chance. That Jessie might have found it. 'What did I do to deserve you?'

'There might not be anything, Eden. We've got to be prepared for that.'

He nodded. 'Just give me a few minutes to say goodbye to Billy before we go.'

'Eden, you don't need to come with me. It won't take two of us. It's better you stay here.'

'You think I'm going to let you go back there alone?'

'I can be in and out in a few hours tops. I'll take Sorran and one of the others with me. The army are still up north for now, but we know the risk of fourth species out there. If one comes knocking, it's me who's going to hear it coming before anyone else.'

He pressed his palm tighter against the doorframe. 'You're *not* going without me, Jess.'

'And you're not coming with me, Eden,' she said, her unflinching gaze telling him there was no room for discussion. 'You know the risks out there. Kane won't let us do it. You're too important.'

'And you're not? Jess, I either go alone or we do this together.'

'Let me do this,' she said, the plea in her eyes melting him. 'Let me put this right.'

As a glimpse of tears reappeared, held back only by her sense of purpose, he reached up to cup her face.

'Let *us* put it right. We're a team. We've always been a team.' He brushed the tear from her cheek with his thumb. 'And don't you dare feel guilty for this. Don't you dare blame yourself. I was wrong back there. I was wrong to accuse you of keeping it from me. Without those tears, I'd already be dead. Honey, Billy and Amanda would never have got here. They wouldn't have the best protection they could have right now. And Honey sure as hell would have been too weak to deal with any of this.

'Even those lycan kids would have been dead if it wasn't for what you did, and we know what would have already erupted across Blackthorn if that had happened. You bought us time, okay, Jess? *All* of us. And if we get there and we don't find what we need, we'll find another way to sort this. Okay?'

'And you know what Kane will say. He'll tell us to wait until we've all headed further south together. He won't let us do this.'

'We're not accountable to him, Jess. And as *you* said, we'll be a few hours tops. Straight in. Straight out. I don't know about you, but I don't think I can wait another day or so to find out if it's there or not. And if anything happens in the interim. . .'

Jessie studied his gaze for a few moments before eventually nodding.

'Good,' he said, kissing her lightly on the forehead. 'I'll tell Kane we're going whether he likes it or not.'

'Are you going to tell Billy before we leave?'

Eden shook his head. 'I can't, Jess. He's got to stay focused. He's got to stay positive. They're going to need all the hope they can get.'

# Chapter Five

Despite the milling about in the communal area, the hush amongst the crowds betrayed everyone's anxiety at the change of events.

After the attack from the morphed lycans, they'd only just been shipped further along the tunnels into temporary safety and for a few hours' sleep before now being moved on again.

Everyone knew it was likely to have been the last time they'd rest for a long while. From then on, they'd all be on high alert in preparation to run at any point if Sirius's army got close.

Billy was already looking tired. Eden knew the signs well enough, could see he was trying to keep upbeat for Amanda and Honey, but it was taking its toll. The compound should have been their home for a while longer – maybe even a few days. But no sooner had they settled than they'd needed to move into the tunnels as the extent of Sirius's plan had become apparent.

Regardless of the stress around her though, Honey looked more resilient than she had in years. With Jessie's tears in her system, she'd changed from the fragile, pale shadow Eden had come to know to a bright, vibrant and energised little girl again. She'd even bounced back from the fourth-species attack in the tunnel without so much as a physical scar, even if the emotional damage was no doubt temporarily delayed.

For her he would do this.

For her he would find the solution.

For them all he'd find a way through that barrier.

The feel of Jessie's soft hand lacing into his brought him back to the reason he was there.

'We really need to make a move,' she reminded him as she gently squeezed.

Throat tight, hopeful he could conceal any hint of the truth from his older brother, Eden made his way through the milling bodies with Jessie by his side.

Looking up from packing his backpack to see them, Billy's subsequent hug was warm and reassuring before he offered the same to Jessie.

'You guys okay now?' Billy asked, his gaze switching between the two. 'I didn't mean to walk in on the middle of something earlier.'

'Uncle Eden!' Honey squealed as she simultaneously collided with his leg.

'Argh, the limpets around this place,' Eden muttered playfully as he grabbed her ankles and gently tugged her away so she hung upside down in mid-air.

As her laughter erupted, Eden grabbed her by the waist and cradled her in his arms before finally lifting her onto his shoulders so she was sitting above the crowds.

He smiled despite the pain in his chest as he held the lively legs of his little niece oblivious to what her uncle had done.

'You know how it is around here,' Eden said, as he readdressed Billy. 'One crisis after another. There are a couple of things I need to go and do so I might miss you before you leave.'

Reaching for his daughter to move her down into Jessie's arms, Billy cocked his head over his shoulder as an indication for his brother to take a walk with him.

'Are you holding up okay?' Billy asked, after he'd led Eden away from the crowds.

'Better than you by the looks of it. You look exhausted.'

'We're all tired, Eden.'

'How's Amanda doing?' he asked as he looked back over his shoulder to see she was now engrossed in conversation with Jessie.

To his relief, they'd hit it off quickly back at the compound. Jessie had been laden with concern as to how they would react to her – both as a third species and as a person. He sometimes forgot how isolated she'd been during her fifty years at the row during Pummel's reign. She wasn't used to normal interactions, conversation, anyone having no agenda other than to talk to her. She'd even forgotten how it felt to be liked. And, as he'd come to realise, had actually come to think of herself as incapable of being liked.

To the contrary, falling in love with her had been beyond easy. He hadn't seen it coming. He hadn't thought it possible to love anyone outside of his family. He'd never been willing to put his heart on the line. He'd even prided himself on being able to harden himself to the prospect. But then no one had ever made his heart pound like Jessie did. No one had ever burrowed into his soul like Jessie had. No one had ever made him feel as complete as Jessie did. And he'd spend every spare minute he had undoing the damage left in Pummel's wake. But even that, he was sure, would never feel enough.

'She's doing amazing,' Billy said, recapturing Eden's attention. 'I think she could get through anything now that Honey's going to be okay.'

Eden dropped his gaze, unable to sustain eye contact amidst his secret.

'But I'm glad you came to see me,' Billy added. 'I know we're all up against it. There are things I need to say. . .'

'Don't,' Eden said, meeting his gaze again. 'We're not talking as if this is final.'

'We both have to face the fact it might be. I know Kane's got a strategy and he's keeping us positive, but we all understand the extent of the threat. We all know what it's going to take to survive these next couple of days.'

'We'll find a way out. I'm working on it.'

'And if anyone can, you can. But I need to say what I need to say, Eden. And if I don't say it now, maybe I never will. The way you've stuck by my side, by Amanda's, by Honey's. . .'

'Billy,' Eden said, shaking his head as he recoiled.

'No. Listen to me,' Billy said, catching his brother's arm. 'This is what you do, Eden. Behind the charm and the smile and the wise-cracks, you never think you're worthy of a real compliment.' Billy cupped the side of his neck with his other hand. 'But I'm telling you now: I'm proud of you, little brother. There were so many times over the years that you could have given up. It would have been so easy for you to slip into a different life. Even after our mother died, even after our own father gave up on us, even with me a waste of space. . .'

'You weren't a waste of space, Billy.'

'But I wasn't the one out putting myself on the line in Lowtown and here in Blackthorn just to help us keep our heads above water; to help us survive. I'd have been dead years ago if it wasn't for you. And where would Amanda be? We probably would never have even had Honey.'

'But you did. What's the point of looking back?'

'Because sometimes you need to do it to see how far you've come. I know what it took you to sign up to the Curfew Enforcement Unit. I know how tough it was to stand your ground those first couple of years. I know how hard you had to work to prove yourself. I know how some of those people judge people like us – people without their privileges, their education, their background. But you made it anyway. More than that, you became the best they ever had. So take a compli-ment, all right?' he demanded with a smile. 'And now seeing you help lead this. . . I'm so *very* proud of you, little brother. I'm proud of the kid who came good despite the odds: just a kid off the streets who never gave up the fight and who's still fighting now. You're not just Honey's hero but mine.'

'For fuck's sake,' Eden muttered under his breath, casting his gaze down again as he blinked to rid himself of the forming tears.

'That's how that beautiful girl over there sees you too,' Billy added, indicating Jessie. 'And I can't tell you how much you deserve to have someone who finally appreciates how special you are.'

Jessie glanced over with his little niece still in her arms, the former pretending not to have heard. But Eden knew better – he knew just how attuned her angel hearing was.

'You're embarrassing me, Billy,' he said, casting his brother a warning glare.

Billy smiled and tapped him playfully on the cheek. 'Yeah, well don't let it go to your head. I haven't decided which of you is the luckier one yet.'

'She is,' Eden declared. 'Hands down. She's the luckiest girl in the world.'

He glanced over to see Jessie attempt to conceal her smile – proof that she had indeed heard every word.

'Mum would have loved her,' Billy said, recapturing his gaze, his words lacerating deep. 'All she ever wanted was for you to be happy. And you're going to get there. We *all* will.'

# Chapter Six

Rob Doyle stared at the dungeon's metal door.

Tick.

Tick.

Tick.

Tick.

He closed his eyes and clenched his jaw as the incessant clock continued to echo around the stone chamber he'd been imprisoned in for the past ten hours.

The guy he knew as Hade – Caleb's sidekick – had brought him water in the interim, which he'd given to him as opposed to undoing the restraints that bound him to the chair.

Hade had only freed his hand after he'd dragged him down the slope to the far end of the room, near the drain, as an indication for him to urinate directly into there from some awkward position half strapped to the chair. He wasn't convinced he'd be able to do it but nature had taken its course.

Hade had strapped his hand back in, ignoring his questions, before throwing a bucket of soapy water down the drain afterwards and dragging Rob back into position in the middle of the room to face the door again.

Back to the ticking clock.

Tick.

Tick.

Tick.

His yells had achieved nothing. His demands for Caleb's presence had achieved nothing.

It hadn't taken him long to detect the camera nestled in the stonework in the right-hand corner above the door. The sadistic bastard was probably watching him. Was probably enjoying watching him sweat.

And sweating he was amidst his increasingly irritating cough. The red patch on his arm was driving him to despair with its incessant itch – an itch he could not scratch.

With gritted teeth he glowered back up at the camera.

Tick.

Tick.

Tick.

But he wasn't going to plead. He wasn't going to beg. Despite the tightness in his lungs, he wasn't going to give Caleb the satisfaction.

Rob flinched as the alarm rang out, his heart pounding at the ominous sound, his attention snapping back to the door.

Shrill in the empty dungeon, the echo grated on his last nerve to the point he clenched his teeth, his bound hands preventing him from covering his ears from the horrific sound.

Eventually the door clunked open.

He drew shallow breaths as Caleb sauntered in, leaving the door open behind him.

Rob looked anxiously past him before watching the vampire approach. He felt a trickle of perspiration tease his temple, heat flushing his face as his hands and feet turned numb. His instincts kicked in and he struggled to free his wrists, despite knowing it was futile.

The vampire crouched down to pick up the clock.

Rob wanted to scream at him to turn it the fuck off, which, eventually, in his own time, Caleb did.

He placed it back down on the floor again.

As his green eyes locked on Rob's, Rob braced himself.

'I meant to unset that,' Caleb declared with a taunting glint in his eyes as Rob sat there palpitating in his restraints.

The vampire turned and sauntered back towards the door, leaving Rob to catch his breath.

'Are you fucking playing with me, Dehain?' he yelled, because he knew as well as Caleb did that it was no accident. 'Why don't you get on with it, huh? Whatever you're going to do, just do it. Is *she* a part of this? Is that why I'm here? Is it because I wouldn't work for her? Is it because I turned Feinith down?'

Caleb stopped.

Rob's heart skipped another beat.

Caleb turned on a slow pivot and sauntered back towards him.

He stopped less than a foot away, meaning Rob had to crane his neck to meet his cold gaze.

'What did you say?'

Rob took another steadying breath at the quiet but deliberate tone that exuded from the vampire. 'A couple of weeks after the trial, she came to see me. She said she could have arranged for Sirius to let me go if I agreed to work for her on my release.'

'Doing what?'

'Helping her catch Kane.'

'Sirius, you say.'

'Yeah.'

Caleb held his gaze for a moment longer. He said nothing more before turning away.

'Hey!' Rob called out again. 'You want me to talk, I'm talking!'

But once again, without another word, Caleb closed and locked the door behind himself.

# Chapter Seven

Eden paced the twenty-foot space between the two tunnel doors.

Sorran, Nico and Jed had all headed above ground to check if the coast was clear. Sorran had been anxious about accompanying them there without Kane's permission, but he also knew they'd go without him otherwise.

They'd tried to find Kane, but he'd already headed off with another team somewhere. With no idea how long he'd be, they left a message instead and made a move while they could.

It went against the grain sending out scouts first, but Eden knew they had to be sensible. He also knew they were on a time constraint, which was why he wasn't going to stand around waiting for Kane to return. This wasn't only about his niece – this was about Jessie. This was about giving her the chance to feel as though she was doing something to compensate for what she now felt responsible for, despite him having tried to convince her to the contrary. And that was what he loved about her more than anything else: Jessie had never – would never – sit back waiting to be saved or wait for others to play saviour on her behalf. Jessie was more than capable of stepping up to the mark, and she always would. She was stepping up to the mark for him right now – and for Honey. The least he could do was be by her side.

She stood leaning against the wall by the steel door. Head down-turned, her ringlets concealing her profile, she scuffed her ballet shoe against the concrete floor. Though brimming with determination to find a solution, they both knew there was no guarantee that the files were still there. They hadn't been back to that part of the row since they'd accompanied Leila to temporarily close the gateway to the fourth dimension. He hoped for Jessie's sake as much as for Honey's that they were.

He could already see the seeds of doubt affecting her composure as they waited to find out. But whichever one of them was plagued by doubt, the other stepped in to be the bolster. They worked in perfect unison; they were the perfect team.

He instantly captured her attention as he stepped over to join her.

He caught hold of her hips and stepped backwards, pulling her between his legs as he rested back against the wall. In the subtle light from the lantern left by the door, her eyes already displayed a subtle hint of forest green that reflected her concern.

'Whatever we find, we'll sort this,' he assured her.

'We'd better. I can't lose you, Eden.'

'You're not going to lose me.'

'We lost Alisha. Jake's gone. We nearly lost Caitlin. Nearly lost Jask. We might even have lost Leila. What if we're not so lucky this time? Shit happens, Eden. Reality happens. This is Blackthorn. What if *we're* the ones who don't get our happy ending?' She pressed her lips together, the subtle tremor in them telling him he'd left her to be locked in those thoughts for too long. 'I'm scared.'

Eden released her hips to push her ringlets back over both shoulders before clutching both sides of her neck and brushing his thumbs upwards along her jaw.

'Hey,' he said gently, holding her gaze. 'This is *us*. We escaped the cons together. We've killed fourth species together. We even battled those morphed lycans Sirius set loose. We've got this, okay? We do what we always do when we're scared: we face up to the fear and we do something about it. Together.'

Jessie broke into a smile and nodded.

Wanting nothing more than to give her that added reassurance, that sense of connection, he kept his kiss slow, lingering, tender, letting her lose herself, and lose himself, in the moment; letting everything beyond the door melt away.

Instantly her breath was taunting against his mouth, the pliability of her soft lips evoked a stirring in the confines of his jeans. He savoured every second: her taste, the warmth of her reciprocation. More so, as his tongue teased hers, her sensual playfulness had him clutching her jaw tighter and then her neck, his thumb brushing her lobe and then under her ear.

'How long do you think they'll be?' she asked, pulling back.

Catching her hips, not ready to let her go yet, he turned her away from him. 'They've only been ten minutes.' He slid down to the floor, taking Jessie down with him to nestle her between his spread thighs. He wrapped his arm across her shoulders and collarbone, keeping her close against him as he rested his jaw against her temple.

She captured his wrist that rested against her shoulder and rubbed her thumb caressingly back and forth along it as the seconds ticked by in silence.

'I hope you didn't mind that I heard earlier,' she said.

His heart skipped a beat. 'Heard what?' he asked, though he knew exactly what she was referring to.

'You know what.' She paused. 'I knew you didn't have it easy. . .'

'It's in the past, Jess. My brother prefers to dwell. I don't.'

'But it made you who you are. It helps me understand who you are.'

'You know who I am. Just as I know who you are without needing to know everything about *your* past.'

She kept her gaze ahead as a few more silent seconds ticked by.

'I talked a lot to Amanda and Billy back at the compound. They told me how much you'd done for them.'

'They're my family, Jess. Looking out for your own isn't worthy of an accolade. I've done a lot of things I'm not proud of too. Billy remembers things as though I was permanently some kind of hero, but he's not remembering the arguments, and the drunken nights, and having to clean up my cuts and bruises, or me disappearing for a couple of days at a time, or the string of women who subsequently brought trouble to our door.'

She looked over her shoulder to meet his gaze. She raised her eyebrows slightly in playful accusation. 'That many, huh?'

'Come on, Jess,' he said, the connection he felt looking into her eyes reminding him just how empty his past encounters had been. 'Don't remind me.'

'With who you've become, I don't think you should have any regrets from your past.'

'You wouldn't be saying that if you'd met me back then.'

'You don't think I would have liked you?'

'You would have hated me.'

'How can you be so sure?'

'Reckless, opportunistic, volatile, impulsive – a promiscuous bastard too. I was a very different guy, to the point where I could easily have ended up in one of those rows myself.'

'But you didn't.'

'By luck, Jess.'

'No,' she said with a slight shake of her head. 'Because of who you are. Because you made a better life for you and Billy regardless. Where you are now is not by accident, Eden.'

'Where? Still trying to save Billy's arse but now the rest of Blackthorn and Lowtown too?' He flashed a hint of a smirk. 'Nothing changes.'

'Except now you have me,' she said, her gaze lingering on his. 'That must make you the luckiest guy in the world, right?'

As her lips curled into an irresistible smile amidst her taunt, as she echoed his earlier conversation with Billy, he caught her jaw just before she turned away.

'Count *your*self lucky,' he goaded back. 'Who would want a master vampire or a lycan leader when they can have Eden Reece? And you're the one who snagged me.'

She laughed.

And he didn't realise how much he'd needed to hear that.

As she rested her head back against his shoulder, he ran the back of his fingers along her jawline.

'No matter how someone behaves,' she said, looking back at him, 'it's their eyes that reveal who they really are. No one and nothing can take the depth out of yours. I saw it from the outset.'

The way her gaze lingered made his heart pound, the hardness in his jeans forming an immediate distraction.

'So you were able to see beyond my exceptional good looks and incredible body then?' he asked.

She laughed again. 'But obviously it was your infallible modesty that finally won me over.'

He smiled from deep within as she continued to play along.

'With you it was your arse,' he teased. 'And all those glimpses of these sexy mid-thighs.'

She chuckled as he ran the back of his free hand up her inner thigh – a move that led to a playful wrestle to the floor as she let him overpower her.

But then she glanced anxiously at the door.

'Behave,' she warned with a smile as she looked back at him. 'They could be back any minute.'

'Just like the old days,' he said, reciprocating her smile as he unbuttoned her shirt to reveal the left cup of her bra. 'Sneaking around.' He nibbled her ear lightly, knowing how it gave her goosebumps, before nipping his way down her neck, over her collarbone, down to the upper curve of her breast. 'Misbehaving.'

'If they come back. . .'

'They're not going to hear anything through three inches of steel – third species or not.'

'Eden. . .'

But he tucked his forefinger over the cup of her soft cotton bra, despite her low-level protest, and eased it down to free her breast to his mouth.

His erection stiffened at her instant gasp, her nipple hardening first from its exposure to the cool air around them then from the heat of his mouth, the stroke of his tongue.

As her fist knotted in his hair, as she instantly lifted her groin against him, he opened his mouth wider, consuming her more hungrily, sliding his hand up beneath her breast to squeeze tenderly.

'You have no shame,' she whispered.

'Of what?' he asked, keeping a hold of her and brushing his thumb across her damp nipple as he gazed back up into her eyes. 'Making love to the girl I adore?'

'Adore, huh?' she said, her eyes glinting, her smile broadening.

'I'd die for you, Jessie. And you know it.'

The instant evaporation of her smile told him his choice of proclamation hit home too hard amidst the reality they were facing. Her frown deepened as her gaze rested on his, her eyes turning the deepest shade of crimson amidst her sadness.

He berated himself for letting it cross her mind again.

'But not today,' he declared, as he pinned both her hands gently back either side of her head to veer her back to light-hearted playfulness.

'How about never?'

'Deal. But only if we stick to our pact right now: making the most of every spare moment. Live each one like it's our last.'

She glanced back at the door before meeting his gaze. 'They could knock any minute.'

'Then best not waste anymore time,' he said, lowering his lips to indulge in another lingering kiss before caressing her neck, his lips brushing the metal chain of the necklace that now fell across her shoulder.

He loathed the sight of it: the vial-holding chain that bound her through a curse that had been placed on her by her own. A curse that had not only wiped her memory of her past and any sense of her identity with it but had led her to be imprisoned by Pummel when he'd taken possession of her necklace.

With the necklace restricting her to within five miles of its presence, they'd had no choice but to take it with them in order to get back to the row.

'How was it you described yourself?' she asked, bringing him back to task. 'Reckless, impulsive. . .?'

'Looks like you bring out the best and worst of me then, Jessie Reece.'

It rolled off his tongue without him even thinking about it.

She stilled beneath him. 'Jessie *Reece*?'

He tentatively met her gaze. They were in it for the long haul, they both knew that, but neither of them had talked much about their futures.

'It's about time you had a surname,' he said. 'And I'm claiming first dibs over choices.'

To his relief, she smiled again, her crimson hues changing to violet. 'First *dibs*? You're such a kid sometimes, Reece.'

'The way I can satisfy you? I don't think so, sugar.'

He popped the top button on her loose-fitting jeans before sliding the zip down.

Her breathing instantly notched up to an almost human rate as he slid his hand down into the front of her knickers to find her sex, his own arousal peaking as he discovered hers too.

'Why do I let you talk me into this, Eden?' she asked with a heavy, sated sigh, her free hand clutching his upper arm as he eased his finger inside her.

'Because I'm irresistible?' He pushed his middle finger deep into her heat, Jessie instantly closing her eyes, breathlessness leaving her parted lips. 'Because I can do this to you. . .' He simultaneously brushed his thumb across her clit, making her jolt. 'Because you love me *almost* as much as I love you?'

She prised open her eyes to give him a sultry gaze that had his erection throbbing.

'And one day,' he said, 'I'll be able to offer you more than back-alley dives and tunnel floors. I'll be able to give you what you deserve.'

'I don't care where I am as long as I'm with you, Eden.'

A spark ignited deep within his core. He gently withdrew his hand to lay it flat beside her head and gazed down at the perfection lying willingly beneath him.

'We should be going for gold,' he said, tugging down her jeans and her underwear.

'For *what*?'

'For first place for fitting in a quick, furtive shag whenever possible.'

She laughed again.

Discarding her shoes, her jeans and her underwear, he lifted her into his lap as she simultaneously slid his jacket down over his shoulders and tugged his T-shirt off over his head too.

Resting back against the wall, keeping her thighs spread either side of his, he guided her to sit astride him as she unfastened his fly.

'Maybe I was a *little* bit attracted to this body too,' she said, referring to their previous conversation. The feel of her soft hands gliding firmly down his shoulders, down over the tattoo of his shoulder armour and both pecs, made him harden to the point of discomfort.

'Just a *little* bit?' he asked, unable to take his eyes off her as he rested his head back against the wall; watched as she unbuttoned her shirt with one hand whilst simultaneously wrapping her hand around his erection.

It tipped him close to the edge every time: the way she watched herself toy with him, handling him with a tender but firm caress as she interchanged between feather-light touches and long, lingering strokes.

He raked his hand through her hair, entwining her ringlets through his fingers as he observed her every expression, her eyes glazing over with her own escalating arousal.

He closed his eyes, absorbing the sensation of her touch, opening them only as she slid further down his legs to replace her hand with her mouth.

He inhaled deeply, his breath trembling as it left his body again. His hand on the nape of her neck, he rested his head back against the wall, letting her take control.

But he couldn't handle it for more than a couple of minutes before he caught hold of her upper arms; pulled her to him.

He gazed into her still-glazed eyes, her soft swollen lips glossed with his pre-cum.

He caught hold of the nape of her neck again and slid his free hand back between her legs, her thighs still spread either side of his.

She pressed her forehead against his, her palms flat to the wall either side of his head, her heavy breaths resounding around the tunnel as he caressed the folds of her sex interchangeably with teasing her clit.

His hand tight on her nape, he captured her mouth with his, slid his tongue inside her mouth at the same time as he gently eased his middle finger into her sex again, her breath catching again at the intimacy of it. And he teased her further by using the same pressure, the same rhythm with both, making the most of the sensitivity of her mouth and sex simultaneously.

'You didn't learn that kind of trick being good,' she said breathily against his lips. 'There are definite pluses to your past.'

He smiled again. His middle finger still inside her, he slid the pad of his index finger back and forth along her sex for a moment before easing it inside her alongside the other.

Jessie jolted and grasped his shoulder, her nails embedded in his flesh, her gaze meeting his again.

Grasping her behind with his free hand, squeezing hard enough to leave finger marks, he lowered his mouth to her breasts, toyed with her hard nipples with his tongue, Jessie's grip on his shoulder intensifying, her breathing becoming more ragged.

Sensing her moving close to climax, her gasp caused his erection to strain, his own breath hitching as he heard her sigh of pleasure, of her absolution at his touch.

And time was short – potentially too short to play for too long.

Removing his fingers, he clutched the firm flesh of her behind to lift her and pull her into position, his other hand then clutching the nape of her neck again as he lowered her onto him and he eased himself inside her.

It got better every time. He never thought he'd find anyone who he could think that of, but every time with Jessie intensified his love for her more.

And he knew that was the difference between the empty, soulless fuck he'd wasted too many years indulging in and being with her – being with the only girl he could ever imagine being with ever again.

As he filled her to the hilt, he closed his eyes to sate himself with every exquisite inch of entering her, connecting with her, consuming her.

And as he opened his eyes again, opened them to look into hers, he felt his arousal peak, his tension soar.

Finding their rhythm was effortless; the most natural feeling he'd ever experienced. Clutching her waist, he rotated her subtly amidst thrusting up to meet her as she pushed down onto him again and again.

She lowered her head, her hands grasping both sides of his neck, her short, curt breaths reinforcing what he already knew: that this was going to be one of those times when they'd both come quickly whether they wanted to or not.

And as she clenched around him, as her eyes met his, his breathing jarred, a sating ache rushing from his fingers to his toes as his climax peaked, as he held himself on the brink for as long as he could before finally spilling inside her.

He clutched her neck and gazed into her eyes, letting her catch her breath as he caught his own.

'Do I tell you enough that I love you, Jessie Reece?'

This time she barely batted an eyelid at him saying it. 'Everything you do for me is enough. You couldn't give me anymore, Eden.'

'When I know I've given you all that I'm capable of, then it'll be enough.' He ran his fingers down her vial-holding chain. 'Including finding a way to free you from this.' He met and held her gaze. 'Once and for all.'

# Chapter Eight

Jessie followed Eden as he followed Sorran up through the manhole.

Nico and Jed, the two vampires who had accompanied the lycan, had remained on full alert outside.

Once Sorran had received the signal that the coast was still clear, Eden took her by the hand and they headed out of the alley and across the street to the burned-out row.

The same queasiness struck her stomach as when they'd returned only a few days before to temporarily seal the fourth dimension in the lock-up in the alley behind.

She looked up to where her room once was, nestled in the attic. Now nothing but night sky loomed back at her. The window she had stood at on the landing and first seen Eden through was gone. Every part of her fifty years in that row was gone, except the memories. Memories of the evil of humankind laid bare around her; memories of isolation, emotional abuse, being used by Pummel for her blood, that cupboard under the stairs where he used to lock her away on the rare occasion she overstepped the mark. . .

'You okay, Jess?'

Jessie tore her attention from the blackened remnants to meet Eden's concerned gaze, not having realised she'd come to a standstill.

'Yes,' she said, adding a nod to reassure him, reminding herself that they needed to get off the street as quickly as possible.

Sorran waited in the recess of the corner shop. 'We'll keep watch outside.'

'We'll be quick,' Eden reassured him as they brushed past him, having as much intention as the rest of them of hanging around.

Jessie scanned the dusty interior of what had once been a thriving local shop in an equally thriving residential area, before the regulations came into being. Thirty years later, the cons had moved into the south.

Now the place was littered with graffiti, empty alcohol bottles, used condoms and whatever else the cons who resided in the area had seen the building fit for.

They stepped over and through the debris that remained, remnants of what had clearly been more than one ransacking over the years. Moving plasterboard aside from the broken ceiling above, Eden shouldered his way through the door at the back.

The dusty office brought pangs of a whole other kind as she saw the desk was still there: Toby's desk.

When the regulations had come into being, having run the business well and meeting the standards required, Toby had been offered a place in Midtown. Moving to Midtown would have meant leaving Jessie, a third species, behind though. She could potentially have furtively relocated to Lowtown, but the chances of her being discovered at some point were high.

Compelling her to stay even more was her connection to that exact location. That was the place where she had first woken a century and a half before, knowing nothing but her name and that she was an angel. That was the place where she'd channelled the prophecies. She didn't understand it, she couldn't explain it, but she knew she needed to be there. And Toby had opted to stay with her.

From the moment he'd found her on his lock-up floor, to the years he'd spent before the regulations finding out as much about her kind as he could, he had been her only friend. He had been her best friend.

Even after the regulations, Toby had spent thirty years researching all he had discovered to try and put as many pieces about her together as possible. Then the cons were moved into the area – a backup to the overspill from the penitentiary across the border.

Pummel had picked that row. He'd picked that house. He'd brutally murdered her best friend right in front of her, the only friend she'd had, slayed and gutted by the con who had broken into their home.

And she had been trapped in squalor on the row for five decades under Pummel's subsequent oppression, bound helplessly by the necklace that had condemned her to his ownership.

She snapped back to the present day as she tuned into Eden's curse.

He was crouched amongst the paperwork that littered the room from the open and buckled filing cabinets that lined the back wall.

'Don't worry, it's not in those,' she reassured him, stepping over to join him. 'They just hold the official accounts.'

Jessie squeezed between two of the cabinets and, using her behind, put her weight against one, pushing it backwards until, eventually, she'd exposed the air vent behind.

'Toby kept all the research hidden away,' she explained, hoping no one had taken the time to look beyond the cabinets.

Slipping her fingers into the vent cover, she dislodged it from the wall, pushing it inwards along with a cut-out square of plasterboard.

Crouching and stepping through the three-foot-square gap, relief washed through her as she saw the narrow, secret room had remained untouched. She hurriedly rubbed away a tear from her cheek. It was hitting her even harder back here than it had in the office, vivid memories flashing through her mind of Toby spreading his paperwork out over the floor, talking through his findings after every trip.

Some trips had taken him away for months at a time as he travelled the world, following lead after lead into some of the darkest and most secretive places around the globe. Every time he came back with something new – urban legends, folk tales, whispers in small, reclusive communities insisting on the existence of angels walking amongst them; of both their healing *and* destructive powers. Angels weren't always spoken of with awe – sometimes they were feared.

Having followed through behind her, Eden's reassuring hand on the nape of her neck told her he had noticed and had understood. He pulled her into him, wrapped his arms around her and gave her a gentle squeeze as he kissed her on the temple.

Amidst his empathy, she could also feel his relief that a solution might still be within reach. And that, right then, was what they both needed to focus on.

She kissed him lightly on the lips. 'Let's do this.'

Eden removed the two torches from her rucksack. Despite their eyes being able to adjust to the pitch blackness, it would take too long for them to adjust to read and scan quickly enough. As well as the torch, he handed her a set of pins to pick the lock.

As soon as Eden broke the first cabinet open, he worked his way through the papers, Jessie opening hers moments later.

'There's so much here, Jess,' he said. 'This is going to take hours. Hours that we don't have.'

She hadn't wanted it to cloud them getting there. She knew Toby's research had been immense by the end of it. She didn't know where to start looking either, the prospect of them having to take reams of paper with them increasingly likely and her rucksack looking increasingly defunct with it. They were going to have to rope Sorran in, as well as Nico and Jed. They'd have to get as much as they could below ground. There was no way they could carry it all the way back, or keep carrying it with the movement plan that was being instigated. They'd have to risk staying put for a few hours. They'd have to get the message back to Kane as to what they were doing.

'Let's check the tabs first,' she said. 'There might be some files that seem more relevant than others.'

She ploughed through each tab in careful succession, searching for anything that would indicate a specific section on angel tears.

Eden did exactly the same, both needing to make initial snap judgements about what was relevant and what was not.

Recollections of overhearing Billy's words to him caused a knot in Jessie's throat, especially having watched the way Eden had met his brother's gaze – like a little boy whose older brother's approval still mattered. It had added to the vulnerable side of Eden that he seemed to only show to her. Because beneath the hard street kid and the even harder CEO exterior, things and people really did matter to Eden. His family certainly mattered. And the knowledge that she had unwittingly poisoned one of the most precious people to him cast another shadow over her hope, like a cloud over the sun, the reminder that *she* had poisoned him too creating a total eclipse.

She knew with every instinct that she could never be without him. She may have known him less than a week, but life without Eden Reece was unthinkable. Even amidst the darkness in that room, surrounded by dust and decay, she never felt more alive, safer, more full of hope than when she was right next to him.

There *had* to be a way to undo what she had done.

Failing that, the doctor would know. Sirius had given the tears to his entire army, which meant he had eventually got the balance right. He knew how to manage whatever condition angel tears evoked.

Sensing her stillness, Eden caught her gaze, his brown eyes locking on hers with concern. 'You okay?'

She nodded and reverted her attention to the papers, more determined than ever – if that was possible – to find what they were looking for.

She flicked through a few more irrelevant files before closing the top drawer and opening the second.

'You have to stop blaming yourself for this, Jessie. I gave those tears to Honey. It was me she trusted. It was *my* choice to give them to her.'

'I will if you will. Because you *had* no choice, Eden. She was a victim of this system. She was one of thousands of others *still* a victim of Sirius's greater plan. And until we change it, that's how things will remain. But we *will* change it. We'll find a way out of here, I promise. Sirius won't get Kane. He's not going to get anything he wants. For as long as Kane is in these walls, we have hope. He's certainly not going to nuke the place with him in it.'

Eden's eyes narrowed slightly, his frown suddenly pensive, his gaze locked blankly on the paperwork as if lost for a moment.

She knew that look. She'd seen that look cross his eyes more than once.

'Eden what is it?'

'He has a wormhole,' Eden muttered, primarily to himself.

Her heart skipped a beat. 'What?'

Eden snatched his gaze back to hers, his ignited with hope. 'It's so obvious. How did we not see it? That's the weakness, Jess. Needing Kane out alive whilst keeping us contained is Sirius's weakness.'

'I don't understand.'

'Sirius is here to *collect* Kane, which means he's got to be able to get him out before he can do anything else. But he can't risk bringing that barrier down for a second, especially in the middle of a war, so he *has* to have an entry and exit point – something that bridges Lowtown and Blackthorn – or how else is he going to get Kane out once he has him? We don't need to be focusing on how to bring the barrier down because a passageway already exists.'

'But you explained to us all that for the electromagnetic field to work it has to run on a complete circuit – that it can't be broken. That's why we can't get the EMP through.'

'Unless you have something of a denser property or even another electromagnetic field that's stronger than the EMF already in place, something the field simply moves around before continuing.'

'A rock in a stream,' Jessie said, finally understanding. 'The wormhole is the rock in the stream.'

'And my bet is it's also the source of the barrier.'

'The circuit battery.' Jessie's heart pounded a little harder. 'And if it's not protected by the electro-magnetic field, an EMP can penetrate it, which means we could collapse it.'

'*Or* leave the barrier intact and get those we need to through the wormhole without Sirius suspecting a thing.'

Jessie let out a small squeal as she wrapped her arms around Eden, pulling him close. 'You're a genius, Eden Reece.'

'And a sex god, Jess. Don't forget genius *and* sex god.' He eased her away from him, his hands tight on her hips. 'But let's not get too overexcited. We still have to find where it is. We're potentially talking about a tunnel system within a maze of tunnel systems. Tunnel systems that are already being invaded. And even if we do find it, we can guarantee it'll be more heavily guarded than the border itself. But as they came in from the north, I think that's our best place to start. They're most likely covering their backs whilst driving us forward. That's going to limit our time for checking it out, though.'

'But we have a plan, Eden,' she said, squeezing his hands. 'We have to get back. We have to tell Kane.'

'I'm going to get Sorran and the others to help shift as much of this into the tunnel as we can,' he said, stepping back over to the gap in the wall. 'We can carry on reading as they get back to Kane.'

Adrenaline pumping, Jessie took the folders out of the cabinet one by one, stacking them on the floor in preparation to be collected. With five of them it would take less than twenty minutes to carry them all back across to the alley.

But as she crouched down, as she lifted the third folder, she stopped. She stared at Toby's writing across the front cover: *Tears*.

She fell onto her knees. She hurriedly pinged back the elastic on the cardboard folder and grabbed the top pieces of paper. With a quick skim, she saw references to angel tears were made throughout.

Her heart pounded; her hands trembled.

She slid all the pieces of paper back into a pile, slamming the folder shut again. Clutching it in her hand, she hurried back through the hole in the wall.

'Eden!' she called out, nearly tumbling over the debris in the office amidst her eagerness to get to him, before she burst into the shop.

She saw the shadow in the doorway. She snatched back a breath at the crossbow poised in her direction.

Her heart plummeted and her stomach flipped as she saw Eden lying motionless on the floor.

Pain shot through her thigh.

And her world turned black.

# Chapter Nine

Caleb sat at the head of the table. As he leaned back in his chair, his green eyes fixated on the spaghetti he twirled and knotted around his fork with a precision Feinith had never seen anyone else achieve, every mouthful not allowing a drop beyond his lips.

His gaze had remained lowered for most of dinner. In some ways she was grateful because when he did look at her, his eyes steady and penetrative, it had taken all her strength not to look away.

He'd barely talked to her since Jake's death. She'd caught him standing, whisky by his side, gazing red-eyed at the hallway that led to Jake's bedroom. A couple of times, she guessed she should have felt guilty, but what she was doing was for the greater good, and Jake had always been the unwelcome conscience.

But rather than be tempted straight into the rampage she had hoped for, Caleb had developed a troubling amount of silence. He'd kept the shutters down ever since, throwing them into a cocoon with the rest of the world blocked out.

'I know you're still distressed about Jake, Caleb, but we need to talk.'

He placed his fork diagonally on the plate before wiping his mouth on a napkin and leaned back in his chair, one hand casually in his lap, the other turning his whisky glass on the table before he took a mouthful.

Her slow vampire heart skipped a beat as he finally met and held her gaze, his expression remaining impossible to read.

As well as the army having moved in and the barrier having gone up, she'd already told him she'd had it confirmed from Hess that the entire Higher Order had been moved to an unknown location.

She'd been in touch with Hess not long after Caleb had found Jake. Hess had told her the Higher Order house had been raided and that they had all been taken in. She'd told her Jarin had been accused of being the prophesied vampire leader. She'd been warned to stay away. She knew they'd be looking for her too – especially Sirius.

'We're on the brink of war,' she added, 'and on the brink of losing everything we have waited for with it. I need something from you, Caleb. I need to know what you're planning to do. I need you to act.'

He took a steady mouthful of whisky. He placed the cut-crystal glass on the table again and pushed his chair back, the scrape across the floor grating through her every nerve as he stood.

'Try to take it easy,' he said as he strolled towards her.

The urge to stand as he stepped behind her was overwhelming, but she remained seated.

She flinched as he placed his hands on her neck.

'You're too tense,' he added as he slid his thumbs simultaneously up the nape of her neck, his fingers spanning her shoulders.

The pressure he applied verged on the rough side of sensual as he worked her with a firm and precise massage.

'You need to relax,' he said, sliding his fingers up her throat to the point he was circling her neck. 'To trust me.'

She tightened her grip on the armrests of the chair before forcing herself to place her hands in her lap.

He rubbed his thumbs along her shoulder blades before dragging his hands across the upward curves of her breasts, close enough to make her close her eyes to relish the feel of him. But it was impossible to suppress her awareness of him behind her. Of not being able to read his face.

'How can I when you give me nothing? You should have an entire army out there looking for that serryn. If we lose her, we lose our guarantee of winning this, Caleb. With Sirius's army already on the streets, her chances of survival are depleting by the hour.'

'I have Rob Doyle downstairs.'

Her stomach flipped. 'Who?'

'Everyone knows who Rob Doyle is. Ex-TSCD Rob Doyle, supposedly doing time for killing Arana Malloy.' His pause was painful. 'You went to visit him in his cell to make a proposition a couple of weeks after the trial.'

She stared ahead at the empty space in front of her and forced herself to stay calm. 'In a bid to up our chances of getting our hands on Malloy,' she said, hurriedly justifying herself as Caleb resumed his firm massage.

'And work with Sirius to do so.'

'We've been through this: to secure the best chance for us. To get close to Kane. To persuade him to work with us.'

'Before you knew about me? Before you knew your vampire leader was already in the wings.'

'We had a potential serryn on the loose, Caleb. You know why I was doing what I was doing. If you had told me then what you were, I would have played it differently. I left believing she had power over you; had made you vulnerable. There was every chance she would warn her sister. I couldn't have our key to the prophecy on the run out there. I've explained this.'

'But Doyle turned you down. You were going to plead for his release, let him use the victim card for being a young, naïve rookie under the control of two more senior agents, and you were going to have him working for you. But it seems Sirius recruited him from under your nose instead. So what lie did you spin Sirius then, Feinith? Because it sounds to me like you're rapidly becoming entangled in your own web.'

A web that was fast taking a stranglehold. A web that had left her with no choice but to remain within Caleb's domain in order to retain sanctuary.

He kissed her on the top of her head before taking her by the hand and sauntering across to the bedroom.

'How did you get your hands on him?' she asked, when all she really wanted to ask was what exactly Doyle had told him.

'Like I keep telling you,' Caleb remarked, not turning to face her. 'I never sit around doing fuck all.'

Feinith glanced at the bed as he let her hand go. She watched him crouch in front of the bedside cabinet to unlock its door.

He removed the phone from within, its landline cable trailing as he placed it on the bed.

He sat against the headboard, his legs casually splayed in front of him, the phone at his feet.

She looked back up into his steady green eyes, and her heart picked up a notch to an almost human rate. 'What is this, Caleb?'

'My bet is you have Sirius's direct number.'

She searched his gaze, looking for any kind of clue as to what he was thinking. 'And?'

'I want you to make a deal with him.'

'What kind of a deal?'

'I want you to tell him I'm still sticking to my side of the deal. I want you to tell him I have Kane. I want you to tell him I'm willing to exchange him for Jarin.'

# Chapter Ten

Jessie woke to the thrum of blood flow in her ears.

She forced her heavy eyes open, the room swaying around her, and tried to blink away the blurriness, her breathing loud against the leather roll that was fixed between her teeth and secured behind her head.

Although she couldn't see properly, she knew she was seated. In what exactly, she had no idea, but she couldn't move her arms or her legs. She tried to look down, but something cold and hard held her head in position as if she was in a head clamp.

Jessie strained her arms to try and free her wrists, but the leather straps held them down – her palms upwards, inner arms exposed. Her parted legs were also restrained by the leather binds around her ankles. She flexed her fingers and tried to blink away more of the blurriness; shake off the woozy sensation.

She flinched as a figure came into view directly ahead. The girl staring back at her was clamped into what looked like an execution chair, lit by a single light on the wall either side.

Her heart pounded harder as she realised she was staring at herself.

The room was cold and bare and, from what she could see of the reflection staring back at her, maybe twenty-by-twenty foot. The walls were mottled with a mixture of peeling mint-green paint and damp, the corners riddled with dead flies. Somewhere in the corridor directly behind, beyond the open door, a dripping tap echoed, telling of further empty and bare rooms.

She took steadying breaths as, whatever room she was in, the mirror ahead indicated some kind of observation chamber – and that meant someone could be looking in; could be watching.

Cons.

Her breaths were involuntarily ragged again.

Cons who didn't only have her but Eden too. Cons who had taken Eden right from under her.

A tear trickled down her cheek as panic – not for herself but for Eden – and even anger consumed her. She clenched her jaw and gritted her teeth against the leather, breathing heavily through her nose as she fought to curb her frustration; as she did everything she could to conceal her emotions from whoever would, no doubt, be watching on with amusement from the other side of the two-way mirror.

She glared directly at it – glared directly at whoever was hidden beyond.

She had spent too long – fifty years – staring day after day into the faces of pure evil. Staring into the eyes of the sickest and most depraved side of so-called humanity.

She fought to suppress the thoughts tumbling through her head of what fate awaited them both as the helplessness of her situation became an increasing reality. She fought to block out all that she had witnessed during her decades trapped in Pummel's row. Fought to repress the conversations and stories that had plagued her nightmares and given her nights of sleeplessness. Blinked away visions of the scenes she had been forced to watch just so Pummel could entertain himself with her subsequent distress and horror: the beatings, the assaults, the murders, the rapes, the humiliations, the mutilations – all in the name of a good night in for Pummel's row. All the sideshows that had earned him lucrative deals and taken him up the next rung of the ladder in control of the south.

But now he was dead. Long gone.

Where one con was removed though, another would replace him. Cons were like mould in a damp room, the spores always finding a way.

She clenched her hands amidst no choice but to await her fate then twitched her head as she heard footsteps. Light footsteps. Female footsteps.

What should have been preferable to heavy male footsteps did nothing to relieve the unease in her chest. There was no sexism in the south of Blackthorn. No fairer sex amongst the cons. The murderers, the rapists, the assaulters could be female in equal measure to male. She knew from Tatum and Mya – back in Pummel's row – how the female cons thrived on the depravity, the cruelty, as much as the males.

Women that could already have Eden in another room.

She squeezed her eyes shut and clamped down hard on the leather roll, her need to know preferable to the running thoughts of what could be happening to Eden somewhere nearby.

The woman stopped in the doorway. Maybe in her late twenties, she was unassuming in her jeans and sweater, her simple ponytail of fine, fair hair brushed forward over her shoulder to mid-breast.

As she approached, she was void of the swagger or lethal seduction that tended to accompany female cons. Instead, there was an unassertive edge to her small strides.

She stepped in front of Jessie, a small contraption that looked like eyelash curlers in her right hand, a needle in the other.

Jessie's heart beat a little harder as she gazed up into the woman's eyes.

She instantly knew what she was. She'd seen eyes as intense as hers before. Except the eyes she'd looked into then had been of a newly found friend: Caitlin.

These shadow reader's eyes were anything but.

Jessie's breaths turned shallow as she realised the shadow reader's intention.

This shadow reader was under command as if from the old system, back when shadow readers were owned by third-species lords who utilised their skills to control their dominions.

Or, as seemed more likely considering where she, Eden and the others had been captured, this shadow reader was now owned by a con.

Regardless, she was there to garner information – information Jessie couldn't afford anyone to have. Information of her team's plans, of their whereabouts, of Caleb being the pending vampire leader, of Leila already rushing to him to change things. . . and now them having worked out the existence of a wormhole. . .

*Sirius.*

Her heart skipped a beat. The prospect was a fate worse than cons – something she'd never thought possible.

There was every chance he hadn't given up looking for her; that he hadn't given up looking for Eden, who he'd sent in to get her. And now Sirius Throme was about to know *everything*.

Jessie looked pleadingly into the woman's eyes but, taken from the impassiveness in the gaze that looked back at her, it was futile.

With her mouth gagged, she could do nothing to put forward a case. She could do nothing to beg for the lives of those she cared about – for the chance at freedom that had finally been within their grasp.

The woman slipped the tip of the syringe into Jessie's inner arm.

Jessie knew the sedative was to make her shadow more accessible – to stop her fighting back against the shadow reader once she was inside her thoughts, her memories.

Because the shadow reader would be. She would see everything that Jessie had seen; everything Jessie had ever heard as far as her memory allowed. As far back as 150 years, to the point where her memory had been wiped: stolen from her as punishment for a crime she couldn't recall.

The shadow reader would see the most intimate recesses of her mind. She would see and feel all of Jessie's encounters with Eden and subsequently burrow into the most private and precious parts of her thoughts and memories.

And, with it, the shadow reader would know what Eden meant to her. Sirius would know what he meant to her.

This was what Sirius was planning to do with Kane once he got him. He would sedate him to the hilt and use the most powerful shadow reader he could get his hands on to penetrate the master vampire's knowledge and find the secret he wanted. He had intended that to be Caitlin until his plan to turn her against Kane had failed. But Sirius was the type who always had a back-up plan.

As the sedative seeped into her system, her vision and the room were thrown off-kilter again. It was a powerful sedative to have had such a fast effect on her, its application no doubt trialled and tested on others of her kind before her.

'If you don't already know,' the woman finally said, holding up the delicate-looking metal device in her hand, 'this process is most effective when I can look into your eyes to read your shadow. You can opt to comply, or I can peel your eyes open,' she added, the purpose of the lid clamp then apparent. 'And keep them open. Which would you rather?'

Jessie glared back at her before indicating downwards towards her hands.

The shadow reader glanced down.

Jessie clenched her hands into fists before raising the middle finger on both.

The shadow reader lifted one thin fair eyebrow as she looked back into Jessie's defiant eyes.

'So be it,' she said, and stepped forward.

# Chapter Eleven

'You expect Throme to give you Jarin?'

Jarin: her betrothed. Feinith could barely even believe Caleb had made the suggestion.

'And you want *me* to make the deal?' she added.

His gaze broken from hers, Caleb removed the packet of cigarettes from his shirt pocket. He placed one between his lips before igniting his lighter then looked back at her as though he'd asked for nothing more than a coffee.

'He's not going to give you Jarin,' she added. 'I told you what Hess said. I told you he's been accused of being the vampire leader. There's no way Sirius will allow him into Blackthorn.'

'He will if he wants Kane.'

He left his exhalation of smoke to linger with her shock before he moved off the bed.

As he strolled back out of the bedroom, Feinith stared down at the phone.

Pivoting on her heels, she hurried behind him.

'You can't give him what you don't have!'

'*Yet*,' Caleb said, not turning to face her. 'What I don't have *yet*.'

Entering the lounge, he stepped behind the bar and reached to one of the shelves beneath it.

'If you give him Kane, he will destroy Blackthorn,' Feinith said. 'This will all be over.'

She moved in front of the bar as he topped up his glass.

'Caleb, are you listening to me?'

'Are *you* listening to *me*, Feinith?' he demanded, his green eyes locking on hers, his arms braced on the bar.

Her anxiety peaked at his steady gaze. 'This is personal, isn't it, Caleb?'

He knocked back a mouthful of drink, his gaze still not leaving hers.

'Caleb, you can't afford to let that cloud your judgement – not now.'

'Who are you thinking of now, Feinith? Me? Your people? Or *Jarin*?'

'You know I have no allegiance to Jarin anymore.'

'But does Jarin know that?'

'What are you planning?'

'You *do* know Sirius's direct number, don't you?'

'This is a mistake, Caleb.'

He stepped out from around the bar. Closing the gap between them, he caught hold of the side of her neck. He rubbed his thumb gently across her lips. 'What would be a mistake, Feinith, is you thinking I'm willing to take no for an answer.' He gazed deep into her eyes. 'You better than anyone know what I'm capable of. Those streets are a lonely and dangerous place to be abandoned to right now.'

'You wouldn't.'

'Wouldn't I? Do you really want us both to find out?'

# Chapter Twelve

Jessie sat bolt upright on the bed and braced her arms behind her.

Her hair was damp around her neck. Hair that felt as fresh and clean as the rest of her.

She stared down at the thigh-skimming black satin kimono-style negligee she had been put in, the low V-neck reaching her waist.

She slammed her hand against her bare flesh and found her necklace had been removed. She looked down at her thigh. The wound from the crossbow was already healing, telling her she'd been there a handful of hours at least.

She drew the fabric at her chest together to cover herself and scanned the room. It was the polar opposite of the clinical hovel she had first woken in, the large octagonal room draped with luxury.

She slid off the satin bed sheets, her bare feet instantly sinking into a deep pile rug before meeting polished floorboards as she hurried over to the open window.

The cool breeze wafted against her hair as she stared out across the long, sun-dried grass, it sweeping towards her like waves from the iron fence in the distance.

She leaned out of the window and looked right to see an identical octagonal turret to the one she was in looming back at her against the cloud-laden sky – matching turrets that were cornerstones above the otherwise three-storey building.

Looking left, a chapel was nestled amidst an overgrown churchyard, the headstones only just skimming above the grass and weeds.

In the distance, a cool chill of familiarity crept over her like a long-forgotten dream as she surveyed the outline of familiar urban buildings.

She was still in Blackthorn, and the skyline told her she was still somewhere in the south too.

She leaned back out of the window to double-check the building she was in. She'd only ever seen it from a distance many decades before: the old asylum. It had been abandoned fifty years before the regulations came into being, closed down for demolition amidst threats of it collapsing at any point.

It had remained empty for 130 years now. When the cons had moved into the south, not even they had been interested in taking it over. Not only was it too far from centralised activity and utilities, talk of hauntings and mysterious deaths kept even the most hardened cons from wanting to use the defunct building for anything more than temporary activities.

But clearly someone had moved in – someone unbothered by the reputation of the building. Either that or they were cleverly making the most of it.

She looked down over the windowsill at the sheer ninety-foot drop below. With nothing to climb onto below or above, it was no wonder the window had been left open.

Already chilled from the breeze, she padded back across the rug to the bed as she kept her arms folded around her chest, not to mention the rest of her naked body beneath the kimono.

She yanked the sheet off the bed and wrapped it around herself as she headed to the threshold of the ajar door ahead.

Some fifteen feet away, domineering mahogany doors mirrored each other on parallel sides of the extensive hallway, wooden panels continuing to stretch another twenty feet beyond those to another open door ahead.

Jessie clutched the sheet at her chest knowing that, at some point, she was going to need to head in the direction someone intended. For all she knew, Eden was already in that room waiting for her. And if he wasn't, whoever lay beyond that door most likely knew where Eden was.

She stepped out onto the deep-pile runner and hesitated only a moment longer before making her way warily towards the room ahead.

She tried the closed doors to her left and her right in passing. Finding them locked, she padded onwards.

As she reached the threshold of the open door, she saw the floorboards beyond were as polished as the ones in the hallway. About thirty feet away she could see the corner of what looked like a dining table and stool, and the back of a navy sofa beyond that.

Jessie hovered, her heart pounding painfully.

'You can come in, Jesca,' the masculine voice declared.

She flinched. Her breathing caught in her chest.

*Jesca.*

No one called her by that name. No one ever called her by her proper name. She'd been Jessie ever since Toby had first started calling her that.

She glanced back over her shoulder at the two locked doors and back to the room she had emerged from with nothing but a ninety-foot drop beyond.

Grasping the sheet more securely at her chest, she stepped into the room, recoiling instantly at the sight of the figure facing the window.

His wings were relaxed and unfolded behind him – wings free of the adapted backpacks his kind wore when out in Blackthorn in order to conceal their identity. Wings that signified the main difference between the two classes of angels: she was an envoi, her wings taking shape only as an electric lightshow when receiving a prophecy. The angel standing before her was a warrior.

And contrary to the misleading pre-Raphaelite paintings where flying humans were best explained with feathers, this angel's wings were the same colour as the rest of his olive skin, betraying a bone-china-like transparency in the weak afternoon light.

And unlike the lone wing of Ziel – the only other angel Jessie had encountered since losing her memory – this angel's wings were covered in black markings.

Black markings that could only be described as tattoos.

# Chapter Thirteen

'What the *fuck* were they thinking?' Kane muttered as he ploughed along the tunnel.

'Jessie had access to something back at the row,' Caitlin explained.

'So they leave without running it past me first?'

'They tried to find you,' Caitlin said as she stepped in front of him, her hand pressed firmly to his chest. 'Apparently there are records back there. Records that Jessie's previous guardian had access to. It might give them the answer of how to help Eden. Of how to help Honey.'

As Kane searched her gaze, she could see the glimmer of relief nestled within his irritation. 'They still shouldn't have gone without my permission,' he said, continuing with his strides. 'The last thing we fucking need is those two going missing.'

Caitlin quickened her pace as she followed behind him, veering right into the open room.

'What have we got?' Kane asked Keele.

The vampire instantly stood from the table. He handed him the arrow with navy fletchings that Caitlin knew belonged to Kane.

'We found this propped against the doorway. And we also found these.' Keele opened his cloth-protected palm to reveal three blood-ied silver discs, the five-pointed arms around each of their perimeters looking unnervingly lethal.

Caitlin stared from the discs that resembled ninja stars back to Kane.

His jaw clenched more than it already had since he'd heard the news of two of his crew going AWOL, except now the irritation in his eyes was replaced with dread.

'We removed these from Sorran, Jed and Nico,' Keele explained. 'They were in major arteries. None of them made it.'

Caitlin knew what Jed and Nico meant to Kane, reinforced by Kane closing his eyes for a moment followed by a sharp, regretful shake of his head.

As for Sorran, he'd been Jask's rock after Corbin had been taken. He was going to be devastated when he woke up.

'Jessie? Eden?' Kane asked.

'No sign,' Keele said.

With an acknowledging nod of appreciation for the update, Kane cocked his head as an instruction for Keele to leave.

'Kane?' Caitlin asked, her pulse racing. 'What are those things?'

'Angel stars.' His navy gaze met hers only fleetingly before he braced his palms flat on the table, his head lowered for a moment. '*Fuck*,' he hissed before pivoting away. He raked his hands back through his hair before grasping the back of his neck.

'Kane, tell me you got around to warning Jessie that the Angelic Parliament has a call out for her. Tell me she knew.'

His sigh followed by his silence said it all.

Caitlin stepped in front of him. 'You didn't, did you?'

'The last thing we needed was her and Eden going off on Ziel for information.'

'You promised me you were going to tell them.'

'And I was – and then all this stuff about the angel tears came to light. I was going to get everyone moving and then tell them.'

'So could this be down to Torren? He's the one who's been looking for her, right? Do you think he has them?'

'I don't know, Caitlin. But I think it's a safe bet.'

'So where are they? Where would they have taken them?'

'Like I told you before, I don't know. No one knows where the fuck the Angelic Parliament reside.'

'You've got to talk to Ziel.'

'I could break him into a thousand pieces and he still wouldn't tell me. It was only the threat of me taking his other wing that got him to break over Torren having the call out for Jessie – and he only told me then because he knew there was nothing I could do about it.'

'Then let me shadow read him.'

'And then what? In the midst of everything else, I'm going to take on the angels as well as Sirius's army? They're fucking warriors – air-skimming, skull-crushing warriors who don't give a shit about anything but their own survival. If we hunt them down, if we descend on wherever they are, then we're going to war with them. You know why that can't happen.'

'This is Jessie and Eden, Kane. This is two of our team. You can't seriously be suggesting we do nothing? More than that, we need them. Even if we get out of Blackthorn, Eden's the only one who can get access to this Cassandra. Without her, we can kiss goodbye to any exposure. I'll have nothing to work with other than Claire's diary. I need evidence, Kane. I need backing. I have to build a case. We have to take Sirius down properly. We'll have one shot at this. One chance or it's over.'

'You think I don't know that?'

She caught hold of his hand. 'There's got to be something we can do. You must be able to think of something.'

When he looked away with a sigh, Caitlin tightened her grip on his hand.

'Kane? What aren't you telling me?'

He looked back at her, his gaze lingering for a few moments. 'They didn't need to leave those stars behind, Cait.'

'What do you mean?'

'They could have removed the evidence they'd been there.'

'So they *want* us to know they have Eden and Jessie?'

'What do you think the arrow propped in the doorway was about? That had to be one of the ones I used to take down the fourth species in the lock-up. Torren knows I was there. And if he was in the lock-up, he's seen Jessie's murals of the prophecy. He's seen Leila's markings when we temporarily closed the dimension. He would have seen the angel blood on the floor. He knows we're all involved. And for some reason he wants me to know he knows.'

'I don't understand why the angels are being like this, Kane. They're third species too. They must know what's going on out here now more than ever.'

'Which confirms one thing: they don't want to stop it.'

'You think Torren *wants* you to come looking for Eden and Jessie.'

'I think it's a trap, Caitlin. I think we've got another player in this game. And I think they've just made their first move.'

# Chapter Fourteen

'Take a seat, Jesca.'

The angel's deep voice complemented both his stature and his stance. He was easily six foot three. His arms, braced on the window frame, betrayed biceps – both adorned with leather ties strapped around them – that it would take three hands to circle. His trousers were tight but not unappealingly so considering the form beneath. The top he was wearing was backless and tied at his slender waist to account for his wings. His black hair was also tied back, shimmering in the weak daylight.

Whoever he was, it was obvious she was going nowhere fast without his say so.

Jessie glanced to the lengthy food-laden table to her right, where he most likely intended her to take that seat.

She'd never seen a display of food like it in her life. She scanned the rest of the room – she'd never seen such opulence and luxury either: the heavy curtains, the thick-pile rugs, the crystal chandelier, the rich mahogany that lined the walls and floor, matched by the ornate furniture.

Kane had warned her what her kind were like. He'd spoken of their detachment from the poverty and struggles within Blackthorn. He'd told her of their indifference to the rest of the third species' plight. And the evidence now laid before her did nothing to warm her to the male who remained with his back to her.

'Where's Eden?' she asked, trying to avoid any inflection of anxiety leaking into her tone.

When he turned to face her, she instinctively took a step back.

His eyes were a shocking amber against his olive skin. His jaw was as strong as the rest of his angular chiselled features, his face as hard in expression as the body below.

'Still the same old, Jesca. *Never* able to follow a simple instruction.'

The hairs on the back of her neck prickled at the edge of familiarity in his words, in his intonation.

As he assessed her too – from foot to head – she clenched the sheet tighter to her chest.

'Yet suddenly so modest,' he said, his broad, thin lips curling in amusement.

With steady bare-footed strides, his eyes not leaving hers, he crossed the room, stopping less than a foot away, and stared deep into her eyes, looming over her with his additional six inches in height to the point she wanted to recoil – not out of fear but from her repulsion at his proximity.

'Which isn't like you, Jesca. There was a time when you were rarely clothed in these very quarters.'

A shiver of unease crept down her spine at his proclamation, not to mention the way his eyes glinted as he said it.

'Do I know you?'

'In every sense of the word, Jesca.'

He brushed her hair behind her shoulder in a move that was too reminiscent of Eden, a ripple of revulsion flooding her at a male touch other than his.

She instantly shrugged him off and backed up to forge some distance, glaring at him.

He smiled again. 'Yet you still have the same petulant streak – which was certainly apparent this morning during your dealings with my shadow reader. Those are quite some gestures you've learned.'

'Who are you? What do you want?'

'Considering the ladies put quite some time into bathing and preparing you, I would at least like to see the benefits of their efforts.'

Her skin crawled at the suggestion, but she avoided biting. 'I asked you a question,' she said as calmly as she could.

The angel jutted his chin up and stared down the length of his nose at her as she dared to glower back at him.

Her entire body heaved a sigh of relief as he finally stepped away. 'Take a seat, Jesca.'

She looked back down the hallway once more, back to the room with no way out.

The angel took his seat at the head of the table. Perching straight-backed on the stool, he reached for pieces of fruit whilst waiting for her to comply.

'The longer you take, the longer answers take,' he remarked as if addressing an uncooperative child.

'You can at least tell me who you are.'

'My name is Torren.' His eyes locked squarely on hers again. 'I'm the one who bound you.'

# Chapter Fifteen

Jessie remained rooted to the spot as Torren declared the fact without an iota of emotion. Worse, he instantly returned to grazing on the food in front of him as if he'd uttered nothing more than the time, as opposed to having confessed to being the one who had cursed her for a century and a half, fifty years of which she'd spent imprisoned in a convict row.

She clutched the sheet tighter to her chest, uncertain whether fury or fear would win out.

The shadow reader would have learned everything and would no doubt have passed that information on to him. As such, Torren would have known the horrors she had been through. He would have known of her darkest, loneliest moments. Moments *he* had inflicted. And yet there was no remorse in his eyes and no comfort in his tone. It was as if the horrors were not even worthy of noting.

He picked fruit from his teeth as if even her presence was insignificant, and she stared at him in disgust.

'I want to know what I'm doing here, and I want to know where Eden is.'

His eyes snapped to hers again. Only then did she see the utter lack of compromise. 'And I will ask you *one* more time to take a seat.'

Jessie looked across at the stool closest to her, at the opposite end of the table.

If there was one thing she had learned first-hand from her time in the row, it was that acquiescence was often smarter than a smart mouth. She had to think of Eden. She had to remember him in all of this.

As the shock subsided, she berated herself for not realising sooner that Torren could know how to undo the damage she had inflicted on both Eden and Honey. One thing was for sure, having had her read, Torren had to know of their predicament.

She drew out the padded stool and sat down.

'I know you'll have forgotten how it works around here, but I give an instruction and you follow it, Jesca. That's how it is. That's how it's always been.'

'Because I'm an envoi?'

His eyes snapped fleetingly to hers. 'Because I'm in charge.' He cast his attention back over the array of food in front of him. 'But it's good to know you have some awareness of our hierarchy without me needing to remind you of that too. Those were some extremely fascinating findings your friend Toby had stashed away.'

His knowledge of her ex-guardian's name further confirmed that Torren had left no stone unturned in his instructions to the shadow reader.

'So you also know where I've been these last fifty years?'

'Why do you think I've been looking for you ever since that row burned down?'

Her stomach somersaulted at the realisation that his finding of her and Eden was no coincidence. 'You've been *looking* for me?'

'Blackthorn is a dangerous place at the moment. Increasingly so. I couldn't have you lost on the streets, especially not knowing if you had managed to take your bind with you or not.'

'You knew where I was? For how long?'

'I've always known, Jesca. I'm not negligent,' he added with a hint of arrogance, as if insulted by the mere suggestion to the contrary.

But it was a declaration too much. Heat simmered through her body. She tightened her grip on either side of the stool. 'You knew for *all* that time?'

'No one foresaw the cons moving in to the south, Jesca. You were fine before then.'

To her frustration, anguish clogged her throat. Worse than him having known was the fact he'd done nothing about it – that her own had abandoned her to that cesspit.

'And for fifty years, *fifty* years, I was anything but,' she said. 'You must have known that. Everyone knows what those rows are like.'

'You were bound for a reason, Jesca. I couldn't be held accountable for the change of events.'

She refused to let her pending tears overwhelm her rage at his insubstantial excuse. 'For *what*? What could I possibly have done to deserve that? What did I do that was so bad it deserved you not just abandoning me to that cesspit, but stealing a century and a half of my life?'

'Which is barely even a life sentence for our kind. Count yourself lucky it wasn't death or, worse, banishment to the Brink – both were options at the time.'

Because despite their life expectancy, like all members of the third species, angels were no more immortal than humans.

'There were times when I would have gladly taken either alternative,' she said.

'And clearly that was my mistake. I was too lenient on you. I let my feelings get in the way.'

'Your *feelings*? *What* feelings?'

'You were special to me. You were *always* special to me. And I to you. At least, I thought I was.'

She assessed him more warily. 'We were *involved*?'

'As I said, you were never so modest with me, Jesca.'

'*How* involved?'

'Involved enough for me to break rank and allow you into my bed.'

She didn't know what hit her harder: facing someone who had clearly meant something to her once, or discovering that someone arrogant enough to state that he had 'allowed' her into his bed had actually meant something to her.

'You were quite the seductress, Jesca,' Torren added, reaching for more fruit. He took a large bite.

'We were involved and you *still* did that to me?'

'You look at me with such disappointment in your eyes, such indignation, yet *I* was not the one in the wrong, Jesca. I did what I could to save you.'

'What did I *do?*' she persisted.

He held her gaze as the seconds ticked by before casting his half-eaten fruit aside.

She braced herself as he stood, as he strode around the table towards her.

He picked a black satin robe from the back of the sofa and held it out for her to take. 'I'll show you.'

❄ ❄ ❄

Mya trudged along Blackthorn's streets, her arms folded around her chest, the cold afternoon air penetrating her low-cut top beneath her black, cropped leather jacket. The chill had turned her bare thighs numb, her sockless toes frozen in her biker boots.

The con took another drag on her cigarette as she stopped for a moment. The south was usually like a ghost town at that time of day, but after the events back at Pummel's row a few days ago, whispers of the threat of fourth species had leaked everywhere. There had been enough witnesses that night to spread it fast – and far. All the cons were on their guard – especially after it had been plastered all across the TV and radio that there were morphed lycans on the loose too.

*Fucking Homer*, she hissed in her own head.

He'd sent her out there as punishment. She'd saved his life back at Pummel's row. She'd dragged him from the bottom of the stairs out of sight amidst the chaos. She'd resuscitated him and given him the contents of one of the syringes that she'd stolen from Pummel one drunken night some weeks before – syringes she'd seen Pummel use after he'd been in one of his fights. And this was the fucking thanks she got?

*One* mistake. One *fucking* mistake.

All she'd done was let slip to that Rob guy about the lycans being involved with Jessie, and mentioned Reece's name too, but that was it.

Homer had banged on about none of them grassing to the authorities and given her a couple of slaps for good measure. She knew the only reason he'd kept her alive was that she'd done it to save his fat arse. *Again.*

But Homer needed to mark his territory in Cyclops's row since taking it over. He needed to lay down the law, to set boundaries.

And she had nowhere to go that would enable her not to take it. It was the only reason she'd saved him in the first place. It had been an impulsive act after she'd watched the rest of Pummel's gang drop like flies. She wasn't willing to start again from scratch. Getting a roof over your head as opposed to being play fodder on the streets was one of the toughest challenges in con row. There was a lot to be said for a bed and four walls in a place no fucker dared raid.

She'd fucked up because Homer had been looking for Eden and Jessie too, and the last thing he needed was the authorities knowing they were still alive. Now she had to work twice as hard to find them.

And if she didn't go back with something soon, Homer was going to start rethinking her purpose – and then she'd be back to the start. Back to where she was years ago but now at a time when she needed protection most.

She continued to curse Homer with every breath as she wrapped her cigarette-holding hand back around her chest, the pictures of Jessie and Eden still clutched beneath her arm.

Mya stopped for a moment and tapped her biker boots on the pavement, trying to get the blood flowing as she scanned the empty street.

Getting the sense that she was being watched, she looked left towards the alley opposite.

He was just leaning there, shoulder to the wall, his stance telling her he was looking in her direction.

She blew out a curt stream of smoke as she watched him through narrowed eyes. The cons often worked in packs – one distracting whilst others came from behind. It was a trick she used herself. It was a trick she'd tried to use with Eden Reece when she'd spotted him on the shop roof opposite Pummel's row.

She pushed up her jacket sleeves, wanting her numbers on display; wanting to let them know she wasn't some easy target, and glanced around, looking for signs of an ambush, but only dull afternoon light and empty streets lingered.

She took a few casual steps closer, stepping down off the pavement and into the gutter. He was tall. Athletic build. And not bad-looking from what she could make out so far.

He could have been another con. He could have been a rogue lycan or a vampire even, as rarely as they ventured into the south. There were certainly plenty of non-con humans who worked for vampire sires looking for new feeders.

But amongst all that, there was potential: potential new interest. Potential *better* interest. A better bed.

And potential answers too.

She cast aside her cigarette and folded her jacket back to show off her best assets. Putting on her sexiest stride, a picture in each hand, she sauntered across the street towards him.

Taking in his six-foot-two body to die for, Mya rested her shoulder against the wall to mirror him.

'Seen something you like, handsome?' she asked, placing her hand on her hip.

His gaze wandered over her – clearly he had.

She indicated his backpack. 'Heading somewhere?'

'Nowhere in particular.'

'If you need a roof over your head, I know a place. *If* you can help me out, that is.' She held up the pictures. 'You seen either of these two while you've been lurking in dark alleys eying up young girls?'

He looked at the pictures and raised his eyebrows slightly.

When he looked back into her eyes, she had no idea why he was smiling.

# Chapter Sixteen

Torren didn't need to open the door – it was opened for him.

Stepping into the quadrant, Jessie glanced at the angel who instantly made eye contact with Torren. His height and stance were similar to Torren's, and he too had markings on his wings, though not in the same abundance as the latter's.

Torren sent him a nod as he strode past.

As he led her along corridors, through rooms and past angels reclining, chatting and mingling, it reminded her in many ways of the compound: the hotel the lycans had turned into their home. Except this place echoed nothing of the basic and minimalist lifestyle of the lycans. This wasn't just a haven – it was a whole other world. This was an oasis of luxury amidst deprivation; riches amidst poverty; nonchalance and indifference set against a backdrop of others fighting for survival in the world beyond.

Her blood simmered – it was abhorrent in light of what her friends were struggling against.

'How have you lived like this?' she asked. 'How has all of this stayed hidden?'

But Torren didn't respond, indicating instead towards the door at the end of the hall.

Again the double doors were opened for him.

The room within was vast enough to take Jessie's breath away. Filling its space, canvas panels were spaced out like dividing shelving units in a library.

Torren walked her through the maze of sketches not dissimilar to the ones she'd produced back at the lock-up in the row. And amidst those canvases, wingless angels busied themselves. Envois: the class of angel who were conductors of prophecies.

'This was where you used to work,' he told her. 'These were once your friends.'

She made eye contact with a couple of them, but they quickly resumed their focus on their drawings.

Her throat tightened at the glimpses of who she once was – of which she had no recollection.

'I used to live *here*?'

'You were born here, Jesca,' he said, glancing across at her.

She met with more envois' curious stares as she struggled to comprehend that this had been her life. More to the point, *this* had been her lifestyle.

He stopped at one of the panels.

'I've seen your drawings in the lock-up.' He pointed to one part. 'This section, I do believe.'

She stared at the same image drawn by a different hand. It felt like a lifetime ago that she had first shown the prophecy to Eden.

'Already it's changing,' Torren said. 'From the interference of just a few, what is meant to be is altering.'

She knew he meant her – her, Eden, Kane, Caitlin, Jask, Sophia; even Leila and Caleb. He would have known about them all from her shadow. And from his choice of the word 'interference', it was safe to assume he didn't approve.

'According to the original prophecy, what was meant to happen was a peaceful truce between humans and third species,' Jessie responded. 'A direction changed eighty years ago when the Higher Order outed the third species too soon.'

'Far from it, Jesca. That is all you remember. The peaceful truce was itself a veering off track. There is only one intended outcome. There was only ever meant to be one outcome.'

'According to *who*?'

'Destiny. Fate. Some higher power. What does it matter?'

Torren wandered a little further through the panels towards the back of the room as Jessie followed.

'Do you recognise the handiwork of this one?'

Jessie's stomach flipped as she recognised her own drawings – and, with it, proof of what Torren was telling her.

Heart pounding, she homed in on one aspect in particular. Staring at the drawing of Eden, she finally knew why she'd recognised him the moment she'd first laid eyes on him in the alley.

She *had* seen him before. She'd seen him in her visions.

'You once drew him,' he said. 'You drew him as the threat that he was.'

Jessie's attention snapped back to Torren.

'He exposes our existence to the world,' Torren added. 'According to the change in prophecy, he does it through revealing Sirius's work. We can't let that happen.'

'Without exposing what Sirius has done, without exposing our existence, we can't bring down this system.'

'We don't need to bring it down, Jesca – the vampire leader will do it for us.'

Her pulse picked up to a human rate as she stared back at the angel. 'You're talking as though you *want* this to happen?'

'It's not about what I want, Jesca. It's not about what any of us want. It's about the prophecy.'

She looked back around the room at the luxury surrounding them. She glared back at him. 'Easy to say when you're amidst all of this.'

'It never used to bother you, Jesca. In fact, you used to enjoy it.'

'With ignorance as my only defence by the sounds of it, if I was willing to listen to this bullshit.'

His eyes glowered down into hers. 'We do not act outside what the prophecy dictates. It is our place to do *as* is dictated. None of us interfere,' he declared with that edge of tone, as if he was talking to an uncooperative child again – one he was now treating as if she was struggling to understand.

'So we stand back and do nothing? With all the power you have at your fingertips?'

'Your job is to record the prophecy. My job is to ensure it comes to fruition.'

'And what if the very foundation of your understanding of the prophecy is flawed? Have you ever stopped to ask yourself that? What if it's merely reflecting the choices you make, rather than giving you a path to adhere to? What if the recordings are self-fulfilling prophecies?'

He stared at her as if he believed the world to be flat and she'd just announced it was a sphere.

'You've had my shadow read, Torren. Sirius knows soul transference is possible. You know what the impact of that will be should we fail. He's planning to keep key figures of the human race alive for centuries and cull thousands more.'

'*If* he gets his hands on Kane – which he won't.'

'You don't know that. You could help us.'

'Have you not been listening?'

'It's not about interfering – it's about fighting for what's right. It's about adapting. It's about change. It's about progression for a better outcome.'

'For who?'

'Have you even stepped beyond these doors to see what's going on out there? Have you any idea? Has anyone in this building?'

'We don't need to.'

'So instead you opt to sit up here in your tower and let the world burn around you?'

'Until the time is right and then we'll step in. We will intervene as is destined and regain control. We're not going to allow total annihilation, Jesca. Merely a. . .' he pondered over his words for a few moments, 'reduction in population.'

The missing piece of the prophecy – the section she didn't complete after the devastation.

She shook her head at his matter-of-fact statement, the indifference in his tone. 'And become the heroes? Become gods amongst men again? You're advocating this war for your own selfish ends. You're as brutal as Sirius.'

'As I keep saying, unlike him, this is not my call, Jesca. Or any of ours. That's why by siding with *them* you are going against the rules. You've been caught up in things you shouldn't have been caught up in. Eden, Kane, Jask: they are the thorn in the prophecy's side. And *you* are helping them succeed. Once again, you are defying our laws.'

'*Once again?*'

'Yes, Jesca: *again*. And, once again, Eden Reece is behind your defiance.'

'Where is he?' Jessie demanded. 'What have you done to him?'

'Concern for the human you've known less than a week. The human who now carries a lethal dose of angel tears in his system. And the very reason you were back at the row, it seems, accessing information that Toby should never have got his hands on in the first place.'

Jessie clenched her teeth as she struggled to swallow her pride. 'And do *you* have the answer?'

'For saving Eden? And his niece of course.'

'Yes.'

Torren's gaze rested steadily on hers. 'And why would I want to do that, Jesca?'

'Because he's a good man.'

'Really? Has that always been the case?'

'He's courageous, selfless, compassionate. . .'

'With a background of being promiscuous, negligent, volatile, ruthless, manipulative. . .'

'And what about Honey? That little girl doesn't deserve this.'

'You should have thought of that before you decided to commit such a sacrilegious act.'

'*Sacrilegious?*'

'The humans' striving to get as close to immortality as possible will always be their greatest downfall. Churchyards are littered with the statues of those who thought they could overcome their human fragility. The very quest in itself is why the sacrament exists.'

'Eden wasn't striving for anything and you know it. He was dying, Torren. He was dying after trying to defend those who could not defend themselves. I gave him my tears to save his life. This is not his fault. How was I to know after you stole my memory?'

'Your instincts should have told you, Jesca. You should have listened to them. Instead you chose to save him. He should be dead. I tried to avoid this. I tried to help you. But it always comes back to him.'

'What are you *talking* about?'

'Have you not realised? Eden Reece is the reason I had to bind you in the first place.'

# Chapter Seventeen

Kane knocked on the door three times and waited.

It was more irresponsible going there than he was happy with, even though he'd used the underground systems and more backup than he should have been wasting. He was the only one who *could* go there though. He was the only one who could ask.

Eventually the basement door opened. Duke stooped his seven-foot frame to look through the low doorway, his grey eyes squinting down at Kane from below white tufty eyebrows and a mop of silvery hair.

This was now his fourth visit in forty years – the second in less than a week. It was going to be tough to persuade Shiver to engage, but he had no choice but to try.

As unvocal as ever, Duke stepped back silently to allow Kane inside, his master-vampire status granting him automatic access where others would have to have bartered – and most likely failed – to have even a moment with the record keeper.

Duke led Kane down the maze of corridors, through the familiar doors of warped shapes and sizes, down declines and up inclines, before reaching the depths of the terrace of adjoining subterranean basements.

When the final door was opened to him, Kane stepped into the poorly lit room, the musty, damp smell overwhelming his nostrils just as it had a few days before – the scent of paper from the library beyond.

In the centre of the room, Shiver was working busily at her desk as she always was, the quill in her hand, books lying open around her.

Her white-blonde hair cascaded down her childlike body onto the chair and desk just as it always did when in her chosen, unshifted state.

And just like last time, her small face looked up with almond eyes almost too big for her elfin face.

'Hello again, Shiver,' Kane said to the shape-shifter.

Except, this time, instead of addressing him with her shrill, child-like voice, she returned her attention to her paperwork.

He stepped up to the desk regardless, only to be blocked by Duke.

Kane reached into his pocket and opened his palm to reveal the collection of marbles he had brought with him.

Duke turned to face Shiver and placed them in the bowl on her desk before stepping away again.

Despite trying to hide it, Shiver's eyes widened in delight at seeing the small, glass spheres, the bright colours that lay trapped within these ones like injections of luminous paint as opposed to the primary colours in the ones Kane had brought with him last time. He knew he'd had to find something extra special.

But this time she didn't instantly wrap her thin fingers around them before hurriedly stashing them away from view in her desk drawer. This time she reverted to ignoring both them and Kane's presence.

'Come on, Shiver,' he said. 'Cut me some slack. You know I wouldn't be back here if I didn't have to be.'

But to his frustration she didn't respond. She did nothing at all but raise her tiny arm, pointing her lengthy finger directly at the door behind him as she continued to scribble with her quill.

Duke stepped forward, assuming his guardian role.

'Just hold on,' Kane said, holding his palm up to Duke, his full attention still on Shiver. 'You know the shit that's going on out there, Shiver. You know what I'm trying to do.'

Silence descended again, broken only a few seconds later by her small voice. 'Helped you once,' she reminded him.

'Then help me twice.'

Her eyes shot to his – eyes that betrayed that, despite her small, childlike frame, there was nothing childlike in the ancient creature within. And there was nothing childlike in the power behind her eyes.

'Leave,' she commanded quietly.

'I'm going nowhere.'

Lightning couldn't have struck quicker. The desk flew sideways, the small child erupting into a creature three times Kane's height, its scaly arms extended outwards from its fat body in its rage, a jaw that could have swallowed Kane blowing hot breath in his face as it roared in his face. 'LEAVE!'

Silence descended, and a couple of stray marbles tapped against Kane's boot as he wiped spittle from his face.

He sighed heavily as he looked back up into the creature's panting face as it loomed inches from his. Reluctantly, he removed the vial of sparking ashes from his back pocket, holding it up for Shiver to see.

She recoiled, her hand held to her eyes as she instantly shrunk back to her childlike form, her eyes wide and troubled.

Duke did the same, looking from one to the other as if not knowing what to do.

'I'm sorry to have to do this,' Kane said. 'You know how I hate to pull the master-vampire card. I know it means our relationship is over from here on, but I have no choice. I need to know how to summon an angel, Shiver. I need to know how to summon Torren. Tell me and I won't need to use this.'

'Impossible for you,' she said, squinting warily at him from behind her hand.

'You know I believe in that word as much as I do Santa Claus.'

'Only one way to summon angels,' Shiver said. 'Only be done by sacrifice. Sacrifice the heart of one you love.'

# Chapter Eighteen

Jessie's stomach flipped. She stared at Torren aghast. 'How can you possibly blame Eden for *that*? I didn't know him when you bound me. He hadn't even been born yet!'

'It still didn't stop you betraying me. Betraying the parliament.'

'I don't understand.'

'Once you started seeing him in your visions, you became infatuated with him. Your job was merely to record that but, instead, he provoked questions in your mind. You developed a compulsion to save.'

Jessie took a step back as she stared at him.

'You were mine, Jesca, in every sense. Then after you saw him, it all changed. A few visions and you were obsessed with him. Obsessed with saving the enemy. You saw he wouldn't survive the prophecy, and you didn't like it. You wanted to interfere – for *his* sake. You started to develop a compulsion to save humanity. You tried to talk members of the parliament into supporting your cause. You wanted us to become proactive. You wanted us to change the course of the prophecy rather than let it become what it was meant to be.'

'You're telling me I tried to do the very thing I'm trying to do now 150 years ago?'

'But never for the right reasons, Jesca. Just like now.'

'So you bound me in order to *stop* me?'

'An envoi is a conduit, nothing more.'

'And I dared to have an opinion?'

'One which opposed your purpose. One which opposed the purpose of us all. Trying to rally others together. . . you were dangerous,

Jesca. You were breaking every rule. The punishment was death. I did the only other thing I could. You look at me like I'm the enemy when I have done everything to try and help you. And now I find you've been doing it all over again.'

His gaze was as berating as his tone.

'Giving your angel tears,' he added, 'revealing the prophecy to non-angels, now intervening in that very prophecy – this is all damning evidence. I find your blood on a lock-up floor next to a witch's symbol telling me you've played a part in suppressing the fourth-dimension fracture; I find an arrow belonging to Kane Malloy in the space right next door telling me you've been fraternizing with vampires. And then I get you shadow read and discover even *more* revelations – that you know who the vampire leader is and that you conspired to kill him. Conspired to halt the prophecy *again*. I saved your life without question the first time. I cannot make such a generous choice again.'

Her heart beat harder. 'What are you going to do?'

'You left me with no choice. I had to intervene to ensure there is no further damage.'

Her legs threatened to give way beneath her. 'What have you done to him? What have you done to Eden?'

# Chapter Nineteen

Torren guided her back the way they'd come before taking a left onto a landing. One of the two angels guarding the stairs unhooked the roped barrier that marked the top step. Beyond, the stairwell was empty, the walls chipped and stained with damp and graffiti, replicating the first room she'd woken in.

Taking the first step down, Jessie felt as though she had walked through a spider's web, something as light as gossamer brushing against her face, the cause of the sensation invisible.

When she looked over her shoulder back up the stairs, she nearly lost her footing. The opulence, even the two guarding angels themselves, had vanished. Nothing but a blank wall stared back at her.

'An angel barrier,' Torren explained as he caught her arm before she tripped. 'Only we can pass. There has been many a fateful accident on these steps for others who have tried.'

She could feel it to be true. As she stared up at what felt like empty space, she could feel angel eyes looking back down on her. Beyond the barrier of invisibility, the world remained. Like the van she had been in that had smashed into an invisible wall as a result of the bind around her, this was a similar trick.

'Even Sirius's technology can't penetrate what we have here. To them the whole place is empty, just like it has been to humans and third species that have ventured here before them.' He glanced across at her. 'And once inside, no one can find you.'

He led her left, down more corridors and past rooms that were stripped bare of any sense of the world that once lived within. Nonetheless, broken windows hinted at sounds on the breeze, as if distant rooms were still occupied by bodiless voices – as if some were reluctant to leave the once-active asylum.

Torren took another left before opening the first door he came to.

He indicated for Jessie to enter first.

She stepped into the darkness to see the dimly lit room beyond.

Sitting on the floor, one leg bent to his chest, his free arm resting across his knee, his other leg stretched out in front of him, Eden leaned his head back against the wall.

She all but threw herself at the glass, a tear trickling down her cheek at her relief that he was still alive.

He rose the second he heard the thunk of Jessie's contact with the glass, his brown eyes narrowed quizzically, proving that he couldn't see her: that the glass was not two-way.

He headed in her direction regardless, the manacle that bound his right wrist sliding along the metal handrail that extended around the perimeter of the room at waist height. It ran the length of three walls, even venturing into what looked like door-less wash facilities. The only wall it didn't reach was the one that housed the exit: a secured metal door with a viewing window that sat in the wall to her right. If not even his angel strength could rip the handrail off the wall, the windowless room must have been designed for the very purpose it was serving: keeping its occupant confined and controlled.

'What are you going to do to him?'

'Now that he's here, I don't need to do anything to him. One thing you need to understand, Jesca, is that Eden was intended to die. You tried to thwart that and all you did in the process was inflict an even worse death on him. That's how the prophecy works. You try to divert it and those you care about will suffer. *That* is why we do not interfere.'

She turned to face him. 'Sirius is giving his army angel tears, do you know that? He already knows about your existence, Torren. And he's found a way to manage those tears.'

'To merely delay the inevitable. There is no cure once they're in the human system, Jesca.'

She shook her head. 'No. There must be a way to save him.'

'He's a dead man walking, Jesca. At least now he's out of the way.'

Her chest ached, her breath involuntarily leaving her body. Jessie pressed both palms flat to the glass as she gazed across at Eden before dragging the pads of her fingers down the glass to form fists against it.

Holding back her tears, she turned to face Torren. 'Then let him go. Do whatever you want to me, but *please* let him go back to his family.'

'And risk letting him continue on the path he's hell-bent on pursuing? I cannot do that.'

Her hands turned numb, her legs heavy. She didn't care at that point how much pride she had to swallow. '*Please*, Torren.'

He looked through the glass at Eden, his gaze pensive.

Her heart pounded, her queasiness escalating with every second as she lived on the blade-edge of hope.

'Together he and Kane Malloy are a lethal combination,' Torren said. 'I cannot allow them together again. He's too integral to the prophecy's outcome, as I've explained.'

'Screw the prophecy, he has done *nothing* to you!'

Torren's eyes snapped back to hers. 'Based on what the shadow reader exposed, I beg to differ. He has very much been straying into my territory.'

'Your *territory*?'

'Yes, Jesca: you.'

She forced herself to contain her rage at his arrogance as it became abundantly clear this was about more than the prophecy. 'Whatever we had in the past, whatever you *claim* we had, you abandoned me a century and a half ago. You left me to wake alone on a concrete floor knowing nothing but my name and why I had the scars on my back. You let the cons, Pummel, rule over me for fifty years in that pit of depravity when you could have intervened at any point. Even the Brink would have been better than what you subjected me to there. So please don't tell me you're punishing Eden out of some sense of jealousy, of revenge.'

'But Eden is here as a result of *your* choices.' He glanced pensively back at Eden. 'So it is therefore only appropriate that *you* decide his fate.'

Her chest tightened. 'Meaning what?'

'I cannot let him go again with Kane still out there. Kill Kane, bring me proof and then I'll release Eden.'

Her breaths were shallow as she stared back at him. 'Do you have *any* idea what you're asking?'

'I know exactly what I'm asking,' he said, turning to face her, 'which is why it will also secure your redemption for all your crimes.'

'The things I have done are not *crimes*.'

His eyes darkened at her dismissal. 'They are crimes against our angelic laws. Against this parliament. My job is to see that you are punished, Jesca. Instead I'm giving you a chance to save Eden as you have pleaded. What more do you want from me?'

'And screw over my friends? Screw over Blackthorn? This isn't be-cause I requested your help: you're using me. The second you found the arrow in the lock-up, you saw an opportunity and you're taking it. That's why you were looking for me, or you would have left me abandoned on the streets. You could have killed Eden outright in that lock-up but you saw potential leverage.'

'Mixing with their kind has darkened your perspective.'

'No, being left in the cesspit of the south by *you* is what dark-ened my perspective. Being surrounded by the dregs of humanity for fifty years. And, right now, you're not coming across much better.' She stepped up to him. 'In fact, you're *worse* than the dregs of humanity.'

The slap to her face was hard and sharp and knocked her to the floor.

She took a steadying breath, her arms braced, grateful that her ringlets hid her face, her shock, from him.

She'd experienced enough blows in her time from Pummel but that could never ease the humiliation.

She stood up and turned to face him. 'Like I said,' she said as calmly as she could, 'not much better.'

He tilted his chin up again as he glowered down at her. 'I'm trying to save your life. Gratitude would be appreciated. The penalty of giving away your tears is abandonment to the Brink, where you will know the true price of eternity. The penalty of trying to thwart the prophecy is death. I am offering you a chance to undo the damage before you do any more.'

'You're trying to get me to betray those I care about for a cause I don't agree with or believe in. And only because you can't kill Kane yourself, right? You can't kill either of them – Eden or Kane. Kill them and you'd be directly responsible for altering the outcome. You'd be no better than me. You're trapped by your own rules. That's why you need me to do it for you: the fallen envoi who's condemned anyway. Then it's ultimately my choice, isn't it? And you can't be held accountable for the choices I make, even if you're the one to present them to me.' She folded her arms. 'So what if I refuse to play your sick game? What then?'

Torren held her gaze as the seconds scraped by. He shrugged. 'Then I'll let him go.'

'But you said you couldn't. With all that he knows?'

He stepped up to the glass. 'At least giving him your tears has created one advantage for him. I can't bind him, as he's not technically one of us, but I do have other options now.'

Jessie's attention snapped back to Eden, before she looked back at Torren. 'You're going to take his memory.'

'I have no choice if you won't do what you need to do.'

She looked back through the glass, pain searing through her chest.

If Torren wanted to be rid of Eden's knowledge of the prophecy, of Kane, of the existence of angels, it would be a chunk enough that Eden's memory of her – of everything they had been together – would be taken too.

'How much?' Jessie asked, her eyes narrowing on Torren. 'How *much* are you planning on taking?'

'Ten years should do it. Maybe just a little more.'

Her stomach flipped. Hot anger flooded her body.

She knew why he had chosen that unnecessary number. She knew how much the shadow reader had seen.

This was not angel law – this *was* personal. This was revenge. This was Torren stripping Eden back to before the turning point in his life. Stripping Eden back to who he once could have been.

She looked back to Eden, to his arm – to the numbers he would assume were real. A fate he'd have no reason not to believe was real without anyone or anything to tell him otherwise.

'You're going to dump him here in the south,' she said, horror coiling through her as she stared back into Torren's merciless eyes. 'Just like you did me.'

Torren could dump him anywhere in the lethal maze, just as he'd done with her. And Torren knew he wouldn't last. Lone cons rarely did. She'd warned Eden of that from the very first moment she'd met him: of how it was especially cons who looked like him. Cons who were too much competition. Or who attracted too much of the wrong attention.

Eden wouldn't be given time to fight for his place in a row. He'd done it once with Pummel but he'd had motivation: to save Honey. This time he wouldn't even know Honey existed. He wouldn't even know he was a CEO. He wouldn't know about Amanda. He would know nothing except Billy, who he wouldn't know was in Blackthorn too. He wouldn't know about the rest of the group and what they were fighting for or, more importantly, *why* they were fighting for it. He wouldn't even know about the danger looming from the north and the fourth species already crawling the streets, or if more morphed, genetically modified lycans were on the loose.

And he wouldn't know her. He wouldn't know who she was. Why they fell for each other.

Jessie glared at him in the silence. She could barely breathe.

'But he will still be alive, Jesca – if that's what you choose. Isn't that what you want? Or is that not good enough now either?'

The discomfort in her chest intensified. 'You were going to take his memory all along! You've been playing with me, you sadistic bastard!

You'd already decided what you were going to do! Persuading me to kill Kane would've just been a bonus.'

Torren looked back through the glass. 'Your disrespect of the rules, your lack of acceptance, is the very reason you were bound in the first place. And yet still you stand there with the same insubordination. Still wanting everything your own way. Still insisting you get to choose what is right.'

'That's not what this is!'

'Then choose, Jesca, before my patience wears out.'

The knock on the door made her flinch.

The same angel who had made eye contact with Torren upstairs strode in. He leaned into Torren's ear and whispered something that was beyond even Jessie's hearing.

Torren looked back at her but said nothing more as he stepped away and slammed the door behind himself, leaving her alone in the room.

Jessie stepped up to the glass.

She watched Eden tentatively approach it and wondered if he sensed her presence.

As his brown eyes searched blindly, she placed her palm flat on the glass, inches from his face, as a tear escaped down her cheek.

'I love you,' she mouthed, hoping he could somehow sense it.

He placed his hand on the glass almost directly over hers. But as she stared back into his eyes, she saw it was just a coincidence, him testing the glass as much as she was.

She moved her hand over his regardless, knowing she'd give any-thing right then to have him look back into her eyes, to feel that con-nection; to be able to do something to show him she cared.

Anything, as she faced the horrendous decision Torren had left her with.

# Chapter Twenty

Caleb dragged the metal chair across to rest squarely in front of Rob's, just as he had the first time.

Except, this time, there was no apple in his hand, no knife, merely a small, chrome cylinder the vampire toyed with between nimble fingers.

It was a cylinder Rob recognised – a cylinder that Caleb would have removed from his uniform. As a rule they didn't need to carry the antidote with them, their morning and evening doses sufficient. They would only need the cylinder when it came to the barrier being raised – when they were potentially going to be in Blackthorn for longer. Rob had carried his regardless though.

Rob squinted through his migraine to look warily into the vampire's eyes as Caleb leaned back, the forearm of his cylinder-holding hand resting on the back of the chair, his ankle resting on his opposing knee.

A chill shot through Rob as it had the first time. But perspiration trickled down his forehead for an entirely different reason, just as his chest was tight for an entirely different reason. The frequency of his cough was fast becoming unbearable, especially the way it echoed around the empty, stone chamber.

'You don't look so good, Doyle,' the vampire remarked.

'Fucking tied to chair in this place for what, fifteen hours now? What do you expect?'

He coughed again, his outburst having aggravated it further, making his head ache more than it already did.

Caleb bent forward in the chair. He unscrewed the lid on the cylinder and slid out a familiar syringe. 'We both know it's nothing to do with the room.'

The small vial followed into his hand and he proceeded to screw both items together.

Rob's heart pounded as Caleb leaned back again; toyed with the loaded syringe between the fingers of his right hand.

The syringe contents he so desperately needed.

'You know,' Rob said quietly, not knowing if it made him feel better or worse. 'Don't you? That's what the clock's about. How the fuck do you know, huh?'

'I've been around a while now, Doyle. I've met a lot of people. I've had a lot of different conversations. I've been up close and personal with one or two species, including angels.'

Caleb's green eyes were steady and resolute as he held the syringe up between his thumb and index finger.

'So this is what Throme gives you? To keep it all under control?'

Rob glanced at the syringe before staring back at Caleb. 'If you need me for questioning, you know you need to give me what's in that syringe.'

'Has Throme also told you what will happen if I don't? Has he told you the full extent of the side effects?'

'Sarcoidosis. I'm more than aware.'

'I won't pretend to know what the fuck that is, but you're having shortness of breath, right? An irregular heart rhythm. A persistent, irritating cough that tightens your chest. Aching joints. Headache.' He glanced down at Rob's hands. 'Tender, red bumps all over your body. But that's only the beginning. Because it's not sarcoidosis, Doyle, and Throme knows it. They might be claiming to give you a cure in a tube, but in the long run, it's fatal. Not that Throme is going to tell you that.

'You're nothing but expendable to him, Doyle. He only needs you for as long as he can gain control of Blackthorn and control of Kane. Then he'll withdraw whatever this magic potion is. He'll build himself a new army again until he no longer needs even that once all the third species are destroyed.'

'So what's *this* about? You want me to sit here and suffer? You want to watch what happens to Sirius's army if we're not treated?'

'As if I'd be that predictable. No, I want to make you an offer, Doyle.'

'What kind of offer?'

'The chance to work for me. And with it, the chance to not be dependent on this anymore,' he added, holding the syringe up again. 'In fact, I want your entire army to work for me. General.'

# Chapter Twenty-One

She was behind the glass – he could feel it.

Eden flattened his palm against it; searched beyond his own reflection.

He'd definitely heard the thunk from the other side. There had been no clues that it was Jessie, but his senses ignited the way they always did when she was close.

He curled his palm into a fist as he was met with a wall of silence beyond.

If they were hurting her – if anyone was hurting her. . .

He slammed his fist against the reinforced glass with frustration, his helplessness causing his rage to escalate.

He knew he was breaking his own rule: never show weakness in the face of the enemy. But he also knew that, from where they'd been when they'd been taken to the nature of the room he had woken in, it was most likely cons who had kidnapped them.

He turned his back on the glass and paced away, dragging his manacle along the handrail as he went, his healing thigh still aching from where he'd taken the arrow.

Even during his highest point of rage – just after he had woken on the floor in the empty room – he hadn't been able to yank the rail off the wall. But he tried again regardless, his hands gripping the steel, willing it with every ounce of his strength to buckle, bend or detach from the wall.

A trickle of perspiration leaked down his forehead, the minutes scraping by as he worked his way back and forth along the rail, looking for any point of weakness. Finding nothing, he slammed his fist into the wall again, growling in frustration, his knuckles still grazed from the last time.

He spun to face the door as it clunked open behind him.

'Jess!'

Eden almost wrenched his shoulder from its socket as in his eagerness as he lunged forward to greet her. But Jessie was already there, both her arms wrapping in a stranglehold around his neck.

The feel of her body was his only reassurance. His forearm pressed against her spine, he clutched the nape of her neck beneath her hair, never wanting to have her out of his sight again.

He glanced at the open door as two angels stepped inside, their wings loose and relaxed behind them.

Suddenly things were starting to make sense.

He entwined his fingers in her hair to ease her a couple of inches back from him so he could look into her telling eyes. 'Are you okay?'

They were glossy; her irises crimson with her sadness.

She offered an unconvincing nod. 'He's trying to trick us,' she whispered breathily. 'Torren. He was the one who bound me. Don't fall for it, Eden. He knows everything. They shadow read me.' Her eyes reflected the dismay coiling in his chest. '*Everything*. He wants me to go after Kane. He wants to stop the prophecy. If not, he's going to take ten years of your memory, Eden. The prophecy dictates you find the way out, and he knows it.'

A split second later, the angels were peeling Jessie from him, yanking her backwards despite her struggles and protests, both physical and verbal.

With gritted teeth, Eden lunged forward again, the manacle digging deep enough into his wrist to make him bleed. 'You fucking hurt her. . .' he hissed in warning.

They forced her to her knees regardless, though his girl, his Jessie, still refused to go down easily. If they had been human, he knew she would have wiped the floor with them by now. But these angels were too big in bulk and in height, overpowering her easily, especially two on one.

He was distracted only by the figure that stepped through the doorway next. His wings skimmed behind his knees, their width when extended no doubt spanning at least nine feet to hold his weight up when he glided – not flew. He knew from Kane, from Ziel, from what he'd learned from Jessie, that angels didn't fly.

And this angel's wings were covered in tattoos, telling stories Eden didn't have the remotest bit of interest in right then. There was only *one* thing he was interested in: making sure Jessie remained unhurt.

The swagger grated, as did the hint of both disdain and triumph in the angel's smirk. *This* was Torren. He was a bulky bastard and dominated Eden by at least three inches in height. Neither phased him though. He still coiled his hand to a fist in his restraint, ready to take him on.

Because *this* was the angel who had bound Jessie – the angel who had subjected her to fifty years of hell in the process.

But Eden warned himself to be on his best behaviour, to think smart – for Jessie's sake. Unable to judge his opponent so far, silence remained his best option, especially considering, from what Jessie had told him, his opposition knew everything about *him*.

'Eden Reece, the con who's not a con but a Curfew Enforcement Officer. *Ex*-Curfew Enforcement Officer now.'

Eden stared into the piercing eyes of the angel.

If his pack of mints hadn't been taken from the back of his jeans pocket, he'd already be chewing on one, flipping it over and over with his tongue to remind him to stay calm and focused.

The angel took a couple of steps closer. He raked Eden slowly with disdain. 'I'm going to keep this simple and quick. I need *you* out of the equation, or I need Kane Malloy out of the equation. I requested the latter from Jesca in order to save *you*.'

'He can't kill you himself,' Jessie called out. 'Nor Kane. Doing so would be a clear breach of the prophecy. He's not allowed to interfere if it leads to finality.'

One of the angels restraining her clamped his hand over her mouth, silencing her.

Jessie's revelation did nothing to ease Eden's tension as he looked back at Torren.

'But since then,' Torren continued. 'I've resolved that testing *your* resolve would be more interesting. Who would you choose, Eden? Blackthorn, your family and this quest of yours, or Jesca?'

The angel held up the necklace: Jessie's necklace.

Eden's heart skipped a beat.

'Because if this gets destroyed, Jesca dies,' Torren said. 'I know you're aware of that.'

Tension took a claw-hold throughout his body as he watched the chain dangle from the angel's spread fingers like he was holding a puppet, the vial glinting in the weak light.

The manacle around his wrist became an even greater weight, an even more significant bind. He didn't dare look at Jessie. He didn't need to. He could sense the replicated tension in her from where he stood.

'I know what a dilemma this will be for you,' Torren added. 'Having had Jessie shadow read, I know *all* about you. When was the last time you felt this helpless about a woman you loved, Eden?'

Eden's jaw tightened. He clenched his hand in its restraint. Childhood memories flooded back of being unable to save his mother that night. Of being hit, overpowered, helpless.

'Not the *same* kind of love obviously. But that night left you damaged enough to affect everything, didn't it, Eden? Some might say broken to the point you never allowed yourself to love a woman after that. You took a look around the dangerous world that surrounded you and became too scared to put yourself in that situation again. Because you can't handle feeling helpless, can you, Eden? You've never been able to handle feeling helpless. That's why you've done nothing more than fuck your way through life – until Jesca here, that is. And now here you are again, facing the very regret you knew you'd have if you veered from your rules.'

Jessie struggled, her glare locked on Torren.

'She's certainly learned a trick or two since being with you,' Torren added. 'You bring out the slut in her almost as much as I used to.'

Eden slammed his hand against the manacle, his jaw clenched as he took a step forward.

Despite the tiny knot of jealousy in the pit of his stomach should it be true that this was who Jessie had spent her past with, it was overwhelmed by his rage at the derogatory edge to Torren's tone.

Eden glanced across at Jessie, who lowered her head as if wanting to deny it had ever happened.

'The question is, how *much* do you love her?' Torren asked. 'I want you to test your convictions.' He stepped closer until he was less than a foot away. He stared deep into Eden's eyes, deep into his soul, to the point of discomfort. 'I want to know if you can face what you dread becoming the most: your own father.'

Eden had no idea how he didn't swing for him, but he retained his composure. He retained his silence.

'You despised him for so long, didn't you, Eden? For choosing to take his own life after your mother died instead of seeing through his responsibilities to you and your brother. Now I wonder if you'll become exactly the same: choosing Jesca over your responsibility to your team, your own family, to all those lives out there you're supposedly trying to save.'

'Get to the point, Torren,' Eden warned.

'Jesca has broken too many rules. It is my job to see to her punishment.'

'She wouldn't even be in this situation if it wasn't for you.'

'She's in this situation because she's never learned.'

'So what's the choice you're offering *me*? You want to know if I'll die for her? Is that it?'

'I know you'd die for her, Eden. Having that knowledge means I can't give you that choice. It would be against the rules. You're too integral to the prophecy, but *she's* not. I could stamp on this necklace right now and I wouldn't be breaking any laws.'

Every ounce of Eden's being ached under the weight of the threat as Jessie's life literally dangled from Torren's fingers.

'In fact, anyone can destroy the bind. But only *I* can undo it. Only I can unscrew the cap *I* placed on the vial. And by spilling the contents, I can free her from it.'

Eden's heart skipped a beat. 'At what price?'

'You forgetting you ever knew her.'

Eden's attention shot to Jessie, to the horror creeping across her face. He stared back at Torren. 'She's right. You want to do the same to me as you did to her.'

'If you love her, Eden, set her free.'

'To what fate?'

'Banishment from this parliament. Her freedom.'

'For ten years of my life, right?'

'Ten of the best years of your life, Eden. There's got to be something in it for me. So which is it? Would you rather retain your memory and lose Jesca right here and right now. Or would you rather lose your memory, and your mission, but let her live? More to the point, free her.'

Eden looked back to Jessie, who shook her head, her eyes damp with tears.

Torren let the chain drop an inch, enough to make Eden flinch.

'Five. . . four. . . three. . .'

'Do it,' Eden said, glaring back at him.

The smugness across Torren's face had Eden clenching his hands into fists again.

He looked to Jessie, the tears trickling down her cheeks.

'He might be able to make me forget, but my love for you will always be there, Jess,' Eden said. 'And I'll find you again. I promise.'

Jessie shook her head, her plea silent for him not to agree to it.

'We'll see about that,' Torren said.

Holding out the necklace, he unscrewed the cap and poured the contents onto the floor.

Jessie baulked in the angel's grip.

She cried out against the hand clamped over her mouth.

Eden yanked his wrist against the restraint again, desperate to get close to her, to comfort her as tears of pain streamed down her cheeks.

'What the fuck is happening to her?' Eden demanded, his glower snapping back to Torren.

'It's just her memory returning. Be glad it was less than twenty years she was missing. I've seen angels die from this when it's been longer.'

'Twenty years?' Eden could barely even utter the cruelty of it. 'You gave her a seven-times-life sentence at *twenty* years old?'

'For you, Eden,' he said. '*Because* of you. Because she was mine before she was yours. Because she chose *you* over *me*.'

Eden stared back at Jessie as she lay on the floor, the angels having now released her in her weakened state, her body trembling on the cold concrete, her breathing terse and shallow.

*His* Jessie.

He looked back to Torren.

'*After* I've found her, I'll find *you*,' he said to the angel. 'We're not done, Torren. We're far from done.'

# Chapter Twenty-Two

Sirius Throme stood looking through the one-way mirror where Jarin sat manacled to the interrogation table.

The higher order vampire at least looked downtrodden if not defeated, his sullen blue eyes laced with indignation and resentment beneath his low, dark eyebrows.

Sharner closed the door behind himself as he joined his boss in the small observation chamber.

'Still denying it,' Sharner declared. 'Still claiming he's not the vampire leader and that he has no idea who is. He could be telling the truth, Sirius. Jask could have lied. Or the soldier who'd overheard heard wrong. With no way of knowing for sure. . .'

'We don't need to know for sure. For as long as he's the scapegoat, we have all the justification we need to keep the Higher Order contained. The vampire leader is amongst them. They won't be evoking much of an uprising from inside their cells.'

'And Feinith? She's still out there in Blackthorn, Sirius. How do we know it's not her? How do we know Jarin and the rest of them aren't covering for her? We know she's in with Dehain. If anyone's capable of inciting an uprising, it's him. You can't afford for Kane to be caught in the crossfire.'

'Which is why we can afford to take our time over this. Let my army do their job. Keep that one sweating,' he said, indicating Jarin. 'And keep finding out what you can.'

Since Jarin had been brought in, Sirius had read his file extensively to remind himself of as much as he could about the potential threat. In name alone, he had the makings of the leader. His father, dead some fifty years now, had been a supreme governor in the Higher Order, attributing Jarin, his only child, with an instant status within their hierarchy.

Jarin had never been one of the vocal Higher Order though, frequently swerving mediation meetings between them and the Global Council. His votes were as rare as his presence beyond the safe and luxurious confines of the Higher Order's haven in Midtown. Jarin, it seemed, liked the easy life; Jarin who had always exuded a laziness, albeit one laced with overindulged arrogance.

Not anymore though.

As Sharner left to return to task, Matt Morgan slipped through the door in his place.

Sirius acknowledged the acting head of the TSCD with only a fleeting glance before returning his attention to Sharner's re-entry into the interrogation room.

It still grated that Caitlin Parish had got one over on Morgan. When he'd appointed the VCU agent into the temporary role, he'd expected more. Instead Morgan had let Caitlin Parish and, subsequently, Kane Malloy slip through his fingers. Now he needed to make up for it. He'd already taken steps in the right direction by making sure Meghan met her demise for interfering in the takedown of Kane, but the agent still had more to prove.

So far, Morgan had remained in his position only because he was the media guru: the familiar, trustworthy face heading up the façade of the barrier being used until the situation with the morphed lycans was resolved; of the army moving in to protect the civilians within. It would make no difference what those on the inside witnessed. Once he had Kane, he would ensure there were rebellions within that would justify and explain the loss of countless lives.

'What is it, Morgan?'

'I have information you're going to find interesting, Sirius,' he said, placing the folders on the workbench in front of him. 'It appears Jarin might not be all he seems.'

It was enough of a statement to capture his attention fully.

Morgan opened up the folders. 'I was clearing up all of the evidence from Caitlin Parish's investigations, making sure there's nothing that could fall into the wrong hands, and I discovered she was due to collect some results from the lab the day she went missing – samples taken from the spate of murders she was investigating. I know you were hoping to find something to allow us to convict Caleb once he's got his hands on Kane.'

'And you have?'

'I found more than just *something*. DNA traces were found on all of the murder victims. Interestingly the same DNA traces were found back at the hideout of a vampire called Marid. Caitlin seems to have been following a couple of leads.' Morgan pointed to the photograph. 'That's Marid now. It took a while for the boys to bag him up so he could be identified properly.'

Sirius looked up from the photograph of the bloodied room to meet Morgan's gaze. 'Tell me it was Caleb's DNA you found.'

'There wasn't a single trace of it.'

Sirius glowered back at him. 'Then *why* interrupt me?'

'Because it was Jarin's DNA, sir.'

Morgan's gaze remained steady despite glinting with excitement.

Sirius looked back through the one-way mirror to where Sharner was hitting Jarin with another stream of questions.

'Caleb wasn't responsible for killing The Alliance – Jarin was. That also means it's highly likely he was responsible for trying to assassinate Caleb Dehain and his brother. We don't know why—'

'Feinith is obsessed with Caleb Dehain. She has been for decades. She's tried to keep her liaisons with him quiet but not well enough. I'm guessing Jarin here was a little affronted by his betrothed being bedded by the local lower-class rogue.'

'That's the interesting thing though, sir. Caleb Dehain isn't a lower class of vampire.'

Sirius's attention snapped back to Morgan.

'Obviously we had a blood sample taken from him when he was brought in for questioning,' Morgan said. 'His blood contains the same unique strain as the Higher Order vampires.'

'You're telling me Caleb is of Higher Order origin?'

'Yes. His brother Jake was too. Obviously we had a blood sample from him as well.'

'If they were Higher Order, why would they opt to live in Blackthorn?'

'Maybe they don't know.'

'Or maybe they do.' Sirius's heart pounded at the implications. He glared back through the mirror at Jarin as the sense of a set-up crawled through him. 'How do we know they're not working together?'

'Who?' Morgan asked.

'The third species!' Sirius snapped. 'How do we know the Higher Order aren't working with Jask? What if it was all a set-up? What if they wanted Caleb and Feinith in there and Jarin's the red herring?'

'Sir. . .'

'I knew she couldn't be trusted,' Sirius hissed. 'Wanting Caleb out, choosing him to track down Kane. The entire third species could be working together right now. Or they could be going after Kane for themselves. . .'

'Sir. . .'

'They think they can get one over on me *again*. Feinith is finished. She is dead after this.'

'Sir, both the Dehain brothers' blood types match Jarin's.'

'What do you mean "match"?'

'As in related. They're the closest relation they could be. The DNA thread proves unequivocally that Jarin is the Dehains' brother. I think you might be right, sir. I think a more clever game is being played here than we thought possible.'

# Chapter Twenty-Three

Eden woke to stare at the peeling paint of a damp ceiling. Mould dominated the top corner to his left, above what looked like a door to a bathroom. To his right a blonde lay facing the wall away from him.

He pushed himself up onto his elbows to take in his surroundings, which were subtly lit by the weak light permeating the thin curtain across the window at the foot of the double bed jammed against the wall.

There wasn't much in the room other than a low, wide chest of drawers beside him and a wardrobe on the far side of a closed door next to the bathroom.

None of it felt familiar – but that was nothing unusual.

He looked back down at the girl. He couldn't see her face beneath her bobbed mop of hair, only the side curve of a breast that seemed too big for her skinny frame. From what he could see from a partial showing of her bare arse, the rest of her was naked too.

And so was he.

'Fuck,' he hissed, pressing the heel of his palm to his forehead as he wracked his brain as to where he was and how he had got there.

He looked across at the half-empty bottles of alcohol beside him, the lingering scent of other substances dominating the room. His grogginess, the thumping headache and nausea, confirmed another wild night.

He placed his feet on the thin rug, a couple of used condoms sticking to his feet as he stood.

At least he'd been sober enough to be safe.

Grimacing, he peeled them off before heading around the foot of the bed to the window. Not in the mood for conversation, he parted the curtains only slightly so as not to wake her.

All he could see beyond the bars was a brick wall opposite and an alley below. There were plenty of brick walls in Lowtown and more than enough alleys. He looked back across at the bed. There were plenty of willing blondes there too.

He reached for the shorts and jeans on the floor and slipped them on as quietly as he could, fastening the belt that was the only item he recognised as his – confirmed as his finger skimmed the extra hole he'd added once.

Amidst the poor light, he scanned the floor for any sign of his wallet, his phone, his keys.

He moved over to the chest of drawers and searched among the array of bottles, used glasses, unopened foil packets and stubbed-out cigarettes. But there was still no sign of his wallet. There was no sign of anything else that belonged to him, not even his mints.

He looked back across at the girl. He nearly woke her to find out if she'd got one over on him, but instead he quietly slid open the top drawer to search amongst items there first, wincing as the sex toys clinked and clunked, producing too much noise for his headache.

And then he froze.

Twisting his arm, he stared down at the unfamiliar markings – markings that, in the poor light, looked like numbers.

He stepped over to the bathroom and closed the door more clumsily than he would have liked. He searched for the light switch. It pinged on at the same time as irritatingly activating the rattling extractor fan.

He stared down at the numbers under the subdued glow of the artificial light. Grabbing the flannel on the side of the sink, he ran it under warm water and scrubbed his inner right forearm frantically until his skin burned from his fervency.

But the numbers weren't coming off. Even with soap, there wasn't so much as a smudge. This wasn't temporary ink, henna, kinky role play. This was no joke. These numbers were real. The numbers marking his arm were real fucking tattoos.

Con tattoos.

His heart pounded. The room swayed more than it already did, and he clutched the sides of the sink.

But this wasn't a prison cell. He wasn't in the penitentiary. The room beyond, not to mention the woman in his bed, told him that much.

If she was a woman at all – as in a human female. Having not examined her for extra incisors to know if she was vampire, or extended and broader canines to know whether she was lycan, he could have gone to bed with anything.

He checked his neck, his arms, his chest and his thighs for bite wounds. He looked in the mirror. His eyes widened in the reflection, his heart pounding. He grasped the sides of the sink again as he leaned closer. Stared closer. His heart beat faster at the subtle lines around his eyes, the maturity of his whole face.

He tried to steady his breathing; placed his hand over the tight spot in his chest.

He looked down at the glass shelf, at the clear plastic packets of powders and pills – substances that would account for him being smashed out of his mind.

He lifted one of the packets of pills to examine them more closely. His stomach churned. He couldn't even be sure if the woman he'd spent the night with – or however long – was there willingly; whether she would remember anything either.

He stared back down at the tattoos. He knew what every single number signified. Having grown up on the rough streets of Lowtown and having ventured across the border into Blackthorn on numerous occasions, he knew the cited list of crimes he'd been prosecuted for: arson, GBH, ABH, possession of illegal substances, armed robbery, attempted murder. . .

Crimes he couldn't remember.

Crimes he didn't want to believe himself capable of.

He stared down at the other tattoo laced delicately on his left inner wrist. One simple word: *Honey* with a capital 'H'. It was a name that meant nothing.

He clutched the sink and lowered his head again, perspiration breaking out on his temples as he struggled to recall what the fuck was happening.

The last thing he remembered was working a job near the hub in Blackthorn. He'd been transferring some goods he'd acquired from a contact in Lowtown who, in turn, had access to Midtown. It was going to make him enough money to keep him off the streets for a few weeks. To take the worry off Billy for a few weeks.

Billy.

His brother.

The door clicked open, and he turned to face the naked blonde who stood in the doorway. She looked in a worst state than him as she squinted against the light, heavy make-up smudged across her eyes.

As she braced her right arm on the doorframe, he saw the numbers on her too.

He'd been in bed with a fucking con. According to one of the numbers, a murdering con.

'*Fuck*, Deep,' she hissed as she used her left hand as a visor to shield her eyes from the light. 'What's with the fan? I've only just got to sleep.'

Maybe five-foot-four, her underweight body – looking even more so due to her oversized breasts – wasn't his usual taste.

As she ruffled her mop of bobbed hair and smudged a little more of her heavy eye make-up as she rubbed her eyes, he didn't need his memory to know nothing about her was to his taste. She wasn't unattractive, but her features had an edge as hard as her blue eyes. And she couldn't have been a day over twenty. The guy in the mirror was at least in his mid-thirties.

*He* was at least in his mid-thirties.

The room spun a little; his breaths were harder to draw.

'Baby, come back to bed,' she said, closing the gap between them as she reached for his hand, her skin rank with cheap perfume.

As he pulled his hand away, her eyes narrowed in disapproval at his rejection. She took a step back and scrutinised him for what felt like minutes. Laced with suspicion, her gaze held his with a wariness he didn't comprehend considering her initial familiarity.

'What's my name, baby?' she asked, watching his every reaction like some kind of professional interrogator.

'Did I take the time to ask? Where am I?'

He was sure he saw her eyes smile from beneath her ruffled fringe, but it dissolved within a split second.

'Fuck,' she said with a sigh. 'Not you too.'

'Me too what?'

'It's okay, baby,' she said as she closed the gap between them again. She slid her hand up his chest, her term of endearment already beginning to grate as much as the stranger – the con – caressing him. 'It's gonna be okay. The barrier they've put up around Blackthorn has affected some of our microchips, that's all. It's fucked with our memories.'

The microchips: the neural implants all cons had before they were extradited out of the penitentiary into Blackthorn. If they tried to step beyond the border back into Lowtown, they would implode. It was the only thing the Global Council had stuck to in terms of protecting the predominantly human population beyond – the Lowtown population he had grown up in.

'We're in *Blackthorn*?'

And he was chipped.

And chipping wasn't the only thing the authorities did to the cons they sent in. There was also the additional course of action: the snip. They couldn't castrate them, but they could stop them reproducing – both the male and female cons. The last thing the authorities needed was the complication of con, or half-con, kids running around the rotten and depraved core. Worse, kids that were half vampire, half lycan or half whatever other species lurked in Blackthorn. Chances were minimal but genetically it wasn't impossible.

Cross-pollinated kids made the Global Council's perfect system of segregation complicated. After all, no one in the privileged districts of

Midtown and Summerton beyond wanted to admit they didn't give a shit about innocent kids born into that world. But neither did they want kids blighted with con blood – or third-species blood – defiling their perfect streets. Or, more to the point, defiling their perfect offspring.

Offspring that, now, he would never have.

Kids had never been a priority, barely even a thought. But instantly the sense of something having been stolen lacerated deep.

As the rest of her information sunk in, he looked back into the woman's eyes. 'What barrier?'

'There's a whole fucking barrier that's been put up around Blackthorn as of last night, Deep – some kind of electromagnetic field to keep everyone in. It was all across the news. Something's gone wrong with the lycans. The fuckers have morphed and are running amok in the north and heading this way. There's shit going down with the vampires too. The authorities have a warrant out on Kane Malloy. He's involved in it all apparently. You were high and out of it last night. You passed out before it all happened. A few of ours collapsed. They woke up not remembering hours, days, some even months. What do *you* remember?'

He held out his forearm. 'It's more what I don't. Like getting these.'

Her eyes widened a little. 'Shit, Deep. Are you fucking with me?'

'Do I look like I'm fucking with you? Who *are* you?'

At first she looked concerned, but her lips broadened to a sultry smirk, adding to his unease. 'I'm your honey, baby.'

He looked back down at the delicate tattoo on his wrist.

He stared back at the blonde.

He'd only ever had three tattoos: the shoulder amour that partially engulfed his left pec and the left side of his neck; the emblem to the left of his stomach; and the Celtic knot a little way above it on his side.

He'd never had a woman's name. He would never have a woman's name. Tattoos were permanent – women were not. No girl ever mattered enough for him to plaster their name permanently on his skin. He didn't do permanence. He didn't do commitment. But it was a well-established tattoo – not some recent drunken decision.

If he was with her, there was every chance he'd done it for survival. If he'd done it for survival, he had to watch his back.

'Where are we?' he asked.

'South.'

Where all the cons notoriously congregated, away from the hub and away from the third species.

'In a row?' he asked.

Because memory or not, he knew how it worked. Cons opted for safety and, more importantly, power in numbers. They'd taken over several rows of residential terraced housing, knocking through to make their own dominions, each ruled by a different leader. To be in one meant you were an approved part of the gang. If he was in a row, he had earned his place there somehow. And he knew *how* those places were often earned.

Part of him hoped she was going to say no. Part of him hoped he had continued to stand on his own two feet as he always had done.

'Too fucking right,' she said.

His scum credentials were growing by the second.

Worse, he knew every penitentiary in every locale had a different number. He knew the pen number on his arm wasn't the Lowtown pen, which meant he'd done time in another locale. Only the worst of the worst were shipped out of their own locale – gang leaders primarily, to lower the risk of uprisings within the pens – or those who needed protection.

'Under who?' he dared to ask.

'Pummel, until a few days ago. Our row got burned down. Him with it. We lost all of our loyal crew in it. Everyone else dispersed. We moved in here. It used to be owned by Cyclops but Homer took it over.'

'Homer?'

'He used to be Pummel's second-in-command. Now he's in charge. And considering you're Homer's best buddy, you're the next in line, baby.' She grinned with pride. 'You're the boss around here too.'

# Chapter Twenty-Four

Jessie twisted her wrists in the cuffs that bound her outstretched arms to the low crossbeam spanning the dusty attic. The beam that dug into her stomach.

To add to her humiliation, her sense of helplessness, she'd woken standing and bent forward at the waist, her behind facing the door. The jeans she'd redressed in had been removed by the time she'd regained consciousness – the clothes Torren had given back to her, along with the contact lenses he'd instructed her to wear to conceal her identity.

Her shirt barely covered her dignity, but at least she'd been granted her underwear. Her gut told her it was nothing but a further goad though. She knew what pleasure the con would get from stripping her the rest of the way – and how he'd want her awake for that final bonus.

She rested the side of her head on the rough wood as she blinked away tears of frustration.

She thought they were simply going to be dropped off in the south. She knew she should have known better. But her third-species heart had pounded to an almost human rate as she'd seen Homer enter the warehouse some hours before. Homer, who was supposed to be dead – killed by Eden before their escape from the row.

Gagged, bound and held on her knees by two of Torren's mob, she'd been unable to do anything but watch as the con had headed across the outbuilding towards them. And his smirk as he'd spotted her had sickened her to her gut.

He'd come backed up by ten of his own crew, outnumbering the four angels who stood around the periphery.

Not that Homer had known that's what they were. And Torren had had no intention of revealing it either.

To Homer they'd been nothing more than a gang from elsewhere in Blackthorn – some species that was insignificant in light of the offering they had brought him.

'Mya tells me you want to talk,' Homer had said, as he'd pulled level with Torren.

There was only one logical explanation. Having survived, knowing him like she had for twenty years, Homer would have been consumed by revenge. He would have been looking for her. More than looking for her, he would have been looking for Eden. With Torren's crew out looking for them both too, at some point the two search parties had collided – and Mya had been core to that.

Mya, who had spent years on the periphery in Pummel's row, never failed to seize any opportunity to better her situation – and whatever she had done to make this happen, it must have brought Homer's approval in droves.

She'd stood not far behind Homer, arms folded, one skinny leg cocked outwards as she'd adopted a triumphant stance. It was identical to the stance she'd taken when she'd played the honeytrap for Eden on his initial arrival to Pummel's row days before, spurring on her gang to beat the shit out of the new boy.

Jessie's chest had burned as she'd glared up at her.

Mya had to have known how much Homer despised Eden. How he'd hated him from the second he'd made his presence known to Pummel; from the second Pummel had started to take a shine to him.

And undoubtedly knowing Eden had tried to kill Homer, knowing his part in bringing about the downfall of Pummel's empire, Mya had known exactly what fate would befall him.

'Mya tells me you want to make a deal,' Homer had added.

'More an *offering*.'

'No one offers anything for nothing around here.'

'Oh there's definitely something in it for me,' Torren had said.

Not that any of it had made sense at the time – until two more angels had entered with the wooden crate the size of a coffin.

As Torren had flipped the lid, as Homer had stepped up to look inside, as a sadistic smirk had crept across the con's face, she'd nearly retched as her worst nightmare came to fruition.

She'd clenched her hands into fists as Homer had reached inside the crate, no doubt to check for a pulse.

With a glint in his eyes, he'd looked first to Jessie before returning his full attention to Torren.

'And still alive,' Homer had said.

'I thought you'd prefer it that way. Mya explained what a special bond you have with Eden, as well as Jesca here.'

Bile had risen at the back of her throat as the horrors of what Torren had planned had become clear.

Death was too quick. Death was too easy. For both of them.

'A *very* special bond,' Homer had declared, his eyes having narrowed in suspicion. 'The question is, where do *you* fit into all of this?'

'You and I have the same issue, Homer. I need him to pay for what he's done. I need her to pay for what she's done *with* him. You and I both have rules about what's ours, Homer. Eden Reece crossed the line. So did Jesca.'

Homer's small eyes had narrowed in suspicion. 'She was yours?'

'A *long* time ago.'

Homer had glanced back at Jessie. His frown had deepened as he'd met Torren's gaze once more. 'You're third species. I don't fucking deal with third species.'

His crew had moved forward and squared up.

'There's no catch,' Torren had said. 'Killing him would be too easy, that's all. And *far* too kind on Jesca. I came to realise from Mya that you're in a much better position to see this to its best outcome, that's all. I want her to suffer, Homer; I want them both to suffer. I know you're the man to do that.'

Homer had remained silent, wary, pensive as the seconds had scraped by painfully.

'We know it's only a matter of time before trouble comes to all of our doors. We both know Jesca has certain *innate skills* that will prove useful to you when that happens. A certain natural substance, shall we call it?' Torren had added.

'And what makes you think I won't kill Eden outright?'

'Because you have more style than that. Because where would be the pleasure? Especially as I've made things a hell of a lot more interesting for you. Considering you know of Jesca's past, you'll know of a trick I inflicted on her. I've taken Eden's last ten years, Homer. When he wakes up, he won't have a clue about how he ended up in your row, or a clue about Jessie. Do you see where I'm going with this?'

A leaden sensation had taken hold in the pit of her stomach as the full extent of Torren's cruelty became apparent.

This was most definitely, undoubtedly, personal.

Struggling to free herself, she'd locked her glare on Torren. And the calm, satisfied gaze that had stared casually back at her had made her want to burn his eyes out.

Worse, Homer's sadistic smirk had broadened as the potential had unravelled before him.

'Now I can see you understand what I mean about you being in a more advantageous position, Homer. 'Quid pro quo. This enables me to get my own message out there that I see my threats through. I know you appreciate how important that is.'

Homer had stared back down at Eden then reverted his full attention back to Torren.

The con's smile had confirmed that the deal had been done.

Jessie didn't know where she'd woken. She didn't know how long she'd been out or how long she'd been awake. Her only measure of time had been the recent ecstatic feminine gasps from below the bare floorboards, the rhythmic thudding of a headboard.

She was back in the nightmare she had escaped from only days before – escaped from because of Eden, who she'd yet to see or hear anything of.

She yanked against her restraints, gritting her teeth in frustration as they remained immoveable, then flinched as the attic door opened behind her.

She'd heard the footsteps enough times over the decades to know it was him. And every slow and steady footstep echoed Homer savouring her knowing it was him who was approaching.

'When I think of all the years I spent waiting for this moment,' he drawled. '*All* those years of Pummel's no-touch policy on that fine arse.'

She blinked away her tears. She turned her head from left to right to wipe away what she could on the rough beam, unwilling to show him even a moment of weakness.

'What, is that the extent of the struggle?' Homer goaded. 'No screams? No begging? No smart mouth now you haven't got Pummel to protect you?'

As she felt his jean-clad thighs touch the back of hers, she clenched her jaw.

'And to think of all those *wasted* decades believing that breaking your celibacy would make you lose that precious healing skill of yours.' He paused. 'Not anymore though.'

Jessie squeezed her eyes shut, sickness lodging at the back of her throat as he mock grinded against her for a moment.

She clenched her hands to fists as she shuddered with repulsion.

He laughed curtly as he smacked her lightly on the behind. 'But there's plenty of time for that.'

As much as she resented giving him the satisfaction she knew she couldn't not ask. 'Where's Eden?'

'She speaks,' Homer said, his voice laced with amusement as he circled round to the side of her and crouched down. 'Don't you worry your sweet little self about him. Eden's doing fine. Mighty fine it seems. Can't you hear that for yourself?'

Jessie's pulse flatlined as she homed in again on the female's ecstatic, climactic groans echoing up towards her, her stomach flipping as she searched his gaze in the desperate hope it was a cruel joke.

It seemed impossible. But she had to remind herself that Eden would be clueless.

And if it *was* true, it was the cruellest thing they could have done to him. The cruellest thing to the man for whom loyalty and faithfulness, once commitment was given, was unshakeable. If his memory came back, it would break him knowing what he'd done.

Right then, she couldn't be sure it wouldn't break her – *if* they survived that long.

Homer rested his elbow on the beam. 'Mya is certainly having the time of her life with him. It's my way of thanking her for helping me out like this.'

But Jessie knew it was about far more than that. Homer knew Eden wouldn't have touched her with a bargepole; that Eden had turned her down previously.

That wasn't something Mya was going to forget either.

'They've been at it for hours,' Homer added. 'Just one quick one I told her. Break him in. I'll admit his stamina has impressed even me. Especially as she's not the only one he's been fucking. He's been like a kid in a sweet shop ever since he gained consciousness. He's sure got a taste for bad girls, hasn't he? The skankier the better, it seems.'

Jessie turned her head away from him to conceal the pain searing through every inch of her as the female groans below peaked.

'Is that what he did for you, Jessie, huh? Is that what persuaded you to fuck him behind Pummel's back and betray your crew? Betray those who put a roof over your head and food in your stomach. Who protected you?'

He rested his arm on the beam, his hot breath against her hair chilling her.

'I hate to admit it, but I'm actually liking this side of him,' Homer continued. 'What do they call it? Self-fulfilling prophecy? Surround a man in where he thinks he belongs, convince him of who you want him to be and, in time, every man will start to buckle – especially one with his past. We've simply got to give him a few more shoves in the right direction.'

Jessie snapped her head back towards him. 'If either of you hurt him. . .'

Homer grabbed her hair and yanked her head back. 'You'll what?' he demanded, spittle escaping his thin lips. 'Mya can slip a blade into his heart any time she wants. We both know she's done it before – more than once. So do tell – what *are* you going to do?' His grip on her hair tightened. 'I'll tell you, shall I? You're going to take a shower, you're going to slip into something more comfortable and you're going to keep me company downstairs. Because you're *my* bitch now, Jessie and, unlike Pummel, we both know I can do *whatever* I want to you; just like I can do whatever I want to Eden. You'd do well to remember that before you even think of mouthing off to me again.'

For decades under Pummel's control, she'd had no one but herself to think about. She'd kept herself isolated. She'd even tried to keep Eden away from the moment they'd first met. And *this* was why.

Pummel had had her necklace to control her. Now Homer had Eden.

She should never have allowed Eden to accompany her to collect Toby's notes – then it would only have been her. Torren would have had nothing to trade with, Homer wouldn't be able to use Eden as a hold over her and she could have ripped the whole fucking place down and torn Homer apart in the process.

'And that's why, for your boyfriend's sake, you're going to sit and watch as Mya continues to have her fun with him – and as I entertain myself watching you watching him. And then I'm going to entertain myself watching him with *you*. I'm going to see to it that he hurts you too, Jessie. I'm going to see that he does things to you that you would have never thought him capable of. I'm going to destroy everything you have with him.

'And if you try to give him a single clue as to what's going on, I'll kill him. If I see one fragment of doubt or suspicion in his eyes, he's a dead man. And if you try and run on me, let alone even *attempt* to persuade him to go with you, I will make you watch what a gang of cons can do to a traitor like him.

'And then you'll be back up here in this position with that door wide open for any con, or group of cons, I choose to send up here. And you *know* I don't make false threats. You've *seen* that I don't make false threats.'

Worse, over the years, she'd witnessed just how few boundaries Homer had. How non-existent moral limitations were for him, whether it was a man, woman or child he was dealing with.

'I warned him once what I was going to do to you,' Homer added. 'We're back to the old game but with new rules. I hope you're not out of practice. Talking of which. . .' He slammed the roll of syringes onto the beam. 'You know how this works.'

He released her hair and turned her arm inwards to reveal the crook.

'I'm going to make you pay for what you did, Jessie. I'm going to make you pay back *every* last drop. You think Pummel treated you bad? Welcome to the real hell. I'm going to see to it that you burn, bitch. And I'm going to see you watch Eden die in the flames first.'

# Chapter Twenty-Five

Billy.

He needed to know where Billy was in all of this.

But tattoo of her name or not, Eden still didn't know this woman. And revealing family was revealing weakness. He could only hope his brother was still in Lowtown, keeping a low profile.

He needed his phone, his wallet – anything that would give him a clue without needing to ask her.

He'd been in the south for two years according to her. He'd been with her for the entirety of that time. Before that he'd done six years in the penitentiary. The two years previous to that remained a mystery because he'd lost ten years according to the dates she had given him. Ten years of his life gone. And there was the girl he had supposedly chosen to be with, who supposedly cared about him, who had only one thing on her mind.

'I've left a message for Homer,' she said, discarding her phone before giving him a playful shove onto the edge of the bed.

Mya, having finally revealed her real name, was already ripping open the foil packet.

Pregnancy may not have been an issue between cons, but there were plenty of STDs to worry about amidst the community where sex was as much about sport or punishment as it was pleasure. It was the only other good measure to come from the authorities: a free, never-ending supply of rubber excuses to indulge in whatever they saw fit as long as disease spreading was controlled.

Eden braced himself on his arms while she tugged down his jeans and shorts as if they were the familiar lovers she proclaimed them to be.

But as she knelt down between his thighs and wrapped her hand around his barely stirring erection, he was more than experienced enough to know hers was anything but a lover's touch.

Whatever it was between them, it was purely sex. And clearly having no intention of getting her mouth anywhere near him until he was covered, she relied on wrist action to get him aroused enough for her to do something about it.

Her efforts were being wasted though. Despite her being naked between his knees and clearly willing to give him whatever he wanted, he still wasn't so much as stirring.

He grabbed her forearm. 'Just slow down, huh?'

'Since when have you ever wanted to slow down, Deep?' she asked with a smirk.

'I don't even know you.'

'You didn't know who I was the first time either,' she said as she slid her hands up his thighs to lean in and kiss him, seemingly growing impatient as he failed to harden sufficiently in her hand. 'It didn't stop you fucking me face-first up against an alley wall for an hour non-stop before you even asked my name.'

He might not have remembered the encounter, but he could believe it.

All he could ask himself was what had driven him to that kind of low: being jerked off by some con he was barely even attracted to in a dive of a row, not to mention what had driven him to commit those crimes in the first place.

'Why do you keep calling me Deep. . .?'

He knew cons didn't go by their real names. He knew there was some kind of logic behind their redesignated ones.

She bit into her bottom lip as she raised herself up from her haunches, her hard nipples brushing his bare chest. 'You're nicknamed Deep because you think deep, baby. And you wound deep,' she added, her lips tasting of alcohol and smoke as they consumed his. 'And my personal favourite,' she declared breathily as she met his gaze again, 'you sure as hell fuck deep.' She licked the underside of his upper teeth before entwining her tongue in his. 'Hopefully this'll bring it all back to you.'

He'd tried to convince himself he could go with it. He'd tried to convince himself it would bring something back. After all, functional sex was an art form to him. And it might even bring some of his memory back.

But instantly he grabbed her shoulders to force her back away, breaking from her kiss. 'Give me some headspace, yeah?'

'For *what*?' she asked curtly, sinking back to her haunches with a scowl.

It was a scowl he could do without, especially as, so far, she was his only source of information. Maybe even the only one he could trust.

'This isn't like you,' she added, as she knelt back up again. 'You need to relax, that's all.'

She caught hold of his left wrist. She kissed his tattoo, the act inexplicably repulsing him as her tongue swept along the length of it.

'You had this done for me, baby,' she said. 'Because you say I taste as sweet as it.' She gazed into his eyes. 'Because you told me you loved me.'

Discarding the foil packet for the moment, she pressed her hands to his chest to lay him down. Her hands were barely able to encompass his wrists but her grip showed determination as she eased his arms either side of his shoulders before sitting astride him.

She ran her hands down his pecs and abs and back up his biceps as if she was feeling his body for the first time; with a hunger as if he'd been away for months. 'Just go with it, Deep. We'll have a good time. Release some of this tension.'

She grabbed his hands to place them over her breasts, her hands on top as if he needed guiding as to how to handle a woman – breasts that were soft and feminine and pleasurably weighty in his hands.

'You know me, Deep. You know how good we are together.'

She squeezed his hands tighter, using more pressure than he would have applied, her fingers brutal on her own nipples as she encouraged him to do the same. Leaning over him, she teased his lips with them, encouraging him to take her into his mouth.

He tried to force himself to relax, never having been reluctant to sample a woman's body. And, to his relief, it wasn't long before nature brought him to hardness, even if he was being worked as if he was nothing more than a tool for her end gain.

Finally Mya was able to slide the protection over him. Lowering herself, she pushed him fully inside her without hesitation.

Eden caught his breath at the feel of her heat closing around him. But that's all it was – just a basic, physical response.

Her head lowered, she writhed above him, her moans something he listened to with mild interest rather than any kind of connection.

Because there was none.

He felt nothing. No, worse than nothing, it felt wrong. And sex had never felt wrong.

She grabbed his hands again, cupping them back over each breast as she rested her hands on his pecs, mercilessly toying with his nipples.

As she groaned and picked up the pace, saying his name over and over again, louder and louder, he did nothing but lie there. He couldn't even bring himself to touch her anymore. Despite the temptation of her naked body, her heavy breasts jolting, he felt no desire to reach out and touch any part of her.

When she jerked minutes later, when she clenched around him, her body shuddering, her lips wet and parted, when she finally cried out with the pleasure of her orgasm, all he felt was relief that it was over.

Finally she fell onto her back beside him.

As she lay panting, her eyes closed, Eden wiped her saliva from his cheek and swept the back of his hand across his mouth to rid himself of her lust-fuelled kisses.

He sat up and slid the condom off to conceal how little she had done for him. Hiding the evidence in his hand, he made his way back across to the bathroom.

Opting to flush it, Eden rested his hands on the sink as his erection, aching with unsated arousal, quickly waned.

Feeling something on his cheek, he rubbed it away with his forefinger before glancing down to see the remnant of a tear.

He was crying.

He hadn't cried post-sex since he was a teenager. And now he was crying over a meaningless fuck with some girl he'd apparently been giving it to for months.

He rubbed his hand under his nose, trying to gather himself as he looked into the mirror, angry at the emptiness he felt inside.

'You okay, baby?' Mya asked as she opened the door.

He lowered his head for a moment until he'd completely blinked away any remains of his tears.

She rested her hand on his back, and he almost shoved her away. But, thinking better of it, he let her linger.

She chuckled. 'Don't worry, baby – it made my eyes water too. That good, huh?'

He met her gaze, unable to believe he had chosen to be with someone so utterly unattuned. Whatever they had, it was the final confirmation that it was about sex – or power – and nothing more.

'Yeah,' he lied as he looked her in the eyes. '*That* good, honey.'

She leaned back against the wall and bit into her bottom lip, her hand straying down between his legs again. 'I'm ready for round two whenever you are.'

He eased her wrist away.

He could no longer not know.

'What about my brother?' he asked. 'What do you know about him?'

'Billy?'

His heart skipped a beat at realising she knew his name. He stood upright, hanging on a thread, waiting for her response as her eyes searched his.

'Billy's dead, baby,' she finally said. 'Billy died years ago. It's just you now. Just you and me – and Homer. *We're* your family now.'

# Chapter Twenty-Six

After the rage, the despair had set in.

Amidst his knocking back several glasses of whatever spirit had been on the chest of drawers, Mya had given him a couple of the pills from the bathroom to help calm him. They'd barely touched him though. He'd had a chain of roll-ups in the hope they'd succeed where the pills had failed. Instead he'd coughed like he hadn't smoked in years, so he'd finally opted to down as much burning liquid as was available.

He knew he should have passed out, but his brain kept ticking and his body remained resilient despite the amount he had inhaled and swallowed.

Mya had been banging on about something in his ear to the point he'd encouraged her to go down on him just to shut her up; just so he could wallow in his grief in peace.

He didn't recall when she had finished. He wasn't even sure if he'd managed to come this time. For all he cared, she could have ended his life right there and then – he wasn't sure he would have even been bothered to stop the bleed.

Everything from the point she'd told him Billy was dead was hazy. She'd told him it had happened during a job Eden had taken him on; that Billy had been shot by a Curfew Enforcement Officer. Since then, his whole world had been a blur in front of him – a meaningless, purposeless blur.

The last thing he remembered was Mya muttering something before finally leaving him alone, before finally leaving the room. His inclination should have been to follow her, but he no longer gave a shit as to what lay beyond the door.

Even as he heard the voices outside it, it took him a while to care enough to tune in. It was only hearing his brother's name that had him lifting his forehead from the crossed arms resting on his knees.

'He took it real bad about Billy. . .' he heard Mya say.

The door clicked open. The male con stepped inside.

He was maybe five-eleven, just a little shorter than Eden. He couldn't have been much older than him either. But where Eden had an athletic build, he was the chubby side of stocky, and the look in his eyes made it clear he wasn't one to mess with. The plethora of numbers down his inner right arm reinforced that – as did the scar that ran down his neck before disappearing into his T-shirt.

Stepping in behind him, Mya closed the door.

'Fuck, Deep,' he said, shaking his head slightly. 'I've been waylaid dealing with a few issues. Mya's filled me in. Ten fucking years, mate. Ten fucking *years*?'

He could only assume the con to be Homer, his so-called best mate. Never having been one to judge by appearances – his survival instincts too strong to be misled by those – the shaven-headed con nonetheless looked to him like the indicative thug.

Eden glanced to Mya.

This was his life? These were the two closest to him? The girl who would rather shag him than give him five minutes to grieve, and the guy who looked like he'd rather gut someone who crossed him than wait for an explanation.

'It's me, mate: Lennie. Homer to everyone around here,' the con added, confirming his identity.

Eden kept his knees drawn to his chest as he watched Homer take a seat to his right, on the end of the bed, less than a couple of feet away.

Mya clambered on a few seconds later, kneeling to Eden's left. She ran her fingers through his hair with what felt like mock affection, though he knew his emotional numbness could be responsible for his paranoia.

'He's really not good,' Mya declared, her playfully girlish voice grating through him. 'Are you, baby?'

'Fucking Global Council,' Homer hissed.

'Mya said I'm not the only one,' Eden forced himself to say rather than sitting there like a mute.

'It's affected five others in this row as far as we know. Three of them are back to normal now. None of them have been hit as hard as you though, Deep.' He shook his head and hissed, 'Fuck,' again. 'We're going to have to handle this carefully. There'll be plenty of bastards out there who want to take advantage of this. We're going to have to keep a close eye on you until your memory comes back.'

'You think it will?' he asked, as he searched the con's gaze for something familiar about him.

At the back of his mind, rooted somewhere inaccessible, to his relief, there was – as if he'd seen him in a dream or suchlike.

'If it did with the others, it can with you. We just don't know when. Mya tells me she's explained to you about us losing most of our crew in that fire, about setting up here and about all the shit going down on the streets.'

'The lycans and Malloy?' Eden asked.

Homer nodded. 'The focus is still up north, but they're going to come this way – the third species and the scummy Global Council army. And the south's going to be caught right in the middle.'

'Do we have a plan?'

'I'll refill you in on that later. You've got enough to be getting your head around with getting through the next few hours. With us being new to this row, the cons round here are still learning where they stand with us at the helm. They don't know us well enough yet, but we're making progress. There's a lot of resentment about what we did to Cyclops—'

'*We?*'

'Me and you, mate. Mainly you. You were the one who chose this row. You were the one who did Cyclops in.'

'*I* did?'

Homer smiled in a way that chilled him. 'Too fucking right you did.'

'What did I do to him?'

'Let's just say we fitted him in a freezer in cling film by the time you'd finished.' Homer's eyes glinted, sending a shiver of repulsion through every inch of him. 'That's why we've got to watch your back, Deep. If we were back in our old row this wouldn't be a problem, but I still don't know where anyone's loyalty lies in this place. Treat everyone as the enemy, all right? Except me and Mya here. Keep your head down and keep yourself to yourself for the time being. Don't talk to anyone, don't answer any question and, for fuck's sake, don't let on. For now, stay off the streets too. Mya here will look after you and keep you entertained.'

He looked down to see Mya smirking at him, the toxic smoke of the room sending his senses hazy again.

'I sure will,' she said.

'You come to her or me if you need anything,' Homer added. 'But I'm going to need your presence down there, mate. We've got to look like everything is normal, but I'll take all the heavy stuff for now. We'll get through this. And we'll get you back, Deep. I promise we'll get you back.'

# Chapter Twenty-Seven

Nestled in the corner of the sofa, Mya draped her skinny bare legs over him, her arm resting on the back of the sofa behind him.

As she toyed with his hair, Eden sussed out the array of unfamiliar faces sitting in various clusters around the room. His presence had caught the interest of a few, but their glances were subtle and guarded.

Indicative of the multitude of terraced rows the cons had taken over, the room they sat in had been knocked through to the lounge of next door and into the hallway and room beyond that too. But despite the vast space, not many occupied it, most remaining across the other side of the hall. Those who were in the same area kept their distance as they minded their own business amidst card games, drinking and mumbled conversations.

Regardless of the evidence in front of him, something still didn't feel right. He'd always been a survivor, but he'd also always been a loner, choosy about his acquaintances and even more selective with those he'd call friends.

He was also smart though, a chameleon when he needed to be, and he knew enough about Blackthorn to know cons who went it alone rarely survived. But *this*. . .

Billy had been dead for over ten years according to Mya and Homer though. *Ten years.* His brother had been the only thing keeping him on the straight and narrow. Billy had been his only reason to play the system instead of immersing himself in it. He could stay in denial as long as he wanted, but Billy's death had clearly been the tipping point.

'Like I said earlier,' Mya whispered in his ear, having also picked up on the glances in his direction, 'most of them don't know you – not yet. But you'll change that. Reputation's what it's all about, remember? You'll be back on track stamping your authority around here soon enough. Homer will see to that.'

Homer, who was mid-conversation a few feet away. But with the backdrop of music playing from a stereo somewhere, Eden couldn't distinguish what he was talking about.

Eventually rejoining them, opting for the sofa opposite, Homer unscrewed the lids on a couple of bottles of home brew before handing one to Eden.

As Mya annoyingly sucked on his neck while massaging his groin, he met Homer's gaze, the con promptly smiling back before blowing a smoke ring into the air.

But the glint in the con's eyes was more unsettling than reassuring, his own uncertainty about what the hell he had become making his head ache and numbing him to the sensation of Mya's hand in his jeans.

He didn't know what caused him to look across Mya's shoulder – probably some basic survival instinct – but his heart skipped a beat as stunning brown eyes stared right back down into his.

Large, intense and uncharacteristically gentle in that place, the girl's eyes perfectly complimented her delicate features. As an added bonus, a cascade of dark curls framed her beautiful face, sweeping down over her chest to her waist.

And then there was the body. Her breasts were no more than a handful, her hips curved out subtly from her slender waist and her shapely legs were lengthy on her five-foot eight-inch athletic frame.

He instantly hardened despite her looking wrong in the short, strapless hot-pink dress that clung to her. He didn't know why he thought that, but her stiletto heels looked just as cheap and misplaced on her as the rest of her attire. Even her make-up looked too heavy, especially as it was clear she didn't need a scrap of it. And if her clothing reflected her personality, she was anything but his type. But those soulful eyes betrayed an entirely different story.

More curiously, her gaze dropped immediately to where Mya was still working his groin. Her eyes flared. Her full lips parted as if she wanted to say something, as if she had somehow walked in on something unexpected.

Even *more* interestingly, her hands subtly trembled as she held the bottlenecks between her fingers.

But she averted her gaze a split second later, her heavy swallow too detectable to him not to make him wonder what the hell had just happened as she made her way over to Homer's side.

Mya, seemingly interpreting his semi as her success, breathed more heavily in his ear. But suddenly the compulsion to remove her hand was more overwhelming than ever.

Placing the extra beers on the table, the girl perched on the edge of the sofa. She clamped her knees together with a modesty that contradicted her attire, seemingly uncomfortable in the length of her dress as she tried to subtly tug it further down her thighs, her gaze downturned.

Homer, however, grabbed her hip and slid her back against him, indicating his ownership. But as the con draped his arm over her shoulder, his hand hovering an inch away from her breast, not only was it clear she wasn't relishing in their intimacy, she instantly tensed.

Glancing at her inner arms, seeing they were free of con tattoos, her reluctance made some semblance of sense.

But then he saw the needle marks instead.

Addiction was hard to survive in Blackthorn. For a beautiful woman like her, those who could provide what she wanted, what she needed, would want both her body and soul in payment.

Either that or she'd been a feeder sating some vampire's need somewhere to the west or east.

Either way, everything about this girl screamed that she was complicated. And the stirring in his jeans added to that sense of trouble. He didn't need his memory from the last ten years to know how it worked. If she was Homer's – under whatever circumstance or pretence – she was way out of bounds. Aside from hierarchy, Homer was his mate. Loyalty counted for something. She was Homer's even if she didn't agree. And there was nothing to say they hadn't simply had a spat. Neither were his concern.

The problem was, he wondered how the hell he'd managed to adhere to that rule when just one moment of eye contact had made him feel more alive than he had since waking; had been the only thing to distract him from the grief that made his chest ache.

Thankfully she didn't look at him again though. Instead, the raven-haired beauty kept her eyes downcast as if purposefully avoiding looking in his direction.

'This is Jessie,' Homer said.

She finally looked up to meet his gaze again with eyes that could melt an iron heart.

'She's aware of your situation now too,' Homer added. 'But she's going to keep her mouth shut.' He squeezed her bare thigh harder than was necessary. Hard enough to inexplicably trigger the tiniest sense of protectiveness in Eden. 'Aren't you, Jessie?'

✤ ✤ ✤

Jessie clutched the bottle between her hands in order to have something to hold as opposed to having any intention of drinking.

Her heart had broken as Eden had met her gaze as if she was a complete stranger to him. Any hope she'd gathered, any romantic sense of his instantly recognising her, seemed painfully naïve.

Without even a fragment of familiarity in his eyes, Eden had given her nothing more than a swift once-over. There'd been no glint or any sign of the smile she'd come to love. Worse, she'd sensed the intense sadness emanating from him as if he had suffered some recent emotional wound. Being so close to Eden yet totally unable to touch him, to even look at him, to do anything to help him, tightened her chest to the point of pain. Any other time she would have been capturing his hands to find out what was wrong; encouraging him to share what was weighing him down, not just as his lover but also as his friend. Except now she was neither. After days of building their trust, their friendship, their love, she was nothing to him.

Adding to the ache in her chest was the fact that he hadn't even the remotest hint of guilt in his eyes as Mya remained draped over him – more so, had blatantly continued to grope him in front of her.

It was like the déjà vu of watching Tatum all over him again: a flashback of a nightmare from the week before. A time she'd thought they'd escaped with the destruction of Pummel's row.

And just as Tatum had been Pummel's partner in crime to manipulate and control Eden, now it was Mya serving the same purpose – this time for Homer.

It was like she'd never escaped at all: a new row, a new leader, but the same putrid pack mentality – not for good, like Jask's pack. This was about standing together to oppress, to control, to destroy.

Back then though Eden had been *pursuing* Jessie's attention. Eden had been knowingly and willingly playing the game – playing Pummel, playing them all, to get close to her. It was a game he had been adept at. And, eventually, she had been willing to engage. She had been willing to take the risk for the handsome, kind and attentive stranger who promised her only escape from the living hell she was trapped in.

Now it was her turn to return the favour. Except this time Homer was tuned in, and worse, Eden was an oblivious participant.

Unlike last time, she now also had no room to call her own. No place she could sneak him to safely disclose the truth. Even if she could, she had no idea where she'd start.

*You're not a con, you're an ex-Curfew Enforcement Officer. The tattoos are fake. You had them as part of an undercover mission to Pummel's row. Since then an angel – a species you don't even know exists yet – took your memory as revenge.*

*Oh and because they're also hell-bent on blocking you from preventing the apocalypse. The apocalypse you're trying to stop with the help of Kane Malloy and Jask Tao – a master vampire and a lycan leader who are now your friends.*

*And by the way, I'm an angel too. I saved your life whilst in Pummel's row. More than that, I'm an envoi who recognised you the moment I met you because, as I now know, you were always destined to save us.*

*I'm also your friend. I'm the one you love.*

*And I love you too. More than anything in the world, I love you with everything I am.*

*You're here because of me, and I'm going to get you out of here. But right now I have no idea how the hell I'm going to do it.*

The challenge felt impossible. An impossibility that became even more palpable as Eden placed a cigarette between his lips.

It was a habit he'd given up years before. He'd resolved never to touch one again after Honey was born. But this was Eden without Honey – four years before she existed. This was the Eden who didn't know love beyond that for his brother. Who, out of self-preservation, had purposefully refrained from knowing any other type of love. This was Eden with his barriers up. This was the impenetrable Eden that somehow, as a stranger, she was supposed to gain the trust of.

In the meantime, Homer was going to do everything he could to corrupt him, revert him back to the path he had been on all those years before. Homer wanted him to die in that cesspit, and the longer she took, the more likely it would become. And the more likely the world out there was going to crash and burn.

Eden was going to be destroyed knowing nothing of what made him good, nothing of their fight for survival beyond those walls, nothing of the team they had become. Nothing of the hero he was.

The urge to reach out and touch him was overwhelming, as if contact alone could bring his memory back. Then they could flee onto the streets of Blackthorn and back to their friends.

Instead she watched him ignite the tip with the swift expertise of a familiar act and, as he fleetingly met her gaze again amidst a cloud of smoke, the indifference in his eyes made her heart ache. Something inside her broke as he looked away again, as he accepted Mya's kiss, sending a further shock wave to her resolve.

As Homer laughed and smoked and drank, his body odour lingering in her nostrils, his clammy hand far too high on her thigh for comfort, tension soared through her body.

Homer could do anything to her, and he wanted her to know that. As yet, he'd refrained though. Homer was a sadist through and through. He wanted to make her sweat. He thrived on the anticipation. And he was savouring her humiliation and distress along the way.

Even as he'd lain on his bed upstairs, watching her as she got dressed – Jessie skilfully not revealing anymore flesh than she'd needed to as she'd shimmied into the clingy strapless dress he'd chosen – he'd done nothing beyond leering.

Thankfully he'd let her leave her hair down to cover the scars on her back – the side effects of receiving the prophecies – her biggest weakness; her greatest sense of insecurity. Scars that Homer had laughed and grimaced at, mocking her by Pummel's side when the latter had first seen them.

Scars that Eden had handled so tenderly; somehow even having managed to make her feel beautiful afterwards.

But that was then. She had the feeling Homer had let her keep them covered not out of a sense of kindness but as part of whatever sick crescendo he was planning.

As part of that, he'd wanted to make her feel cheap. He'd wanted the other cons to look at her like she was cheap. He'd even forced her look at her own reflection in the mirror. She'd hated seeing herself with her poorly applied dark eyeshadow and thick mascara, and the horrendous shade of pink lipstick he'd selected. Unlike Pummel, Homer wasn't going to let her wander around in her oversized jumpers and her face free of make-up as she hid under the mask of her hair. He was putting her on display. He was objectifying her. Ultimately that's how he wanted Eden to see her. More than that, he wanted to use her to tempt Eden. He *wanted* to set him up. He wanted to use *her* to set him up.

And the way Mya's hands were all over Eden amidst her sneaky little triumphant glances in Jessie's direction, she was willingly as much a part of it.

'What do you reckon?' Homer asked, his hot breath repulsive against her ear, his sweaty, clammy hand on her becoming even more unbearable as he slid it up to squeeze her bare behind. 'Shall we give them a little show too? I reckon Eden would like to watch.'

Amidst the horrifying thought of Eden bearing witness to her with another man was that her friend, her lover, her protector would have no reason to do anything about it. Worse, could be unwilling to do anything to help her.

'Maybe he'll even fancy a foursome,' Homer added, amusement lacing his tone.

And that was what Homer ultimately wanted just as he'd threatened. That was how they would hurt her: they would get Eden to do it for them, the man who had become her hero becoming her enemy. And Eden's ignorance was definitely his greatest disadvantage, his lack of knowledge of the truth behind the situation his biggest vulnerability.

When she couldn't breathe anymore, when she felt the intense sensation that she was going to vomit, she prised herself away, muttering that she needed the toilet.

'Make sure you give him a wiggle,' Homer whispered in her ear before she had a chance to stand, his grip on her arm tight enough to bruise.

The compulsion to shrug him off was overwhelming, but she knew better.

'Get some more beers while you're at it,' he added more loudly as he let her stand.

She stepped over the array of legs, almost Eden's included, had he not been the only one with the manners to retract them out of the way.

She shot a glance sideways in his direction and found his eyes ready and willing to meet hers.

And it was a gaze that lingered a second longer than it should have.

Some things would never change about Eden Reece.

Her heart skipped a beat. Her skin prickled as his gaze lingered on hers, as she lost herself in his eyes, just as she always did with him.

And she searched them in the frantic hope that it was his cryptic message back to her: that he *did* know the truth. That the spell hadn't worked; that he was just wearing the mask he'd worn so adeptly the last time he'd been in the row.

But any semblance of hope instantly dissipated as the glint in his eyes remained as absent as all the rest of the non-verbal cues they had shared.

There was no connection with this stranger – from his side, at least. This was not *her* Eden looking back at her.

He was still in there though, trapped behind those beautiful brown eyes by an angel spell he didn't deserve. And she would free him from it – somehow. But first she had to get him out of that hellhole.

# Chapter Twenty-Eight

'Your memory might be screwed for now, but that's no excuse for not knowing where your loyalties lie,' Mya stated.

Eden snatched his attention from watching Homer converse with a small group two rooms away. Jessie had failed to return as yet, leaving him alone with Mya.

'Meaning?' he asked, looking down at her as she stroked his chest, her hand under his T-shirt.

'Meaning memory or not, some things shouldn't need to be said. Me, I'm not bothered if you play free now and again as long as you come back to me, but Homer doesn't like people checking out what's his. I'm just looking out for you, baby.'

'So she *is* his?'

'Has been for years.'

'So how come he didn't mention her in the names I could trust?'

'He likes having her around, Deep. She makes him look good. She makes him feel good. And from what I hear, she's a slut between the sheets. That doesn't make her trustworthy though.'

'Homer doesn't strike me as fool enough to keep a pretty face without loyalty.'

'He's just selective with what he tells her; what he lets her overhear. She would have soon worked out there was something going on with you though, so he had no choice.'

'So how come she didn't look happy to be his?'

'Because she's a mardy bitch who doesn't know how to appreciate what she has. Homer's done a lot for her over the years. He's done a

lot for us all. You more than anyone. You and him are close, Deep.
Just you remember that. Anyway,' she said, tracing her index finger
around his nipple. 'We've been down here long enough. Give me ten
minutes then come back upstairs. We'll keep working on that memory
of yours.'

Placing another cigarette between his lips, he cast a glance at her as
she left before returning his attention to Homer.

*He's done a lot for us all. You more than anyone.*

Eden struck a match to light the tip of his cigarette. He inhaled a
couple of lazy drags as he watched the con; as questions lingered in his
mind of how they had met. Of what exactly he had done for him to
constitute that level of loyalty.

Sensing he was being watched, Homer sent him a pally nod. If
he was disgruntled about his buddy eyeing up his girl, there was no
evidence of it yet.

But that was exactly what he *had* been doing. She clearly wasn't
worth the hassle though. From the way Mya had described her, Jessie
was even less his type than Mya was. If anything in his past had dictated to the contrary, it would have no doubt been Jessie's legs wrapped
over him, not Mya's.

He reclined back into the sofa and placed an ashtray on the seat
beside him, nudging aside a couple of bottles so he could put his feet
on the table.

Feeling it was his turn to be watched, he glanced up to see a pair
of pretty eyes staring right at him – eyes belonging to an attractive
redhead.

To that point, he'd only seen the back of her head, the sofa she'd
been sitting on having its back to his. Up to that point, she'd been
nestled in the neck of another con. The con she now straddled. And
her subtle movements, the glazed look in her eyes, her hitched breathing, told him exactly what she was in the midst of.

From fifteen feet away, across the dimly lit room, she smiled at
him. And it was a smile that was as languid and seductive as her

moves. A smile that was an invitation for him to keep watching her performance, even if her partner was oblivious to the fact.

A smile that told him exactly who she was *really* fantasizing about at that moment.

Eden reciprocated her smile, enjoying her brazenness, her playfulness, and realised it was the first time he'd smiled since hearing the news about Billy.

He dropped his gaze, a tightness forming in his chest again, his stomach knotting.

He inhaled deeply, closing his eyes to let the toxic fumes consume him as he drew on his cigarette again. Right then he didn't give a fuck about the effects. Right then he didn't really give a fuck about anything at all.

Resting his head back against the sofa, he slowly opened his eyes to a cloud of smoke as he looked at the redhead again, the increase in her pace telling him she was close to climax.

He stared right at her, willing her to come as he watched, needing that moment of escape, of control. Sex games had always been his release, especially when the participant was as willing as she was.

She smiled again as he played along, her eyes becoming hooded, her hands clutching the nape of her partner's neck as she drew closer and closer to climax.

He stiffened in his jeans knowing what she wanted him to do but, instead of tucking his hand into the front of his jeans, he exhaled another taunting stream of smoke.

His defiance and self-control had the bigger impact that he'd hoped for. Her lips parted as she reached the cusp of her orgasm, a small groan echoing towards him.

But her climax wasn't enough to maintain his attention, not when a familiar figure stepped into the doorway to his right.

The redhead instantly faded into insignificance as Jessie paused at the threshold. Clearly taking in that he was alone, she scanned the room before she located Homer in the distance, his presence seeming to make her hesitate more.

After a few moments, she joined Eden at the sofas anyway.

She placed the bottles on the table exactly as she had last time, the condensation leaking down the glass telling Eden they'd been out of the fridge for a while.

Jessie resumed her seat, holding down the hem of her dress as she did so. Keeping her knees locked together again and pointed away from him.

Again, her grace, her elegance, her modesty contradicted her outward appearance, making him wonder if maybe she dressed that way for Homer's benefit.

As she kept her gaze downturned, as she remained poised on the edge of the seat, he exhaled a slow stream of smoke and waited to see what she'd do next.

No doubt feeling him watching her, Jessie met his gaze, those brown eyes inexplicably burning deep.

'Is there something you want to say to me?' he asked.

Her grip on the hem of her dress tightened.

'Only I'm feeling some tension here,' he added.

'You think so?' she said eventually, assuring him she wasn't mute.

He flicked ash into the tray beside him. 'Are you telling me I'm wrong?'

Her terse breathing added to his curiosity. More so when she glanced across her shoulder as if needing reassurance that Homer was out of earshot.

Meeting his gaze again, she kept her voice low. 'We need to talk.'

His heart skipped a beat, exacerbated by her caginess. Clearly he'd been right in sensing something.

'About what?' he asked.

'Something you don't want anyone to hear.'

Her additional glance across her shoulder made it more than clear she was referring specifically to Homer.

He leaned forward and rested his forearms on his knees as he looked squarely into her eyes.

'Clearly I'm missing something here. You know this barrier has fucked with the chip in my head and affected my memory.'

She frowned a little as if processing his claim.

'So you're going to have to be a little less cryptic with me here, angel,' he added.

Her eyes flared. Her lips parted. She looked as if she was about to speak, but her gaze shot over her shoulder instead. This time in the opposite direction to where Homer was located though.

The stranger glared down at him with the kind of sneer Eden instantly wanted to wipe from his face.

'This one not enough for you?' the con asked, indicating Jessie.

Eden looked past her shoulder to where the redhead was now standing amidst the horseshoe of sofas, watching the con she had been straddling challenging him.

The redhead he'd forgotten all about the second Jessie had appeared.

Another con stood next to her – no doubt his challenger's backup. Two more kept to the sofa but watched on with concern.

Remaining seated, Eden leaned back and looked squarely up into the eyes of the con clearly spoiling for a fight. But the very pit of his gut told him today was a bad day for anyone to be picking a fight with him.

Today was the kind of day when he deserved the numbers on his arm.

❋ ❋ ❋

Jessie's attention snapped from the con to Eden and back again.

She'd seen that look in Eden's eyes before. She'd seen it the very first time he'd laid eyes on Pummel across the room and Pummel had dared to glare directly back at him.

Despite the stand-off, Eden, being Eden, didn't flinch.

She looked back to Homer, now watching on too, his eyes meeting hers only fleetingly. The minor upward curl of his lips was unmistakable.

This was what he wanted as much as he'd wanted Jessie to entrap Eden. He wanted Eden to play the part. And Eden was on the verge of succumbing.

Despite wanting to stand and forge a barrier between them, Jessie remained seated, aware that even a minor glimpse of her third-species strength could make it difficult to gain Eden's much needed trust.

'If you're referring to the girl watching *me* whilst fucking *you*,' Eden responded, 'I would suggest that's a clue you should improve *your* technique rather than questioning mine.'

Jessie cast a glance over her shoulder to see the girl standing at the sofa behind her, the scenario becoming clear.

The cold directness of Eden's words, not to mention the challenge they presented, were not the words of her Eden though. Her Eden knew when to keep his mouth shut and play it smart. This Eden seemed to be spoiling for a fight.

'Leave it, Coplan,' one of the other cons called out. 'It's not worth it.'

'First they take over our row and now they want to take our women too? I think it's worth it,' the con counter-argued, his attention fixed on Eden.

'There's no 'want' about it,' Eden said, still maintaining his steady glare. 'If I wanted her, mate, she'd have been straddling me – not you.'

Confident, yes. Playful, yes. But antagonistic. . . arrogant even. . . Jessie's heart pounded harder. This was someone who looked like Eden but had been possessed by a stranger. And with this understanding came the realisation that it was no longer just a question of whether he could trust her, but whether *she* could trust *him*.

The con clenched his fists and lunged.

Eden was on his feet a split second later. His counter shove sent the con sprawling.

The room fell to silence.

Jessie didn't know who looked more shocked by the power behind his shove: the con, the rest of the room or Eden himself – all of them oblivious to the angel tears in his system.

She knew she had no choice but to stand between them.

She pressed her hand to Eden's chest as his glower remained on the con sprawled on the floor. She could feel the tension tearing through him – the anger even.

Eden was never that quick to the edge of temper. He was always so composed, so strategic, so mindful. And worse, whereas before her touch would have been enough to grab his attention, terrifyingly she couldn't even capture his gaze.

Instead he placed his hand on her hip and pushed her aside.

She needed to hold on to one thing: he was not one of them. He was not a con, even if self-fulfilling prophecy was threatening to take effect.

'Eden,' she whispered firmly as she grabbed his arm.

His gaze shot to hers.

He frowned.

It was a moment's distraction that was a mistake on her part. The con was on him a moment later, taking him clean over the back of the sofa.

Jessie clutched the back of her head, horror consuming her as the fight broke out properly. The compulsion to tear the con off Eden sent her to the edge of despair, the pounding of flesh and the grunts and groans she heard unbearable.

But the con was no match for Eden, as she well knew. What she didn't expect was Eden to go at him so angrily, so aggressively, so brutally.

He'd overpowered him within seconds, but he wouldn't stop hitting him. The crunch of bone, the smacking of a fist against flesh, had her looking to Homer in desperation.

But Homer merely sent her the slow, warning shake of his head. A warning that told her if she intervened, the consequence would be worse for Eden.

She blinked away her tears, grateful only that the sofa formed a barrier that prevented her seeing fully what Eden was doing.

Moments later he stood, his T-shirt and his face splattered with the con's blood. He wiped the back of his hand across his mouth and looked across to Homer before scanning the rest of the room.

The room that was stunned to silence.

And when his eyes met hers, it was as though his soul had temporarily vanished. The dismissal in them as he looked away again chilled her, as if he hadn't seen her there at all.

She looked over her shoulder as Mya wandered in. Striding straight over to see what had happened, her eyes flared. Her attention shot to Homer, a subtle glimmer of panic in her eyes. But his subtle nod back at her had Mya reverting her attention to Eden.

'Anyone else want to argue with Eden here?' Homer called out, his glower marking every con in the room.

Silence.

'I'll take that as a no,' Homer said. He looked across to the con's companions. 'Get him the fuck out of here.'

They hurried over and lifted the limp body from the floor.

Jessie stared at the bloodied form of the con as they carried him out, every breath leaving her body as she stared back at Eden, at the man she loved. At the kind and gentle – yes tough and hard but fair and clean-fighting – man she had given her heart and her body to.

Now *his* body was draped with Mya's as she crooned over him.

Crooned over her brutal warrior.

'Looks like you earned yourself an extra prize tonight,' Homer said, his grin broadening as he drew level with Eden. He indicated the redhead across the room. 'Two's company, three's a party.' Homer slapped Eden's upper arm as he passed and whispered, 'It's good to have you back, Deep.'

And just as he was out of Eden's view, the con grinned again, this time in Jessie's direction, triumph glinting in his eyes.

# Chapter Twenty-Nine

Jessie remained perched on the sofa as she trembled with a concoction of shock and despair amidst the anger burning through her veins.

Homer sat opposite her in the now empty room, blowing rings of cigar smoke into the air in way that was too reminiscent of Pummel not to make her blood freeze. He might as well have been him back from the dead, still lording his power over her with that same arrogant sanctimony.

Eden had left with Mya. Worse, he'd left with the redhead in tow too. He hadn't even bothered to send her another glance as he'd done so.

It was as though he hadn't seen the shock in her eyes, the disappointment, nor the sadness at the betrayal of his principles as he simultaneously handed the baton of triumph to his enemy.

'Not quite the hero now, is he?' Homer goaded, his cruel, predatory eyes locked on hers. 'I wonder if he feels the same disappointment in himself as you do right now or whether he's too busy fucking two hot young women to care.' He smirked again. 'My bet's on the latter.'

Despite trying to hold it in, she couldn't suppress her glare any longer.

'He's quite the bastard underneath it all, isn't he?' Homer added after blowing out a few more smoke rings. 'It's almost a shame I'm going to have to kill him. I think he's settling in nicely already.'

Teeth gritted, her jaw clenched, she refused to give him the satisfaction of sustaining eye contact.

'Scrapping, slaughtering and mindless screwing – I'll make a man out of him yet.'

She coiled her fingers around the edge of the sofa.

'Is it feeling like home again yet, Jessie?' He leaned forward and blew a few taunting smoke rings in her direction. 'I saw you chatting to him before it all kicked off. Have you been a naughty girl already?'

Her gaze snapped to his. 'You set me up.'

'Oh, so you *have*, haven't you?'

'He spoke to me first. What was I supposed to do?'

'So it's Eden's fault. Is that what you're telling me? Do you *want* to get him killed, Jessie?'

'It's what you're planning regardless.'

'Then I'll rephrase it: do you want him to die *tonight*, Jessie? Would you *like* to witness his execution *tonight*?'

'Damned if I do and damned if I don't, right, Homer? Just like the old days? You want to take it out on me then take it out on me. Eden's suffering enough.'

'*Suffering*? Maybe you should see for yourself.'

He slid three unopened bottles towards her.

'Take those up to his room, Jessie. Hand deliver them for me.'

Her breath caught as she looked into his eyes. He was going to make her witness it. He was going to engrain it in her brain. This was how he was going to operate: inflict the emotional scars, the sense of doubt, first.

But there was no way Homer was going to succeed in brainwashing her. Nothing could change how she felt about Eden. Whatever was happening with him, it was an act, a performance. Whatever Eden was doing, he was doing it as someone else, not himself.

Fifty years she had survived this life. *Fifty* years. And she was going to be smart, just like she was back then. She was going to play the game. She didn't just need Eden out for himself, or for her, she needed him out for Blackthorn. And no cons – no bullying, putrid cons – were going to cloud her judgement to the contrary. Because no one knew Eden like she did. *No one.*

And no one was going to steal who he was from her – or from himself.

She swiped the bottles up against her chest and stood, staring defiantly down at Homer.

And then she turned her back on him.

# Chapter Thirty

Jessie knocked on the door three times, but there was no answer. All she could hear was a low, rattling hum from within that blurred the distant, indistinguishable blend of voices.

She felt Homer's gaze burning into her back as he waited on the stairwell, and her fingers trembled as she reached for the handle.

The room was subtly lit by a combination of the bedside lamp and the light coming from the ajar bathroom door – the latter's extractor fan the source of the low hum and rattle.

This was his room. This was Eden's new haven – a haven littered with empty bottles of alcohol, torn foil packets and used condoms discarded on the floor.

The room tilted off-kilter as she stared from the rope around the headboard down to the sex toys amidst the ruffled bed sheets.

She held her breath. Her legs turned leaden. She couldn't move as she took in the nightmare playing out in front of her; the soundtrack of groans resonating from inside the bathroom. The groans of *two* women simultaneously.

One voice in her head told her to let the tears flow and to run. The other demanded she kick down the bathroom door and drag Eden out by the scruff of his neck.

As Mya stepped out of the bathroom wet and naked, Jessie nearly dropped the bottles she still held clutched to her chest.

Mya glanced at the bottles then met Jessie's gaze. She smirked. 'Room service? I think your man is already getting enough of that, don't you?'

The heat of her rage burned her chest and she glared at the con who, only days before, had been a honeytrap for Eden. Who would have allowed him to be slaughtered if Jessie hadn't intervened. And now there she was, using an act so intimate, so precious, to break the man he was.

'And I sure don't hear him protesting.' Mya took a couple of steps closer, her eyes narrowing to a disturbingly piercing stare. 'Not that it would have made a difference if he had. He still would have been a good time to be had by all. Might still be.'

As the threat of rape leaked easily from the con's lips, Jessie clenched her fists. She knew enough about the sickening things Mya had done in the past. She knew how devoid of empathy she was. Of compassion.

Mya had grown up in Lowtown as the only sister to four older brothers. She had been used for whatever they saw fit from an early age. She'd been left screwed up beyond repair amidst her warped sense of masculinity. She'd learned early on that sexual blatancy was better than feeling the victim. She'd learned to hit first before being hit.

But the past didn't excuse the present.

'You don't have to do this,' Jessie said – her sole attempt to get through to the con.

Mya smiled. 'I know. But I *want* to.' The con closed the gap between them. 'Because who'd have thought that when you peeled back those layers to see the rawness beneath that he'd be just as twisted and depraved as the rest of us.' Her gaze didn't flinch, her smirk remaining at the heightened climactic groans of the redhead mingling with the heavy sighs of the man Jessie loved. 'Have you seen that side of him yet, Jessie? Or was he pretending to be something he's not?'

At Mya questioning his integrity, their relationship, her insides bubbled with jealousy, with possessiveness.

'You know *nothing* about him.'

Mya glanced at the aftermath on the bed before looking Jessie square in the eyes again. 'I reckon I know more about him than you do. What he *really* likes. And he *loves* it cheap and nasty.'

It took all of Jessie's self-control not to lunge at her, especially when Mya gave her another smirk of triumph.

'And that *body*,' she added. 'The way he can just keep going and going and *going*. This has to be the best job I've ever had.'

As the redhead's final exultation echoed around the bathroom, Mya glanced at the open doorway before meeting Jessie's gaze again.

'I'd best get it there. Sounds like he's ready for dessert,' Mya remarked. 'Is there anything sweeter than his honey?'

Bile rose at the back of Jessie's throat as she understood what Mya was saying.

'He calls me it now, you know, when he's fucking me,' Mya declared, getting right up in Jessie's face. 'Honey! Honey! Hon-ey! Hilarious or what?'

Everything went red.

Jessie grabbed Mya around the throat and slammed her up against the wall.

But Mya fought back. With lengthy nails, she swiped and scratched, punched and kicked. Getting a hold of Jessie's hair, almost ripping it out at the roots, she shoved Jessie forward over the chest of drawers, glass bottles smashing against each other, to punch her in the kidneys again and again before attempting to slam her forehead down onto the hard surface.

Jessie thrust her backwards though, both of them slamming from wall to wall before she gained the upper hand, pinning Mya down with the power of her legs and squeezing her throat again.

Mya retained her grip on Jessie's hair and yanked for all she was worth. Pain swept across Jessie's skull until she felt arms wrapped around her. Familiar masculine arms that peeled her from Mya, that overpowered her quickly despite her rage – a move that could only come from someone of equal strength.

'Whoa!' she heard Eden say against her ear. 'What the fuck is this?'

Mya lunged at her again, eyes blazing, and Eden had barely turned Jessie away before she'd pulled free again.

But as Jessie grabbed hold of Mya once more, as she caught a glimpse of Homer bursting into the room, Eden got a hold of her again.

As he pinned her face first against the wall, her wrists flat against it either side of her head, her stomach flipped at the feel of his warm, naked body against hers. The tiny hairs on the back of her neck stood on end as his grip tightened on her wrists, his groin to her behind to keep her against the wall. Her pulse raced as she felt his breath against her ear.

'Feisty little thing, aren't you?' he whispered. 'Surprisingly strong too.'

As reality of what she had done struck, she realised she couldn't fight back. Despite the rage flowing through her, she had to let him succeed in keeping her there. She couldn't place any suspicion in his mind as to what she was.

No sooner had she feigned calmness than Eden pulled her from the wall and shoved her into another's arms – large, clammy arms.

Homer's arms.

Eden helped Mya up from the floor amidst her curses and attempts to lunge at Jessie for more. But he held Mya back with ease as she bucked against him, fury still igniting her eyes.

'Take it easy, baby,' Eden whispered in her ear as he all but carried her over to the bed.

His words of affection, the fact he had chosen Mya over her, the touching of their naked bodies threw the room off-kilter again.

The scratches and red marks on his behind, his upper thighs and his back from their sex play sunk her heart – more so when she switched focus to the wet redhead standing aghast in the bathroom doorway. A woman he'd barely finished having sex with. A young, pretty, *human* female he'd been banging up against the bathroom wall within less than an hour of meeting her.

*'Reckless, opportunistic, volatile, impulsive; a promiscuous bastard too. I was a very different guy. . .'*

His words came back to haunt her, adding to the sickness of anguish deep in the pit of her stomach..

'Chill,' Eden commanded as he forced Mya to sit on the edge of the bed, catching her jaw to make her look him in the eye.

At the flick of Eden's head instructing her to leave, the redhead gathered up her clothes and walked out in silence.

Jessie's heart shattered as the only man to ever defend her beyond Toby now defended another in her place. Defended another who she had attacked in defence of *him*. In defence of his beloved niece.

Mya's breathing was still ragged, but after a swift glance at Homer, she started to calm.

'Big mistake,' Homer whispered against Jessie's ear, the proximity of his hot breath making her skin crawl, his grip vice-like enough to bruise her upper arms as he held her back against him. 'Big, *big* mistake.'

# Chapter Thirty-One

'What the fuck was that about?' Eden asked as he pulled on his shorts and jeans, buttoning them sufficiently enough only to stop them falling down.

Homer had yanked Jessie outside and closed the door behind them, but Eden could still hear his voice even if he couldn't decipher what he was saying.

'*Bitch*,' Mya hissed under her breath. 'You should have let me finish her!'

'Looked to me more like she was going to finish *you*,' Eden said as he turned to the chest of drawers.

It had taken effort to peel the girl off Mya. But one thing that had left him far more unsettled than her strength was that there had been something familiar about feeling her in his arms. More interesting was how she had eased the second he'd had hold of her.

'Take this,' he said, holding the pill up for her – it was the same kind she'd given him after she'd told him about Billy.

'I don't need one of those,' she said, pushing his arm away.

'And I'm not getting it on with you in that state. I don't know what you'll do to me. You're trembling like a fucking vibrator.'

She may have been half his size, but he'd seen the extent of Mya's temper now. The bottom line was he didn't know her; he had yet to work out the bundle of simmering psychosis who chuckled as if he'd just given her a good idea.

'So put it in your mouth and swallow or I'll fucking force it down your throat,' he warned.

She tongued her teeth, her blue eyes glinting darkly as she held his gaze.

She leaned back on braced arms and, feet still on the floor, spread her legs. 'Ask nicely.'

Placating her with his smile, his acquiescence, he placed the pill on the tip of his tongue as he knelt in front of her. He caught hold of her outer thighs before sliding his hands up to her behind to yank her close to his groin, only to then slam her down on her back.

Tongue exposed, he leaned over her. Just as he'd hoped, she took his tongue deep into her mouth, taking the pill with it before swallowing as he'd instructed.

'Prefer me this way, do you?' she asked, her eyes glossy with lust. 'Subdued?'

'I prefer to call it "manageable".'

She smiled again, but he kept her wrists held to the bed.

'So what was it about, huh?' he persisted.

'She thinks she's queen bee around here. Sometimes she needs reminding she's not.'

But there had to be more to the spat than that.

'And that's how you do it?'

'That's how we all do it, baby. You better than most,' she added, freeing her wrists to curl up against him, her hands grasping his behind.

But seeing her cussing and blinding like a hellcat wasn't exactly top of his list of turn-ons.

He peeled away her hands and slid behind her. Arm around her waist, he eased her back against his chest as he rested against the headboard.

He'd only just started to get used to the feel of her, but suddenly she felt alien in his arms again. To his unease, Jessie had felt the exact opposite.

He'd forced himself to let her go to get his focus back on task, his instant stiffening as he'd pressed himself against her behind a reaction he could have done without, especially with Homer having entered the room.

And now he was stiffening again simply at the recollection of it.

He fancied his best mate's girl. Deny it all he wanted to, it was there. And that attraction could lead to a beating, a death sentence or banishment.

He *had* to shake her out of his head.

But that was easier said than done when the door opened and Jessie stepped back over the threshold again.

❊ ❊ ❊

'We're a little busy here, Homer,' Mya said from her reclining position against Eden, her blue eyes glowering into Jessie's again at the interruption.

'Not too busy for an apology, I'm sure,' Homer said. 'I do believe Jessie owes you one.'

They'd set her up.

Homer had wanted to create the exact sense of insecurity that she was feeling right now. He'd given her a glimpse into the Eden he wanted her to see. The Eden he wanted her to believe was beyond hope.

In turn, Mya had purposefully wound her up to make her attack.

She felt sick to her gut that she'd allowed it to happen – that she'd broken her golden rule about never being provoked. She felt even sicker at the sight of the naked woman nestled between the thighs of the man she loved, Mya sliding her hand behind her to grasp Eden's groin – no doubt also for Jessie's benefit.

The only sense of control and power she'd been left with was to refuse to indulge in the feelings of betrayal the situation had been set up to evoke. To refuse to be drawn into Homer and Mya's manipulative game. She would even swallow her pride and apologise there on her knees in order to get out of there – to prevent Homer gaining satisfaction from further punishment, from her further humiliation.

But she knew it was never going to be that simple.

This was just the beginning of Homer's plan to make her suffer. And he knew nothing would make her suffer more than Eden's betrayal, whether of their love or their trust. And in that moment she could almost believe either possible.

Lighting a cigarette, Eden took a steady inhale before handing it to Mya in a further show of intimacy, barely acknowledging Jessie as he did so; treating her as if she wasn't even there. In turn, Mya grabbed his hand and placed it over her breast, her palm wrapped over the back of his hand.

Jessie dropped her gaze and clenched her jaw again, her pulse thrumming with the urge to challenge Eden, to yell at him to snap out of it.

'My girl went for your girl, Deep,' Homer said.

*Deep*: clearly the con name they had given him.

'We can't be having that kind of behaviour,' Homer added. 'Especially as solidarity is more important than ever right now. Jessie here needs to make up for it. It's your call as to how she does that.'

Tendrils of disgust unfurled as Homer revealed his test for her *and* a test for Eden.

If she'd had any doubt of the extent of Mya and Homer's putridness, it had just evaporated. This would be the ultimate for him: watching Eden hurt, humiliate or degrade her.

Eden barely flinched at the suggestion, staying silent as he toyed with a matchstick between his teeth, before raking her with a sweeping gaze of indifference. Jessie had never felt more alone in his presence.

'It's nothing to do with me,' he said dismissively.

Her heart skipped a beat, her relief at his reluctance to participate dampened by her fear of the repercussions for him.

'But it's to do with *me*,' Mya counter-argued as she turned her head to meet his gaze. 'This is how it works, Deep.'

'It's a one-off,' Homer said. 'Make the most of it.'

The compulsion to elbow Homer deep in the groin before knocking him out cold – of slapping Mya hard enough to do the same – was overwhelming, but Jessie remained silent, passive, as she waited to see exactly what this Eden would do.

Eden chewed the match as his gaze lingered on her more pensively before returning to Homer. 'Why do I get the feeling a simple apology isn't what you're looking for?'

'Like Mya said, this is how it works, Deep. We look out for each other. It's also about respect. You're not going to insult me by turning me down, are you?'

'Leave her with me,' Eden eventually said, with such resolve, such conviction and such sincerity that Jessie had to question his intention. He lightly slapped the side of Mya's thigh as an indication for her to move. 'You too.'

'That's not how it works, Deep,' Homer said.

Jessie's heart pounded, her attention snapping back to Eden.

'Don't go shy on us now, Deep,' Mya added, leaning back against his shoulder again so she could look up at him. She stroked her hand down his jaw. 'This kind of thing is right up your street.'

'And when I remember, maybe it will be again.' His gaze locked squarely on Homer's. 'But for now I'd prefer some privacy. If you don't trust me or don't think I'm capable, just tell me.'

The blood pumped in Jessie's ears as she awaited Homer's response. He and Eden stared each other down before Eden casually broke away first to reach for the wine bottle beside him.

'Mya,' Homer said eventually. He cocked his head towards the door as a cue for her to step outside.

Despite her disappointment-laced glower, her confusion at Homer conceding, Mya grabbed her T-shirt. She yanked it over her head, pulled her denim skirt up over her hips and left.

'A couple of hours should be enough,' Homer said, looking back over at Eden before his cold gaze rested on Jessie. 'Do as you're told,' he warned her. 'You don't want to get yourself into any further bother.'

As he closed the door behind them, her gaze shot back to Eden.

She desperately wanted to believe it was out of compassion on Eden's part or simply a basic sense of decency. But as he knocked back a mouthful from the wine bottle, exposing the grazes on his left knuckles as he did so, vivid images of him beating the con flashed into her mind.

She glanced at the puddle on the floor where the redhead had stood. The redhead he had been having sex with up against the bathroom wall less than an hour before.

For the first time in a long time, she had no idea what he was capable of. Right then, she wasn't sure she knew him at all.

Eden remained reclined, his hooded gaze assessing her in the silence.

'Come here,' he said eventually and tapped the bed beside him.

# Chapter Thirty-Two

Holding down the hem of her dress, Jessie perched side saddle next to him, her feet on the floor, his proximity making every nerve-ending spark.

Eden knocked back another mouthful from the wine bottle as he assessed her in the silence, the sheets ruffled around him, his legs casually bent behind her.

She wanted to let everything spill there and then – for the nightmare to be over. Except she'd seen the bars on the window. She knew Homer would have someone guarding the stairs, and she had experienced for herself how sound travelled up through the ceiling.

More so, she couldn't trust him. She couldn't trust *this* Eden. Not yet. Not until he knew *he* could trust *her*.

She kept her gaze averted from the body he had so willingly shared with her. The body he had now given to two others – that she knew of. It seemed more plausible than ever that Homer had been telling the truth: that Eden had been with others in the interim too.

But amidst the jealousy coiling in her chest, amidst the even more oppressive sense of betrayal, she continued to repeat the same message to herself: he didn't know; it wasn't his fault; it wasn't *her* Eden.

She could only hope he wasn't going to attempt to do anything stupid enough to necessitate her outing her third-species abilities, because that would bring about an entire raft of new questions, and maybe even more distrust.

But although she knew it was best for him, best for them both, if she kept it concealed for now, she couldn't let him overstep the mark.

She knew if he did and his memory came back, he would *never* be able to forgive himself.

'You called me Eden downstairs.'

And she shouldn't have. It was another of her mistakes. And one that, so far, hopefully Homer hadn't picked up on.

She glanced back at the door, reminding herself they were far from out of earshot.

She looked over to the en suite, the extractor fan still buzzing within, and remembered how the noise had prevented even her third-species ears from detecting more than groans when she'd stood outside that very door.

That was where she needed to get him. That was where they needed to talk.

As he brushed her ringlets back from her shoulder, Jessie's stomach leapt at the intimacy of the move, the reminder of the feel of his touch tying her stomach in knots.

Her gaze snapped to his to search once more for the possibility that maybe he *did* know – that he too had been waiting for them to be alone. Failing that if maybe, at least, touching her would bring back some sense of their connection.

But nothing changed behind his eyes.

'What were you thinking stepping between me and that con?'

'We look after each other,' she replied, thinking on her feet.

'Like Homer's looking after you right now?'

Her heart pounded at the sense of urgency she felt, but she knew she needed to tread carefully. A couple of hours, Homer had said. She knew she needed to make herself transparent as soon as possible though – dragging it out might raise questions in Eden's mind as to why, when she did reveal the truth, she hadn't done so sooner.

'What was it?' he asked. 'A one-off?'

'What?'

'The looks down in the lounge. The need to talk to me. The little spat with Mya. Your response to me when I held you against that wall.

The fact you recoil from Homer, but you didn't even flinch when I touched you just then. What's going on between us, Jessie?'

It was perfect. She would have berated herself for not thinking of it sooner had she not been so relieved at the get-out clause.

'It's not a one-off,' she said, her voice lowered. 'We're having an affair, Eden. *That's* why we need to talk.'

❊ ❊ ❊

It was the last thing he needed to hear. A complication he could do without amidst everything else. More so, he knew it wasn't how he operated.

He wanted to believe he wouldn't have been stupid enough to get involved; that he wouldn't have been willing to risk his arse for a girl. More so, that he hadn't got it on with another guy's girl behind his back – and certainly not his mate's. If she was telling the truth, he was beyond contempt.

Unless Homer already suspected. Unless that was just as much what this leaving them alone together was about.

His head ached with possibilities, but it explained a lot.

Whatever the issue between Jessie and Mya, it had clearly been a long time coming as far as Mya was concerned. There was no love lost between the two girls – on either side if he *was* sleeping with Jessie as she claimed.

It also explained why she had looked at him like she had when they'd first made eye contact in the lounge – and why the tension between them had been so palpable.

And why it had stirred something deep inside him when she'd uttered his real name like it was the most familiar and natural thing to trip off her tongue.

All the same, as he searched her brown eyes, detected her contact lenses, he looked for any hint of nothing more than a get-out clause, of her using his lack of memory to her advantage just as Homer had warned him some would.

But it was a reckless confession without any of them knowing when his memory would return. And it was a confession that put her on the line too should he decide to call her bluff.

Nonetheless the unflinching gaze that stared back at him was laced with sincerity and sobriety. Neither could she conceal the *way* she looked at him. She couldn't hide the edge of genuine sadness that emanated from within and struck him a little too deeply for comfort.

Discomfort riddled his chest at knowing she was yet another in a long line of people who knew more about him than he knew about himself right then. Except this girl potentially had something over on him – and he had no idea how much of a threat she was, or whether she meant anything to him.

One thing he did know, they had *something*. He could feel it even as she sat next to him. And he needed answers as to why he'd been so reckless as to get involved with her in the first place. Because a girl who got involved with a con behind another con's back was one to be wary of. A girl capable of doing that to Homer was capable of doing it to him.

It was risky though. Even giving time to her claim was risky.

'You're telling me I'm fucking you?'

Her eyes flared at his directness. She cast a wary glance at the door.

'I wouldn't put it like that but yes,' she whispered, looking back at him. She moved to stand. 'It'll be safer to talk in the bathroom.'

He caught hold of her arm and tugged her back down onto the bed. 'We can talk here.'

She glanced back at the door. 'We can't risk it. You don't remember what this place is like.'

His hand moved to her wrist and he held her forearm out to expose the track marks. 'This kind of indulgence can make you paranoid, ringlets.'

'I'm not on anything,' she declared, impatience lacing her tone.

But as she tried to free her forearm, he tightened his grip. He studied her gaze for a moment, his survival instincts sparking for him to stay wary.

'Eden, *please*.'

His own patience wearing quickly, he moved off the bed and took her to the door with him, because one thing he *knew* was that this wasn't his style. Loyalty meant something. For there to be any truth in her words, she had to be something special. A mistake one night when he was too drunk or too high to have his senses, he could believe. But an affair was not his thing. An affair that risked his life was most definitely not his thing.

He jammed a chair under the handle. He turned ninety degrees and headed to the bathroom, taking her with him.

Closing the door behind them, the extractor fan buzzing above them, he switched the shower on too before pressing his palms either side of her shoulders – barricading her in against the door – and fixing his gaze on hers.

'Okay, ringlets,' he whispered. 'No one's going to hear you now. So talk.'

# Chapter Thirty-Three

The biceps in Eden's bare arms flexed as he held himself temptingly close, his honed chest inches from hers, his lips even closer as he'd kept his voice to a conspiratorial whisper.

He wanted answers, but Jessie still couldn't afford to give them to him. Once she started, she wouldn't be able to stop. And this Eden was still unknown to her.

The last thing either of them needed was for this Eden to plough downstairs for a confrontation with Homer over the truth, especially with the fight having exposed just how impulsive this Eden could be.

In that very space, he'd not long finished having sex with two other women. It had been less than an hour since he'd comforted Mya instead of her. On top of that, his eyes remained laced with distrust.

'We need to talk properly. Away from here.'

He narrowed his eyes with suspicion. 'Like where?'

'Out of this row.'

'Why?' he asked, his breath mingling with hers.

'You have to trust me when I say I can't tell you, but it will become clear when I do.'

But she knew that look in his eyes – the look that told her he wasn't going to budge.

If she could have knocked him out cold and carried him out of the building unawares, it was exactly what she would have done to save time. The latter was certainly not an option – thunking his unconscious six-foot-one, solid frame down the stairs unnoticed was impossible, even for her. What she needed to do was get him somewhere so she could at least secure him whilst giving him time to process everything she had to tell him.

Until then she had to rely on tempting him to trust her – not an easy feat for Eden Reece when faced with a complete stranger who already had something over on him. Something that already put him at risk.

'So you want to go *where* exactly?'

'Just a few alleys from here.'

As his eyes flashed with more wariness, she knew she had to persist.

'I know you can't remember,' she said, 'but you *can* trust me. I promise.'

'The girl who's fucking me behind her boyfriend's back?'

The harshness of his words lacerated as deep as they had the first time. 'It's more than that.'

It had *always* been more than that. And he had to sense something. He *had* to.

'It's never more than that,' he declared.

And she knew he believed it. She knew that it had once been the case.

'It is with me. I know you have no reason to trust me. But you can, Eden. I'm the only one around here that you *can* trust.'

His fleeting smile cut with its insincere edge. 'I don't need my memory to know I don't fuck around behind my mates' backs – no matter how beautiful their girl might be. I might have made a one-off mistake, but an *affair*?'

The confirmation that he was still attracted to her gave her that extra push of confidence. The urge to tell him Homer wasn't his mate was overwhelming, but she couldn't have the barrage of questioning that would follow. She couldn't let suspicion cross his eyes when he saw Homer again. Homer was far too attuned to miss it.

'If you come with me, I'll explain.'

'How about I call your bluff instead? How about I get Homer back up here and we'll see if he thinks there could be any truth in this?'

'Tell me why I'd risk lying about this for that very reason. I'm trying to save your arse. I'm trying to save *both* our arses.'

'Save our arses from what? Does Pummel know?'

She nearly said yes, hoping to create that greater sense of urgency in him. But again, she couldn't predict what he would do. 'No.'

'Are you only telling me that so I won't go and confront him?'

'No.'

'So what's the issue?'

'Give me half an hour of your time away from here. That's all I'm asking.'

'You know what you're suggesting?'

'I know exactly what I'm suggesting.'

'And you don't think that Mya and Homer might find it a little suspicious if we *both* disappear?'

'We've done it enough times before,' she declared, knowing she needed to keep her claim of their affair forefront in his mind. 'We haven't exactly been doing it right in front of them.'

'Where have we been going?'

'Never too far.'

His pensive eyes narrowed. As unpredictable as he was right then, she knew how his mind worked. All she needed was to give him that extra little shove. Time was too short for her not to.

'You think it was a one-off?' she asked. 'Let me *show* you how well I know you.'

❈ ❈ ❈

He knew he should have stopped her unfastening his jeans. He knew he should have grabbed Jessie's hand the second her fingers wrapped around him, but he *wanted* to call her bluff. He wanted to continue calling her bluff.

The buzz of her touch on his already throbbing erection was more intense than anything he'd felt with Mya that past day. The fact that Jessie kept her gaze on his added to it, creating a sense of intimacy he hadn't felt with the con. More noticeably, her deep brown eyes looked at him in an entirely different way.

Jolts of pleasure shot through him as she wrapped her hand partially around his girth, the pads of his fingers involuntarily clawing at the door either side of her head, his teeth clamped down on the matchstick between them. And as her thumb brushed his tip and then under his ridge, the tenderness with which she did it caused his breath to catch.

Within a few seconds of her working him, she had him on the brink of coming. Worse, the instant desire to kiss her troubled him even more.

Whatever there was between them, they were familiar lovers. She was far too attuned to what he liked – everything from the pressure, speed and technique that he loved. And as if wanting to add to that point, she withdrew her hand as if she knew exactly how close to the edge she had taken him.

'I know you better than you know yourself right now, Eden.'

He wetted his lower lip as he kept his hands barricaded either side of her, partially in frustration that she had chosen to stop. 'One decent partial handjob and what, I'm convinced? What's your next trick?'

He almost felt guilty for the uncertainty that crossed her eyes but the threat of what she might be playing at still weighed too heavily.

'I need you to listen to me—' she began.

'No,' he said, curtly cutting her off. 'I need you to listen to *me*. Whatever issues you've got with me, you can wait until my memory comes back. Do you understand me? You needed to make your point, maybe you needed to make sure I didn't do anything nasty to you – I get it. But this ends here. If there's more between us like you say, whatever it is can wait.'

But as he moved to pull away, she grabbed his forearm.

'We don't have time, Eden.'

He looked back at her, at the genuine alarm in her eyes.

'Things have happened. Things you need to know about. If you come with me, it will make sense. I promise.'

'And if I don't? Is the world going to fall apart in the next couple of days?'

It was a statement that left her lips parted.

'I didn't think so,' he said, pulling his arm free.

But as he reached for the door handle, she slammed her hand over it first, her gaze resolute as she stood steadfast between him and his exit.

Either she had guts or he'd given her credit for being smarter than she was.

He placed his palm flat beside her head again.

'Let me make myself clear, Jessie. I believe something has happened between us. I just don't trust you. I don't trust anyone right now. And I'm *not* going to trust you until my memory comes back. Until then, you need to practice a little patience because, based on the way I'm aching right now, I might end up doing something we're both going to regret if not.'

❄ ❄ ❄

That same look was back again: the one Jessie didn't recognise. She should have known better than to think he would drop his guard so quickly.

Her pulse escalated with nervous anticipation. Eden was still looking at her like she was a stranger, making her anxious that he would treat her like one – and how it would feel. Because she didn't know *this* Eden's rules. She didn't know *this* Eden's technique. And she certainly didn't know his boundaries if she called his bluff.

She wondered whether it would feel different; if it would feel like the first time all over again. Whether it would spoil what they had. Whether she would feel differently about him or, if his memory returned, he about her for allowing it to happen.

More to the point, if sex would trigger something in him – whether it could even bring his memory back.

That look certainly triggered something in her. Something more than just wanting the chance to save him. The deep-rooted need to wipe the thoughts of those other girls from his mind overwhelmed her. To reclaim him. To reclaim *her* Eden. To rid the poison from her mind of him being with them before it took hold; to remind herself that what they had was so much more. To convince herself that not even Torren could steal it from them.

She couldn't let him walk out of that door. She couldn't throw away what might be the only opportunity they were going to get.

But she couldn't afford to alienate him either.

When he reached for the handle again, she let him open the door. She leaned back against the sink as he wandered into the bedroom and over to the chest of drawers. His back to her, he placed a cigarette between his lips and gazed down at the bed.

The minutes scraped by to the point she was ready to try again but he broke away, disappearing out of sight.

She watched warily as he wandered back into view, an item of clothing she couldn't distinguish in his hand as he headed back over to the bed to remove the piece of rope from the headboard.

She braced her arms on the sink as he strolled back over to join her. Her eyes searched his as he assessed her for a moment, letting out a contemplative stream of smoke before tossing the remains of his cigarette in the toilet.

Assessed her in a way that she couldn't read.

She glanced down at his rope-holding hand before her eyes snapped back to his. Her pulse raced, and her stomach flipped as his gaze remained composed, steadfast, unflinching.

He handed her what she could then see was a T-shirt. 'Strip,' he instructed. 'And put this on.'

'Why?'

'You want me to trust you? You're the one who supposedly knows me, so prove it. Take your dress off.'

She slipped the black T-shirt over her head, letting it fall to mid-thigh before wriggling out of the strapless dress beneath.

He held out his hand to accept it off her.

'Only good thing about cheap dresses,' he said, locating the split at the back of it before tearing upwards in one easy move. 'Weak seams.'

He cast it out of the door before closing it behind him.

Her usually slow-beating third-species heart was hammering in her chest, her pulse racing as he unravelled the short section of rope.

'What's that for?' she asked.

'The most effective way to create quick and easy marks.'

Evidence for Homer – just like the dress.

Her heart pounded as his intention became clear and, with it, her first semblance of proof that her Eden still lay beneath. The Eden who wasn't like them. Who wasn't a con. Who had no intention of seeing Homer's threat through.

'Wrists in front of you,' he said.

As she held out her arms, he slid his hands from her elbows, down her forearms to her wrists as he guided them together, the brush of the rope almost purposefully taunting.

Her thoughts flashed back to the first time he had bound her, using his belt with the extra notch to gently restrain her in order to protect himself. Heat gathered between her locked thighs at the recollection of what had followed: her first time being with a male for as far back as she could remember.

The same thrill rushed through her again – that not knowing, that unpredictability. Except unlike with his belt, he pulled this rope tight, purposefully letting it bite into the fragile skin of her wrists.

She flinched from the discomfort, but as their gazes met again, as she saw the matter-of-fact look in his eyes, the clench deep in her abdomen intensified.

'Ready?'

She frowned. 'For what?'

He ripped the rope away with lightning speed, Jessie gasping at the shock of it. She stared down at the scorch marks on her wrists before staring back at Eden. There wasn't even an inkling of remorse or apology in his eyes – as if he'd done nothing more than rip off a Band-Aid.

As she comforted each wrist in turn, the shock settled in, an edge of unease at the reminder that despite the glimmer she might've seen, it still wasn't her Eden she was dealing with.

He held her gaze for a moment longer.

But confirming the decision he'd made, he pulled away again.

Jessie let go of the sink behind her. 'Wait!'

# Chapter Thirty-Four

Hand poised on the handle, Eden knew he should have ignored her request. He should have left the bathroom regardless.

And as he turned to look at her again, he wished he had.

He was in deep shit. Deeper than even he had realised. Because, as she gazed back at him, his erection was already stirring again at the sight of her in the masculine black T-shirt, her nipples hard against the cotton, her slender, shapely thighs locked together. Worse were those eyes – they inexplicably burned right into his soul again.

'It would be a bad idea, Jessie.'

Because he knew that look. He'd seen it often enough. He knew what she wanted.

'He will check,' she said. 'It'll take more than rope marks and a torn dress.'

'So what – I leave you bruised in all the right places?'

'Homer knows what to expect of you. Anything less will raise questions neither of us need.'

He didn't know why he was hesitating. He didn't know why he hadn't made the excuse already for himself, because it sure had crossed his mind.

And at least he'd know. He knew sex with her would be more telling than anything else, memory or not. More telling than her words, the way she looked at him, even her clever foreplay tactic.

'You want me to fuck you, angel, I will. But only because I'm as willing to protect both our arses as you are. It doesn't mean anything. It doesn't mean I'm going to trust you.'

'But it means I trust you,' she said, her gaze not flinching.

Now it felt like it was her calling *his* bluff – a risky move based on how he was feeling right then.

Whatever game she was playing, whatever mind-fuck, it was working. He knew then that this was far more than screwing behind Homer's back. This was something *much* more dangerous.

Unfastening his jeans the rest of the way and dropping them to the floor with his shorts, he reached to the shelf behind her and tore open the foil packet with his teeth before one-handedly sliding the condom down his length.

Grabbing her behind, he lifted her with ease onto the edge of the sink. As her smooth thighs brushed his, his erection instantly jolted with the need to be inside her – a need more powerful than he had felt with Mya. Mya, who he'd barely been able to get a hard-on for compared to the straining ache he felt the second he made skin-on-skin contact with Jessie again.

Heat surged through his veins and his adrenaline pumped. He felt light-headed as he looked at the beautiful woman who stared back at him.

He already knew it was going to feel different to banging the red-head against the tiled wall in the shower or screwing Mya on the crumpled sheets on his bed.

But deep in his gut, he knew he couldn't afford to feel that way. Amidst the grief still lingering in his bloodstream, the acknowledgement that he'd already lost everything he cared about, he couldn't put his heart on the line again. If there *was* something between them, it was about time he came to his senses and pushed her away.

It wasn't easy entering her at first, something that sent his pulse racing. Her hot, wet tightness sent him to the edge, as did her ragged breaths echoing against his shoulder as he didn't allow her time to adjust.

Despite that, it felt effortless, her mutual arousal eventually aiding his entry.

As he fucked her to the hilt, a shiver of satisfaction washed over him whilst she gasped and shuddered against him, her nails digging into his back, her groans resounding deep into his neck.

And as he clutched the hair at the nape of her neck, tugged her head back slightly so he could look at her, the temptation to kiss her parted lips was compelling.

Dangerously compelling.

But he wouldn't let himself do it.

Grabbing her behind, he instead carried her to the wall beside the sink. Slamming her against it, he withdrew only to lower her to her feet and to turn her away from him.

Clutching her jaw with his right hand hard enough to leave finger marks, he grabbed her behind with his left hand hard enough to bruise as he thrust himself into her again.

❆ ❆ ❆

Sliding his hand from her jaw to her throat, Eden guided Jessie's head back against his shoulder.

Her pulse picked up another notch, his own heavy breathing inciting her further as she lost herself to the sensation of him entering her again and again.

As he yanked down the collar of her T-shirt and clamped his lips onto the tender flesh of her shoulder, as he sucked with a fervency she knew would leave one hell of a love bite on her flesh, she squeezed her eyes shut. She fisted her hands against the wall as he pressed his teeth in just enough to make her wince, his grip on her jaw again no doubt already leaving the impressions he had hoped it would create.

And as he slid his lips slightly further up her neck, just below her ear, a tingle shimmied down the full length of her spine, her body instantly responding to it – to the brush of stubble against the tender flesh of her neck as he consumed her with his mouth, lips and tongue.

She let out a steady exhale. Heat pooled deep in her abdomen as he sucked hard enough to hurt. Goosebumps broke out over her skin from head to toe as he released her behind to grip her breast hard enough to make her eyes water, the firmness of his thumb across her nipple taking no consideration of the sensitivity of her flesh at all.

It was nothing like their lovemaking had ever been. It was nothing like she'd ever felt from him before, even during their row on the stairs to the cellar. The first time he'd handled her up in his room, as he'd held her against the chest of drawers, he'd been so gentle, exploratory. But there was nothing cautious about his exploration this time as he squeezed and tweaked, digging his fingers deep into her flesh.

She nearly asked him to stop, it being the first time she had felt pain at his hands – actual pain as the coarseness of his fingers and thumbs with her tender nipples became unbearable, his mouth, his lips, his tongue, his teeth, his hands becoming a paradox of tenderness and ruthlessness. Any other time she would have pushed back and warned him to take it easy, but she was too lost in the moment. Too lost in him.

Instead it only intensified her need, her body's sensitivity under his expert manipulation gradually overwhelming any other thought, any other sensation. What at first felt uncomfortable, painful even, soon started to subside. His fingers releasing her jaw to dig deep into her inner thigh became a further taunt to her sex.

And as he slid his hand between her legs to grasp her sex, his blatancy, his overt sexual claiming of her swept her somewhere unfamiliar; somewhere she wanted to linger to test her own boundaries as the absorbing blend of pain mixed with pleasure incited an alien high.

A high that was so addictive she ached for him; almost pleaded with him to put her out of her misery and make her come. As his thumb brushed her clit, her knee jerked against the wall in response – a reaction that only seemed to incite him more. Sliding himself through his own parted fingers each time he entered her, she let out a sated groan as he indulged in his own pleasure maybe more than he was indulging in hers.

His clear mutual arousal sent a flood of adrenaline through her system, the rush of blood to her most sensitive areas creating the most intense sensation as he picked up his pace, each thrust harsher, more purposefully invasive.

❊ ❊ ❊

Whatever they had, it was electric once they got going, adding weight to her claims.

Taking a hold of her wrists, he pulled her arms behind her back, holding her forearms together as he fucked her harder and harder against the wall, losing himself to the sensation, to the sounds of her sated moans.

He tightened his grip, parted his thighs further to part hers with them, the compulsion to be as deep inside her as possible consuming his every thought as he increased his pace even further to the point he knew was veering on brutal.

Blocking out any care of anything beyond the room, he understood why he might have been risking everything for her.

He couldn't explain it. He sure couldn't justify it. But something about being with her made him feel more like himself.

The 'himself' he realised he was searching for.

As he felt her clench, as he felt her shudder, as he heard her muffled cries against the wall, he came hard and fast with a force that was painful.

And he didn't come quietly – but neither did she.

He all but growled through clenched teeth as he spilled, his fingers digging deep into her arms as he thrust again even as he came, wanting to hold on to that moment for as long as possible.

Even as his climax waned, she remained trembling enticingly as he kept her locked in position against the wall.

Reluctant to move, he kept his temple against hers, his free hand against the wall as he caught his breath. His other hand dropped to her thigh to brush it tenderly with his thumb.

And as she turned in the tiny space he had allowed her so she could look him in the eyes, he knew he shouldn't have let her do it, shouldn't have let her cup his jaw and lift her lips to his.

Because those lips were toxic – they transported him somewhere else for a few seconds with an affection that made his heart ache. That made him feel even more as though he had forgotten or lost something.

His tongue found hers easily in a kiss that had been as easy and natural and satisfying as sex with her had been.

But he couldn't cross that final barrier of full reciprocation, not with the intensity that was burning in his chest.

This girl meant something. He didn't need his memory to know that. And that just made everything a hell of a lot more fucking complicated.

They were on the brink of a war. The streets were too dangerous to enter. There was nowhere to go. There was nowhere to take her. And Homer. . . Homer would kill them both if he found out.

Regardless he nearly held her. He nearly held her as if it was the most natural thing for him to do.

Everything about her felt so right.

*Everything.*

And it nearly made him forget himself.

*Nearly.*

But instead he pulled away.

# Chapter Thirty-Five

When his thumb had tenderly brushed her skin, mindless on his part or not, Jessie's heart had skipped a beat at the small display of affection that reminded her so much of *her* Eden post-sex.

The familiarity of his touch made her instinctive physical responses impossible not to act on, made it impossible for her not to want to pull him closer – to kiss him. But as soon as she had, he'd instantly pulled away.

She wanted to tell him everything there and then, but his reaction proved the man she loved couldn't possibly feel love back when she was still a stranger to him.

It was as though she were learning about him all over again – learning how the old Eden used to deal with things as opposed to the new Eden who had gained a sense of purpose, not to mention awareness of how significant the threat was beyond.

Now he leaned back against the sink, both hands opting for the cold ceramic rather than her.

From one show of affection to a move that was blatantly about regaining distance, the warmth that had spread through Jessie instantly chilled. It was bad enough that he lowered his head to avoid looking at her. She never thought it would feel worse when their eyes finally met again.

The high was over, the excitement gone, the act completed.

It had never been like that with him: that complete sense of isolation afterwards. She swallowed a little harder than she wanted to as she clenched her hands.

'Is this how it's been?' he asked. 'Is this what I've been risking my life for? A quick fuck in a bathroom somewhere?'

The iciness of his words diminished everything that had been between them, tearing deep despite her knowing it wasn't her Eden speaking.

'I told you it was more than that,' she said. 'And I know you felt it. You may not remember, but you *must* have felt it.'

She stared into the depths of his dark eyes as if searching for her soulmate in there, willing him to come back to her; for it all to be over already. All she needed was his belief, his trust, and then she knew they would get out of there. Together.

'I swear I'm telling you the truth, Eden.'

He sighed heavily as he pulled away from the sink.

She knew it could be her only chance. That it could be *their* only chance.

'I'll even let you choose where we go and when,' she suggested.

His gaze lingered on hers for what felt like a lifetime.

'I'll think about it,' he said. 'For now, let's hope you're as good an actress as you've led me to believe.'

# Chapter Thirty-Six

The lounge area was quiet again, most of the hustle happening elsewhere in the row.

There were enough cons in close proximity for him to have to worry though. There were at least fifteen in the lounge from his swift count. Fifteen for Homer to give the signal to if he didn't like what he saw.

And, for him, that meant he would soon find out just how convincing she was.

The sense of having to put his trust in someone else for his own survival made him feel uncomfortable. He always looked after himself – himself and Billy. Billy who he didn't have anymore; Billy who he'd let down. After over twenty years of protecting him, he'd finally failed.

Eden's grip on Jessie's arm involuntarily tightened to the point he felt her gasp. But her genuine shock and discomfort would only add to the effect as he escorted her over to where Homer waited on the sofa.

Eden left her standing in front of Homer before taking his own seat opposite.

He knew how to play the game. He knew how indifferent he had to look. But he still didn't understand why he was playing the game at all. He didn't understand why he couldn't do what they all clearly thought he was capable of. Why they thought that torturing some girl was common practice to him. Because it wasn't. It never had been. It least it hadn't been as far back as he could remember.

And that was when his head started to ache again at the frustration of not knowing who he had been for the last decade. As he looked around the room, he still couldn't bring himself to believe he was a part of them. He had never been one of a pack. He had always, *always* been a loner. Except for Billy.

He reached for a bottle to pour himself a drink before reclining back in the sofa as Homer scrutinised the girl who had been placed in front of him, her torn dress in her hand as she stood there in Eden's T-shirt.

She kept her eyes downturned, her expression unreadable as if she'd been playing the game herself for decades. She even flinched as Homer touched her. And it was a genuine flinch laced with even more loathing than he had witnessed earlier. For someone who shared her bed with the con, Eden could almost believe there had been no intimacy between them at all.

Or there had been once. And now she had fallen for someone else.

*Him*, if her story was correct.

Yet she'd been right about the connection they'd experienced in the bathroom. He'd fought it, but he'd felt it. He just needed to work out what the fuck it was that she was risking her life for in trying to convince him to get out of there.

He watched as Homer pushed back her hair to examine her neck, the marks on her jaw. He saw her cringe as the con brushed her T-shirt up to examine her thighs.

He felt his grip on his glass tighten for reasons he couldn't explain, as if just watching the con touch her made him want to slam him halfway across the room.

Because if he'd *chosen* to have an affair with his best mate's girl, then he had chosen to sit back and watch her with another every night. He should have been used to it by now, so whatever it was between them, as little as he understood it right then, the intense burning inside him told him she was telling him the truth.

He waited for the result as Homer finished his examination. His pulse raced as adrenaline flooded his system in preparation for the fight. Because it would always be fight with him – never flight.

'Go and take a shower,' Homer instructed her. 'Clean yourself up. Get dressed.'

She didn't look back at Eden as she left the room. She didn't look back over her shoulder once. She simply left the room in silence, leaving him feeling as though she'd taken a little part of him with her.

'That was a one-off, Deep,' Homer remarked, reaching forward for his own glass to join him in his drink. 'You know that, don't you?'

'What I don't get is why you let me handle it at all. Anyone would think you cared more about Mya than you do your own girl.'

'That's not all it was about,' Homer said, his gaze lingering invasively to the point Eden wondered how the hell he could have wanted to associate with him at all, let alone be so-called mates.

Homer stood up. Glass in hand, he moved over to sit alongside Eden. 'How was she with you?' he asked, keeping his voice low so as to be unheard by the others in the room.

Eden's heart picked up its pace a little, though he was far too adept at concealing his feelings to give Homer even a glimmer of a hint. 'What do you mean?'

'It looked liked you went hard on her. Did she struggle much? Object much?'

'No more than you'd expect.'

He held the con's gaze without flinching as Homer gazed back, his eyes painfully scrutinizing as if he was trying to dig into the depths of Eden's soul.

If Homer suspected the affair, if he was waiting for a sign of panic in Eden's eyes at being confronted, he had another thing coming.

'But this is me, Homer. When do I never live up to my namesake? You need to be careful or she might start wanting me more than you.'

And Eden smiled. He dared to look into the con's eyes as he lifted his glass back to his mouth – and smiled.

Homer's eyes searched his for a few moments longer. Then he laughed off the back of a terse exhale before taking a mouthful of his own drink. He savoured it as he stared pensively at the table.

'Now are you going to tell me what that was *really* about?' Eden asked, still needing those answers. Still wanting to look into Homer's eyes as he asked the questions. Because despite Homer's sudden ease, there was still something simmering beneath the surface – he could feel it.

Homer knocked back another mouthful of his drink. 'I think we've got an issue.'

'What kind of issue?'

'Disloyalty.'

As the con's calculating eyes met his, Eden reminded himself of all the positions of the other cons in the room; where the exit was. Homer would be the first to go down, the reason he'd picked up the glass – as a defensive measure – in the first place.

'From who?' Eden asked.

'From Jessie.'

Eden's heart skipped a beat.

'She's been seeing someone behind my back, Deep.'

Eden reminded himself to stay calm. He stared at Homer in silence as he waited for him to elaborate.

'She's betrayed us, Deep. And by doing so, she's put us all at risk.'

'Betrayed us how?'

'She's trying to out. She's trying to defect to another row.'

Tension coiled in the pit of his stomach. 'What the fuck are you talking about, Homer?'

'Creating disloyalty amongst our own is our enemy's greatest advantage, Deep. She's been targeted by another row. Someone comes in here and makes eyes at Jessie and offers her better elsewhere. Us losing members of this row makes us look weak; makes it look like I can't hold my shit together. And one fracture of loyalty, especially from those closest to me, and this place gets hit. We get taken over, just like we did with Cyclops and this place. Jessie's seeing someone from another row.'

Eden knocked back another mouthful to ease his dry throat. 'And you've got these suspicions because?'

'Because you saw her, Deep.' His eyes locked on his again. 'She doesn't know you did, but you saw it with your own eyes. You told me you saw her with someone from Milton's row.'

'Milton's?'

'Next biggest row to ours. It was always Pummel's at the top, then we took over Cyclops's. Now it sounds like Milton's coming for us – and she's helping them.'

'So you sent her to *me* for punishment? This was nothing to do with Mya?'

'I sent her to you because you're vulnerable, mate. Because this memory loss has made you vulnerable. She's going to see an opportunity. That's the only reason I told her about your memory.'

'You used me as *bait*?'

'I couldn't let on to you. I sent her in to see if she'd say anything to you.'

'Did Mya know about this?'

'Do you think she would have left you alone with her if she didn't? That's one who *does* know where her loyalty lies.'

Homer rested his hand on Eden's shoulder as he leaned in a little closer.

'You'd be her prime target, Deep,' he said quietly. 'Taking you down – my wingman – would send out a clear message. They take you out and this row is finished, and they know it. I think she's coming for you, mate.'

Eden glanced back at the sofa – at the ghost of where she had been sitting only a short while before. A convincing actress, though not convincing enough to hide that she was repulsed by Homer – the con she was supposedly 'with'. The actress who had tried to convince him they were having an affair he couldn't remember and had wasted no time trying to get it on with him in the bathroom. Trying to convince him to leave. Trying to *seduce* him into leaving.

Trying to get him out there on the streets away from the protection of the row.

His hand tightened on his glass for a whole other reason.

She was trying to convince him that it was *him* who was being disloyal.

'I definitely saw her with someone?' Eden asked, dragging his attention back to Homer.

'No one gets near her without one of us knowing, Deep. Plenty have tried their luck. You were fucking furious.'

'Does she know I know?'

'You told me she didn't.'

But it was real. He'd felt it. That had not been their first time together. She'd been playing him even before his memory loss; convincing him to trust her. Maybe she'd even been guarding her infidelity to the row by distracting him with her infidelity with him.

'If you're so sure, why haven't you intervened already?' Eden asked.

'Because this isn't just some small-time runt trying to get in on what's mine – this is big-time warfare. And we need to be prepared. Sometimes you've got to give them enough rope to hang themselves. But I'm warning you to watch your back. We've got enough going down out there.'

'Exactly, so why the fuck are they pulling this now?'

'Because of what we've got, Deep. Because *we've* got a plan.'

# Chapter Thirty-Seven

Eden surveyed what could only be described as a workroom, the tables laid out like some kind of packing factory. There were at least forty cons at work in the small space, their tabletops littered with equipment.

As Homer led him through the rows, Eden glanced over the piles of disposable cameras, copper wire, iron rods and soldering tools. The biggest giveaway was the rubber gloves they were using to safeguard against electric shocks.

Because Eden knew exactly what they were creating. He'd made enough of his own. He'd made his first when he was only a kid – using a disposable camera just like one of those, the double-pronged capacitor that triggered the flash the final component he'd needed.

Eden Reece knew an EMP emitter when he saw one. Just as he knew anyone could make one with a few basic tools like they had there. And those tools would have been easy to find in a residential area like the south if you had enough time to scavenge.

'Turns out our row burning down and us ending up here worked perfectly in our favour. And it's all thanks to you,' Homer said.

His gaze lingered for a second longer than Eden found comfortable until the con broke away again and continued on his journey through the tables.

'Cyclops has had his crew on this project for months,' Homer added.

'What project?'

'To disable the chips in our brains.'

As Homer continued on his way, Eden stopped abruptly. He stared around at the mechanisms already piling up.

'Are you fucking kidding me? And risking them going off?' he called after Homer. 'Blowing your own fucking head off without the authorities needing to press that button for you? Do you not think if a simple EMP could do that, they'd have thought of it and accounted for it? This lot would disable your phone, maybe a few machines. . .'

'You know that. I know that.' Homer stopped and turned to face him. 'Cyclops learned it too after losing a few heads in the process from what I hear,' he said with a smirk. 'But that doesn't stop us using it to our advantage now.'

'For what?'

'For the soldier boys, mate. For all those fuckers hiding behind uniforms and weapons. What can I say? I'm old school. If they want to come into our territory, they're going to fight like men – one on one.'

'You're going to disable their equipment?'

'Unfortunately we don't have anything big enough to take them down in one go, but one advantage we do have is that their guard isn't up as much around humans as it is the third species. That means we can get closer than they can.'

'You want to pick them off one by one.'

'An ambush,' Homer declared with a broader smirk. 'We're going to cut them off before they get here. Judgement day is coming one way or another. We either die like the insignificant cockroaches they think we are, or we take as many down as we can in the process. All of us versus all of them. All those soldiers, all those *CEO*s,' he said, lingering on the last one, 'just like the one that killed your brother. We're going to see them all burn. And amidst the chaos, we're going after Malloy, Tao and every other rancid third species in our territory.'

'You kick off like that and the authorities will end up nuking this place.'

'Not if they want Malloy,' Homer said with a grin. 'And if not, it sounds to me like one hell of a fun way to go out.'

# Chapter Thirty-Eight

Caitlin's legs weakened at the graveness in Kane's eyes as he stared into the distance, his elbows on the table, his interlaced fingers tight to his mouth.

'Kane?' she asked as she stepped over to join him.

His navy eyes met hers and her heart skipped a beat.

'I got the message you wanted to talk to me,' she said. 'Please tell me it's not more bad news.'

'There's a way we might be able to find out where Jessie and Eden are – maybe even get them – without having to go to war with the angels just yet. I emphasise "just yet".'

She reached out to slide her hand over his as he placed them on the table. 'But that's *good* news.'

He reciprocated, interlacing their fingers as he gripped her a little too tightly.

'Except there's another but,' she said, able to read him too well now.

'I can summon Torren to a secure location. We can keep him there without any of the rest of the Parliament knowing where he's gone.'

'What do you mean by "summon"?'

'One minute he's wherever he is and the next minute he's behind bars.'

'A spell.'

He nodded.

'I'm guessing he's not going to be happy about that,' she said.

'I'm going to try and get him to talk voluntarily. I'm going to try and persuade him to give them up.'

'And if not, I can shadow read him. Kane, this is perfect.'

'Caitlin, you have to remember you're not as strong as you were when we first met. That protection around your soul has already weakened because of your intimacy with me, as you well know. You're not exactly celibate anymore.'

'But I can still read. We know that from what I managed to do with Jessie.'

'Which she was *willing* for you to do. This is Torren, Caitlin. He's not your regular angel. And he's going to be just a little bit fucked off to say the least about you forcing your way in there – especially with all the angel secrets he holds.'

'And amongst those secrets could also be how to help Eden and Honey. Kane, I've got to do this. I'm still strong enough. I know I am.'

'With a soul more exposed than ever before.'

Caitlin searched his lingering gaze. 'I'll know if something's wrong,' she assured him. 'I'll pull back if it happens.' She squeezed his hand. 'They're our friends, Kane. And they're essential to us pulling this off.'

'We don't even know if they're still alive.'

'We *have* to do this.'

After a painful few moments of silence, he met her gaze again.

'I told you what Shiver said to me about you not making it to the end of this,' he said. 'What if I hadn't actually saved you from it back in that tunnel. . .'

Her heart pounded a little harder as his trepidation made sense.

'None of us know what's waiting for us,' she reminded him, clutching his hand tighter. 'What is it you once told me: that being brave isn't about not being afraid, that it's about facing what we're scared of? We're all scared, Kane. That's why we *have* to keep going.'

'We also have to accept that by summoning Torren, I'd be crossing a line that not even I've ever crossed. I'm a master vampire. By doing this, I *will* be declaring war on the angels on behalf of my kind. I will be declaring war between the entirety of my species and theirs. There will be no going back from this. We will be instigating this at the worst time possible.'

'Or maybe this is the only time we'll ever have. The only chance we'll ever have. We're a team. We're all in it together. And we *never* leave anyone behind. I can do this. I promise.'

He dropped his gaze again.

'Kane?' She reached out to cup the side of his face. 'What else are you not telling me?'

'The summons involves something very specific. Something that's in place to be a preventative measure to ensure no one's ever tempted to go ahead with it.'

'Go on.'

'To summon an angel, you have to sacrifice the heart of one you love.'

He reached down to the seat of the chair beside him and placed the wooden box on the table.

A wooden box she instantly recognised.

'Oh, *shit*,' she muttered under her breath.

She instantly squeezed his hand again.

'Arana's heart. But, Kane, you were going to bury that in your parents' grave when this is all over.'

'Then I guess I'll be burying her ashes with them instead.' He offered a glimmer of a smile but it never made it to his eyes. 'She'd be telling me to do it, Caitlin – not only because she would have liked Jessie and Eden, but because Arana sure as fuck would have wanted to stick it to the angels right now. She hated them more than I do.'

# Chapter Thirty-Nine

Eden was standing at the bedroom window with his back to her, staring out through the bars at the brick wall opposite.

The night breeze skimmed through his dark hair, wafting and dissipating the smoke from the cigarette he held by his side.

Homer had taken her aside in the kitchen, out of earshot from everyone.

'Well?' she'd asked Homer. 'What happened? Did it work or what?'

'He brought her back in one piece.'

'Yeah, but did it *work*?'

'She came back with some convincing marks.'

'I still don't get it. I thought you wanted them sneaking around so you could catch them at it. Why are you dragging this out?'

'You're a part of this because you made the deal with Torren,' Homer had reminded her far too curtly for her liking, his eyes flashing darkly. 'And because you're the only woman around here I can trust to carry this out properly. That doesn't mean you can question me.'

As per usual, she was nothing more than convenient. For the plan to work, Homer needed to keep the network around Eden small. The few who had made it out of the row had already dispersed across several rows. Those in the inner circle who had known who Eden really was were dead – which basically left her.

Based on that, she knew Homer needed her more than he liked to admit – something she could challenge him about if she chose to. But at most, Homer would drag this out no more than a couple of days. She had to think of her situation beyond that.

Besides, Eden Reece was proving to be more enjoyable than she'd anticipated. As insulting and irritating as it was that he wasn't into her, that he never had been, it only made it even more worthwhile, even more fun, knowing how she'd make him suffer for it eventually.

'But if you must know, I told him she's trying to defect.'

'*What*? Why?'

'We're getting him onside remember? The more Reece believes we trust him, the more he trusts us and the less he trusts her. That way she has to work harder for him – and the harder she works, the more likely she is to fuck up. She's tying her own noose.'

'You're going to get *him* to drop her in it, you sick bastard,' she'd declared with delight. 'And drop himself in it in the process.'

Homer had puffed out a few smoke circles from his cigar in a way that had reminded her of Pummel. There was security in that familiarity – reassurance.

'No man likes to be played, Mya. You know that better than anyone. Nice guy or not. Con or not. That boy's got pride if nothing else. He's not going to like thinking some bitch thinks he's thick enough for her to get one over on him, not when he's feeling as vulnerable as he is right now. And that's where you come into your own. You just make sure you're his rock. He's going to need it.'

'Why?'

'Because it's time for the next stage, Mya. And this one's going to be even more fun than the last.'

Mya closed the door behind her.

Eden didn't flinch beyond casting a glance over his shoulder in her direction. Lifting his cigarette back to his lips, he looked ahead again.

Her gaze lingered on his jeans-clad arse – as hard and toned and powerful as the rest of him. In discovering that, she'd also discovered an edge to him. The edge of someone who, underneath it all, belonged with them.

If he had been a real con, he would have been a formidable one. She'd watched him enough from the sidelines the entire time he'd been at Pummel's row to know that. A time when Tatum had had him in her clutches and no one else had been able to get close.

No one but Jessie.

But only because he'd wanted her to. Because Eden, as had become apparent, was the kind of man who always got what he wanted in the end.

And he could have had her too. He could have had her from that first second she'd wandered up on to the roof to talk to him. Honeytrap though she had been, if he'd shown her any interest, she'd have got the others to back away. But Eden hadn't. He'd turned her down. He'd *dared* to turn her down.

He wouldn't have looked at her twice now either if it hadn't been for the lies or the circumstances. He thought he was too good for her – or that she wasn't good enough for him. They all thought she wasn't good enough for them. Good old Mya: useful for a quick fuck and nothing more until something better came along.

Something like Jessie.

And now she'd make him suffer for it. For now, he was hers. That had been the deal. That was what she had told Torren she'd wanted before he'd made the deal with Homer. That was her payment. Doing whatever she wanted with Eden in the interim was her payment, her reward.

Closing the gap between them, Mya skimmed her hand across his behind before leaning back against the wall to his right to face him.

Again, he hadn't flinched even when she'd touched him. Instead he remained with his right arm braced on the window frame, his biceps and forearm flexed as if he were intentionally teasing her.

She reached to take the cigarette from his left hand, taking a drag before handing it back to him.

As he met her gaze, she felt the rare sensation of her stomach flipping in response. He was looking at her differently now – less lost. And whatever place he had found himself instead, he had that darker shade to his eyes that she'd seen creep over everyone eventually in that place. Her pulse raced a little with the excitement of it – of what she was seeing being moulded in front of her eyes.

Either Homer had successfully weaved that sense of betrayal into him, or something really had happened between him and Jessie. Something that had nudged him a little closer to the side of him his soul was reluctant to embrace.

But that soul was hers now. And Eden Reece was already on the precipice of his own tipping point. He simply needed everything good in his life peeled away.

'You look tense, baby.'

He didn't answer, his gaze remaining fixed pensively ahead.

'Homer told me he's let you in on it. That he's told you about Jessie.'

His dark eyes met hers.

'He was worried about telling you too much too soon with your head being all screwed up. He only used you as bait because he had no choice. He's only doing it to protect what's ours. To protect you.'

'Do you also know about Homer's scheme to take on the Global Council's army? To go after Malloy and Tao?'

'He's not going to sit back and do nothing. And neither would you.' She slipped between him and the window. 'Just think,' she said, as she closed the gap between them, 'with this plan Homer's got, you can get every last one of those bastards back for what they did to your Billy. You can be the Deep we know: the Deep that takes no shit from anyone.'

She ran her hand up his chest, up under his T-shirt, to explore every hard curve of his perfectly honed abs.

'Talking of which,' she added. 'Did she say anything to you?'

'Who?'

'Jessie.'

He took another inhale of smoke before offering it back to her. 'Like what?'

She let the absorbing cloud of smoke penetrate her system as she tried to remain focused on her task. 'Like trying to get you out of this row.'

'I wasn't in the mood for talking.'

She slid her other hand down between his legs to massage him. 'So tell me about it. You know how I love all the sordid little details.'

Homer had asked her to check. He'd asked her to see if she could get him to talk.

'You couldn't have left her too roughed up. She's up with Homer right now.'

She searched his eyes, looking for a glimmer of a reaction – a hint of resentment or jealously or concern even.

But there was nothing.

Not even a stirring beneath her palm.

'He sure didn't need to ask her twice either,' Mya added. 'Must have been all that foreplay you gave her. Did she pull the sweet and innocent card? She's good at that one.'

Frustratingly, still no reaction.

He exhaled another steady stream of smoke instead as he gently caught her jaw with his left hand, tilting it upwards so he could look into her eyes. 'Can I trust you, Mya?'

'You know you can trust me, baby,' she said, as she stared squarely back into his eyes. 'You'll always be able to trust your honey. That's what that tattoo is, Deep. You had that done *because* of our trust.'

'Then why do you call me Deep even when we're alone? Why don't you ever call me by my real name?'

She impressed even herself with her unplanned response. 'Because you hate it, Deep. You told me to never call you it. You told me you'd stopped being Eden the day your brother died.'

She glanced towards the door.

She wouldn't have long before Homer arrived, but irritatingly she could only bring on a semi again.

'How about you cover my back instead?'

She snapped her gaze back to his. 'For what?'

'For when I go and talk to Jessie.'

It wasn't the direction she'd been expecting him to take. 'What do you want to talk to her for?'

'Homer wants to know if she's double-crossing us. *I* want to know if she's double-crossing us.'

His eyes glinted more darkly than she had seen up to that point as he held the cigarette to her lips, inviting her to take another inhale.

And she did so, her gaze not leaving his the entire time as his lips curled into the subtlest yet sexiest smile she had ever seen.

Her stomach leapt at the possibility that Homer's plan was already working: that Eden wasn't only already doubting Jessie, but he was ready to act upon her playing him. She knew she shouldn't have been surprised having seen his short temper in the lounge, but Homer wouldn't want him to move too quickly. They had at least another day or so left to play with before all hell broke loose with the army getting there.

Most of all, they couldn't risk Eden killing Jessie. They were still going to need her blood. And Homer still wanted to leave her languishing in her own grief after he gutted Eden in front of her. Torren had given specific instructions that she was not to die. Torren had given *her* specific instructions that Jessie was not to die.

'We need to run this past Homer,' she said.

He'd be there any minute. She needed to stall longer.

'Why? I'm his second-in-command, right? Homer wants answers – I'll get him answers. You know he'll thank me for it later. This is my row as well as his. It's my job to protect it, right?' His grip tightened on her jaw. 'If that bitch is trying to play me just as Homer and you think she is then that makes this personal. Are you going to cover me or not?'

Despite the authenticity of the irritation behind his eyes, she warily searched his gaze knowing this could have been something cooked up between him and Jessie. Eden could already have been aware of what was going on, despite what Homer thought. They could have already been planning their escape, and *she* could be helping it happen.

There was a knock on the door. Her heart leapt with relief.

Homer opened it halfway. 'Deep, I've got a job for you.'

# Chapter Forty

The wooden steps they descended were poorly lit and narrow. Each tread creaked under Jessie's weight as well as that of the two cons who led her down there.

The dark and musty cellar smelt of damp and mould. The sight of the stained mattress under a spotlight in the centre of the room had her heart pounding, light-headedness taking over as blood rushed to her heavy-laden legs.

She looked from one con to the other. Neither made eye contact with her.

Their silence confirmed they were under instruction – something she'd assumed from the way Homer had grinned at her from across the lounge as he'd sent the two goons over to collect her.

She looked back at the mattress, over to the blacked-out windows behind it.

This was test number three. This was the next part of Homer's plan. First was to leave her alone with Eden in full view. Then was leaving her alone with him in his room. Now there was this. Whatever *this* was.

The mattress made her skin crawl and chilled her to her core. Possibilities raced through her head amidst hundreds of memories of things she had witnessed and heard of in her fifty years under Pummel's rule. Sickening, depraved, brutal, cruel things that came under the banner of either punishment or entertainment. In this instance, in her case, Homer had cause for both. And the mattress, no doubt, was the core prop.

She screwed her hands into fists either side of her hips. The threats Homer had laid down while he had her strapped down in the attic played through her mind. Visions of being forced down onto the mattress, of lying helpless as con after con used and abused her – maybe even Eden witnessing it, or amongst them, if Homer wanted to use that to persuade her to comply.

The corners of the room faded into further darkness. She swayed enough on the spot that she stumbled. Both cons flinched and glanced to her, but she regained her footing; pleaded with herself not to pass out.

*This* was part A of the third test: being left there to wait. Being left to ponder the prospect of what was to come next. Being dared to run.

She looked ahead at the windows. The chill in the room told her they were made of single-glazed planes. And that sort of glass was easy to smash. For her, it was effortless.

Beyond the glass was Blackthorn. Beyond the glass were her friends. Beyond the glass was escape from the pain, humiliation, degradation and depravity about to be inflicted on her.

But within these walls was Eden. Within these walls was the man she loved. The man who had remained at Pummel's row to help her when he could so easily have walked away and left her. The man who would now suffer in her place if she ran. If she abandoned him.

Footsteps echoed down the stairs behind her.

Another con she didn't recognise led the way, followed by Mya and then Homer.

But as a fourth set of footsteps echoed behind them, the room swayed off-kilter again.

Eden descended with slow, purposeful, calculated steps.

So many times in the past, her heart would have leapt for joy. Just the sight of him would have been enough to know everything was going to be okay. Now the prospect of why he was present filled the pit of her core with the deepest sense of horror. Participant or willing bystander – she didn't know which would be worse.

Ultimately he was no doubt there to be a reminder to Jessie to take what was coming.

Or this was it. This was the place where Homer was going to slaughter him in front of her. This was the moment. This was why Homer had the others cons there too – as reinforcements.

Thoughts of Pummel murdering Toby hit her in a nightmare-like stream. How quickly it had happened – the blade slicing through his throat. Her friend – the only person she had in the world – bleeding to death in front of her.

Homer wasn't going to make it that quick or that simple.

She'd once heard him boast of killing one enemy whilst the latter was mid-sexual act, too distracted to notice the knife coming at him from behind. That would be the ultimate for Homer: slaughtering Eden whilst Eden betrayed her – the memory of which would only be the start of the suffering Homer had planned.

She wanted to yell at Eden that he was about to die. She wanted to throw Homer into action so Eden would see for himself.

But Homer wasn't that stupid. Homer would laugh it off, probably accompanied with a pally pat of Eden's back as they mocked her attempt to escape.

A futile attempt that would be Eden's death sentence.

When Eden's eyes locked on hers, any hope she might have had left evaporated. Whatever glimmer of her Eden she'd seen back in his room was gone again. It was as if there had been no breakthrough at all. It was as if that moment of intimacy they'd shared was non-existent – wiped from his memory. Now he looked more than distant: he looked detached.

Eden had never, *ever* looked at her the way he did then. Even dismissal or indifference was easier to handle than the distrust, hatred even, that she saw as his eyes narrowed on hers, toying with the matchstick between his teeth: the substitute for the mint that reminded him of who he was.

Her heart stuttered as she wondered what the hell Homer had told him. What the hell had happened between Eden telling her in the bathroom that he would consider her proposition and now.

Jessie balanced on a knife-edge, the air squeezed out of her lungs as they strolled past her.

Homer walked over to the door on the left-hand side of the room, and it rattled on its metal track as he slid it back.

The cons grabbed an upper arm each and led her behind them into the room beyond. In the centre of the room knelt a gagged man, his fair hair ignited to almost a halo by the spotlight. His hands were bound behind his back, his ankles secured together.

He couldn't have been very old – early twenties maybe. He already looked as though he'd suffered one severe beating. From the vibrancy of the bruises on his face and the scar tissue, it had been a few days ago.

She didn't recognise him from Pummel's row. She couldn't see his arm to tell if he was a con.

'This here is Dominic,' Homer announced to Eden, who stepped up alongside him.

Out of the corner of her eye, Jessie saw Mya cast her a glance, the malicious glint in the con's eyes confirming this was the next stage in Homer's horrific plan.

'Or "Dom", as he's known. Dom and his sister have been running a store not far from here. They leased the business from Pummel. When he found out they were making profits on the side, he sent us to deal with it. You helped us handle it at the time. Since then, I've heard he's trying to defect.'

The guy's blue eyes flared.

'Thinking it's all coming to an end, people are starting to run amok,' Homer said, meeting Eden's gaze across his shoulder. 'We have to deal with this or many more will be defecting. We both know this is ultimately going to be about strength in numbers. We need to protect what's ours. That's why this is the kind of behaviour we can do without.'

Beads of perspiration trickled down Dom's temples.

Jessie closed her eyes to his trembles, to the ragged breaths behind his gag, and tried to block out the horror of what she knew was to come.

'This is about your leadership role, Deep. It's about those around here knowing you're my second-in-command. If something happens to me, they have to be able to take you seriously or someone else will step up to the mark.'

She opened her eyes to see Homer handing Eden the six-inch gutting knife.

Her legs nearly gave way beneath her.

*This* was part B: to see whether she would stand there and let Eden slaughter an innocent man. Whether she would allow an innocent man to die in place of Eden.

As Homer glanced over his shoulder to meet her gaze, she shook her head in the shadows as she silently and futilely pleaded with the con.

To add to her sense of hopelessness, he sent her a wink before he resumed his attention on Eden.

And she knew she had only one option if she wasn't to cause Eden's execution there and then: to hand the gauntlet to Eden. To hope that his strength of character, ten years of memory gone or not, Homer's toxic influence or not, would win out – that *her* Eden was still in there.

That, underneath it all, he was still the man she loved, respected, admired. Who strived to make the right choices. The Eden who could get himself out of impossible situations time and time again.

Her heart plummeted as Eden accepted the knife.

She willed him with everything she had to see right through Homer, to reach out and slice clean through his throat instead. She would take the two cons either side of her down a second later. Eden would have no problem with the third. And then *she* would handle Mya.

'Get rid of the audience,' Eden said, his voice low.

She didn't know if he specifically meant her.

'I want to see this, Eden,' Homer replied.

Eden looked across his shoulder at him with a look that terrified even her, given the darkness in his eyes. 'You'll see the evidence soon enough.'

Silence descended on the room.

She knew when Eden wasn't open to debate. Seemingly Homer did now too.

It was the first time she'd seen the pecking order change since she'd got there. This was an order from Eden – and, to her surprise, Homer agreed.

The cons grabbed her upper arms. As they led her back through the sliding door, she wanted to strike out and make her plea to Eden. But she knew it was out of her hands.

This time Eden had to redeem himself.

The door was slid shut with a clunk, leaving him to face his own demons beyond it.

# Chapter Forty-One

Loosely holding the blade handle across his thigh, Eden crouched to one knee a couple of feet away from Dom. Homer had briefed Eden on the situation before he'd got there. The spiel when they'd arrived had been purely for Dom's benefit.

Homer's instruction had been simple: make an example of him. He was going to be hung outside the store as a message to anyone else who thought about double-crossing them at a crucial time when loyalty meant more than anything.

Homer had also told him that was the reason for Jessie's presence: a reminder to her of what happened to traitors.

That was the next phase: Homer wanted a confession from her. He wanted Eden to get that confession. Trick her into giving it, beat her into giving it – Homer had told him the game was open.

As far as Eden was concerned, the jury was still out. Homer had put forward a convincing case, as had Mya, but he was going to look her in the eye when he asked her directly. He'd planned to do exactly that before Homer had called him in on this.

One thing was for sure: this was going to make her think twice about lying to him.

He could have done Dom in quickly. He could already be out of there and back on task. But Dom was another insight into his past. Dom had answers he wanted too.

As Eden peeled down Dom's gag, his blue eyes flashed, his breaths still ragged. It was hardly surprising considering that the state of his face was apparently evidence of their previous encounter.

'You recognise me?' Eden asked.

Dom nodded.

'I came to visit you with Homer and Pummel?'

Dom nodded again, his eyes squinting a little in confusion at the line of questioning.

A part of him had hoped Dom would claim to the contrary. He didn't know why.

Dom looked anxiously to the door as he trembled before he looked back at Eden. 'Do you know they came back for her?' he said, the tremor in his voice matching that in his body. 'Homer came back for her. He finished what they came to do the first time.'

'Came back for who?'

'Jem. My sister. Did you know? Was that part of the plan? You smooth talk us, make us promises, win favour with Pummel and then let them come back for her? She trusted you. She believed what you said.'

The kid talked like he was making sense. Eden knew he couldn't reveal to the contrary. 'What did I say?'

'That you'd get them to leave her alone.'

'And why did I say that?'

Dom frowned amidst his confusion at Eden's continued line of questioning. 'I don't know. To gain kudos with being the new recruit?'

Eden's heart skipped a beat. He swiftly scanned the kid's days-old wounds. '*New?*'

'Just fucking end this quick, all right?' Dom pleaded. 'Don't drag it out like they did.'

A tear trickled down Dom's cheek. Eden's grip tightened on the blade.

'We hadn't met before?'

Dom shook his head.

'That didn't make me new.'

'Pummel called you his new friend. He said he was breaking you in.'

Eden's stomach coiled. 'Breaking me in? That's what he said?'

Dom nodded, his eyes wide with confusion.

The kid could have been lying, but it would make no sense.

'*I'm the only one around here that you can trust,*' Jessie's words echoed back to him.

'Tell me *exactly* what happened that night.'

'Why?' Dom looked anxiously to the door again. 'What does it matter now?'

'You want this ended quickly, you *tell* me.'

'Pummel, Homer, you, Chemist and Dice came to get the goods from us. They came to do what they wanted to do to Jem too, as warning. You intervened. You talked them out of it. You spoke to me and Jem on the quiet. You said if we gave you the goods and helped you out, there would be mutual benefits. Jem trusted you. You took the goods. You left.'

'I didn't touch her?'

'No.'

'Did *I* do this to you?'

'No.'

'Who did?'

'Pummel. You didn't touch us.'

Eden stood.

'*Please,*' Dom begged more fervently, looking up at him. 'I know I ain't getting out of here alive, but don't let Homer be the one to do this. I know what he'll do. Please just get it over quickly.'

Because Dom was right: he wasn't getting out of there. If he didn't kill him, Homer would. One way or another, this was Dom's resting place.

As more tears trickled down Dom's face, Eden turned away and stared at the door.

He shouldn't have been hesitating like he was. If everything he'd been led to believe about himself was true, this should have been easy. The numbers on his arm told him it should have been easy.

'You're not fucked up like him,' Dom said. 'I can tell that. You wouldn't have helped us like you did if you were. You're not like them. Jem said you weren't like them, and Jem knows people. She gets people. She always did.'

The knife loose by his side, Eden rubbed his hand across his mouth, his jaw.

'Just let me go with some dignity,' he pleaded, his tone strained and wretched.

Eden turned to face him again.

'I can't handle the pain.' Dom's blue eyes rested squarely on him. 'Let me go quick.'

It wasn't like him to tremble, but that's exactly what Eden's hand did as he tightened his grip.

He stepped around the back of Dom so he wouldn't see it coming.

And stared ahead at the door.

❊ ❊ ❊

Jessie flinched as the door slid open, the ominous rattle echoing around the cellar.

Eden strolled out, one slow and steady footstep after the other.

Heart pounding, she stared down at his knife-holding hand in the shadows.

He threw the knife onto the mattress, the spotlight igniting the blood-stained blade, the blood that now stained the mattress too as it landed in the middle.

As his dark eyes met Homer's, Eden didn't say a word. He barely even hesitated before walking past them all back to the stairs.

'Deep!' Homer called after him.

But Eden ignored him as he ascended the stairs in silence.

'Stick with him,' Homer ordered Mya and the con who had entered with them before hurrying over to the sliding door and bracing his arms on it.

Jessie held her breath. Breath that escaped her body sharply as Homer turned to face her.

He stepped back over to her and grabbed her arm before indicating for the other cons to leave them be, then he dragged her over to the sliding door and shoved her across the threshold.

Dom lay on his side in a pool of blood, his chest too much of a mess for her to be able to tell exactly what had happened.

His eyes were wide and glassy; his soul snatched from within.

His soul stolen by Eden.

Homer's grip on her upper arm tightened. 'You didn't think he'd do it, did you, Jessie? But this is your proof. See how easy it is to bring out someone's true nature? That's all I've done. He's no different to the rest of us. He's a part of this place as much as we are. Those CEOs are no better than cons – they just get to wear a uniform and receive a pay packet for doing what they're told to do. So tell me, has the knight in shining armour been tainted, or was he tainted all along? Because it looks to me like scum always rises to the surface eventually.'

But she didn't want to believe it. Even as she stared down at the brutalised body, she couldn't believe it. 'What lies did you tell him to make him do it?'

'Does it matter? The fact is he did. And it looks to me like he enjoyed it. Just like he's going to enjoy what I'm going to persuade him to do to you next. Unless, of course, you'd like to run now and leave him with me?'

# Chapter Forty-Two

Jessie sat at the kitchen table, unable to even be in the same room as them. She didn't know why Homer had allowed her to separate herself, and she didn't care to ask anymore.

One look into Eden's eyes had left her questioning her resolve once and for all. When she'd stared into the eyes of a stranger again down in the cellar, the sense of loss had been gut wrenching and overwhelming. A wealth of ten years' experience that had made him the man he was, the man she loved, was gone. And any semblance of soul left within was lost beneath the surface. Lost amidst lost hope. Hope she couldn't give back to him until she got him out of there. Until she reminded him who he was and all that they were fighting for. A prospect that felt more impossible than ever.

She laid her cards out for clock patience for the eighth time. Dealing the cards out in a circle to represent the twelve numbers on a clock face, with one in the middle, she layered them four times until all the cards were gone.

Starting in the middle, whatever number she turned over, she placed in the appropriate place on the clock face before taking a card from that pile and repeating the action.

In each of the previous seven rounds, she'd lost, all four kings appearing before she'd managed to turn the rest of the cards over and place them all in the correct position: four aces, four twos, four threes, four fours. . .

It almost seemed ironic that the four kings coming together signalled her losing the game when, out there, the bringing together of Kane, Caleb, Jask and Eden would secure their win – and *Sirius's* loss.

But her king, right then, was laughing and joking and smoking and drinking and partying with the enemy. With *his* enemies.

Hours were passing. Hours they didn't have. Hours they were wasting. The deepest sense of panic was already embedded in the pit of her stomach that the team would no longer be where they'd last left them. They could be anywhere in the tunnels by that point.

Kane was bound to be looking for them by now though. They were probably risking themselves out on the streets trying to find them, exactly as they had when Leila had gone missing.

She looked right towards the utility room. On the other side of the toilet cubicle was the back door. A door that was padlocked but that she knew, thanks to what Eden himself had taught her, she would be able to unpick.

As she'd already told herself through all previous seven rounds, she could leave right there, right then. She could be gone. She could be making it across Blackthorn alone.

She knew what her Eden would want her to do. Her Eden would be telling her to get away the first chance she had. He'd be telling her to leave him to handle himself.

But she couldn't.

Even if she could find Kane and the others, they'd never make it back before Homer found out she'd gone.

She couldn't leave without him. She couldn't subject him to the fate she knew would await him when they found out that she'd left.

She couldn't leave her Eden. She couldn't turn her back on him now. She would die there before that, a possibility increasing with every hour.

And Eden would *never* leave her.

They *would* find their way back to their friends. They *would* find a way through the barrier. They *would* find a way to save him and Honey from the angel tears in their system.

Jessie wiped away a stray tear as she reverted her focus to her game. She turned over a three and placed it where it needed to be before turning over a five in that pile and placing that where it needed to be.

She *would* find a way to get him out of there, even if she ripped the place apart in the process. She would have to give him an ultimatum.

Her attention snapped to the door.

Eden stood alone, toying with a matchstick between his teeth as he watched her.

Her stomach coiling, she dropped her gaze back down to her cards and continued with her game in silence as she awaited him to make his move.

She glanced warily at the empty doorway as he strolled past the table to the utility room. He closed the door behind himself. The minutes scraped agonizingly by. She heard the distant flush; the pipes clunk.

This time he left the utility door open alongside her.

She held her breath as he walked back past the table then flinched as the chair scraped out in front of her.

She looked up to see him sitting directly opposite, his gaze steady on hers as he reclined slightly, still chewing on the tip of the matchstick.

Her spine tingled at being alone with him again, and she held his gaze for a moment, but the distance in his eyes made it too difficult for her to sustain it.

He slid the packet of pills towards her.

Her stomach jolted, heat forming low in her abdomen as his little finger brushed her thumb in the process, the thrill of skin-on-skin contact again too intense for her not to look up.

'They're sedatives,' he declared. 'Easy to slip into drinks. I've unlocked the back door. Are you ready to go and have that talk?'

Heart pounding, she glanced warily back to the empty kitchen doorway before meeting his gaze again. Two hours before she would have leapt at the chance. Now, as she held his gaze, uneasiness spread over her.

'*Now?*'

'They'll be out of it for a couple of hours at least.'

Her heart should have been leaping for joy, but her nerves were as hard to suppress as her distrust.

She'd never been anxious at the prospect of being alone with him, even in the early days – especially as she'd always known that, physically at least, she could always win out in the end.

But Eden was no ordinary human anymore, even if he was oblivious to it.

Something didn't feel right. Something niggled. But if he was genuine, she knew it could be their only chance.

And the fact he'd drugged Homer and the others would make it harder for him to go back.

It could be the turning point they needed.

She glanced back down at the cards – at the three kings now sitting in the middle, the fourth remaining elusive.

Abandoning the game, she stood.

And nodded.

# Chapter Forty-Three

There was an unnerving quietness across the south of Blackthorn once they'd left the row behind.

Eden strode alongside her, his lack of conversation exacerbating the silence. He knew better than to talk – they both did. Making it anywhere in the south was challenging enough without drawing attention to themselves. The possibility of a fourth species or morphed lycan appearing on any corner added to it.

The mist didn't help. It reached into the south now too as if gradually taking over the entirety of the district.

Eden was at full vigilance, even though he didn't yet know he would hear things before others did, that he would smell things before others did, due to the angel tears within him exacerbating his senses.

Angel tears that were in his system because of her.

He had still to find out about the power that flowed through his veins – and hers. And for now it was safer to keep it that way.

It was hard not to reach out and take his hand. Hard not to feel his fingers interlace with hers. Hard not to have him grab hold of her and cradle her in his arms, or playfully throw her over his shoulder to spin her and bring her to ground; or give her a piggyback only to shamelessly use it as an excuse to squeeze her behind.

Because Eden hadn't only become her hope in Blackthorn's darkness, he'd become her light relief too. He'd reminded her how to smile and how to laugh. How to play.

But now he walked alongside her with a foot-wide gap between them, still toying with the match between his teeth, his focus kept on every nook and cranny as he avoided the alleys as much as possible, keeping to the main road.

He led her further away than she thought he would have risked for their initial conversation, but she wasn't going to question it. Instead her relief increased step by step as they headed in the direction of the hub and away from the south.

But it was relief that was eventually quashed as a rhythm of footsteps that had followed behind them for over five minutes continued to close in no matter how many twists and turns they took. Twists and turns that proved that Eden had also realised they were being followed.

To her disappointment, they weren't third species. It wasn't Kane or the lycans. If it had been, they never would have heard them coming. These were definitely humans in pursuit. And if they closed in on them, Jessie could be on the brink of showing Eden exactly what she was made of. Her cover would be blown, any iota of trust she might have gained potentially lost.

Moving in close enough for his hip to brush hers, Eden rested his hand on the back of her neck, the tiny hairs on Jessie's arms instantly standing on end with the intimacy of it. 'Do you know we're being followed?'

'Three at my last count,' she whispered back as she kept her gaze ahead.

He tightened his grip a little as he veered her left. 'Be smart and leave it to me.'

Looking down she saw the glint of metal in his left hand and her pulse picked up a notch.

There was nothing to stop him hightailing it and leaving her behind, deciding she wasn't worth the effort after all. Eden – *her* Eden – would never leave her behind. He would never leave anyone behind. But for this Eden, the jury was still well and truly out.

Taking a sharp left, he led her deep into the depths beyond the mouth of the alley, taking his chances in the darkness as opposed to the open street now.

The intermittent moonlight partially paved their way but did nothing to illuminate the multitude of recesses. Regardless, Eden led her through the foot-wide gap between two walls.

As it opened into another narrow alley – maybe no more than five foot wide – he opted to nestle them into a recess only three feet from where they had entered.

The small gap necessitated his body touching hers as he pressed her backwards against the wall. Swapping the blade to his right hand to have it ready for the only way the three humans could enter, he clamped his left over her mouth as he pressed the back of her head to the wall.

He stared deep into her eyes in the shadows as he lifted the flat of the blade to her throat. 'If you make a sound. . .' he whispered.

He didn't need to finish his sentence. The look in his eyes and the pressure of the cool blade were enough to convince her it wasn't an empty threat. It felt surreal that Eden – the one person incapable of hurting her – was on the end of it. If it was anyone else, any other circumstances, she would have ripped their arm from her throat. Even in that tiny space she would have overpowered them.

Instead she flattened her palms to the wall either side of her hips, his proximity a painful reminder of what his closeness did to her, her heart faltering at how clinical his eyes were; how focused.

As Eden switched his focus to potential sounds coming from around the corner, she realised that's why he'd led her there. In the narrow space beyond, their pursuers' clothes would brush against the walls and the sound of their breathing would be exacerbated by the tunnel effect, pre-warning Eden of their presence.

It was a calculated risk, a clever and strategic move, instinctive to having survived on the streets for so many years. Either that, or his Curfew Enforcement Officer training was too instilled despite his memory loss.

She felt him hold his breath as he heard, at the same time she did, the rustle of clothes scraping against stone.

He removed the blade from her throat to hold it poised and ready, his left hand still cupping her mouth to keep her quiet

Every inch of her tensed in preparation as whoever it was moved closer. If Eden lost control of the situation, if they even *tried* to hurt him, she would kill them *for* him – just as she had done the very first time they'd met.

But for now she'd play the helpless female. She'd keep her third-species identity concealed for as long as she could.

She listened as intently as he did to the rustle closing in, his hand still pressed over her mouth, his knife-holding hand raised.

When he finally moved, a cold chill instantly replaced his presence. In the distance, there was a grunt – and not from Eden.

A split second later, they both appeared right next to her. Eden's hand was clamped over the con's mouth to keep him silent as he ploughed the blade into his side once, then twice. On the third time, Eden twisted the knife, his teeth gritted and partially exposed, his eyes blackened by the shadows.

It was swift, it was brutal and it was effective.

The con slumped silently to the floor thanks to Eden's adept handling.

But the second con was right behind him.

Moving quickly, Eden tugged him backwards against him and locked his arm around his throat before twisting sharply, instantly breaking the con's neck.

Jessie didn't get to see the third one's demise as Eden stepped out of sight again. She heard only the pounding of flesh, the grunts and the groans, before the gurgling of a blood-filled throat.

*Her* Eden was hard; had always been hard. He'd had to *learn* to be hard. But this Eden was ruthless. This Eden didn't have a glint of remorse in his eyes as he stepped back into view. He didn't even exhibit the slightest tremor.

This Eden truly was a complete stranger to her – a fact that had never seemed truer as he stepped back into the gap.

Grabbing both her wrists, he pinned them to the wall above her head with one hand before holding the flat of the blade to her throat again. She gritted her teeth to refrain from knocking his hand away, from kneeing him in the groin.

'Look me in the eye and tell me they were nothing to do with you,' he demanded.

Startled by his suggestion, she refused to conceal her confusion. 'With *me*? Why would I want to lead them here when I was trying to get us away from them?'

'From who?'

'From the row. From Homer.'

His frown deepened, his eyes laced with suspicion. 'We both know they weren't from Homer's row.'

Her stomach flipped as he retained his grip. Being on the receiving end of it made her pulse race for all the wrong reasons. In that moment, he couldn't have looked more at home amongst the cons.

'What that's supposed to mean?'

'Because Homer's on my side, angel. You're here because I want to know what side *you're* on. As of now, it looks to me like you've been backing the wrong one.'

❃ ❃ ❃

Jessie's gaze didn't falter – she looked genuinely perplexed. 'Eden, I don't know what you're talking about.'

'You sure you want to risk this?' Homer had asked him.

He had.

'We need to know,' Eden had said to him.

He'd needed to know. After what Dom had told him, he'd needed to get the girl alone under his terms.

And now he knew.

Homer had been right: the second they'd left the row they'd been followed. They'd been watching the place just as Homer suspected. His leaving with Jessie had given Milton's crew the opportunity to strike.

'I'm not going to lose you, Deep,' Homer had said. 'You'd better know what you're doing.'

'If you know anything about me, you know I can handle myself out there.'

'Then stray far enough to tempt them to follow,' Homer had said. 'But you fucking make sure you can get back here.'

He stared deep into her dark eyes as she warily, though defiantly, held his. Because the slightest possibility remained that it was a coincidence – that the three cons had simply been chancers.

Too big a part of him wanted that to be true – the same part of him that had pinned her to the wall to question her further instead of dragging her straight back to the row to be dealt with by Homer.

'Who were they?' he asked quietly, his teeth gritted as he held his impatience in check.

'I don't know. *How* would I know?'

'Five minutes,' he said as his final warning. 'And don't be cryptic with me, girl. I'm not in the mood or the mindset. You've got five minutes to tell me why it was so important to do this out here rather than back at the row. And you've got half that time to convince me to give you the full five minutes or I swear I'll drag your arse back to Homer right now. Go.'

'You're not a con.'

His heart jolted at hearing the last thing he'd expected to come out of her mouth.

Her gaze was steady, her breathing a little terse.

'Say that again?'

'You're not a con, Eden. And Homer knows it.'

Her unflinching eyes somehow managed to retain their sincerity.

'So what the fuck are these?' he asked as he moved the blade from her throat to remind her of the numbers tattooed on his arm. 'A fashion statement?'

'You had them done a few days ago. You've been undercover.'

Of all the lies she could have come up with to save herself in that moment, the absurdity of it made it impossible for him to conceal his smile of disapproval.

'Undercover? You make me sound like a fucking cop.'

'You are. Kind of. You're a CEO, Eden. You *were* a CEO.'

'A Curfew Enforcement Officer?'

'Yes.'

He dropped the blade from her throat before he was tempted to do something just for the insult of her expecting him to believe that. 'That's what you needed to tell me?'

'It's the truth.'

He leaned back against the recess wall to calm his impatience, her body still only a few inches from his.

'That's what I needed to tell you. That's why I needed you away from there. I knew it was going to be hard for you to believe me. We were in Pummel's row just before it burned down. You came undercover to get me out. We're responsible for what happened to it. Homer knows that. If Homer knows I've told you, he'll kill you. You can't go back there.'

'So now you're telling me *we* burned down the row?'

'We were a part of it, yes.'

He exhaled harshly before he glanced right out into the moonlit alley.

He looked back at her. Back into her eyes.

A Curfew Enforcement Officer. A kid off the streets of Lowtown. No education, no prospects, no parentage. A kid with a temper. A kid with an attitude. An impulsive, reckless kid who cared about nothing but his and his brother's survival. And now she was telling him he'd got a job working for the Third Species Control Division – reserved only for those with Midtown and Summerton privileges. That he'd got himself a stable job with money and prospects. That he'd actually worked under someone rather than for himself.

He'd last all of five minutes before telling someone who thought they understood how life really was on the streets of Lowtown and Blackthorn to go fuck themselves.

She clearly didn't know him at all.

'We have to keep moving,' she added. 'And I'll tell you the rest.'

'A minute and a half is up,' he said, not sure how he was managing to hold back his temper. 'Doesn't look like you're going to make it to two.'

'If you go back there, he *will* kill you. He'll kill us both.'

'Thirty seconds to redeem yourself.'

'I'll tell you everything, I promise. Just come with me.'

He caught hold of her T-shirt at her chest and scrunched it in his hand as he pinned her back to the wall.

'If I'm not a con, I have no microchip in my skull.'

And that was the cruellest part of her lie: that he wasn't the scum he'd been led to believe he was. More than anything, that maybe he did have hope; that he could get out.

'So what the fuck happened to my memory, huh?'

Her gaze remained locked on his but, this time, she had no quick answer. This time she struggled with an explanation.

It was confirmation enough that she hadn't thought that far ahead. It was an insult too far. He had to get her out of that recess, out of that alley, and back to the row before he proved just how low he could sink right then.

He closed his blade and slipped it into his back pocket before catching her wrist and tugging her from the wall back into the alley.

Jessie pulled herself free a split second later. More to the point, she did so with impressive ease.

He turned to face her as she stood, hands clenched, in the recess. Her composure, her stance, her gaze all spoke of a woman far from intimidated at the prospect of what was about to happen.

No con tattoos. No extra incisors. No broader, slightly more extended canines.

But this was no ordinary woman.

He narrowed his eyes. 'What the fuck are you?'

'I'm trying to save you.'

'You need to be worrying about saving yourself right now.'

'That too. Which is why you're not taking me back there. Which is why I won't let *you* go back there.'

'Cut the bullshit and make this easier on yourself.'

'*Listen* to me, Eden. *Please.*'

He grabbed her forearm and pulled her to him, wrapping his arms around her as he carried her out of this recess this time.

She used the wall opposite to force herself backwards with more power than, again, he would have given someone of her size and frame credit for.

She was quick too. As soon as she'd slammed his back against the wall, she pressed the heel of her hand under his elbow. She pushed upwards whilst simultaneously tucking her head under his arm. Freeing herself with nimble ease, she spun on the spot to face him.

But she didn't run.

She would have had a split-second start for what it was worth, but she didn't move.

'I don't want to fight you, Eden.'

He exhaled tersely. He couldn't help but smile as she misinterpreted his self-restraint as meaning an equal match.

'Fucking do that again. . .' he warned.

But there wasn't so much as a flicker of anxiety in her eyes. Yet neither did a reciprocal threat leave her lips.

It was almost as if she was purposefully killing time.

Deal with the three cons he might have, but there would be more. There would always be more on the south side of Blackthorn, and he'd wasted enough time on her already.

He should have pulled the blade again. He should have made his point swiftly and effectively.

He felt his patience snap like an overstretched band.

Despite her knocking him back three times, the callousness of his brute strength eventually overpowered her reluctance to cause him any damage.

Crossing and locking her wrists at her chest, he wrapped his arms around her in a vice-like grip, preparing to slam her face first against the brick wall to utter a few home truths in her ear if she didn't stop struggling.

'I'm trying to take you to Billy,' she said breathily.

Eden felt the blood rush from every part of him and his grip involuntarily weakened enough for her to pull away again.

She stood with her back to the alley as she faced him again, the three dead cons her backdrop.

His heart pounded. Adrenaline pumped around every inch of his body.

'That's a fucking low blow.'

'*What?*'

Her eyes were startled enough, but then panic ignited in them as she looked behind him.

'That *is* a low blow,' Homer said. 'Using his dead brother is an *extremely* low blow – even for *you*, Jessie.'

# Chapter Forty-Four

As the breeze whipped down the alley, Jessie stared over Eden's shoulder at Homer and the two cons with him.

They'd told Eden Billy was dead.

She stared back at him as he glared at her, a mix of pain, confusion and fury in his eyes.

They'd ripped his brother from him. They'd used that as a way in.

She glowered back at Homer, ready to lay into him there and then.

But hearing the brush of clothing against stone behind her, she glanced behind her to see two more take the rear.

The impassable walls either side loomed over her, closing in as if they were curling inwards on themselves.

Less than twenty-four hours before, she and Eden would have taken the five cons down between them. With their combined speed, skills and strength, it wouldn't have been any competition. Together they'd taken down bigger. Together they'd taken down far worse. With nothing more than an exchange of glances between them, minutes later it would have been over.

But the exchange of understanding between her and Eden was lost. More significantly, his trust in her was lost again too – if she'd ever had it at all.

'You were supposed to wait back at the row,' Eden said to Homer with nothing but a small acknowledging glance over his shoulder.

Her stomach coiled in dismay at Eden's deceit. 'You set me up?'

'Enough,' Eden said firmly. 'I know. I know you've been using my memory loss against me. We know about your involvement with Milton.'

*Milton.*

It was a familiar name. A familiar con name.

'We know you're switching rows,' Eden added. 'We know you wanted me dead. I know they followed us out of that row.'

With fifty years spent amidst the cons, she knew exactly what Eden meant. As the pieces fell into place, her attention snapped back to Homer. Because Eden wasn't the only one capable of deceit.

The initial three cons were down to him. This was Homer's set-up too. Homer was setting them *both* up.

Jessie glanced back over her shoulder at the two cons who hadn't moved from ten feet behind her, awaiting their boss's instruction.

But Homer was seemingly in no hurry. He was too busy revelling in the look on her face.

'And it seems I was right,' Homer declared, addressing Eden, though his gaze barely left Jessie. 'Jessie here was playing a clever game with you, Deep. I did warn you.'

Knowing the latter part of what Homer said was as much a warning to her as it was to him, she looked back to Eden, who hadn't moved.

'But using your brother, Deep. . .' Homer added. His cold eyes locked back on her. 'This is going to carry a heavy price, Jessie. You know how we feel about loyalty around here.'

Jessie glared into Homer's eyes as a glimmer of triumph glinted within them. He truly was sadistic to the core. But the one predictable thing about sadists was they loved to prolong the agony.

Homer wasn't going to end it there, quickly in some dark back alley. Homer was going to take them both back to his row. He'd want a show. Eden would be his key to that. He was going to see to it that she suffered at Eden's hand first, just like he'd promised. And right then she wasn't entirely sure Eden wouldn't comply.

But one thing she did know was that Eden had worked the back-streets of Lowtown and Blackthorn like a pro, even ten years ago. He'd already demonstrated that his CEO training still lingered beneath the surface, memory or not.

And she knew Eden better than any of them did.

She dropped her gaze and lowered her shoulders to indicate her defeat before backing up just a few feet.

She came to a standstill. She lifted her glare to meet Homer squarely and defiantly in the eyes.

He frowned. A split second later she saw him realise that she was going to do the last thing he expected her to do: that she was going to put Eden on the line.

Having backed up close enough to the two cons behind her, Jessie pivoted. She kicked one and then the other clean in the noses, blinding them with their own blood and shock, giving her the advantage she needed to plough through them.

She nimbly leapt over the three bodies Eden had left in his wake, using her slender frame to her greatest advantage as she swept back through the narrow gap.

As soon as she reached the main street, she picked up her pace – but not too much. Everything hinged on Eden keeping her in sight. Everything hinged on Eden being able to eventually outrun the others. Eden, who didn't know his own strength yet or – more importantly – his own speed.

Her only guarantee was that none of the cons, however fit, however determined, would be a match for the angel tears in his system. None of them would be able to match his unremitting stamina. And most of all – the main thing she was counting on – none of them would feel the buzz of the chase as intensely as Eden did. None of them would feel the buzz as much as the CEO who would *never* let a target get away.

This was about a marathon and not a sprint. This was about getting Eden as far away from the row as possible. It was about losing the others one by one until only she and Eden remained.

*If* he'd make it out of the alley at all.

That had been her one calculated risk.

He had to. She *had* to believe he would. She had to believe her punt was right: that Homer killing him in that alley would scupper his master plan.

She looked over her shoulder.

Her heart leapt with relief, with elation, as Eden emerged unscathed. Clocking her instantly, he gave chase just as she'd hoped he would.

She kept to the main streets, staying away from alley openings so as not to be taken by surprise. They were bound to try and corner her off. Their pack strategy was too embedded for them not to.

But she'd learned all there was to know about strategy from the best and most effective pack there was. On top of that, she'd learned how to navigate an effective getaway from the very man who was now chasing her.

Adrenaline pumped as she managed her breathing as she'd been taught. Light-headedness was as much a danger as her muscles seizing up or her lung capacity weakening if she didn't control her breathing. Breathing, Eden had taught her, was key to everything.

She needed to stay focused and keep her attention as much on her peripheral vision as on what was directly in front of her. She had to watch for trip hazards and plan in advance whether to lose time skirting around them or leap over them. For every move she made, she had to be at least three thoughts ahead. Nothing could get in the way of her momentum. And she always, *always*, had to keep that spurt in reserve for the sprint when she needed it.

But the cons in pursuit were fast – as fast as Eden himself just now – because they loved the chase too. More to the point, they loved the hunt. They loved the capture.

But where their pursuit would have usually involved whooping and jeering as they wore her down, or veered her to be cornered, there was silence instead. This was not solely entertainment for them. They'd been instructed to catch their prey at all costs. This was the result of Homer's determination to catch his prey at all costs.

To her immense satisfaction though, ten minutes into the run, Homer was the first to fail.

For the second her advantageous distance would allow, she glanced over her shoulder to see him doubled over as he gasped for breath.

Good living coupled with the arrogance of thinking he was untouchable had led him to become too lax physically.

The other two were still in pursuit though – as was Eden. But the other two were leading the way – and she knew why. Eden knew how to play the game. He was using them to keep her pace up, to help tire her, as he held back to build his own reserves. Once the two front-runners had weakened her, he would start sprinting. He would be the one to bring her down.

Eden, as always, was strategic to the last, exactly as she'd hoped he would be.

They could sprint all they wanted though – she had yet to reach full pelt. All she had to do was match their pace and stay twenty feet ahead. When she wanted to weaken them, *then* she'd sprint.

She needed to form a plan in the interim though. She needed to find somewhere to go where she could have a stand-off with Eden without an audience.

Despite the looming threat beyond the south, as well as the fourth-species stories, there were still some people mingling on the streets and hanging around the alleyways. Some jeered as she ran past to encourage her pursuers. Some tried to block her way so they could watch her get caught. Others even joined in at one point until their stamina or, more likely, their interest, faltered in the face of an easier buzz.

All she could keep doing was running as the sun rose, as the night breeze ebbed into dawn, a muted grey light creeping across the streets ahead.

She looked back over her shoulder to see another of her pursuers had faltered, leaving only one con and Eden left.

If she'd been a regular human, she would have already been run into the ground. But she wasn't, and she *was* going to succeed.

❀ ❀ ❀

Eden felt a familiarity in the chase, as if he'd done it loads of times before. His blood and adrenaline pumping as he hightailed it behind her, the buzz was addictive to his core. He was good at it too, as if he could sense her when the others couldn't.

The girl's agility and speed betrayed what he'd already suspected was something third species. But as long as he kept her in his sights, he was satisfied for now. She was fast and she was quick, but so was he. Clearing objects was effortless, as was scaling walls.

Before they'd given chase, Homer had said she'd try and get back to Milton's row now that her plan had unravelled. Eden had no idea where Milton's row was, only that there was no way he was letting her go back there. An alien sense of possessiveness crept through his veins amidst his need to be the one to take her down.

And he would be.

As the other con finally conceded, Eden pulled on his reserves. This needed to end, and it needed to end quickly. After a thirty-minute sprint, even he was starting to feel it.

But he was not going to lose her.

He picked up his pace into a full-on pelt as the dead end ahead gave her no choice but to veer left.

She leapt over obstacles with grace and ease; used walls and objects for leverage to enhance her agility. But interestingly not once did she throw something in his path; not once did she try to trip him up. For someone who was adept at getting away and so clever at navigating away from four unremitting cons, she did nothing to derail his chase, despite the opportunities. As they ploughed deeper into the alley, she even seemed to be easing her pace.

She wasn't the type to give up though – that much was obvious. But refusing to be distracted or put off by second-guessing her, Eden ran for all he was worth.

She made her first fatal mistake – if that's what it was – as she glanced once more over her shoulder. She lost her footing a second later, something she may have recovered from if his response hadn't been quicker.

He took her down face first amidst the debris – the cardboard the only thing to soften the impact – and slammed her wrists either side of her head, pinning her legs with the strength in his lower body as she panted beneath him.

The sudden stop had caused him to catch his own breath; to realise just how long and hard they had been going.

Feeling no fight from her, thinking she had weakened enough, he loosened his hold just a little.

Only to have her slam her knuckles back hard into his nose.

He recoiled but refused to move.

Jessie took full advantage of his blurry eyes though and rammed her elbow into his stomach before thrusting him off her.

He rolled and tumbled with her, though he could barely see a thing. Flat on his back, her thighs locked either side of his hips, he felt her tuck her feet and ankles over his knees to stop him kneeing her in the back. With astounding strength, she pinned his wrists to the ground.

He blinked away his tears to finally meet her gaze.

She was panting, clearly struggling as much as he was to keep her momentum going, but she locked him down as if she was fighting for her very life.

'Bet you wish you hadn't taught me that,' she said breathily. 'Going for the nose.'

He blinked away the remains of the tears to enable his eyes to focus.

'Please don't make me knock you out cold, Eden.'

It was a threat too far. Five more seconds of recovery and he'd have her flat on *her* back. He'd have her pinned down so hard she wouldn't even—

Her attention snapped behind her and her breath caught. A second later, she slumped onto him.

Eden lay there in shock for a moment before easing her unconscious body off him to lay her on her back beside him. With her out of his eyeline, he stared at the helmeted figure clad head to foot in black leathers ahead, at the gun pointed in his direction.

The breeze in the alleyway whistled around him as he stared down the barrel – a barrel that was lowered a few moments later.

The CEO grappled with his helmet before clumsily tearing it off.

'Shit, Reece!' the blue-eyed stranger exclaimed. 'Of all the fucking chances! I was starting to think I'd never see that pretty-boy mug again!'

Eden's heart pounded as the stranger smiled broadly at him.

Not taking his eyes off the CEO, Eden reached to search for a pulse on Jessie's neck, surprising himself at his level of concern.

'It's just one of our sedatives, mate,' the CEO declared, closing the gap a little more. 'Looked like you needed some help.' He smirked as he tucked his gun back in its holster. 'Just over a week out of the unit and you're already losing your touch.'

The CEO looked down at Jessie with curious eyes.

Jessie, who recaptured Eden's attention for an entirely different reason.

*You're not a con, Eden. You're a CEO.*

'Nice find though,' the CEO added. 'Cute.' He stepped closer still. 'Maybe you haven't lost it. Just enjoying the scuffle a little too much, huh? Let's take a proper look.'

Eden stood to block his way, surprising himself again as his protective instincts kicked in. He kept his left hand behind his back where he removed the blade from his back pocket.

The CEO's blue eyes instantly narrowed in confusion. 'Whoa! Protective much?' He frowned. 'You okay, Reece?' He took another step closer.

Eden instantly made the blade visible at his side by way of warning.

'What the fuck?' the CEO said, further uncertainty crossing his expression. He glanced around warily as if he expected to see someone else. He met Eden's gaze again. 'There's no one else here.' He held the helmet up as though imparting shared understanding. 'You two are the only ones out on the street in a quarter-mile stretch around here. It's how I picked you up so easily on the tracker. I can't keep it switched off for long though. They've tweaked things. We go out of range for more than fifteen minutes and questions are asked. Not like the good old days.'

'Who are you?' Eden asked. 'How do you know my name?'

Confusion sparked in the CEO's eyes. 'It's me: Sean. What is this, Reece? What the fuck's happened? Why are you looking at me like you don't know me?'

'*How* do I know you?'

Sean stared at him bewildered. He looked to Jessie and back again. 'Mate,' he said, lowering his voice, 'I'm telling you she's out of it. I'm not blowing your cover here. She'll be out for at least twenty minutes. She can't hear us.'

'I asked you a question,' Eden reminded him.

'Maybe you should be asking yourself why I haven't popped you as well as her. You're quick, Reece, but you're not quick enough to dodge a bullet at close range. I should know – we've worked together long enough.'

Eden's heart skipped a beat as, again, Jessie's claim echoed back to him.

More to the point, the CEO *could* have shot him – easily.

'I think we'd better take this off the street,' Sean said, checking his watch. 'I'm ahead on the sweep but more will follow.'

And he cocked his head back the way he'd come.

# Chapter Forty-Five

It was basically a living room with a double bed against the right-hand wall. Directly ahead was an open-plan kitchenette. A door to what Eden discovered was the bathroom sat to the left. It was bare apart from the bed, a stray chair and the faded curtains over the boarded-up window.

Eden lay Jessie down on the bare mattress as Sean removed a pair of cuffs. He passed them to Eden to allow him to fasten one of her wrists to the metal headboard.

'Feels like old times,' Sean remarked with a grin. 'Sharing a bit of bounty now and again.'

Eden stood upright on the opposite side of the bed. 'You're saying I'm one of you?'

'Not just one of us – the best of us.'

'You said you saw me less than a week ago, so how do you explain this?' he asked as he held out the tattoos on his forearm.

'Last time I saw you, you said you were on some kind of under-cover mission.' Sean's frown deepened. 'You're really not bullshitting me about this memory loss, are you?'

'I've lost the last ten years.'

Sean's eyes flared then narrowed again. 'Ten *years*?'

'How long was I a CEO?'

'About that long. Fuck,' he hissed. 'How has this happened?'

'Just tell me who I am. Tell me what you know.'

'You're name's Eden Reece. Like I said, you've been a CEO for ten years. We've been partners for over five of those. We've got the best haul-in record the CEU has ever seen. Over a week ago you disap-peared. A few days later you showed up at my apartment telling me you needed access to the CEU – that you needed the updated code because you were on some kind of undercover mission that had gone wrong. You know we've always got each other's backs so I stupidly didn't ask too many questions.

'Next thing I knew, there was word that you'd broken into the de-tainment unit and had pulled out suspects linked to a spate of recent murders. You nearly dropped me right in the shit. But if there's one thing we both know how to do after all we've got up to together these past few years, it's how to feign innocence.'

Eden couldn't move as Sean and Jessie's stories coincided, their le-gitimacy reinforced by the authenticity in the CEO's eyes, by the fact that it was a scenario that made more sense, as unrealistic as it still felt, than him ending up in the row.

He looked across at Jessie, still lying unconscious.

'So who's she?' Eden asked, looking back at Sean.

'I don't know, mate,' he said with a shrug. 'All I know is that there's a call-out for you – and the girl you've got there too. I don't know who the fuck she is or why you're involved with her, but you're in serious shit. You're lucky you came across me.'

'A call-out for what?'

Sean checked his watch and lifted his helmet from the bed. 'I don't know what's going on here, but I'm your mate and I'm telling you right now to hand yourself in and take the girl with you. You've spent half your career in deep shit, so this will be no different – you'll get out of it somehow. Whatever's happened here, it can be sorted. Think of Billy. Think of Amanda. Most of all, think of Honey.'

'What do you mean "think of Billy"? You talk like he's still alive.'

A flash of concern crossed Sean's eyes. 'Are you telling me he's not?'

'Are you telling me he *is*?'

The concern in Sean's eyes intensified. 'He was two weeks ago.'

'Two *weeks* ago?'

Eden stepped away, uncertain how he was keeping what was left of his composure. He spun to face Sean again. 'You mentioned Honey. You know her too?'

'Sure. But how do *you* if you've lost ten years?'

'She's back at the row. Is she working the job with me?' Questions spiralled through his mind. 'If I'm not a con, then I'm not chipped. How the fuck did I lose my memory then?'

Sean rubbed his forehead, his gaze even more wary as it held Eden's. 'Shit.'

Eden's heart pounded faster. '*What?*'

Sean held his gaze for what felt like minutes. He looked at his watch again then anxiously at the door behind him before looking back at Eden.

'Eden, I don't know what the fuck is going on here or what's happened. I don't know who you think Honey is. I don't know what's happened to Billy. And I know this is no time to break this to you,' he said with a heavy sigh, 'but Billy's got a kid. That's the Honey I'm talking about. You've got a niece. Six years old. As cute as her mother – if you don't mind not punching me this time for making that remark.

'But Honey's really sick. You've been working extra hours, some side jobs, all sorts of stuff to get her the medications and things that she needs. You've even been fucking your own boss's doctor daughter to get meds you shouldn't be getting access to.'

Sean indicated down at the tattoo on Eden's left wrist.

'You had that done the day she was born,' he continued. 'Honey's the centre of your world, mate. She's the main reason you've stuck with this shitty job. You'd be locked away for real if it wasn't for her,' he added, indicating the numbers on his arm. 'That's why I thought you'd agreed to some undercover work, no matter how risky – because you were being paid well.'

Eden backed up a couple of steps. The room spun. His chest burned. Rage simmered deep at the lie that had dripped so easily from Mya's tongue.

Of the lies that had dripped from Homer's.

'I have a *niece*? They told me Billy was dead. So he *might* still be alive?' Eden asked the one person who, right then, felt like the only person he could trust.

'I sure as fuck hope so, mate.'

Eden looked back to Jessie, who had told him she was taking him to his brother.

'Ah, shit,' Sean said. 'I *have* to go. For your sake – *and* mine. Come with me, yeah? Right now. I can get you out. I don't know how aware you are of what's going on, but it's all kicked off out there. Morphed lycans are on the loose; Kane is this prophesied vampire leader by all accounts. Some major shit is going to break out here soon and you don't want to be caught up in it. The Global Council has brought their best in. They've done the north and east and now they're working west and then south. There's too much other shit for them to worry about besides you having gone off the rails again. If you come with me now, we'll sort this.'

'Come with you where? The border's sealed.'

Sean hesitantly held his gaze. He pressed his lips together in his final move of hesitation as Jessie stirred on the bed. 'This is fucking top-secret information okay? I shouldn't be saying this but, shit, you've got me out of more situations that I can count. You've sure saved *my* life enough times.' He hesitated a second longer. 'We have an entry and exit point. It's through the tunnel they use to transport the cons here from the penitentiary. It's a bridge in this electromagnetic field they've put up. It's the best route-access point considering it has the impassable security in the penitentiary as backup.

'I can get you to the gate, Eden. Give them your number. Hand yourself in. Tell them about your memory – you might get off more lightly.'

'And if I don't?'

'Well I'm hardly going to volunteer to get my arse kicked for the last minute of my life.' But his smile quickly faded. 'Eden, as your mate, I'm telling you that you need to do this.' He glanced back at Jessie. 'If you don't want to hand her in, leave her behind. I can pretend I never saw her.'

Jessie sighed heavily and languidly turned her head as she roused.

'I can't go with you, Sean,' Eden said, looking back at him.

Sean shook his head. 'You always were a law until yourself, Reece. But never over a girl.'

'It's more than that. She told me Billy's in Blackthorn.'

Sean's nod told him he instantly understood. 'Then at least let me warn you, with her in tow, you're going to get caught. We've been told to ignore all humans for now and focus on the third species. We've got some serious equipment on board to detect them. She's going to draw attention to you. You're my mate, Eden, so I'm telling you this as your mate – she's on a no-kill policy, but you're not. Less than half an hour from here is your way out. Find out from her where Billy is then get your arse out of here.'

Sean's gaze lingered for a moment longer before he moved over to the door.

'And keep yourself as far south as you can for as long as you can,' Sean added, glancing over his shoulder. 'That will buy you some time. Good luck. I hate to be clichéd, but you're going to need it.'

# Chapter Forty-Six

One minute he'd been sipping wine and the next minute Torren had woken with his wrists manacled to the crossbeam and his ankles manacled to the floor. A strong scent of incense lingered in the air, but it was the undertones of burning flesh that made it clear what was happening.

Torren stared ahead at the copper bowl where the heart would have been burned to ash. Ash that had been used to write his name on the concrete floor where he now stood.

A summons. Never in over five hundred years had anyone ever *dared* summon him.

He looked to his right into the darkness, where someone stood from a seated position to approach him.

'This is either an arrogant error on your part,' Torren said. 'Or you are already in a pit of desperation. Either way, this will not end well. Release me. *Now*.'

But as the figure came into view, as Kane's navy eyes came into view, Torren couldn't help but chuckle as all became apparent.

'Kane Malloy. I should have known. Only *you* would dare resort to these measures. And in this case, there's no guessing why.'

'I know you took them, Torren. I want to know where they are.'

Torren's spine prickled as the master vampire squared up to him. The master vampire whose notorious edge of unpredictability did nothing to appease his irritation at being unwillingly removed from his comfort zone.

'Let me go now, Malloy, and I *might* consider forgetting this ever happened.'

'We both know you're not going to forget this, Torren. Just as we both know you *will* tell me what I want to know.'

'Over an envoi and a human. My, my, master-vampire standards are slipping of late. Whatever happened to putting your species first, Malloy? Isn't that what you're *supposed* to do? '

'I am.'

'Clearly not effectively considering you've dared to summon me. This is no less than declaring a war between our species, Malloy. Are you *sure* this is what you want to do? Because that doesn't sound like the action of a responsible master vampire to me.'

'And putting your army at risk doesn't sound like the action of a responsible warrior to me.'

'At risk?' Torren laughed. 'At risk from what? A couple of hundred vampires thinking they can take us on? Don't make me laugh, Malloy. Get these binds off me and walk away.'

'I'm going nowhere, Torren, until you tell me what I want to know.'

'You're defaulting on the basic premise of your role, Malloy,' Torren warned again as Kane's glare remained frustratingly unremitting. 'You know there will be consequences – severe consequences – for your kind. Stand *down*.'

But the master vampire's gaze remained infuriatingly calm. 'Where are Eden and Jessie, Torren?'

'Torture me within an inch of my life and you know I will never talk, vampire.'

'But I don't need to torture you, do I, Torren? If you're attentive to the media, even local rumours, you'd know I have other resources at my disposal.'

A coil of uncertainty teased his chest – not that he was willing to display that to Kane.

'The shadow reader?' Torren laughed again. 'The *non-celibate* shadow reader? Considering your antics with her between the sheets, you know as well as I do that her heart is no longer well enough protected. It would kill her if she even *attempted* to read me. Clearly though it's not *her* heart you opted to sacrifice to summons me.' He indicated the remnants in the copper bowl. '*Two* loves in a master vampire's life – you *are* in a mess, aren't you, Kane?'

'Who says she's going to read *you*, Torren?'

He frowned at Kane's subtle smirk.

His frowned deepened as three figures stepped into the room to join them. He could sense the shadow reader from ten feet away. He could also sense his own being escorted in by a lycan.

Ziel was forced on to his knees, his hands secured behind his back, his eyes rightly lowered.

Torren yanked downwards on his restraints before cursing through gritted teeth.

Kane's still-calm gaze burned through the shadows towards him.

'You either tell us where they are, Torren, and – if they're still alive – how we save Eden from what Jessie's angel tears have done, or Caitlin here will read Ziel and find out where you've been hiding all this time.'

The threat stepped much further beyond the mark than summoning him had; the threat of war non-retractable.

'And you're going to send your *entire* army, are you, Malloy? Because that's what it will take. You're going to abandon all of those you're trying to protect and head right into the thick of the battle just for those two.'

'*My* army will be staying exactly where they are. It's not *my* army you need to be worrying about. You need to be worrying about someone who's indebted to Eden Reece and Jessie for saving his young. That's not a debt that's forgotten easily, not where he's concerned.'

Torren stared across the room to where the lycan leader had entered, azure blue eyes meeting his squarely without a glimmer of hesitation.

*Jask Tao.*

Torren closed his eyes and cursed in his own head before he glared back at Kane.

The master vampire merely folded his arms before shrugging, that exasperating smirk subtle but definitive.

# Chapter Forty-Seven

Jessie stirred to the sound of an unfamiliar voice, followed moments later by the noise of a door closing. She tried to sit up by bracing her arms behind her only to find one of her wrists cuffed to the headboard.

Eden sat at her bedside watching her, leaning back in a wooden chair, his feet on the mattress.

Using her free arm for leverage, Jessie rested back against the headboard as she cast a glance towards what seemed to be the only door out of there. Whoever the voice had belonged to was no doubt responsible for whatever sedative had been shot into her system. She'd seen the uniform before she'd passed out – the same CEO uniform Eden had used to break into the TSCD when they'd rescued Leila and Alisha.

Eden was still alive and the CEO was gone. She could only hope he'd said something to back up her claim. Whatever had happened, Eden was at least still there.

He certainly seemed calmer, but there was still the absence of connection in his eyes despite her hope there would have been a hint of progress.

He held up a key, obviously to the cuff that bound her.

'Tell me everything as quickly and concisely as you can,' he said. 'When I'm done listening, the place where this key lands will depend on how convinced I am by what you have to say.'

Jessie warily held his gaze. 'What have you been told?'

He folded his arms. 'You might want to bear in mind that only three things have stopped me walking out of that door already. One is that I've played enough kiss-chase in my time to know when a girl wants to get caught. Two is that you were telling the truth about me being a CEO. And third is that you're claiming to know where Billy is. Now talk.'

Her heart leapt at his words. 'Was it Sean?'

The only friend and colleague he had mentioned to her by name. The one she knew he had gone to for help when they'd needed to break into the Third Species Control Division – when they'd gone there with the intention of killing Caleb.

His eyes narrowed a little at her revelation that she knew Sean's name, something she hoped would help in convincing him to trust her.

'Who are you and how did we meet?' he asked.

'As I told you, you were a CEO sent on an undercover case to Pummel's row. You were sent by Sirius Throme himself to get me out with promises of a better life for your family. You worked out that once you handed me over though, neither you nor your family was going to live – that Sirius would want his undercover work to stay that way. So instead you resolved to get what you could from me in exchange for my freedom and then get your family away from Sirius and into Blackthorn.'

'Get what from you?'

'My blood works like the Higher Order blood they're researching at The Facility. That's what the needle marks in my arm are from. Homer knows. Pummel did too. You thought it could help your niece Honey.'

His eyes glossed but his gaze didn't flinch. 'So it's true that she's ill.'

She wanted to tell him no. She wanted to be able to tell him they'd sorted it, exactly like they'd thought they had. 'Yes.'

'So your blood didn't work?'

It was too much for her to explain there and then, so she simply shook her head.

'You said my brother's alive?'

'He's alive and he's safe, Eden.'

He dropped his gaze for a moment then got up out of his chair and paced away.

She couldn't have him lose it. She couldn't have him heading back to Homer.

'I can get you to him. They're *all* here. Honey too.'

'Why would Sirius hurt them?' he asked, still not facing her.

'The undercover job he sent you on was big.'

Eden turned to face her again. '*How* big?'

'There's so much to tell you, Eden. . .'

'Then do it,' he said sternly.

'Sirius is trying to change the global structure. He wants rid of all third species. He wants an elite human society. And he wants to find a way to make a select cohort of humans as close to immortal as can be.'

'How?'

'Soul transference. He knows third-species blood – Higher Order vampire blood – isn't the permanent cure they hoped for. Nor is mine. He knows the permanent cure doesn't exist, so he's been trying to find another way. All the research at The Facility has been about creating an alternative to prolonging human life instead. That's what all of this is about. It's what it's been about for decades. It's why he wants Kane Malloy.'

'*The* Kane Malloy?'

'Kane Malloy knows how to transfer souls. Sirius has perfected cloning, now all he needs to know how to do—'

'Is omit the frailty of the human body. Are you fucking serious?'

'I'm afraid I am. It's why he sent you for me. I was his last-ditch at a permanent cure before he closed ranks on capturing Kane.'

'How do you know all of this?'

'There's a group of us. You're part of it. We've put the pieces together. You didn't only rescue me from Pummel's row – you rescued nine lycan young too. Nine young Sirius had taken there as his backup plan should you fail.'

His eyes widened slightly. 'Tao's young?'

'Jask's your friend now, Eden. It's his pack that are looking after your family.'

He took two guarded steps towards her. 'My family are with *lycans*? *Morphed* lycans?'

'The morphed lycans are genetically modified. They're nothing to do with Jask's pack. Sirius sent them in to justify this barrier going up. Your family are safe with Jask. I promise.'

He stared at her for a moment, his eyes unreadable.

'I know it's a lot to take in, Eden. . .'

'A lot to take in? My brother was dead this morning! My niece didn't exist. I thought I was the scum of the earth. Not only am I a completely different person to who I thought I was less than two hours ago, now *you're* telling me I'm part of some covert third-species team too?'

'They're not all third species. It's fifty-fifty.'

He exhaled brusquely. 'Like that's relevant. Where are my family? At Jask's compound?'

'They were. We had to evacuate a couple of days ago. We've been under attack from Throme's army. Now they're in the underground tunnel system set up by Kane Malloy.'

He lifted his eyebrows a fraction. '*The* tunnels? The stuff of the urban legends? And Kane Malloy and Jask Tao have teamed up?'

'I told you it was complicated. Half of Blackthorn is down there. The lycans and vampires have teamed up to protect as many as they can. Like I said, there's a group of us. We're trying to stop Sirius. If we fail and he succeeds, Blackthorn will be destroyed. More than that, the devastation will spread far beyond this border. We're on the brink of war.'

'And you're telling me Kane Malloy is trying to *stop* the war he's supposedly instigating?'

'He's not the vampire leader that they're claiming him to be. And, yes, he is trying to stop it. It's all linked to the vampire prophecy that should have stayed under wraps to stop this very thing from happening. Exposure of the vampire prophecy is what caused this segregation, this stratified society we all live in. We're trying to avoid a massacre that will only reinforce this segregation further. And you're a pivotal part of that.'

'How?'

'You have access to a doctor at The Facility who you believe has evidence directly related to the research Sirius has been conducting. Through her, you can get proof to expose what Sirius has been doing. As a result, we'll be able to call into question not only his motivations but also the construct behind this entire system – the system you grew up in and fought not to be a victim of. The system that put your niece's life at risk.'

'So this group I'm supposedly part of is trying to bring down the *entire* global system?'

'Yes.'

'How many of us are there?'

'At the head of it? Seven, including you and me.'

His lips parted, shock emanating from his eyes. '*Seven* people are trying to bring down an eighty-year-old institution on which this entire globe is run?'

'It'll be eight if we can get one more aboard.'

'Eight?' He let out a curt laugh. His gaze studied hers for what felt like minutes. 'How long have I been a part of this group?'

'Less than a week.'

'And you?'

'The same.'

He shook his head before pacing at the foot of the bed.

'How long have I known you?' he asked, turning to face her.

She pressed her lips together as she hesitated over telling him. 'Less than a week too.'

His eyes narrowed pensively as the sense of ludicrousness of how it must have sounded echoed back at her. 'This has *all* happened in under a week?'

'For us, yes. Kane's been planning it for decades though. Sirius has been turning up the heat for about three weeks now, ever since Kane and Caitlin met and he found out he had the option of soul transference—'

'Who the fuck is Caitlin?'

Where to begin on that one. . .

'Like I said, I know it's a lot to take in but it's all true – I swear. This is why I couldn't tell you back at the row. I'm trying to get you back to our friends.'

'*Where* exactly?'

And that was when reality stung even more. 'I don't know. All I know is that we're not safe here. There's *so* much more to tell you, but we've been gone too long already. We have to find the others before the army reaches the hub.'

Eden sat back on the chair. He lowered his head and rested his forearms across his knees as he sighed heavily.

'Eden, you need to untie me. I *have* to get you to safety. You have no idea how important you are. How important you are to what needs to happen.' She hesitated for a moment, but she couldn't help but say it. 'How important you are to *me*.'

His gaze met hers again. 'I've known you less than a week according to what you just told me.'

'You'd be surprised how long a week can feel lately.'

He looked away before his brown eyes rested back on hers. 'Then tell me the one missing piece: why don't I remember any of this?'

❋ ❋ ❋

Of all the questions, that was the one she hesitated over most.

'An angel took your memory.'

'So now angels exist too?'

He didn't know why he'd questioned to the contrary. That morning his niece hadn't existed either.

'Eighty years ago, vampires and lycans were the stuff of storybooks as well. We all know that. We have every reason to believe Sirius has been hiding the angels' existence too.'

'Why?'

'Because he thought *they* were the permanent cure he needed. They've been part of the experiments back at The Facility.'

'So you're telling me Sirius wants global domination. At first, like the rest of us, he thought the Higher Order's blood was the cure. When he found out it wasn't permanent though, he somehow discovered the existence of angels and thought they were the solution. But now you're telling me they're not either?'

'No. The lasting effects are more damaging than good.'

'So now he's having one final shot combining clones and this soul transference using Malloy.'

'Yes.'

'And he's invaded Blackthorn to get him.'

'Yes.'

'Which is what this barrier is *really* about?'

'The fact is Sirius has been involved in a lot of sneaky, inhumane and backhand activity to get us to this point, and we need to expose him before we can effect any kind of change.'

'So one of these angels took *my* memory – why?'

'Because they don't want us to win. They want this war to happen exactly as is predestined. They want the cull as much as Sirius does. And when they're ready, they'll intervene.'

'As the heroes? Narcissism sure is fucking rife in Blackthorn these days.'

'Like you wouldn't believe. All the whispers about the prophecy are true, Eden – but it's latent. The eight of us have all effected change somehow. Now the angels want to get it back on track. Before they took your memory, you were trying to find a way through the barrier. You were destined to work it out, which means you would get to the doctor and some of us would get through too to help expose the truth.'

There was a chance she hadn't been unconscious – that she had heard everything Sean had said, which was why she'd added this fragment to her story to garner validity. But there was something in her eyes, something in the way she looked at him, that spoke to that sense of familiarity he had with her – just like when they'd been together in the bathroom. Just like the first time he'd seen her.

There was something about her that made something deep inside him urge him to believe her. Because if she was right, if she *was* telling the truth, it sounded like he was risking throwing a hell of a lot away by letting himself be swayed by the sheer improbability of it.

'So they're picking us off.'

She nodded.

'And I picked one of the lucky straws. So how did I end up with Homer? Where does he fit into this?'

'It was true he was Pummel's right-hand man. You nearly killed him back at the row.' She hesitated again for a moment as if trying to gather her thoughts. 'You and I were trying to get some information. We were kidnapped a couple of days ago. I was shadow read. Torren, the angel who did this to you, found out everything about you through me. He found out what we're all trying to do. In part, he could be using us as bait to get Kane. . .'

'Because if Kane's out of the equation. . .'

'Exactly.'

'You said "in part".'

'Instead of killing you outright, he wanted to make you suffer. He wanted to make me suffer. So he handed us over to Homer.'

'Why?'

'Because we're together. And because I was once with Torren.'

His chest knotted. Rage simmered somewhere deep inside at the prospect of the truth: what the angel had done to him.

He clenched his hands into fists as thoughts tumbled over each other, each to the detriment of the other. But then, amidst it all, there was her: the girl that his most basic instincts told him to trust.

'Why didn't you escape?' he asked.

'Because Homer threatened to kill you. If I told you anything or if he thought you even had an inkling, he would have slaughtered you.'

'And you need me alive.'

'It's more than that.'

There was an unsettling stirring deep in his gut as he gazed into the eyes of the girl he couldn't deny having a connection with.

'What are you to me, Jessie?'

Her eyes glossed. 'I'm the one you used to love. I'm the one you still loved only a couple of days ago.'

The girl who'd been under the same roof as him whilst he'd been with another. Who'd walked in on him with another.

And yet *still* she had stuck with him. It didn't make sense.

His stomach churned.

'You're not human. What are you?'

Her gaze was hesitant again. 'I'm an angel too. An envoi to be precise. The type of angel that ends up with scars on their back instead of wings. I receive messages about the prophecy whether I want to or not. I first saw you in that prophecy over a century and a half ago. And then a week ago we met. I think I'm here to protect you, Eden. Whatever it takes, I'm here to see that you do what you need to do. I guess I'm the messenger telling you what you need to do. And I'm telling you we have to find the others.'

'It's not safe out there. Not only will the cons be looking for us, it seems we have an entire army looking for us too. Do you know we're both on a wanted list?'

'Sirius's? That wouldn't surprise me. Staying here is as much a risk though. Our team will be looking for us. We need to be out there so they can find us.'

He ruffled the back of his hair before stepping away again.

'Sean told me I'm safer without you,' he said, turning to face her again. 'Being with you is going to draw attention to me.'

Her eyes flared in minor panic. 'No. You're safer *with* me, Eden.'

He flipped the key over his fingers.

'Please,' she said. '*Please*, believe me. I'm the only one who can protect you.'

# Chapter Forty-Eight

They'd been given an hour to rest before they had to move again.

Billy had already asked a few times what was happening with Eden – why he hadn't seen him or Jessie in a while. Eden had said he'd check in at the next stop but that had been hours before. So when he saw Kane and Jask approaching through the restless slumber, he instantly got to his feet and headed over.

'What's going on, Kane? I keep asking about Eden but nobody's telling me anything. Has something happened? Why have I got this sick feeling that something has happened?'

As Kane indicated for him to follow him to the outer tunnel, Billy cast a glance over his shoulder in Amanda's direction. With a frown, she met his gaze over Honey's head, their daughter cradled in her arms.

To reassure her, he sent her a wave before following Kane outside of the room. He tried to swallow but his mouth was as dry as his throat, his eyes searching Kane's and then Jask's in desperation.

'Something has happened,' he built up the courage to say. 'Something bad.'

To his little brother – the brother who he'd spent his whole life failing to protect.

'We don't know,' Kane said, his hands low on his hips. 'But he's in the south, Billy. He's with the cons.'

'The south? What the hell is he doing there?'

'He and Jessie went back to get some paperwork from the row.'

'*Paperwork*? What paperwork?'

But for some reason Kane refrained from elaborating. 'Jessie's ex, the one who bound her, caught up with them. It seems your little brother will find the way through this barrier. Torren is trying to prevent that.'

Fury sparked in him like a gas flame. 'Do you still have this Torren?'

'We do.'

'Then take me to him,' Billy said, stepping forward.

But the vampire's hand was instantly against his chest, blocking his way. A hand he wouldn't stand a chance of budging. Especially as it seemed that Jask was backing him all the way.

'We've got all the information we need from him,' Jask said. 'We don't know where Eden and Jessie are, but we know they're together and we know they're with someone called Homer.'

'Homer? As in the Homer who was with Pummel? But that can't be right – Eden killed him.'

'Apparently not. We need to track down which row he's now at.'

Billy nodded. 'Eden will get out of there. I know he will. He got out of there once. He's smart. And he's so strong now. . .' he said, as if needing to convince himself. But he knew he was deflecting, like he always did. 'Won't he?'

'We need something from you, Billy,' Jask said.

'Like what?'

'I know it's a long shot, but do you have anything on you that's an old keepsake? A piece of jewellery maybe?'

'Why? What's going on?'

'Torren took his memory,' Jask said. 'Ten years of it.'

Billy stared from Jask to Kane and back again.

'Without his memory, waking up in the south with those numbers tattooed on his forearm, he's going to believe he's a con,' Kane said. 'Just as Torren has planned.'

'Ten years? Gone? But that means he won't know about Amanda, about Honey, about his life as a CEO.'

'Exactly,' Kane said. 'Just like he won't know about Jessie or any of us. He won't even know about our cause. That's what Torren wants. He wants him lost in there.'

Fury flooded through him at the prospect of everything his little brother had fought to become being stolen from him. *Everything* that made him a better person. Everything that brought out the best in him and had given him a purpose.

Everything that kept him on the right track.

'This is why this isn't going to be straightforward,' Jask said. 'Even if we can locate him, he won't know who we are beyond what he might have been aware of a decade ago. We know he's faster now, tougher. . . and we can't afford to lose him.'

'Ten years ago he was also dangerous, reckless, opportunistic. Me being with Amanda changed him for the better. And Honey. . . she changed everything for him. Him getting that job with the CEU. . .' He looked back into their eyes. 'What about Jessie? What have they done to Jessie?'

'She has her memory back. Torren wants her to suffer.'

Billy cursed under his breath.

'If you have anything that will help us prove he can trust us,' Jask said. 'It would really help. Something that he'll recognise. . .'

'Amanda has our mother's engagement ring. He would know that instantly.'

'Will Amanda give it to you?'

'For Eden? She'd do anything.'

Jask nodded. 'We'll get him out of there, Billy – just like he got my young out of there. Now it's my turn to do the same for him.'

Billy nodded as he turned on his heels and made his way back through the blankets and stretched legs to Amanda.

'Billy?' she asked, her blue eyes wide, and placed her hand over Honey's ear, despite their daughter clearly being asleep. 'Please tell me it's not bad news?'

'Eden's in trouble, Amanda. Jessie too.'

Her eyes flared. 'What's happened?'

'It's okay. Kane and Jask are forming a plan. They need our help though. They're going to need. . .'

But he couldn't do it. He couldn't bail out on his brother like that. Because there was more that he could do than hand over a ring.

'They're going to need me to go with them.'

Amanda's hand instantly shot to his. 'What? *Where*?'

'To the south.'

Amanda snatched back a breath and slammed her hand over her mouth.

'It's okay,' he said, catching her hand. 'I'll be going with Kane and Jask.' He blinked away tears as he stared deep into his wife's eyes, knowing that, despite her reluctance to let him go, she would understand better than anyone. 'You know why I'm doing this, don't you?'

She nodded as she wiped a tear away from her own eyes.

'And we're going to bring Eden home,' he said. 'I promise.'

❄ ❄ ❄

Kane watched Billy make his way back across the room and sent a glance in Amanda's direction, Amanda who, face ashen, was now holding Honey tight to her chest.

'I'm coming with you,' Billy declared.

Kane exhaled curtly. 'Like fuck you are.'

'He could die at any point, Kane, alone in the row, thinking no one gives a damn. I'm not losing him to that hovel. I'm bringing him back.'

'And he's not going to want you dying in there either.'

'Which is why we're going to stick together. A ring is one thing, but seeing me will be all we need to convince him out of there. He won't be the person you know now. You need to prepare yourself for that. Ten years ago my brother was used to working the streets. He has a strong survival instinct and a poor sense of trust. He's a survivor and now, as far as he's concerned, he's a con. I'm the one person he'll recognise and trust. It *has* to be me who goes in there with you.'

Kane looked to Jask, who appeared as reticent as he was. It wasn't just the risk to Billy himself but the fact he would be baggage they didn't need. A distraction they didn't need. They had maybe a few hours before the soldiers moved to the edge of the hub. That meant only a few hours to wrap this up.

'You have to give us the best shot,' Billy pleaded. 'If we stand any chance of bringing Sirius down. Please. He's *my* brother. I can't even begin to tell you how many scrapes he's got me out of over the years. He was my little brother, and he spent the entire time we were growing up being my protector, but now he needs *me*. For once in his life, *he* needs *me*. We've spent too many years with roles reversed, now it's time *I* stepped up to the mark.'

# Chapter Forty-Nine

As they made their way through the misty streets towards the hub, Jessie desperately wanted to reach out and take Eden's hand in hers. To offer him some kind of comfort as he visibly battled with the confusions in his head, his mind split between trusting her and remaining on guard.

But it had been their biggest step in the right direction. Just having him trust her enough to walk alongside her was huge. Ultimately he had opted to release her and give finding the others – his family – a shot.

Eden stopped alongside her as they stared ahead at where the mist had thickened, the street lamps and phone box masked in an ethereal hue. But while he was only thinking of the potential of cons using it to hide, Jessie was searching for clues of an entirely different threat.

As he moved forward, convinced the coast was clear, she grabbed his arm, tugging him to an abrupt standstill beside her as she continued to search the mist.

Her heart leapt as she detected an iridescent mass moving within it.

It was the mist that Leila had warned them all about: mist hidden in mist.

'*Shit*,' she muttered, grateful she had hesitated, her grip on Eden's arm tightening as the thrumming then resounded deep in her eardrums.

'What?' he asked.

'We need to move,' she said quietly, not taking her attention off the willowy shadows appearing as the mist developed a violet hue. 'We need to go back.'

'We can't go back. We've come too far to go back.'

Her heart pounded as the figures turned to face them.

'*Now!*' Jessie said as she spun on her heels, yanking Eden with her.

'Jess, what the fuck is happening?'

But he ran down the street alongside her regardless.

Jessie glanced over her shoulder to see the mist rolling towards them like a ball, picking up momentum to match theirs.

'Fourth species,' she said. 'Bone feasters. That's acidic mist.'

She felt his gaze burn into her as they ran, but she remained focused ahead.

'We need to get inside,' she said. 'Somewhere with water.'

As they sprinted down the residential street, finally having gained a little distance, they each shouldered themselves against every door they came across.

'We need a flat or apartment of some kind!' she shouted across the narrow street. 'We need water!'

'Why?'

'Just trust me on this! But we can't break in – the lock must stay secure!'

As they continued to race down the street, they tried as many doors as they could to no avail.

'Fuck this!' Eden finally exclaimed and fell to his knees in one of the doorways.

Jessie stared back at the mist as Eden reached into his back pocket and pulled out small metal pins to burrow at the lock – no doubt the same ones he'd used to get out of the back door at Homer's row.

Her mind slipped back to the cellar – the night children approaching as Eden desperately tried to undo the cage lock to free the lycan young. It was something he wouldn't remember – another in a long line of heroic acts he'd forgotten. And just like she had then, she formed a barrier between the fourth species and him, blinding them for as long as she could.

'Ten feet,' she said. 'Eight, seven, four. . .'

'In!' he declared, grabbing her arm and tugging her inside with him.

He slammed the door as Jessie searched her surroundings for the kitchen and bathroom.

The first knock echoed around the room, followed by the second and then the third, all exactly five seconds apart.

'Find any glasswear! Fill it with water!' she said, skidding into the kitchen. She yanked open the cupboards, taking out whatever glasses she could find – a vase too. 'They knock nine times. Three groups of three with a short break between each cluster.'

'What happens after the ninth?'

She met his gaze fleetingly. 'Then they come in.'

She turned the tap but nothing came out. She cursed under her breath.

'Cut off,' Eden said. He reached across her. 'Try the hot-water tank.'

As the water spurted out, she filled two of the glasses, her hands soaked in her clumsiness to do it quickly, before placing them on the side and filling another two.

The fourth knock resounded, followed by the fifth and the sixth.

'Salt!' she said. 'Search the cupboards for salt!'

The ache in her chest intensified as they remained on a wing and a prayer that the apartment had what they needed.

She ploughed ahead regardless, filling as many glasses as she could.

'Salt,' Eden said, slamming the canister on the worktop.

'Place as many glasses as you can on all the entrance points,' she instructed. 'Doors and windows. Start at the front.'

Without hesitation, Eden did as he was asked, circling the apartment and placing glass after glass in front of the door and on the windowsills.

Jessie placed two on the kitchen windowsill and two by the back door before pouring salt into each.

The seventh knock resounded deeply and forebodingly across the room.

She sprinted to the front door, poured salt into the glasses that lined the threshold of the apartment as the eighth knock was struck, then threw the canister at Eden, who was waiting in the bedroom. She skidded to the doorway to see him pouring it into the three glasses on the windowsill.

The ninth knock rang out.

Eden threw the canister back at Jessie, who raced into the bathroom.

'Windowless,' he said, bracing the threshold behind her.

They both spun simultaneously to stare at the door as they caught their breath.

But the knocking had stopped.

# Chapter Fifty

In the couple of minutes that passed, the silence remained.

'Do you think they've gone?' Eden whispered.

Jessie shook her head as she focused her full attention on the door. 'Unlikely.'

She headed back across the living space and over to the boarded-up window to peer cautiously through the slats.

Eden moved up behind her, the feel of his warm body against hers the only welcome distraction as they looked out into the centre of the street.

The cluster of willowy figures stood in a circle, facing inwards, their heads slightly lowered as if in meditation.

'What are they doing?' he asked.

'Waiting, I guess.'

'Fucking creepiest thing ever,' he remarked, his breath caressing her hair. 'How long for, do you think?'

'I don't know.'

He rested his palm against the wall beside her head and leaned further over her shoulder to get the best view possible to the left and right of them.

Seeming to sense her tension at his proximity, he pulled back.

As he wandered around the flat, Jessie forced herself to stop watching him and instead scan what had clearly been someone's functional home. They'd been gone a long time though from the mould in the cup next to her and the thick layer of dust on everything. They were most likely missing alongside countless others who, over the years, had become lost in the depths of Blackthorn.

Knowing there was nothing more they could do for the time being than wait, she took a seat on the sunken sofa, folding her arms and resting them on her knees.

'There's mist out the back way too,' Eden said, re-entering the living room from the kitchen.

'We have no choice but to wait for them to get distracted or bored,' she said.

As he sat alongside her at the other end of the two-seater sofa, she absorbed the silence for a few moments. The urge to snuggle into him as she usually would was overwhelming as the stark reality of the chase set in. Battling alongside him felt like old times – working with him like the finely tuned operation they were. But she was under no illusion that the main reason he had remained with her was because of Billy.

'That was impressive stuff,' he remarked. 'How did you know to do all that?'

'From a friend: Leila. There's not much she doesn't know about the fourth species. If they're inside with you, you throw salt. If they're outside, you can block their entry with water *and* salt – but only if the entry points haven't been damaged, or it doesn't apply. She warned us about the bone feasters as soon as the mist started to appear in Blackthorn. She was the one who told us to look out for the warning sign of iridescent hues in the mist.' She met his gaze fleetingly. 'Melting you with acid makes your bones easier to get to.'

'I always thought the fourth species was about as real as Santa.' He slumped deeper into the sofa. 'I'll remember to leave salt and water next time instead of milk and cookies.'

She smiled as another glimmer of her Eden shone through. He met her gaze fleetingly and then smiled too.

Her heart skipped a beat at his reciprocation but he broke from her gaze to scan the apartment again. 'Is this Leila part of the team?'

'Yes.'

'So who are the others?'

'Leila, me and you, Kane and Caitlin, and Jask and Sophia – or Phia as we call her.'

'Who's the eighth you want to recruit?'

'Caleb Dehain.'

His dark eyes locked on hers again. 'Caleb Dehain as in the *vampire* Caleb Dehain?'

'That's the one.'

'Ten years of my memory gone or not, even I know you don't get involved with Caleb Dehain.'

'We don't have much choice. He's a part of this prophecy too – and we need him onside.'

He turned more fully towards her. 'You really believe you can bring this system down, don't you?'

'So did you a couple of days ago.'

His eyes glazed momentarily – further evidence that he was still struggling to come to terms with all she had told him. He slumped back into the sofa again. 'Yeah, well I've always hated it. They corner you and corner you until you have no fight left and nothing left to fight *for*, whilst those sitting amongst their privileges and opportunities tell people like me to pull ourselves together; that hard work pays off.

'They lay on their inherited inflatables, coasting around their calm, warm pools, dipping their toe whenever it suits, telling us – those dumped in the cold ocean miles from shore amidst the tides and the sharks – that all we have to do is swim a little harder to catch the next boat. It doesn't matter to them that the boat we're swimming towards keeps moving that bit further away each time. That there isn't a ladder to grab hold of even if we get there.'

He looked across at her as she listened in silence.

'But you're going to tell me you've heard all that before, right?'

'It's why you're fighting, Eden. It's why Torren did this to you. He knows you're going to succeed. *I* know you're going to succeed.'

He frowned pensively as his gaze lingered on hers again. 'You told me Sirius sent me to get you out of Pummel's row. What were you doing there?'

'I had the same thing happen to me as has happened to you. I had my memory taken as punishment.'

'For what?'

*For trying to save you.*

'For trying to change the course of the prophecy. It's forbidden for my kind to interfere.'

'Was it this Torren who put you there?'

She nodded. 'A long time ago. Long before the regulations. Then, thirty years after the regulations, the cons moved in. Unfortunately my punishment included a bind that kept me helpless in the hands of whoever had it. And that became Pummel.'

His gaze studied hers, a glimmer of empathy resonating behind his eyes. 'How old are you?'

'About a hundred and seventy.'

'Cougar, huh?'

The relaxed taunt in his smile – reminiscent of her Eden – eased her.

'How did we meet?' he asked.

'I saved you from a group of cons in the back alley behind Pummel's row.'

He frowned. 'Why?'

She shrugged. 'Because they'd outnumbered you and it wasn't a fair fight. Because I was sick of the violence. Because I could. All that matters is that I did.'

Silence consumed the air between them for a moment. 'And then?'

'I became more than a job to you. And you became more than just anyone to me.'

His frown deepened, trouble lingering behind his eyes. He broke from her gaze to lean forward with a heavy sigh. Arms resting across his knees, he stared at the floor. 'If you know me like you say you do, you know why this is hard for me to understand.'

As he looked back into her eyes, she wanted only to slide in close to him.

'I do,' she said.

He looked back at the floor. His eyes remained downturned and pensive as the seconds scraped by.

'You know I've slept with Mya.'

As his eyes met hers again she nodded, her throat tight.

'And still you stuck around,' he added.

'It wasn't you,' she said without hesitation.

'Does *she* know the whole truth?'

After a few moments of hesitation, Jessie nodded.

He leaned forward and raked his fingers down his face before keeping it hidden behind his hands. He took a steadying breath and she braced herself as he looked across at her. 'Including who Honey is?'

It was the hardest truth to acknowledge yet.

Already feeling his tension escalate, Jessie reluctantly nodded.

He was on his feet a second later. He kicked the chair out of the way so it smashed against the wall.

He paced for a few moments before turning to face her.

'You should have told me,' he said, his eyes emblazoned with accusation.

'I tried to.'

'You should have told me sooner. In the living room. The first time we spoke.'

'Eden, you know why I couldn't.'

'If you had told me. . .'

'You would have what? Believed me? Left with me? Marched straight over to confront Homer? Put your life in danger?'

'As opposed to me fucking that manipulative bitch? As opposed to you letting it happen?'

Jessie leapt to her feet to look him in the eyes on a level. 'Don't you *dare*! Do you think I *wanted* that to happen? Do you think I wanted to sit back and watch the man I love more than anything else in this world be with someone else? Do you not think I was tempted? Do you not think it broke me in two? Homer was going to *kill* you. If I screwed up, you were dead. I was trying to save your life. I'm trying to save us all.'

The glossing of his eyes, the confusion and guilt behind them, were the only things that helped rein her temper in.

Crossing the threshold to enter the bathroom, he slammed the door behind him.

Any other time she would have followed. Any other time she would have comforted him. But she knew he needed time. Most of all, he wouldn't want her to see his vulnerability. It had taken him long enough back in the row.

So, as agonizing as it was, Jessie headed back over to keep watch out of the window.

She wiped a couple of stray tears from her eyes, precious time continuing to trickle away. Time she could do nothing to stop. Time that would mean it would make it harder and harder to find the rest of the team.

# Chapter Fifty-One

It was irresponsible for him to leave her out there alone, but the rage burned too deep for him to want to be in the same room as her. He wasn't going to inflict any more distress on her than he already had. He'd been wrong to accuse her, adding to the weight of his guilt.

Now he understood her reluctance. Now he understood why she wouldn't tell him back at the row. His reaction then was the very thing she had been safeguarding him against.

He clutched the sink, his head lowered.

As the extent of Homer and Mya's deceit swamped his head, his grip tightened.

And then there was Jessie putting herself through all of that to get him out. To save him.

His real-life guardian angel.

And he'd been screwing someone else right under her nose. Someone who'd knowingly defiled and mocked his ill little niece's name.

He'd never laid his hands on a woman – not like that – but he could have gladly throttled Mya right then. Mya *and* Homer. The compulsion to return to the row overwhelmed him; the compulsion to look them in the eye before he tore their stone hearts out.

He wiped the tears from his eyes as he pulled himself from the sink to slide down the wall to the floor.

Because revenge wasn't an option. Not yet. Finding Billy was his priority.

Following a gentle knock on the door, Jessie opened it a second later. She hovered at the threshold, a piece of paper in her hand.

No doubt sensing he was calmer, she moved over to join him.

'Being an envoi, the one thing I do well is draw,' she said after a few moments. 'I used to draw pictures of you and hide them under my bed. You broke into my room one time and found them. I was mortified.' She fleetingly met his gaze. 'And you made the most of playing on it.'

He didn't know how he managed to break into a smile, but he did. 'Sounds like something I'd do.'

If she was his as she claimed she was, he wondered how the hell he'd done it. How he'd captured her heart enough for her to put it on the line for him like she had. How he'd snagged someone so beautiful – and, as was becoming increasingly clear, more than just externally.

She placed the A4 piece of paper on his knees.

He stared at the drawing, uncannily lifelike right down to the finest detail. His heart pounded at the sight of a slightly older brother than the one he last remembered seeing.

He raked his hand down over his mouth, down over his stubble, before he looked back at her, uncertain whether to hug her or drag her straight back out the door to get him to his brother sooner.

'He's kind,' she said. 'Hard-working. Loyal. He worships your sister-in-law and your niece. And he loves *you*, Eden. He's so very, *very* proud of you.'

Eden looked away to conceal his tears from the girl who, no matter how he was increasingly feeling about her, was still a stranger to him.

'We've known each other less than a week,' he said, daring to meet her gaze again. 'Why are you doing this? Why did you stay?'

'Some couples can spend a lifetime together and never *truly* know who the other person is. Others simply connect at first sight. When it comes to love, time is nothing more than a socially induced marker of validity. When you simply *know*, time becomes irrelevant.

'After all, sometimes you don't even need to know a person to already know you love them,' she added, reaching for the piece of paper. 'Why else have millions looked a complete stranger in the eyes and promised to love and protect them always?'

She turned the piece of paper over so he could see the reverse of it.

Tears instantly welled in his eyes as he stared at the blonde child smiling back at him. A little girl, maybe no more than five or six years old, with eyes as bright as her smile.

He knew instantly who she was.

A subtle tremor escaped from his fingers as he dared to look back at Jessie. 'This is *her*?'

Jessie wiped away her own tear.

'That's Honey,' she confirmed with a glimmer of pride in her eyes. 'And she's brave and funny and strong – and a fighter, a survivor, like her uncle.'

His chest burning, knowing he could contain his tears no longer, Eden pulled away and stood to turn his back on her, the picture squashed hard against his chest.

'You're a good man, Eden. Those numbers are a lie. They're not who you are. You're brave and kind and funny and compassionate and strong. And you were there when I needed a friend. You stood up for me in a way no one ever had for a very long time. You gave me hope again. You made me believe there are still good people out there. You were my light in the darkness and my warmth in the cold. You were the compassion amidst the cruelty. You saved me when it would have been so much easier for you to leave me behind. And you've saved countless more since. Because that's who you are, Eden. You don't know it yet, but I do. That's who I fell in love with. That's the reason why I wouldn't run. That's the reason why I'd never run anywhere without you.'

Despite the compulsion to face her, he stared at the floor, his chest tight, his cheeks wet with tears at her proclamation.

'And I know you don't remember why *you* love *me*,' she added. 'I don't know if those memories will ever come back, and it's breaking my heart that Torren stole them from us. But he can't stop the way I feel about you, even if he was able to take away the way you feel about me.'

He wiped away his tears, preparing to face the girl who couldn't have made it clearer why he loved her. Why he would have dared love her despite the dangers to his own heart.

Right then, he understood.

But when he finally turned back around, she was gone.

# Chapter Fifty-Two

Jessie pulled herself away from peering out of the bedroom window at the feeling she was being watched.

Eden stood just inside the room, his hand remaining on the door handle as her gaze met his. His eyes were slightly bloodshot, his rims reddened, but his tears had subsided.

'I didn't mean to upset you,' she said. 'I wanted to remind you what you were fighting for that's all; why we're doing this.' She indicated the window amidst his silence. 'They've gone. That means we should get going too.'

He moved over to the window to peer out through the slats.

She backed up to the wall beside it, interlocking her hands and rubbing her thumb over her opposing palm.

In the daylight shadows of the bedroom, he met her gaze again. 'I think we should give it a short while longer to be sure.'

It was a thought that had crossed her mind and one that she would have suggested herself if time hadn't been so crucial. But he was right – it was better to be completely sure.

She stepped forward but his arm was instantly across her body, his hand locking on the hip furthest away from him.

Her stomach flipped at his touch, the tenderness amidst the firmness a sharp reminder of her Eden.

'I know what else I've been fighting for,' he said. 'Torren can take my memory, but he can't stop me falling for you again.'

Her stomach flipped. Her heart pounded. She swallowed hard against her clogging throat.

'I'm not sure anyone could stop that,' he added.

Moving his hand from her hip, he tenderly brushed his knuckles along her jawline, and she instantly closed her eyes at the reminder of the touch of the man she loved.

As he rubbed the back of his hand down her neck, she reached for it. She held his palm tight to her face at his first touch of genuine affection since Torren had tried to tear them apart.

The second she met his gaze again he lowered his mouth to hers.

The deepest part of her core ignited, the warmth of his kiss about more than the heat of his lips. Teasing, coaxing, exploratory, he brushed his lips against hers time and time again before finally clutching the nape of her neck, his palm pressed to the wall beside her head as he backed her up against it, as his tongue met hers.

She instinctively reached for his belt, her other hand sliding up around his neck to run her fingers through his hair before gently clasping his neck.

'I haven't got anything with me,' he whispered against her lips.

'We never use anything. We don't need to.'

As his gaze studied hers for a few moments, she knew it was the biggest test of his trust. She knew there was every chance he would pull back.

She braced herself for him not to take the final leap.

But he had a hold of her behind a second later, digging his fingers deep as he lifted her with ease, parting her thighs around his.

He turned to carry her over to the bed, lay her down and instantly melded into her as though he remembered every single moment they'd shared.

Jessie slid her hands up his back under his T-shirt before tugging it over his head. She traced her hands back down his warm, firm flesh to grasp his behind.

His kiss was instantly deeper, his fingers finding the front of her jeans a second later, reassuring her further.

She lifted her hips for him as he tugged her jeans down her legs and over her ankles, taking down her underwear next, before doing the same with his own.

As she felt his warm thighs between hers, his mouth against her neck, she wrapped her legs around him.

She clasped his neck. She gazed deep into his eyes. And she waited with bated breath for that moment she'd longed to feel again.

❊ ❊ ❊

Eden nudged into Jessie without hesitation, his gaze holding hers as he edged deep into her sex inch by inch.

He exhaled with satisfaction at the absence of anything artificial between them, the sensation like nothing he could remember. He'd never thought it would feel much different, had never dwelled enough to be tempted to try – all the risks too great for what could potentially be no payback.

But it *did* feel different. He didn't know if it was just the physical sensation or because it was her. If somehow, even in that last hour, something between them had reconnected.

The tightness of her sex made his breaths ragged, his need to be inside her as deep as possible overwhelming – his need to thrust harder, to thrust faster, so tempting. But every inch was too exquisite to rush, and no more so when he dragged his gaze to look into her eyes – eyes that looked back into his in a way he'd never seen a girl look at him during sex before.

And he knew he was looking straight back at her in a way he had never looked at a girl before. He barely remembered any time he'd cared to look. Any time he'd wanted to forge that kind of intimacy.

And unlike when he'd had Mya astride him, a recollection that sickened him to his core even then, he couldn't consume enough of Jessie; he wanted every part of her.

He lifted her T-shirt over her head and unclipped her bra, loving the subtle tremors that escaped her body as he pushed a little deeper in the process.

Her lips parted, her eyes glazed, and to his added arousal she trembled a little more as his thumb toyed with the soft pliability of her otherwise hard nipple, a tempting contrast to the smooth softness of her breast.

And as he lowered his mouth to replace his thumb with his tongue, she arched her back and neck, allowing – encouraging – him to push deeper as her subtle groan filled the silent room.

Taking hold of her behind, pressing his fingers in deep, he did what they both wanted and finally filled her to the hilt.

Eden bit deep into his bottom lip and closed his eyes to savour the sensation before gazing back down at her naked, lithe body exposed to him fully as she rested her arms over her head, encouraging him to let his gaze wander down her breasts, down her concave stomach, to see him buried deep inside her, her shapely thighs parted wide around him.

But as he ran his hands up her back, as he felt the raised thread-like bumps on her skin, she froze, her eyes flaring.

He remembered her telling him about the scars on her back – resulting from receiving the prophecies.

As her hesitant gaze held his, he lowered his lips to hers again, taking hers tenderly and lingeringly against his.

'Anything else I should know?' he asked, easing back enough to look her in the eyes.

She bit into her bottom lip. She reached to her eyes and removed one contact lens after the other.

As stunning violet irises gazed back at him, his breath caught in his throat.

'They change colour,' she said. 'According to my mood.'

'Tell me violet's good.'

She smiled. 'Violet's extremely good.'

He looked back into her eyes as he braced himself on his arms, gradually picking up his pace again as she lifted her knees further, encouraging him to fill her fully with each thrust, her hands sliding up his biceps, her thumbs tracing every flexion of his biceps. As he watched himself enter her again and again, his arousal spiralling, hers satisfyingly did the same.

A few more thrusts finally brought him dangerously close to the edge. And as his lips closed over hers again, as he felt her clench, as he felt her breath ragged against his lips, she came at the same time as he did, their bodies perfectly synced, their locked gazes as mutual as their smiles.

# Chapter Fifty-Three

Jessie fastened her jeans as she headed over to the window to peer outside.

The mist had well and truly evaporated in the twenty minutes or so that had passed, their cue that it was finally safe to leave.

'We need to make a move,' she said, turning to face Eden still lying naked on his back, partially bathed in the light through the slats.

'I know how to get out.'

She froze, his steady gaze as he finally turned his head telling her that it wasn't a joke.

'*Out* out?'

Her heart pounded at the prospect of the chance to save him, to save Honey. At the prospect that the prophecy had been right.

He braced himself on his arms. 'But it's not good news, Jessie.'

With hope reinstated, the last thing she needed was to have the rug torn back out from under her.

She didn't know whether to tell him why: that his very survival depended on him being able to escape. That Honey's survival depended on him escaping.

It was a secret she still needed to hold back until she at least got him back to his family; to some ray of hope. Because if they weren't to make it that far, if they were never to see the others again, she couldn't have him believing there was no hope at all. She had to keep him going.

She stepped forward as he tugged on his shorts and jeans.

'Not good news why?' she asked.

'The only way out is through the tunnel they use to bring the cons in here.'

She sat down on the edge of the bed as he too resumed his seat. 'The penitentiary tunnel?'

He nodded. 'It sounds like it was designed for this purpose from the very beginning. The electromagnetic field travels around it, leaving that one hole that they can pass through should it be needed.'

'Like a rock in a stream,' she muttered, recollecting their conversation, forgetting he wouldn't.

He nodded. 'Exactly. But the security is so tight there that no one would think to try and tackle it.'

'But if we know where it is. . .'

'It'll be on total lock-down, Jessie. The only way we'd get through is to blow the entire system.'

'With an electromagnetic pulse. You talked to me about it.'

'One hell of a powerful EMP. But that would mean taking down the penitentiary too. I don't need my memory from the last ten years to know that whole place is controlled electronically. For us to get out means wiping that out – most likely the backup generator as well.'

'It'll disable the *entire* penitentiary?'

'And form an open gateway to Lowtown not only for us but for every con in Blackthorn and every con in the pen. That's hundreds on this side of the wall with hundreds more inside. I don't need to tell you what that will mean.' He held her gaze. 'I grew up on the other side of that wall, Jessie. There are kids over there, Jess. Kids like Honey. There are vulnerable people. People who have been victim enough to this system without the contents of that pen spilling out.'

Jessie rested her head in her hands before looking back at him. 'Who told you this? How do you know it's true?'

'Sean. He told me to get out of here. He said I could report in at the gates.'

'How likely is it that you'd get through?'

'I'd be handing myself in, Jess.'

'But you could get to the other side?'

'And then what?'

She stood up and stepped away, pressing her palm against her forehead. 'You're right. We don't know what Sirius would do. And it's useless anyway,' she said, forgetting the most salient point hindering his escape in the first place. 'You have to locate this Cassandra – the doctor who knows about Sirius's research. You don't even remember what she looks like, let alone the way to her house.' She folded her arms as she turned to face him again. 'What are we going to do, Eden?'

'Like you said, find the others, because we have another problem too. Homer showed me a room at the row where they've been making EMP transmitters. They're going for the army – then they're going for Kane and Jask. If what you're telling me about them is true, we need to warn them.'

# Chapter Fifty-Four

Despite a subtle mist still lingering in parts of the south, the bone feasters were definitely long gone.

As Eden reached for Jessie's hand and interlaced their fingers the way he always used to, she met his gaze, the reassurance of having him back – of almost having him back – overriding any sense of anxiety she had right then.

'We'll interchange between the main streets and the back alleys and courtyards,' he said.

'Sounds good to me.'

'If we get to the hub, we at least need to have some idea where we're heading though, Jessie.'

'I've memorised most of the underground routes. Kane made us all do it. We'll at least be able to see if they've passed through. They'll leave us a sign or something, I know it.'

'It's still a long shot.'

'And I'm telling you they'll be looking for us.'

They veered right, heading down one of the side streets before taking a left. Seeing a couple of figures in the distance, Eden squeezed Jessie's hand, and she took the cue that they were going to duck out of sight to the right.

But no sooner had they turned ninety degrees than a few more figures emerged from the thin mist in the direction they were heading.

Jessie's pulse raced, her grip on Eden's hand tightening. No more so than when she sensed movement behind her the second Eden did.

They both glanced over their shoulders before looking left to see even more figures emerging out of the alley.

She counted fifteen, then twenty.

On the small garden wall less than thirty feet away, the con perched as though attending nothing more than a carnival. A dustbin lid in his hand, he beat a metal pole against it in a slow and steady rhythm. A beat that echoed through the streets and seemingly garnered even more attention.

Twenty-five and then at least thirty cons all moved into clear view, their ice-cold eyes raking over the pair of them like hyenas circling their trapped prey.

Eden pressed his back to Jessie's but wouldn't loosen his grip on her hand as he assessed the opposition – any way out – as silently as she did.

But there was no gap left for them, and the cons closed in by the second.

'There's a weak point in everything,' she whispered before using their interlaced fingers to subtly guide his index finger towards the alley to the right.

There were six in the narrow space, but she knew she could take at least three. Speed was going to be the most important thing before the others caught up.

And so was the element of surprise.

'Jess. . .' he said, apprehension clear in his tone.

'We don't go down without a fight,' she insisted.

'This is one of the reasons I love you, right?' he said, squeezing her hand a little tighter.

'One of many.' She squeezed back. 'If you get the slightest chance, you go. We *need* you alive.'

She met his gaze. She didn't give him a chance to respond.

Eden was a split second behind her as they bolted into the alley. With the six cons not having anticipated the brazen ambush, Jessie and Eden were upon them before the latter had the chance to brace themselves.

Sliding the knives she had taken from their hideout from the back of her jeans, Jessie ploughed into them as if she were entering nothing more than a lycan scrum during practice time. She applied everything she had learned, using both knives simultaneously, taking one con out with a stab to the artery in his thigh and another clean in the neck, as Eden took two down behind her.

Her third was a struggle, snatching the knife from her before kneeing her in the stomach and slamming her against the wall. He wrenched one arm up behind her back, but he struggled to grab the other.

Using the wall as leverage, Jessie managed to slam him backwards, Eden stabbing the knife deep into the con's side before catching hold of Jessie's hand again as the crowd piled in.

They pelted left and then right, Eden freeing her hand to allow them both greater speed and momentum. They skidded around corners as cons appeared at every entrance and exit, trying to head them off, their number allowing them to disperse quickly and effectively.

With hunting down prey one of their most basic instincts, the cons worked as an entirely different type of pack to the one she had grown to love, howling and yelling with delight as they cornered her and Eden off again and again, the cons' intricate knowledge of the south streets of Blackthorn putting her and Eden at an increasingly precarious advantage.

Forced into the open space of a car park, they ploughed around and over the stripped-down cars, each keeping a watchful eye on the other as they worked to keep in sync.

Her lungs burning, her limbs aching, they found that no sooner had some tired behind them than reinforcements had moved in, to the point there had to be at least fifty now in pursuit.

She glanced across at Eden, who was also beginning to struggle.

But neither had the intention of quitting. For the sake of the other, neither was willing to go down. Neither was willing to. . .

As something locked on her ankle, Jessie hit the ground face first, stunning her for a moment. She looked over her shoulder to see the weighted chain that had been swung in her direction and had wrapped itself around her lower limb.

As she was yanked to the floor, Jessie stared up at Eden skidding to a halt ten feet away.

'Go!' she yelled, her hand held up towards him before she felt and heard feet all around her.

Heard the climactic beating of the dustbin lid.

And felt a blow to the back of her head.

# Chapter Fifty-Five

Whatever contraption Eden woke in, it restrained him in a vice-like hold. Bound and gagged, he blinked away the confusion incurred from the blow to his head as he took in his surroundings.

His heart pounded with a mixture of relief and horror as he looked left to see Jessie bound by a similar contraption, but her legs parted in a Y, her hands secured above her head.

Rage suppressing the fear in his veins, he looked to where Homer stood between them, toying with the tip of the six-inch blade he held in his hand.

Eden scanned the twenty plus cons watching from the periphery of the room. In amongst them, Mya smirked back at him.

Eden returned his attention to Jessie. She looked back at him with as much helplessness as he felt.

Unable to contain his rage any longer, he growled against his gag and shook the contraption that he quickly realised was secured to the ground.

'They're extremely sturdy,' Homer announced, stepping forward. 'Apparently Cyclops acquired them from an old brothel down the road.'

Eden's hands tightened to fists as Homer sauntered over to Jessie to slide the flat of his blade up her inner thigh.

'Used to be quite the upmarket whorehouse from what I hear,' Homer added. 'The best of everything to service what was once this nice residential area.'

As Homer slid the flat of the blade up over Jessie's breast to her throat, the first trickle of a tear of frustration leaked from Eden's eye.

'You know all about whores though, don't you, Eden Reece?' Homer exclaimed, finally pulling away from Jessie. 'Tatum. Mya. . .'

'Hey!' Mya protested from the crowd.

Homer grinned across at her.

'And now Jessie too,' Homer added, returning his cold glare to Eden. 'But a wise man did once tell me that all men subconsciously seek out their mothers in a partner. Some kind of twisted Oedipus complex. And your mother was most *definitely* a whore, wasn't she, Eden? I heard all about how she once screwed three men just to pay the rent on that grubby little dive you grew up in.'

His jaw clenched behind his gag, Eden strained his wrists against the restraints that bound him until his veins almost popped with the force of it. Because he may have been a child at the time, but he'd understood too much of what had really happened that night. He'd known his father had failed to pay the rent again. He'd seen the ashen look on his mother's face. He'd comprehended the silent threat that had occurred as she'd been cornered against the wall, the man's glance in his direction telling her it was *him* – her six-year-old son – who was on the line if she didn't comply.

It was because of him that she had gone to the bedroom without a fight. It was because of him that she had humiliated and degraded herself with one after the other. It was because of him that she had cried night after night after it had happened.

He had seen the silent exchange between her and his father as the latter had offered no comfort, forging only a deeper emotional gap between them so he could deal with his own selfish anger.

Homer placed the knife down on Eden's chest and retrieved a packet of mints from his back pocket. Leaning back against the contraption, he peeled the packet open as if uncovering some priceless object on an archaeological dig.

'Apparently,' Homer said, rolling the mint between his thumb and forefinger to examine it as though it was a rare diamond. 'You fought back though. Or tried to. But you were knocked to the ground. You were given a packet of mints apparently.' He looked back at him. 'As compensation.'

He placed the mint in his mouth before making a mocking yum sound.

'Torren told me all about it,' Homer said. 'Just before he handed you and Jessie over to me. I needed to know, you see. I needed to make sure your memory didn't come back too soon. Torren tells me a trigger can make it return – some significant event from your past. And he told me the chances increase the more sensory that trigger is – like taste or, better still, smell. Because that guy made you eat them all in the end, didn't he, Reece? He told you that if you ate them all before the other guy was done, he'd leave your mother alone.'

Eden looked away and pressed his tongue to the roof of his mouth to stop himself from crying in frustration, in rage, at his most vulnerable secret being exposed and mocked.

Homer placed another mint in his mouth before crushing it between his teeth off the back of a triumphant smile.

'But he went in there anyway, didn't he, Reece? He watched you nearly choke on those mints and then he laughed as he headed into the bedroom regardless.'

It had taken him three days to tell Jessie the full story – the mints being thrown at him, how the man had gone back on his word, how he'd knocked Eden out cold when he'd tried to stop him.

How that was why he'd spent the last twenty years flipping mints in his mouth, reminding himself that he wasn't that helpless child anymore, desperately crunching his way through the packet in desperation to save his mother.

'So here we are,' Homer remarked. 'The bad guy, the mints. . .' He indicated Jessie. 'And the female you so desperately want to save from another three guys. For starters, that is. It must be like déjà vu.'

Eden shot his gaze to Jessie, who shook her head slightly as despair consumed her too.

'Because the Reeces might not owe rent this time,' Homer added. 'But you owe me an entire fucking row and crew that you burned to the ground.' He eased the gag down from Eden's mouth and held up a mint. 'And you're going to crush your way through this mint until you remember everything, so open wide,' he said, holding the mint above his mouth. 'Or Jessie will pay the consequence.'

❊ ❊ ❊

Watching Homer's turgid vileness spill out in front of her, Jessie warned herself to take calming breaths. She wanted to catch Eden's gaze, to plead with him not to give Homer the satisfaction, but she knew they would punish him until he did.

This was part of Homer's master plan. This was what he wanted her to witness: Eden's pain as his memory returned. As he realised the true extent of what awaited them both.

Of what he had done.

Through tear-smeared eyes she watched Eden jerk in discomfort, his eyes tightly closed, his jaw tight, his fingers flexed as his memory started to return.

'Torren did tell me it would be painful,' Homer said, stepping over to join her. 'Like one hell of a fucking migraine apparently.' He brushed her hair from her perspiring brow as he loomed over her. 'I did warn you, Jessie. I warned you that if you told him anything, I would make him suffer.

'Now every con in this room is going to play their part, each taking it in turn with those blades they're holding – avoiding all of the major organs, of course, to make it last as long as possible. And then I'm going to gut him, Jessie. I'm going to gut him right in front of you as the last thing he sees is me coming for you.'

Helpless to do anything else Jessie glowered deep into his eyes.

'And I'm going to have it filmed from every angle,' he said. 'Then I'm going to share it far and wide. This is the day Homer rises as *the* badass of Blackthorn – not Kane Malloy, not Jask Tao, not Caleb Dehain and most definitely not Eden Reece. This is the day *I'm* put in charge. And it starts *now*.'

Jessie opened her eyes to the monotonous beat of dustbin lids being struck – not just one now but four.

She looked across to Eden, to meet his brown eyes already awaiting hers.

Her swallow was hard and painful against her arid throat as apologies leaked silently from his eyes. As she saw the sense of failure in them as his memory fully returned.

Her Eden was well and truly back but for the first time she wished he'd been spared the burden.

She wanted desperately to be able to tell him that it was okay. That it was all going to be okay. But as much as they sought comfort in each other's gazes, they both knew it wasn't.

They each broke away temporarily as the tempo on the dustbin lids rose.

Mya stepped away from the wall. The only female aside from Jessie, the con paraded the room in a mock model walk, flipping one foot in front of the other, playing to both the crowd and the phones that were recording it all, forming a couple of poses with her knife to cheers and encouragement.

Relishing in the attention, she lifted her top, flashing the room to further whoops as she circled all the way round to the front of Jessie and Eden.

Her glance in Jessie's direction lingered, that sickening smile broadening before she stepped over to Eden. She dragged her blade from his neck to his chest, her eyes not leaving his despite the camera phones closing in, the increasing exultation of the cheers. Cheers that nearly blew the roof off as she lowered her head to Eden's groin to theatrically act out oral sex on him before sliding the blade down to his crotch.

Jessie's heart rate escalated to the point of pain as she stared across at Eden's wrists straining in their restraints, his glare locked on Mya.

The cheers lifted.

And Eden jolted, his teeth gritted as Mya ploughed her blade deep into his thigh.

Jessie flexed her fingers, almost ripping herself from the restraints as she willed herself across the room to shove Mya away, to silence the cheers as Mya strutted away, flicking her hair triumphantly to whoops of approval and admiration.

Eden closed his eyes, clearly trying to control the pain as the second con moved into view.

As one camera closed in to capture Eden's reaction, another closed in to catch hers.

And as the second blade was rammed into his side, Jessie screamed out behind her gag, only to be greeted with laughter from the con filming her.

She screamed again as she heard the third blade and then the fourth being thrust into the man she loved to further whoops of encouragement. Blades specifically placed to prolong his agony. Agony that would last for hours because of her. Because of the angel tears she had inflicted on him.

She balled her hands into fists. She tensed every muscle. As her heart blazed in a way she'd never known, she slammed her eyes shut and a yell of abject fury exploded from deep within her core.

❊ ❊ ❊

Amidst his torture, Eden felt a wave wash over him like the ripple of an earthquake.

His first thought was that it was death itself – that maybe he had passed out and that the last blade he'd felt had been the final one.

Instead he opened his eyes to a murmur of voices.

He opened his eyes to the same room – to the cluster of cons crowded around Homer with their phones.

'It's stopped working,' one said.

'Mine too,' another remarked.

Eden looked across to Jessie. His heart skipped a beat to see she was still alive. She was breathing heavily though, her complexion ashen. But it was her eyes staring at the ceiling that captured him the most – her pupils so dilated as to make her sockets appear like opals.

'I'm telling you it was a fucking EMP,' another con said somewhere in the background.

He switched his attention back to Homer, who was now staring directly at Jessie, his brow lowered quizzically and pensively.

'Everything in the room's been blown,' another con reported.

Homer held up his hand to command silence, his gaze not leaving Jessie.

'Shall we finish him?' another con asked.

'No,' Homer said pensively. 'Not yet. I believe we've just had a very fortunate turn of events.'

And Eden's stomach coiled as the faintest glimmer of a smile crossed Homer's lips.

# Chapter Fifty-Six

Jessie woke face first on a cold concrete floor, the chill permeating every inch of her skin. Her hands secured behind her back, she forced herself up onto her knees to find a sense of location in the dimly lit room.

'Jess!'

Jessie couldn't get to her feet quick enough before bolting towards the wall of bars that divided her from Eden.

She pressed her forehead and cheeks to the bars either side of her face as he did the same, urging herself closer as her lips finally met his.

'Eden. I thought I'd lost you. Where are we?'

She remembered the rage. She remembered the peculiar sensation washing over her.

'I don't know,' he said. 'I woke a few minutes ago.'

She looked at the blood trickling down the side of his head, at the bloodied clothes betraying the stab wounds that would have caused him to eventually bleed to death had it not been for the angel tears in his system already healing him.

She scanned the room of cages identical to the ones that bound them – there were maybe fifteen or twenty of them from what she could see, the darkness interrupted sufficiently by the cobwebbed, wall-mounted light above the hinged door.

'Did you see what happened?' she asked, looking back at him.

'That static isn't the only thing you can produce?'

The concern in his eyes did nothing to ease the pulse pounding in her ears.

'What did I do?'

'You wiped out all of their equipment, Jess. You gave out one hell of a short-range EMP by the seems of it.'

She'd always been able to produce spurts of static at her command, but never anything that powerful.

'Did you know you could do that?' he asked.

She shook her head. Not even when they'd killed Toby had the rage left her with such overwhelming power.

'Why are we still alive? Why are *you* still alive?' she asked, that being a bigger concern.

'That's what's worrying me.'

He nodded to her feet. 'I got the pins out of my back pocket that I used to get us into the flat when the bone feasters were chasing us. My padlock's too high for me to reach. Can you pick them up?'

Seeing the small, metal shards, Jessie turned her back to him. Sitting on the floor, she felt behind her. She picked them up with her index fingers and thumbs before coiling them into her palms as she pulled herself to her feet again.

'Try and undo yours,' Eden said. 'It'll be easier than trying to get to mine through the bars.'

Her fingers trembled enough for her to frustratingly drop one, losing time as she had to locate it again before getting back onto the floor to retrieve it.

Despite the setback, Eden watched on with patience as she got to her feet again.

'Just remember you were taught by the best,' he said, clearly trying to keep her panic to a minimum. 'It's all about feeling your way.'

As he flashed her a wink, she smiled at the recollection – the moment when they'd first started to form a bond of trust.

But realising he remembered was a double-edged sword.

'Eden, is your memory back fully? Do you remember everything?'

The pain in his eyes was palpable as he nodded. 'Everything.'

Pausing what she was doing for a moment, she stepped up to the bars wishing she could push her hand through to offer him some kind of reassurance. 'I'm sorry, Eden. I'm *so* sorry for what Torren has done to you. For what *they* did to you.'

'What they did to us both, Jess. None of this is your fault. Now just get those padlocks off, yeah?'

He rested his temple against the bars, keeping his voice low.

'Jess, if you can't make it to me in time—'

'Don't,' she said firmly.

'I don't know what Homer has planned, but we both know I'm dead anyway – whether by his hand or what's going to happen because of the tears in my system.'

'No,' Jessie said, shaking her head. 'I don't want to hear you talking like that, Eden.'

'You need to hear me talk like it because we have to work together on this. Homer's eyes lit up when he saw what you could do. He's going to use you somehow. I think I'm alive because he knows I'm the trigger to evoke the response in you.'

'Use me for what?'

'Against the army, I reckon. Those handheld transmitters might work at close range, but what you did was so much more powerful. If I was him, I'd be drawing the soldiers in right where I wanted them and knocking out their defence in one swoop.'

'He's going to use *me* to bring down the entire army?'

'I don't know, Jess. I'm speculating.'

'But at least if that happened, it would give our team a fighting chance.'

'And every one of my colleagues will be wiped out. It's not just Sirius's army out there. I know some of my ex-colleagues are abject dickheads, but on the whole they're good guys trying to earn a living just like I was. They've got families too. I'm trying to tell you that you have to get out of here. I'm big enough and good-looking enough to take care of myself if it comes to it.'

Jessie wriggled the pin in the lock more hastily. 'I'm not leaving without you, Eden. Don't you dare suggest it.'

'Listen,' he said firmly. 'I took that mint because I wanted to. I wanted to remember who I was. I wanted to remember my family. Most of all, I wanted to remember you. I wanted to remember what we are together, and how we got to that point. I wanted *you* to know I remember *all* of those precious moments. And if I don't make it through this, I wanted to go knowing I love you. I wanted you to know I remember why I love you.'

'Eden—'

The door behind her was shoved open. She looked over her shoulder to see four cons enter then looked back to Eden, her pulse racing as she concealed the pins in her palms again.

'We can't let them succeed,' Eden whispered. 'Whatever happens, I love you, Jess. That's all you need to remember.'

The four cons burst into his cell a few seconds later. They didn't give him a chance to protest as they beat him to the floor, Eden hard-pressed to retaliate with his hands bound and his ankles secured less than a foot apart in chains.

'You leave him alone!' Jessie demanded, following them along the periphery of her cage. 'You hear me!'

'Don't worry, chick,' one of the cons said, leering at her through the bars as they carried Eden out face down, each one holding a limb. 'We'll be back for you soon enough.'

# Chapter Fifty-Seven

Eden saw only grubby red carpet swaying beneath him; smelt only damp. They'd given him something. He'd felt the needle go into his arm. He'd felt the slight disorientation, the thickness in his head and vision.

The four cons carried him along narrow corridors and up low, broad stairs, through set after set of double doors.

As they descended into darkness, mustiness consumed the air around him. But it was soon replaced with an entirely different smell – one of sweat and cigarette smoke, drugs and alcohol.

He was brushed through mould-riddled curtains, wooden floor-boards staring him in the face. Then bright lights blinded him, and a wave of voices swept towards him.

Thrown inside another cage, he was held down by knees in his back as his ankles and wrists were uncuffed.

Once he was free, the four cons left the cage promptly, locking it behind them.

Eden stared around the empty thirty-foot-square space, up the full length of the bars crowned with coiled razor wire.

He looked ahead, his eyes adjusting to the spotlight.

And at least three hundred faces stared back at him. Three hundred faces sat in row after row, some in the aisles. He stared up at the dress circle above, then left and right at the boxes: the prime views of the stage.

The Theatre: con-entertainment central. The place where they paid to watch murder, maiming, torture, rape and assault. The place with no limits. The place where you needed an iron heart – and an iron stomach – to even step through the doors.

It was one thing he wouldn't have needed ten years of his memory back to remember. He'd grown up knowing what The Theatre was, even when he was still in Lowtown. There had always been whispers about it. Whispers from young lads without the sense to know just how sick what went on behind the walls was.

And tonight he was clearly the headline show.

His stomach churned as the audience knocked back their drinks and stuffed their faces as they looked on with interest, some laughing and joking like it was nothing more than a night down the pub.

His stomach coiled to a fist at the thought of what would come for Jessie, of what they had planned for her.

As if perfectly timed, Homer brushed through the curtains on the opposite side of the stage to his awaiting audience. Because *of course* it was perfectly timed. This *was* a show. This was Homer's show. This was Homer's finale for him. Maybe for them both.

Cheers and whoops and a round of applause rang out across The Theatre as Homer stepped centre stage, his back to Eden.

'Comrades,' he said, his palms uplifted in greeting like some theatrical televised preacher. 'Thank you for joining me for this momentous night. The night that *you* gain your freedom!'

The knot in Eden's stomach tightened.

Homer swept his arm right towards where he had entered.

The curtains billowed as two cons came through, dragging a limp, naked body between them. A bloodied, battered and castrated male body.

Eden barely recognised him at first his face was so swollen. But then bile rose from the pit of his stomach.

Sean.

'Here is our opposition,' Homer said, pointing his finger at Sean, who was barely conscious, hanging from the cons' arms like a rag doll. 'One of those who works for the traitors that sent us here to Blackthorn to live with the third-species scum. Third-species scum like her,' Homer added, sweeping his left arm towards the opposite side of the stage.

Eden lunged forward and clutched the cage bars in fury as Jessie was forced to her knees near the edge of the stage. Her hands were still bound at the small of her back by the padlocked chains, her ankles locked together by the same. Whether of her volition or just because they'd returned to her too soon, he couldn't be sure.

One of the cons fisted her hair in his hand as he tugged her head backwards with an aggression that made Eden's blood boil. Her eyes turned glossy as she surveyed the cage he was trapped in.

'*We* are human beings, yet our very own treat us as though we are not worthy to share the same air as them. They make decisions over us like they're somehow superior. They abandon us here while those like *her*,' Homer said, thrusting his forefinger in Jessie's direction again, 'are allowed to reside in places like Lowtown, even Midtown, while we are left to rot with the dregs.'

He stepped closer to the edge of the stage.

'But if to err is human,' Homer added, 'then that makes every one of us in here the most human of all.'

A flourish of cheers broke out around The Theatre, the stamping of approving feet resounding through the floor like a mini earthquake.

'Where are *our* rights?' he demanded, his palms upheld again. 'Who are *they* to tell us what's right and what's wrong? Who are *they* to tell us what we can and can't do? All *they* do is judge us and marginalise us. "Judge not lest thee be judged" – is that not what the good book teaches us? Does that not make *them* more sinful than us? Live and let live – is that not our very motto here in the south? Do we judge each other for our needs, our basic instincts? Our God-given right to express ourselves, to *be* ourselves? Yet they segregate us as if *we* are the monsters. They remove our human rights to act as we want to act, to think as we want to think, to be who we want to be. Who are *they* to dictate?'

More cheers erupted as some of the cons rose from their seats in applause, others pounding their boots against the floor.

'Natural selection, my comrades,' Homer continued. 'Are we responsible for others being weaker than we are? Is it not their place to be used to strengthen those of us able to survive? Is that not how nature works? Is that not how the natural order works? Does the gazelle not exist only to feed the lion?'

He indicated for the two cons to bring Sean forward, his knees scuffing on the floorboards as he remained too weak, too dazed, to defend himself.

'They might *think* they control us but *not* tonight. Tonight we will *not* be suppressed. Tonight we will regain our rights. Tonight we will be set free in every sense of the word. We will *all* be set free – through the very tunnel they used to enslave us!'

As cheers erupted again at a deafening volume, Homer stepped up to Sean.

Eden tightened his fists around the bars at the confirmation of his worst nightmare: that Sean had told him. That Homer was now aware of the wormhole too.

With Jessie, with The Theatre being so close to the tunnel, everything fell into place. They weren't only going to collapse the barrier – they were going to collapse everything that controlled the penitentiary. The electronic gates would swing open to announce their freedom into Lowtown. Every cell in the pen would slide back, freeing the cons within.

The army would be defunct without the use of their equipment. The cons would run riot with no motive other than destruction.

*If* Jessie was about to do what they hoped.

If they could drive Jessie to do what they hoped.

That was just as much what Sean's presence was about – for Homer to prove his threat to her.

'Tonight,' Homer said, his voice ringing out across the auditorium. 'We'll show them how it's done.'

Homer plunged the knife deep into Sean's groin before tearing upwards, causing his insides to spill out onto the stage as the con gutted him live for his audience.

Deafening cheers of approval broke out, whoops of triumph echoing into every recess.

Eden took a step back and clasped his head in his hands.

But the horror wasn't over. He opened his eyes just in time to see Homer swinging the fire axe downwards before lifting Sean's decapitated head to the audience.

'*This* is the way mankind began,' Homer said. 'The survival of the fittest, the strongest, the most *merciless*. And so shall it return!'

The whoops and cheers continued, but Eden tore himself away. Raking his hands back through his hair, he scanned the coiled razor wire thirty feet above him.

He could scale the bars, could even risk flipping over the razor wire if he gained the right momentum. Even with the sedatives throwing him off-kilter, he could try.

But even if he succeeded, there would be a hoard of cons awaiting him. And he knew without doubt that Jessie would suffer for his actions.

'And your freedom depends on *one* thing,' Homer added. '*Her.*'

Eden turned to see Homer thrusting his index finger back towards Jessie.

'And to get to her, to gain our freedom, we need to get to *him.*'

Eden narrowed his eyes at the pure hatred emanating back at him from Homer's, the con's face glowing with a smirk that disgusted him.

'Don't let the numbers on his arm fool you. Eden Reece is a Curfew Enforcement Officer through and through. He came here to deceive us. To spy on us. *He* was the one responsible for burning down Pummel's row. *Him* and *her.*'

As Jessie met his gaze again, Eden shook his head slightly, and he knew she'd understand. He knew she'd get the message: they couldn't let this happen.

'The question is: how quickly can we break her? How long will it take to break him before we break *her*? Line up, my friends, my comrades,' he shouted to the audience. 'Line up if you want to give it a go!'

As Jessie blinked away her tears of despair, he mouthed the only three words he could think to utter to her: *I love you.*

# Chapter Fifty-Eight

'It's like a fucking ghost town,' Kane remarked as he scanned the silent houses.

Never had he seen the south so empty. Never had The Circus been so shrouded with silence. His unease escalated amidst the freak occurrence.

The prospect that Torren had lied took hold. But Torren wasn't that stupid. The angel knew he didn't bluff. He knew he was going to find Eden and Jessie one way or another and take down as many angels as it took in the process, starting with their chief.

'Where the hell have they all gone?' Jask asked.

With a quick scan and nod to the scouts they had brought with them for backup in case it was a trap, Kane stepped out of the alley.

'Only one way to find out,' he replied, tapping Jask on the back before heading into what had once been Cyclops's row.

It was even eerier inside than out – no music, no crowds, no activity at all. Nothing but empty sofas and empty rooms.

Kane veered right as Jask took a left with Billy to check out the extended lounge. But nothing changed the deeper he delved into the row. All he saw was empty room after empty room.

Jask had clearly found the same as he was back by his side a few minutes later.

'I'm not liking this, Kane.'

'Tell me about it.'

'Is it possible that the army moved up from the south as well as down from the north?'

'Not according to my sources.'

'Fourth species?'

'Feels more like the second coming. Though I doubt this lot would be top of the VIP list for a priority entrance to paradise.'

Their gazes snapped simultaneously to the con who sauntered out of the kitchen. His youthful blue eyes widened as he caught sight of Kane and Jask before he instantly pivoted one-eighty to run back the way he'd come.

'Why do they always try to run?' Kane asked. 'You'd think they'd have learned by now.'

Jask shrugged. 'Evolutionary habits are hard to break. Talking of which, I'll take this one.'

Kane indicated for Billy to join him as they followed behind Jask.

'They've got to be here somewhere, right, Kane?' Billy asked, his eyes laden with worry.

'Even if they're not, I'll find them,' Kane said, the alternative unthinkable.

By the time they got outside, Jask was already dropping the con to the ground, the latter covering his head as if expecting a beating to follow.

'Anything?' Kane asked, not liking the look in his friend's eyes as he marched back past him.

'Yeah. We need to move faster,' Jask said. 'They're all at The Theatre.'

# Chapter Fifty-Nine

The atmosphere in The Theatre sparked with excitement and anticipation, filling Homer's soul with exultation that *he* had brought them together; *he* had made this happen.

The representatives selected to join Eden in the cage lined up at the front of the auditorium. Weapons weren't allowed in the first round. This was about building the tension, about building the agony, about the slow breaking of Eden Reece. This was about getting Jessie to snap just as she had last time. *Everything* depended on Jessie snapping as she had the last time.

The Theatre was positioned perfectly. All it would take, as he had been reliably informed, was a strong-enough charge to be channelled through the tunnel, the electromagnetic barrier acting like the sides of a pinball machine, guiding the charge to hit the central core. And then they would be freed – every last one of them.

It didn't matter what happened from there. What mattered was that they would be loose in Lowtown. They would disperse. They would wreak havoc. They would have their day, their revenge.

He would be known as the con who freed them all. The con who broke the system. He would be heralded the king of Blackthorn *and* Lowtown by the time he was done.

Soaking up the escalating anticipation, he turned to face Eden, who stood glaring right back at him. He had that same arrogant stance he'd had the second he'd walked into Pummel's row. The same defiant look in his eyes he'd had on the streets outside Jem's store. The same superior glower he'd had when he'd cornered them all with his threat of a lycan descent on the row.

And he had that same cockiness he'd had when they'd had their head-to-head clash at the foot of Pummel's stairs.

Only this time Eden was going to be the one left for dead.

Homer removed the packet of mints from his back pocket as he left his crew to align the waiting cons for their moment in the cage.

He tossed the packet through the bars. 'For old times' sake. Do you remember what I told you I was going to do to Jessie once you were dead?'

He didn't expect Eden to accept the mints, but he did. He bent down to lift them from the floor, unwrapped the packet a little further and placed one in his mouth.

Eden's glare lingered as he stepped closer to the bars, flipping the mint in his closed mouth. 'Because you're *all* man, aren't you, Homer? That's why you're staying safely out there instead of coming in here with me.'

He spat his mint through the bars, and it caught Homer on the side of the face.

With an infuriatingly confident smile, the CEO turned away again. More than that, he tore off his T-shirt and cast it aside. Turning to face the audience, he rolled his shoulders and flexed his arms behind his head in preparation, before casting Jessie a wink.

Homer knotted his hands into fists at the glint of admiration in Jessie's eyes. Even with both her and Eden knowing what was to come, their shared moment of strength infuriated him further.

He'd seen it too many times over the decades – her refusal to break. And now with Eden's nonchalance and defiance, it was being fuelled further.

Homer took a few steps back and nodded for the first to enter the cage.

However long it took, Jessie *would* break.

*Both* of them would.

❊ ❊ ❊

Jessie was torn between the compulsion to look and the need to keep her eyes closed, but the latter only exacerbated the stench of alcohol, of smoke, of other substances that had filled her nightmares for so many decades.

As Eden took blow after blow, though he inflicted more than his fair share too, Jessie knew the only thing she could do for him was to keep a hold of her emotions and make sure he wasn't battling for nothing.

After Homer's revelation she knew Eden was buying them time. By now Kane's feelers would well and truly be out. They were needles in a haystack, but the team would not give up on them. The team never gave up on each other. And the mass exodus of cons to The Theatre would have helped their cause. Word would have spread and, whatever situation the team were currently stuck in, Kane was too savvy not to put two and two together.

At least she hoped so because, right then, there was nothing either of them could do other than stay alive long enough for reinforcements to come.

She had to stay calm. She had to stay controlled. She couldn't give Homer what he wanted.

But it became increasingly difficult as con after con entered the cage, each failing to take Eden down as his street skills – as well as his training with the CEU and the lycans – took effect.

More worryingly, it was becoming apparent to Homer that there was more to Eden's strength, speed and stamina than just the possibility of her having given him her blood. It had evoked Homer's curiosity to the point that he'd sent her more than one suspicious glance.

She needed to retrieve the pins from her back pocket, having been forced to tuck them out of sight when Homer's men had returned to collect her. But the cons restraining her were watching her every move. If she slipped up just once, it would all be over.

She glanced back around the auditorium, back up at the razor-wire-topped cage Eden was held in. She had no idea how she'd get to him even if she did free herself.

No idea how she would get through so many cons.

She wasn't willing to give up hope though. Neither was she going to let Eden die tonight. Recollections of Toby entered her head. There was no way she was losing someone else she cared about. Someone she loved more than she'd ever thought possible.

Homer raised his hand. Raised two fingers for the crowds to see. Two fingers that sent the auditorium into more cheers as two cons entered the cage with Eden.

And this time they entered armed with baseball bats.

❋ ❋ ❋

His body ached, his muscles burned, his vision blurred and his head throbbed. He could barely see Jessie anymore through the blood that masked his eyes, but Eden knew he had to keep getting up.

He'd lost track of how long he'd been in there or how many cons had joined him, but Homer's impatience was beginning to show.

They threw him his own baseball bat but never gave him a chance to pick it up as they kicked it out from under him time and time again, mocking and jeering until he refused to give them any further satisfaction.

From what he could see as he wiped the sweat and blood from his eyes, the whole auditorium were on their feet now, their cheers and encouragement for their comrades ringing in his ears.

But there was still no sign of Kane or the others.

He *had* to stay alive. He *had* to stay strong. He had to give Jessie hope. They had to delay for as long as they could.

For her sake.

For Honey's sake.

For Lowtown's sake.

He would *not* let the bad guys win. He would not let them ransack his home again. He was stronger now. He was stronger than he'd ever been.

Because of Jessie he was stronger in every sense of the word.

Knocked to his knees, collapsing on all fours, he searched once more for her. He saw she was doing exactly what she was supposed to – keeping her eyes shut and her head lowered.

But he should have known Homer wasn't going to let her off that easily.

Eden raked his nails through the stage as the two cons manhandled her over to the bars. They tugged back her head to reveal her face – streaming with tears – before forcing her eyes open.

The cons in the cage came at him simultaneously, each swiping at him with their baseball bats in turn, each knocking him further and further to the ground.

And even when he was flat on the floor, they didn't stop.

He felt another sharp needle in the back of his neck – another sedative to weaken him even further. He could barely feel his limbs, could barely move. And when another swipe of a baseball bat hit him in the lower spine, he could no longer lift himself from the floor.

The cage clunked open. More entered.

He knew then that any reinforcements would be too late.

❋ ❋ ❋

Jessie clenched her hands into fists in their binds, her throat tight with repressed tears, her chest aching with the pain of her self-restraint as any window of opportunity to escape continued to elude her.

With every thud of wood against flesh, her heart broke a fraction more. She clenched her jaw as she fought to keep Eden's wishes at the forefront of her mind – his wish to save the thousands back in Lowtown from the fate that would await them should she fail. Thousands like his family, like Honey. Those who didn't deserve to have cons running amok on their streets. Cons who, right then, were showing the true extent of what would befall all of Lowtown if they were set free.

And Eden took every blow for it – Eden, who knew he wasn't going to make it out of Blackthorn anyway. Eden, who had even relinquished hope for his beloved niece in the process, the pain of which must have been killing him more than the blows cruelly inflicted on him.

'As soon as you've done what you need to, it'll end,' Homer said in her ear. 'We can let him go quickly, or we can drag this out. *You* get to choose how much he carries on suffering. Finishing this is under *your* control, Jessie.'

Fury scorched her every vein and every sinew, but she fought to do what Eden had asked. For Eden, for all he had suffered, she wanted the strength to make sure it wasn't for nothing; her worse betrayal to him at that moment for him to believe it was all for nothing.

'Time's up,' Homer eventually declared curtly in her ear before standing. 'Flip him over!'

She could barely breathe. The two cons holding her tightened their grasp as a third handed Homer the knife he'd used to gut Sean. Her pulse thrummed in her ears, her heart pounding as light-headedness consumed her vision, the room, the cage, swaying in front of her.

'We finish him,' Homer called out to the crowd as he stepped up to the edge of the stage again, 'and *then* we start on her.' He pointed his finger towards Jessie again to another cheer of apocalyptic proportions. 'You *shall* have your freedom, comrades. And *nothing* is going to stop us now!'

Homer moved round to the edge of the cage. The door clunked open.

His eyes leaked with venom as he stared down at Eden, barely on the edge of consciousness, pinned on his back beneath him.

The tightness in Jessie's chest intensified to the point she stopped breathing. She was a split second from elbowing the cons aside and throwing herself at the cage.

But instead of driving the knife down into Eden, Homer looked back out over the crowds. 'We're ready!' he declared to more whoops and cheers. 'To the outpost!'

# Chapter Sixty

The four cons carried Eden face down ahead of her, up the length of the aisle. Amidst more whoops and cheers, with hisses and curses now thrown into the mix, pieces of food were tossed in Eden's direction to a barrage of name-calling and false accusations.

Jessie closed her eyes to the horror of it as she was carried out the same way to even more jeers.

It felt like she was in the midst of some ethereal nightmare as the cons piled out onto the mist-filled streets, missing only their pitchforks and blazing torches held aloft.

She tried desperately hard to keep Eden in view, but the crowds quickly broke them up as three hundred cons headed to some central point that had yet to be identified.

And it was only when those crowds slowed to a standstill, when she was ushered through the parting masses, that the full horror of what was to happen became apparent.

What were nothing more than unassuming, rusting double gates into some distant tunnel took on a whole new significance.

They were giving themselves the best shot they could and with the army probably barely having reached the hub, they were counting on having enough time to storm the exit point. That meant time was up. That meant it was about to be over for Eden.

She was forced down onto her knees again, bile clogging the back of her throat as she watched the con shimmy up the flagpole through the mist, ten feet away from the gates, the coil of rope wrapped over his shoulder.

She looked back to where Eden was lying supine, horrifyingly still conscious but with insufficient strength to fight the four cons who pinned him at the foot of the pole.

The rope was dropped from forty feet above. Dropped to Homer, who proceeded to tie it into a noose.

Everything became a blur as blood thrummed in her ears, as her heart beat so fast, pounded so hard, that she swayed at the rush of blood that left every extremity.

'This is the border that scum like this one think they own,' Homer yelled out to the crowds as he pointed down at Eden. 'Not anymore! As of tonight, this tunnel that was used to imprison us will now be used to free us!'

More cheers filled the cold night air.

'There will be no Blackthorn–Lowtown divide – there will only be Blacktown!'

The cheers switched to whoops and the stomping of feet.

As the two cons that held her remained distracted by Homer's speech, as they released her to clap their hands above their heads, she strained her wrists so she could finally reach into the back pocket of her jeans for the pins.

Keeping a wary eye on both cons, she lowered herself tighter to her haunches and dropped her head back slightly so her long hair would mask what she was doing from the cons standing behind. Then she slipped the pins into the padlock that bound the chains around her ankles.

She'd managed it once but had been forced to click the padlock shut again when the cons had returned, not allowing her enough time to free her hands either. If they'd found the pins, she would have thrown away her only hope of escape.

She knew she needed to blank everything out. She knew she needed to focus. She needed to use everything Eden had taught her that night in his room in Pummel's row: how being able to pick locks was as much about feeling her way through it, and tuning in to every slight hitch of metal, than it was about seeing. How *he* had taught her how to feel her way.

She wouldn't be able to take them all, but neither was she going to die on her hands and knees. Neither was she allowing them to inflict that final cruelty on Eden, that final humiliation. She would die trying to stop it before it got to that.

As the padlock clicked open, she carefully unwound it before clicking it shut again, lying it on the chains so it wouldn't look any different.

She knew she needed to be subtler, but her adrenaline pumped, her need for speed seeping into her clumsy fingers as she fumbled to get them into the right position whilst tucking the next padlock between her hands.

'And like the great warriors, the great leaders, the great men who made this country what it is, we will hang, draw and quarter our enemies at the gates! We will leave our enemy hanging as warning that they do – not – fuck – with – *us*!'

The roar of the cons was deafening.

Homer lowered himself to his haunches and wrapped the rope around Eden's neck before tightening it. He stood again, brandishing the blade he'd used to slaughter Sean, and held it aloft to more raucous cheers and pounding feet.

Jessie fumbled and cursed as Homer moved back to Eden, looming over him. He lifted the knife, and she stopped breathing as a hundred slow-motion images of him gutting Sean tumbled through her head.

Amidst the chants and encouragement of the crowd to slay the stranger who lay at his feet – Eden, who was already judged and deemed the enemy without question or mercy – her fingers fumbled helplessly with the lock, despair ricocheting through every nerve-ending.

And as Homer pulled back ready to stab downwards, Jessie cried out in panic, the padlock simultaneously clicking open.

Jessie broke her wrists free of the chains that unravelled. She slammed her hands onto concrete, her body shuddering with the force of the energy involuntarily sweeping from it like a tsunami.

The crowd instantly switched from a thunderous roar to deafening silence as all eyes snapped from the imminent hanging to her.

Cracks splintered through the concrete from her fingertips, the cons stumbling back to avoid them as the ground shook beneath them. Cracks that fractured the ground all the way to where Homer was standing twenty-five feet away.

Invisible to all but her, the pulse of powerful energy left her like a silver tidal wave. Like a stone had been dropped in a pond, the ripples swept away from her.

And as the electro-magnetic charge reached the gates, there was the subtlest of clinks amidst the silence before the electronic gateway creaked open.

Jessie held back a breath, the horror of what she had caused becoming too stark a reality as she met Homer's gaze through the mist, a sickening smile crossing his lips.

Cheers erupted. The stampede was instant.

The jostling around her forced Jessie to protect her head as the mass evacuation began by those for whom not even a live hanging was a sufficient draw when freedom beckoned.

Cons leapt over the cracks and fissures she had created as they ploughed towards their freedom – into the penitentiary tunnel towards Lowtown beyond.

And as she looked up through the crowds on all fours, Eden now lost in the chaos, the deepest sense of failure consumed her.

This catastrophic turn of events was not supposed to happen. This had never been part of the prophecy. The cons' escape had *never* been on the cards.

Now *she* had changed that. Her interference, her falling for Eden, her weakness, had changed that.

*This* was what happened when angels interfered. *This* was her punishment. She had to stop it. Somehow she had to stop it.

But as the crowds dispersed around her, Jessie saw Homer tightening the noose around Eden's neck despite the stampede. As he looked over his shoulder, ready to give the con up the flagpole the signal, Jessie simultaneously felt a sharp tingle in the pit of her spine.

She gasped at the familiarity of the sensation. The sensation she should have seen coming. The sensation that told her she had seconds left.

This was a major alteration to the prophecy, changing its direction *again*. And she knew what came next.

The flashing lights erupted, shooting pains hit her neck and shoulders, blood rushed to her head.

With every ounce of strength that she had, Jessie lunged forward, losing the loose chains from her ankles.

She knew exactly what she had to do. She knew exactly where she had to go.

As bolts of electricity shot out from her spine as the new message, the new prophecy, arrived, she raced forward.

Because this one wasn't going to bring her to her knees. Not yet. There was no way she was going to be drawn into the hypnotic state that would come. She would die suppressing it if it meant saving Eden.

Homer gripped his blade as he saw her closing in on him, his eyes narrowing as he prepared to take her on.

But it wasn't Homer she was aiming for.

Jessie fell onto all fours over Eden just as the powerful electric current exploded from her spine – lightning bolts charging the air around her in a multicoloured electrical display.

Intensified and strengthened by the water droplets in the mist, the charge carried far and fast, connecting every one of the cons around her like a macabre dot-to-dot.

Cons shuddered and fell as they were electrocuted on the spot, Jessie's electrical wings remaining spread over Eden in all their iridescent, sparkler-like glory, safeguarding him in her self-made bubble.

Removing the noose from his neck one-handed, she brushed her hand down his cheek to see he had regained enough consciousness to meet her gaze, to take in the bright lights cascading around him.

As he smiled, albeit it weakly, as he showed her he understood, she smiled back in relief.

But the headache inevitably hit. The intense headache that wouldn't let up until she recorded the new prophecy. The headache that would only ease once she'd let herself slip into the hypnosis that was demanded of her.

But she wouldn't leave him. Nor could she let her guard drop for a moment.

Looking up, squinting through her migraine, through the translucent display, she watched Homer drag himself to his feet from where he'd been thrown a few feet away.

Only her blood in his system had saved him, that much she knew.

He stumbled towards them, the blade back in his hands, his eyes blazing with the incessant need for final vengeance.

She blinked away pain-induced tears, closed her eyes and gritted her teeth as she forced back the overpowering need to relent to the trance.

She forced it back until everything started to turn black, as the force of the migraine threatened to split her head apart, her wings naturally starting to weaken and disperse.

As droplets of blood landed on Eden's cheek – Eden who had finally lost consciousness – she pressed her fingers under her nose, knowing the source of the bleed.

'No,' she muttered to herself, her tears merging with blood. 'No, *please.*'

She looked up to see Homer standing over her, the con swaying as her strength finally waned.

And then, somewhere to her right, she recognised the voice suddenly demanding Homer's attention.

'You stay the fuck away from my little brother, you bastard!'

# Chapter Sixty-One

Jessie woke to an eerie silence. She stared straight up into brown eyes as Eden gazed down at her.

'You've got to stop this passing out on me just as it gets interesting,' he said.

As he smiled, she smiled back, but it was fleeting. She reached up to touch his cut and bruised face, the relief that they'd both made it overwhelming her enough to bring her to tears.

She pressed the heel of her palm to her forehead at the shock of it all, not even daring to take in the aftermath as she wrapped her arms around his neck, clinging on with every iota of strength she had left.

'Hey, it's okay,' he said, holding her against him.

She looked over her shoulder to where the gates lay open, all the cons having now dispersed, those that hadn't lying dead amidst the fissures.

'How *can* it be?' she asked, looking back at him. 'Eden, look what I've done. I'm so sorry.'

'For saving my life? *Again?*'

'That's quite some snow globe you had going there,' she heard a familiar voice say behind her.

Jessie snapped her attention over her shoulder. 'Jask, you're awake!'

'And just in time by the looks of it,' the lycan remarked. 'I leave you lot unattended for five minutes. . .'

Her relief dispersed as reality struck again. The reality she had caused.

'Jask—'

'No apologies,' Jask said firmly, his azure eyes sombre. 'You did what you had to. We'll sort it.'

As Eden helped her to her feet, Billy came up from behind her to give her a hug, pulling her into him as tightly as he could. He kissed her affectionately on the temple.

'Thank you,' he said. 'My brother's *official* guardian angel.'

She turned in his arms to face him; gripped his upper arms amidst her relief at seeing him. 'Looked to me like you were both of ours. Where is he? Where's Homer?'

Billy cocked his head over his shoulder to where a couple of the cluster of people in the distance moved, revealing Homer on his knees amongst them.

She gripped Billy's arms tighter as the con's icy grey-eyed stare locked on hers.

She looked to Eden. 'What are they going to do with him?'

'They've left it up to us.'

She flinched as a siren broke out. A siren none of them ever thought they'd hear, the breakout in the penitentiary meaning everyone beyond the wall had to be warned to get inside and go on lockdown.

'We've got very little time to get back under cover,' Kane said, joining them. 'The army would have heard all the activity, not to mention seen the lightshow.'

'How bad is it?' Jessie asked.

'Scale of one to ten? Best get a bigger scale,' Kane replied.

Jessie stared around at the aftermath; a particular mop of blonde hair captured her attention amidst the dead cons.

Mya.

She wished she could have felt regret or a glimmer of empathy at least, but she felt nothing.

She grabbed Eden's hand and looked from him to Kane to Jask. 'We can't let the cons run amok in there. What are we going to do?'

'We're forging a new plan,' Kane said. 'At least the tunnels are open again.'

'But do we have the resources to take on the cons as well as the army now?'

Kane's troubled gaze said it all.

'We'll sort it,' Jask said, recapturing her attention. 'Like I said, you did what you had to, Jessie. And though it might not feel like it, you did right. We need this boy of yours – now more than ever.'

'He's right,' Kane said. 'So don't be so hard on yourself. And *you*,' he added, his navy eyes meeting Eden's. 'Enough hogging the limelight for one night. We've got work to do.'

Kane strode away but glanced over his shoulder to send Eden a wink. 'It's good to have you back in one piece though, buddy.'

'Just tell me you love me, Kane!' Eden called after him. 'Stop repressing it!'

Without turning back around, Kane flipped him the middle finger before joining the cluster standing amidst the mist and awaiting his next command.

Jask shook his head, sighing at the pair of them before he clipped Jessie on the chin. 'You fit enough to get moving?'

She nodded.

As Jask stepped away to head in the direction of the cluster, as Billy tapped his brother affectionately on the arm before joining him, she looked back at Eden. 'They came looking for us, didn't they? I told you they would.'

'They knew we were in the south, Jess. They've got Torren. They threatened to have Caitlin read Ziel and him unless he revealed where we were.'

Her heart skipped a beat. 'Do they *still* have him?'

'They sure do.'

Jessie looked back at the gaping tunnel, a faint idea forming.

'Jess, there's something you need to know.'

Her heart pounded as she met his gaze, his thumbs brushing her hips as he held her against him.

The glossing of his eyes had her clutching his forearms. She knew it couldn't have been bad news about Honey or she would have seen it in Billy.

'What?' she demanded quietly, despite being uncertain whether she wanted to know.

'Kane and Jask also got the truth out of Torren about the angel tears.'

She stopped breathing as her eyes searched his.

'Me and Honey are going to be okay.'

Her stomach flipped. She tightened her grip on his forearms. 'What? *How*? For *real*?' she asked breathlessly.

'For real,' he stated with a smile.

She pulled him against her, even the shrill sound of the siren fading into the background. Wrapping her arms around him as he reciprocated, she clung onto him with every ounce of strength, one hand reaching for his neck as her tears of relief dampened his shoulder.

She forced herself to pull back so she could look him in the eyes. She clasped either side of his neck. 'There's a cure?'

'You could say that. Not that me and Honey need it. He was keeping things from you, Jess. The problems the soldiers are facing, that The Facility discovered, are only related to warrior tears.'

She stared deep into his eyes as she tried to take it in amidst everything else. 'But not mine?'

'Envoi tears are the cure, Jess,' he said, brushing his fingers back through her hair. 'Envoi tears are the permanent cure.'

Her relief soon merged with anger to the point she tried to take a step back. 'That bastard!'

'Hey!' Kane called out. 'We're out of here! Now!'

They followed the direction his finger was pointing and saw the mist intensifying in the distance, subtle hues of colour changing within it.

The thrumming in her ears followed a second later.

'Company?' Eden asked her.

She nodded. 'The worst kind.' She glanced back at Homer being dragged to his feet. 'Almost.'

When she looked back to Eden she saw his eyes had narrowed pensively on Homer.

Homer glowered back at him, but Jessie knew fear when she saw it.

Eden glanced over his shoulder at the rope, the noose, still lying on the floor, still attached to the pole Homer was going to hang him from.

He looked back at her. 'Those bone feasters, please tell me they can they climb.'

# Chapter Sixty-Two

'Why is the siren going off?' Cameron – vice chair of the Global Council – asked as he ploughed along the carpeted halls. 'Please tell me it's a false alarm.'

'There's been a malfunction at the penitentiary, sir,' Ranson declared as he marched alongside him, matching his strides on their way down to the control room.

'What kind of malfunction?'

'The electronics have failed.'

'The backup generator?'

'Failed, sir.'

Cameron came to a standstill. 'You're telling me nothing is currently operating in the penitentiary?'

'I'm telling you all systems have failed, sir. One of the guards manually raised the alarm from the tower.'

'How? *How* has this happened?'

'The only thing that could be responsible for wiping out both the main system and the backup is something the equivalent—'

'Of a lighting strike. A very large lighting strike, for which the building is fully conducted. So *how*?'

'We think it was an EMP, sir. An electromagnetic—'

'I know what an EMP is, Ranson. How did it permeate the electromagnetic barrier?'

'We think it went off near the penitentiary tunnel, sir. The EMP bounced off the walls like a pinball. It blew out the circuits along the way.'

'Has this been done on purpose?'

'It was very precisely located, sir, to maximise impact. So, yes, it's possible.'

Cameron carried on walking. 'And what's the current situation?'

'The cells will obviously have opened automatically. The lock-and-key system was done away with years ago, as you know. At the last report, some of the cons have dispersed back into Blackthorn but most headed directly out into Lowtown.'

'How far did this EMP stretch?'

'It hit the Midtown border, sir.'

'*Midtown*? Tell me the border is still effective?'

'We'll need to transfer extra staff from the Summerton border.'

'Decrease security at Summerton?' He exhaled curtly. 'I'm not politically suicidal. What about the army?'

'They're still in Blackthorn, sir. They'd reached the hub on the cusp of the south at the time the EMP struck.'

'What updates have they given?'

'Sir, *everything* is run on technology. It would have wiped out their suits, their communication, everything.'

Cameron came to another standstill. 'You're telling me I have over three hundred soldiers trapped in there with no communication and no leadership, civilians left unprotected in Lowtown, cons running amok, third species goodness knows where and inadequate force to protect ourselves within Midtown too?'

'Reinforcements are on the way, sir, but it could take several hours. We had bled all surrounding locales dry of security for this one cause.'

Cameron marched into the operations room. He stared at the array of blank screens in front of him, the sources responsible for feeding the information into them defunct.

'We're maybe a couple of hours away from having a literal war zone on our doorstep. Loss of life doesn't bear thinking about, sir.'

'Get as many as you can onto the Midtown border now. And get the armoured trucks in to get our soldiers out for fuck's sake.'

'Yes, sir,' he said, marching back over to the doors.

'And Ranson.'

Ranson turned back around. 'Yes, sir?'

'Get hold of Matt Morgan. I need the head of the TSCD here. And get me Sirius Throme on the phone – *now*.'

# Chapter Sixty-Three

'Are you sure you want to do this alone?' Eden asked.

Jessie nodded. 'I have to try and reason with him first. His pride is guaranteed to get in the way if you come with me.'

'You know what I think: you're wasting your time.' Eden shrugged with reluctant acquiescence. 'You're a better person than me.'

'I'd reserve that judgement for after I'm done.'

He smiled. 'That's my girl.'

She slid her hand up his chest to cup his neck; leaned in to caress his lips with a lingering kiss, his reciprocation warm, tender, reassuring.

'Always,' she confirmed.

'Whatever he tells you, you didn't deserve it,' he reminded her.

She nodded, finally knowing it was true. 'I know,' she declared with conviction. 'And neither did you.'

Her thumbs brushed his ears on her way to gently clasping the back of his neck.

She'd never forget seeing him reunited with Honey. She'd never forget the tightness of his grip as he held his little niece against him. His tears of relief would remain engrained in her memory forever.

She kissed his lips once more. 'Unbreakable, right?'

'*Always*,' he declared with a smile. 'And we'll keep proving it.'

'This doesn't mean I've forgiven him though, Eden. Nor will I ever forget what he's done to you. What he tried to do to us.'

'Then go get him, Jess,' he said. 'Because if you don't, you know *I* will.'

The light broke through from the grate above, illuminating Torren with its subtle glow.

Torren exhaled tersely as soon as he saw her. 'You just keep bouncing back, don't you, Jesca?'

She stopped a few feet away from the beam he was manacled to. 'We need help from the Angel Parliament, Torren. The tunnel between Blackthorn and Lowtown has been breached. The cons have spilled from the penitentiary. With the resources we have we can match the army, but it won't be long before they send reinforcements in. We can't handle that and deal with the cons. There are hundreds of them on the loose. And we still don't know how many fourth species are out there.'

'Sounds to me like your little team is fucked, Jesca.'

Jessie stepped closer to him, reminding herself to keep calm. 'Lowtown is full of people, Torren. Humans *and* third species who have done nothing to deserve being caught in this crossfire. I have seen, first-hand, fifty years' worth of what those cons are capable of. They're out there only to wreak havoc and take down as many as they can in the process. This is not the prophecy – this is mayhem.'

'And as I told you, Jesca, we do not intervene. We are forbidden to intervene.'

'You know the consequences if we don't.'

'Yes. Fate,' he said. 'Suck it up, Jesca. The new world order starts today.'

Jessie bit into her bottom lip and folded her arms as she dropped her gaze. When she looked back up into his eyes, she saw the first glimmer of uncertainty flash across them.

'I was really hoping you would change your attitude,' she said. 'I really wanted you to change your attitude so it wouldn't come to this.'

His eyes narrowed. 'Are you threatening me? If you're threatening me, you fucking well untie me and *then* try threatening me.'

She moved a little closer. 'Trust me, I'm not scared to.'

'Let – me – go,' he warned, his glower unflinching. 'They might not have the sense, but you know better. Take a close look at my wings, envoi. Take a close look at the battles I have fought and won over the centuries. Do not think the Angelic Parliament will go down without a fight. They will rip your friends apart, and you will remember your place.'

'My *place*? The hierarchy that claims warriors have supremacy over envois?'

'I have warned you for the last time, Jesca.'

'You lied to me. Eden was never going to die from my tears, and you knew it.'

The utter indifference in his eyes behind what she could only interpret as a glint of triumph nudged her barely-contained rage up a notch.

'Tell me, did he make it too?' Torren asked. 'Did he have a good time in there? Did he enjoy mingling with the natives?'

She drew back her fist, smacking him hard enough in the jaw to graze her knuckles.

His indignant glare shot back to hers.

'I owed you that one.' She took another step closer. 'And guess what, Torren? I love him more than ever. I've *always* loved him, as you well know. And now I know how much, thanks to you giving me my memory back. Best of all, so does Eden. Because thanks to you, I've now proven to him just how much. You failed, Torren. Better still, you've brought us closer than ever. You've made us stronger than ever.'

'And you've just made your biggest mistake.'

'No,' she said. '*You* did. And now I'm here to abide by *your* rules. Because however you look at it, you *did* intervene. The cons are free because of the chain of events *you* started. A chain of events you started not for the good of the prophecy but out of *your* need for revenge.' She stepped closer still, held her gaze steadily and squarely on his. 'That puts a whole new spin on this, doesn't it, Torren? Because being an envoi, being the librarian of our kind, I know a lot of things. More to the point, I now *remember* a lot of things thanks to you giving me my memory back. One of those is that as the chief of the Angelic Parliament, you hold more accountability than anyone else.'

His eyes flared, negating her need to ask her question.

But she asked it anyway.

'And we *both* know what that means, don't we, Torren?'

# Chapter Sixty-Four

'There!' Iona said as she looked down from the turret. 'What is that?'

Novak frowned at the figure moving through the long grass towards them. The figure he'd been called into Torren's quarters to check out.

'Get everyone on standby,' he commanded.

The angel spun on her heels as Novak continued to stare out of the window.

Even his superior vision wasn't clear enough to determine what was approaching. But the closer it got, the more a sense of unease tightened in his chest.

As she drew closer, her long, dark ringlets billowing behind her in the dawn light, she became unmistakable.

Jesca.

And she carried something with her – something that flattened the long grass behind her like the train of a wedding dress.

He scanned the other figures rising from the grass in a peripheral formation. Somehow their hideout had been exposed, their haven on the cusp of being invaded.

And as he heard the creak of the roof tiles above him, he knew there was only one species who could move so stealthily, so adeptly; could scale their walls undetected.

He let out a frustrated and indignant sigh.

*Lycans.*

Novak turned on his heels. He marched out of Torren's quarters, it now being clear where – or, more to the point, why – their chief had disappeared.

'Get armed!' Novak barked to any of the angels not yet moving quickly enough as he ploughed down the hallway towards the top of the stairs. 'We don't know if they have an angel breach. They could be in here in minutes. MOVE IT!'

Nine others moved in behind him, each in strategic formation, their crossbows and spears poised and ready.

Novak braced himself at the top of the stairwell. The likelihood was that Malloy was involved too. Only a master vampire would dare summon their chief, that in itself a declaration of war.

But only one figure ascended the stairs towards them – slowly, calmly and resolutely.

And it was only when she reached the stairwell directly below that the horror of why she was there became apparent.

He didn't know whether to fly at the envoi in rage or indignation.

But reluctantly he backed up, having no choice other than to respect angelic law as she stepped up through the barrier, dragging her spoils of war behind her.

Spoils of war she dared to throw in front of the shocked angels.

Novak stared down at Torren's wings – cut from his body – unmistakable from the tattoos they were covered in.

He glowered back up at Jessie, who stared right back at him.

'What the *fuck* have you done?' he demanded quietly.

'Don't worry,' she said, 'he's still alive.'

'I *won't* let this happen,' Novak warned. *No way* was he allowing an envoi to do this.

'You have no choice,' she said. 'Not unless you too want to defy angel law – like Torren has. You know the implications of that. I've brought you the chief's wings, Novak. That puts *me* in charge now. It puts me in charge of you all.'

'You're an *envoi*,' he reminded her. 'You have neither the right nor the capability.'

'You know as well as I do, as *everyone* stood here knows, bringing you those wings prove otherwise. Just as you know that refusal to adhere to the law will result in banishment to the Brink upon death.'

She scanned the now crowded room.

'You did right to get your weapons together because it's about time you actually did some good around this place,' she said, addressing them all. 'We have a war to fight in Lowtown, and we have people to get safely through to Midtown and Summerton beyond. As of now we're *all* on the front line.'

# Chapter Sixty-Five

Sirius stared down at the busy Summerton streets below as people – *his* people – milled about their daily lives, sandwiches in hand as they rushed back and forth from work during lunch breaks, others chatting and laughing casually on benches.

His people. *His* world. Which he *would* keep safe until the moment he could recreate it.

He glanced over his shoulder as the knock on the door was followed by Sharner entering the room.

'Cameron is still trying to get hold of you, sir.'

'Fuck Cameron. What's happening with my team?'

'Still no contact. All the systems are down. They will resort to plan B.'

Plan B: the reason he'd turned his army superhuman should the eventuality arise that it be necessitated. The equipment was merely the bonus.

'Their sights will remain firmly set on Malloy,' Sharner added.

'Who could be in Blackthorn, in Lowtown or in the tunnels on his way to fucking *Summerton* already if rumours of their existence are true.'

Sirius turned and walked over to the table.

Sharner backed away, no doubt recalling the last time he'd imparted similar news. 'Sir, I'm here because Feinith called.'

Feinith who, as was now abundantly clear, had been double-crossing him all along.

Feinith who was tucked in Blackthorn, no doubt still with Caleb Dehain.

'Ready to hand herself in? With news about Malloy, I hope?'

'With a message to pass on from Dehain. Dr Throme, he says he wants Jarin.'

Sirius laughed, irritation simmering deep that the vampire thought he could negotiate with him. 'Jarin? Does he think I'm stupid?'

'That's not all.' Sharner hesitated for a moment. 'Caleb Dehain's claiming he's the vampire leader.'

Sirius held his gaze as though waiting for the punch line.

'Feinith corroborated it, sir.'

'And we believe everything Feinith tells us.'

'He's also claiming to have Doyle. He said he now has your army under his control, and he's about to get his hands on Malloy too. Apparently he's willing to talk though. He said Jarin's your ticket in; that this is your last chance to stop the war.'

Sirius snapped the pencil he held in his hand. 'Do you have a number? Get him on the phone.'

'Sir, the EMP. . .' But he instantly seemed to think better of providing an explanation. 'He said he'll only talk to you in person. He said he wants you to go into Blackthorn to meet with him face to face.'

Sirius laughed again at the absurdity of it despite his indignation leaving a bitter aftertaste. 'And if I don't?'

'Caleb claims he's going to get through the Midtown border. He said he'll come to *you*. But if he has to do that, he'll kill Malloy before he does.'

# Chapter Sixty-Six

'You're making a mistake, Caleb,' Feinith said, hot on his heels. 'Stop blocking me out of this!'

Caleb strolled down the hallway towards his bedroom, ignoring her persistent protests. Protests that were starting to grate intensely.

'This is an insane plan!' she declared. 'Do you hear me? You think Sirius is going to comply? You've put us *all* in danger by threatening Malloy. For all he knows, he's dead already. And now you've revealed who you are, he will destroy this entire district – and Lowtown with it! What the *fuck* were you thinking?'

He spun to face her and pressed her back up against the wall, slamming both her hands either side of her head in a move that made her flinch with the force of it.

Her grey eyes satisfyingly flared, her breath hitched.

'Still such little faith in me,' he said, the uncertainty in her eyes telling him just how much she was starting to question his sanity. 'After *all* these years.'

'It's not that,' she insisted, switching from accusation to placation at his sudden proximity – and no doubt the look in his eyes. 'But what you're doing doesn't make any sense.'

'You don't think so?'

'Sirius is *not* going to put himself on the line for this.'

'We'll see.'

He let her go to turn and reach for the door to his quarters.

'Listen to me,' Feinith said, sliding between him and the door to block his way. 'Why? Why would you expose who you are to Sirius? What could you possibly gain? Caleb: the great strategist. The vampire of his people. The one who wanted nothing to do with the Higher Order. Who preferred to slum it here rather than secure himself a place in Midtown. Where are your people in your hierarchy of priorities now? Why couldn't you just let Sirius believe it was Jarin?'

'Because I want him, Feinith. Because before I do anything else, I want Jarin.'

'What does it matter anymore?'

The fact she had to ask was yet another reminder that, even now, she still barely understood him.

'Because he came after Jake, that's why it still matters. Because destroying Seth wasn't enough for him.'

'And Seth is gone,' she said, her cold hand cupping his face. 'I'm sorry, Caleb, but Jake is dead. Killed by that bitch of a serryn. It's her we should be trying to find. It's her you should be out there seeking, not Jarin. You have to kill *her* first. You *have* to gain your Tryan status. Only then are you guaranteed to win this.'

She caught hold of his shirt and lifted her lips to his.

'Find her,' she whispered, her grey eyes penetrating deep into his as their breaths mingled. 'Be the hunter you are. Become the *king* that you are. Find that serryn and bring her back here. End this. Make us win. Don't let Jake have died for nothing.'

Her fingers tightened in his black shirt as she took a step back, crossing the threshold into his quarters, into the library, her heel catching the door and making it swing open behind her.

Before her lips were able to touch his, his gaze snapped across her shoulder.

The secret bookcase door lay open. A figure stood motionless in the middle of the room. A girl with russet hair and hazel eyes he had once almost died in.

Except this time there was a whole other type of fire in her eyes.

She had a rucksack on her back – exactly as she had the first time he'd laid eyes on her. Only this time she carried a sword too.

The dormant Tryan in him sparked, every nerve-ending sensing that the serryn in her was back. Not just back, but stronger than ever.

Feinith backed away, but Leila didn't move, though the glance she cast in Feinith's direction was laced with a confidence that made far more than just his nerve-endings fire.

As Leila looked back to him, as she looked him square in the eye, his slow-beating heart skipped a beat.

Her lips curled into a hint of an enigmatic smile.

'Hello, Caleb.'

# LETTER FROM LINDSAY

I really hope you enjoyed re-visiting Eden and Jessie in our penultimate Blackthorn story. Please feel free to get in touch and let me know if you did. Whether via email, Twitter, Facebook or comments on my website, contact with my readers is really important to me.

If you did enjoy *Blood Bound*, I'd also be grateful if you'd consider writing a review. It's a great way to encourage new readers to try my series.

Well, that's almost it, everyone! The finale is on its way. If you'd like to be one of the first to hear about its release, you can sign up for e-mail updates at:

**www.lindsayjpryor.com/lindsay-j-pryor-e-mail-sign-up**

And if you're intrigued to know more about Blackthorn or would like to receive regular updates, please visit my website for all the inside information.

www.lindsayjpryor.com

As for what happens next…

Caleb and Leila will be back as our spotlight couple as my Blackthorn series draws to a close with *Blood Broken*. And, of course, there will many other familiar faces I hope you've come to love (and hate) making an appearance too. Our heroes and heroines have got quite the battle ahead! I do hope you're keeping your fingers crossed for them.

Thanks for reading.

Lindsay

Made in the USA
Middletown, DE
20 September 2016